Vanessa studied English and Australian literature at the University of Sydney and dreamed of one day writing fiction. She then went on to immerse herself completely in writing about real people, working as a journalist for twenty years. Vanessa has been a news, medical, entertainment and arts reporter for the *Daily Telegraph* and her writing has appeared in numerous other publications. She's happy to now, finally, be creating fictional characters. She lives in Sydney with her husband and daughter.

DREAMING
IN
FRENCH

VANESSA McCAUSLAND

HarperCollins*Publishers*

HarperCollins*Publishers*
Australia • Brazil • Canada • France • Germany • Holland • India
Italy • Japan • Mexico • New Zealand • Poland • Spain • Sweden
Switzerland • United Kingdom • United States of America

HarperCollins acknowledges the Traditional Custodians
of the land upon which we live and work, and pays respect
to Elders past and present.

First published in Australia in 2023
by HarperCollins*Publishers* Australia Pty Limited
Gadigal Country
Level 13, 201 Elizabeth Street, Sydney NSW 2000
ABN 36 009 913 517
harpercollins.com.au

A catalogue record for this book is available from the National Library of Australia

ISBN 978 1 4607 6291 2 (paperback)
ISBN 978 1 4607 1549 9 (ebook)

Cover design by Louisa Maggio, HarperCollins Design Studio
Cover images: Woman by Klara Kulikova / Unsplash; beach by istockphoto.com
Back cover image by Linda Xu / Unsplash
Author photograph by Sally Flegg Photography
Typeset in Bembo Std by Kirby Jones
Printed and bound in Australia by McPherson's Printing Group

MIX
Paper | Supporting
responsible forestry
FSC
www.fsc.org   FSC® C001695

For anyone who has ever held a deep fascination for another land and its language

One who speaks only one language is one person, but one who speaks two languages is two people.

– Turkish Proverb

PROLOGUE

The wind whispered through the pines. Only the sea answered. I heard my voice call her name over and over, but it was distant, an echo, no longer my own. He took my hand as we ran, stumbling over tufts of coarse sea grass and pine cones shed from the trees that edged the beach. But there was no one in the dunes, only a still, hovering moon, and I knew, in the same way the water knows the land, that she was gone, and that she was never coming back.

CHAPTER 1

Dry-stone walls and orange trees, searing salt air rising off the Atlantic. I have compartmentalised this part of my life because it happened in another language, in another place. And with the fading of my understanding of the words, I was able to forget.

It was so long ago. I was only nineteen when I left my home and travelled to the other side of the world, to a place of low, hot skies over salt flats, languorous bodies on fine white sands, and a sonorous language I did not fully understand. I knew I must never return. Now I am returning.

I hear my husband and daughters in the living room playing video games, their squeals and shouts have become the soundtrack of my life. And I cannot reconcile myself now − a mother, a wife − with the girl I was then. Because I was a girl, a child myself really. I understand this now that I have children of my own. I was too young to know what I was doing. That is what I tell myself when snatches of that language return to me on the street, in my dreams. Snatches drifting into my subconscious, reminding me that I haven't forgotten, not really. But there's no use in going back, in remembering. Besides, is the person you were so long ago really the same person you are now?

Of course not. That's what I tell myself when I open the letter, which is printed on thick stock, the kind of paper used for important information, and see the stamp. The stamp is French. The only communication then was by post, and I spent weeks waiting for news from home. Thin blue aerograms that could only hold a handful of anecdotes. And the stilted conversation with the kind woman who ran the post office. The word for stamp returns to me. *Le timbre.* Part of the address comes back, as things often do when you don't try to find them: *19 Rue de Concord, Saint-Martin-de-Ré.*

I never tried to find Félix again. I put him in the same place his language went – a subconscious place, a place only found in dreams. But he has returned to me now over wide, deep oceans, over wide, deep years. I read the words in the letter, my throat swelling, a static fuzz filling my ears.

And then I am back there, pedalling hard on *le vélo* against a warm summer wind, legs aching, browned by long hot days, hair streaming back. I am climbing the curve of the bridge that connects the island to the mainland.

But no. It is a bridge that I never allow myself to cross.

I place the envelope on the kitchen bench. My hands are sweaty, and I wipe them on a tea towel and go into the backyard. Evening is falling. The low clang of windchimes, the soft movement of birds in the leaves, the neighbours' voices – the sounds of an ordinary Sydney suburb bedding down for the night. I am here now, I remind myself. I am so far from that place. I am safe.

But I don't know myself as I stand here with a cigarette between my lips, stolen from my husband's emergency stash. The smoke feels foreign, dangerous in my mouth. I haven't smoked a cigarette since I was in France.

Dylan's voice startles me.

'What's this?' He holds out the envelope. 'Looks important ... Are you smoking?'

Instinctively I hide the cigarette behind my back, even though doing so is pointless. I bend down and extinguish it on the pavement, disgusted with myself. I take the letter from him, hoping he doesn't see that my hands are shaking. I wish I'd hidden it, given myself time to think, been more strategic about this. Stupid. Sloppy.

'It's ...' I don't quite know how to explain and at this point lying is futile. It sounds absurd to say out loud. 'It's a will.'

'Who died?' A wry smile. He takes a cigarette and lights it and I get a glimpse of the man I married nearly two decades ago.

I clear my throat, trying to sound normal, as though everything is just like it was before I opened that letter, but my voice sounds too high. 'A lady, no one you know.'

He raises his eyebrows. 'What did she leave you? A fortune, I hope.' He laughs and I do too, because it's actually crazy.

'A house.'

'Are you shitting me?' Dylan extinguishes his cigarette, his face serious.

I shake my head. 'Well, half a house. In France.'

He runs his hands through his greying hair, his forehead crinkling. 'What the actual, Saskia? Are you off your meds?'

I shoot him a look but laugh despite myself. He's always been able to make me laugh.

'What kind of house are we talking about?' he asks carefully. I can practically see his brain clocking over our expenses. Private school fees, potential bathroom renovations, my studio.

'It's a villa.' I want to downplay it, but I'm jostling inside – part disbelief, part excitement, part dread. 'A villa by the sea,' I allow.

His eyes glaze over with desire. I remember when he used to give me that exact look. 'Where?'

What he should be asking is, who? What kind of person leaves their beautiful villa to a girl she met twenty-six years ago?

'Her name was Simone Durant, and I met her the summer I lived on Île de Ré.'

As I say the words, I feel the past stir. It's too near now, filling my lungs and infusing me like salt on a tongue, like a lover's fingers through hair, like the wind whispering in the pines and only the sea answering back.

CHAPTER 2

The house is by the sea. Orange trees flank its crumbling walls and I can almost smell the fruit. The photo is blanched with age. I can't remember taking it, printing it or putting it in this album, but I must have. It's the lone keepsake from that time in my life, the only evidence that it actually happened. And now there is the letter. I suddenly remember the taste of those oranges on my lips. I slip the photo between the pages of my book, turn off the light and close my eyes. It's late but Dylan is still up, in a research frenzy, googling the island, the price of villas, French real estate.

Earlier he pointed to a photo of a single-storey stone house with green shutters, a small courtyard with a square patch of grass, around which sun lounges had been positioned, as though willing a pool to materialise. 'Here, look. This one's two million euros. Is it nicer than this one?'

It's much nicer than that one, but I told him I wasn't sure. The wild look in his eyes made me nervous. I was envious in a way, of his simple flurry of excitement.

I can almost feel feelings. They skim my surface, like an ice skater over thin ice. The blade is there but it never cuts. I never bleed. I know it's better this way, with my little white pills to buffer me, and yet there's something about today, about what has come to me unbidden, the hot and cold surprise of it, that I long to feel. Perhaps it's the lingering brightness of those days in my mind. So bright. But then so dark. Now my life is safe, monochrome.

I feel a small, warm body slip into bed beside me. It's Lara. She smells like milk and apples and her body curls into mine.

'Can't sleep La-La?'

'I can't stop thinking about the turtles.'

I kiss her hair. If it's not the turtles, it's the whales, or the penguins. Every night the same. They showed a documentary on endangered animals at school a few months ago and ever since it's been the same worries, lingering long after sleep should have come. I say a silent apology to her every night, wondering if I've conferred my faulty brain chemistry on her.

I reach for my bedside drawer and take out a tiny pair of scissors and a sheet of paper. I feel Lara's body relax into mine, mesmerised by the small, precise movements of the scissors. It doesn't take me long to fashion a turtle with a string of babies trailing after her.

'The turtles are okay, today they are okay. Remember what we talked about? Not thinking of the future, thinking of now, and right now you're here with me and everything is okay.'

She holds the fragile paper in her hand. 'But one day it won't be … okay.'

'I know it's hard not to worry, honey, and it's beautiful that you care so much for the animals, but you need to sleep.'

'Can I stay in with you tonight?'

'Course.'

Dylan comes into the room. He's noisy and I can smell the several glasses of wine he's drunk during and after dinner in celebration of our windfall.

8

'Out. You're too big to be in our bed.' He ruffles her hair, tickles her under the arms, and she laughs but nestles tighter into me.

'Just tonight,' I say, touching his shoulder.

He sighs and turns over. 'Did you email the lawyer?'

'Yes,' I say, even though I haven't.

'Babe, you need to follow up the lawyer tomorrow so we can get all the paperwork sorted.'

'I will,' I say.

Earlier, he asked me who this Simone was, and why she would leave me a villa in her will when I hadn't seen her in more than twenty years. I didn't have an answer for him. I don't have an answer for myself. He eventually dropped it, but I felt him watching me, perhaps seeing me in a different light, the way I saw him when he smoked that cigarette. It's strange, after so many years of marriage, seeing a little chink of something you don't quite recognise, a tiny enigma piercing the mundanity. That's what this feels like.

I close my eyes and the villa is there, haloed in summer light.

Citrus assaults my nostrils, sun strokes my skin with its long, slow touch. Simone is at the far end of the garden under a canopy of green leaves, under the shadow of a straw hat, on her typewriter. Félix is coming out of the stone pool, his brown skin a contrast with the purple and white wildflowers, his body glistening, and he's shaking water over her and the bright beads strike her skin like beautiful bullets, relentless and annihilating.

I open my eyes to the blackness of our bedroom. Dylan is snoring softly. He falls asleep in the same way he does everything – with blithe ease. Lara's breath is measured on my chest, and I feel it then, a tiny zing. I'm not sure if it's excitement or fear, because as I know so well, the two are intertwined. But I feel it.

*

The studio is quiet at 8 am. I take up my scalpel and let the blade glide through the thick stock. I cannot say exactly how I begin with a blank sheet and find the image within, only that I must begin. The sun through the arched window makes a perfect curve across the brushed concrete floor. There is a vase of white flowers on the black table in the centre of the room. It occurs to me how this room, with its pared-back palette, could be papercut art itself, as though someone had fashioned my life with clean snips, stark pieces strung together, out of a pretty but flimsy medium.

There is something so calming about the process. I don't think, I don't feel, I just slice. I start at the outside and work towards the centre. That's my signature, the thing at the centre. I have commissions for a wedding and a fashion label due this week. The happy couple want roses, the fashion label wants bees and butterflies. I work solidly for the morning, the only measure of time the sun's slow slide across the floor and the lattice of white offcuts that have fallen around me like snow.

I simply hold the central image in my mind and let my fingers do the work. It feels like a letting go rather than a tuning in. It has always felt like the soul of me coming out on thin wings.

I've made good progress on the hero panel for the fashion client. I step back and try to look with fresh eyes. It is a garden scene, with butterflies and bees fanning out from a sun. My eyes are drawn to the only human face in the picture. She is always there; I don't know why. Her face hidden among the foliage, her eyes two tiny scoops of paper.

I take a sip of cold black coffee and dial Petra's number. She picks up before the second ring. She's breathless from just coming back from her morning run and getting her three boys ready for school. Shortly she'll be at the hospital putting someone under anaesthetic with the same easy confidence.

'So, how's your Tuesday going and what the hell? I just read your text. Who in God's name is Simone Durant and why has she left you half her castle?'

Her words are an embrace. 'Villa,' I correct, and I can practically see her eyes rolling in her head while she makes herself toast on her gleaming marble benchtop. 'Do you want the Wikipedia version or—'

'I want all the versions.' Toast crunches in my ear. Sourdough with cashew butter. I can practically smell it down the phone. I read directly from the screen in front of me. '*Simone Durant is heir to the Durant cosmetics empire. Her grandmother, Sophia Durant, is one of the richest women in France. Simone is a model and muse ...*'

'Okay, stop. Stop, stop, stop. Saskia, how do you even know this woman? Why has she left you her house?'

'Half her house.'

Petra makes a strangled, disbelieving sound. 'God, you don't even sound excited.'

She should know by now that I don't do high emotion, I'm not capable of it. 'Well, I'm—'

'Stunned? Shocked? Intrigued?' she asks. Sometimes it feels like Petra is my only direct line to my own feelings. She is a surplus of feeling, unlike her brother, my husband.

'I met Simone when I lived in France that time.' I'm aware that I sound offhand, flippant.

Such a tiny proportion of my life and a time before the internet. A time before the eternal cataloguing of information in the ether. Perhaps that's why it all feels so much like a dream I once had. If there is nothing but our memories, how do we know something existed?

But there is evidence. The photo. And now, the letter.

Petra assumes the breathy voice of a film narrator. 'When artist Saskia Wyle lived in France in her youth, she met French heiress Simone Durant at a gallery. The pair caught up over the years in Simone's Paris apartment in … in the Marais, over red wine and cheese platters … discussing art. Simone never forgot her Australian friend and she felt compelled to include her in her will when she died.'

I laugh. I look around at the sharp, seemingly perfect contours of my life. It would be easy to say yes. That would make sense. That would fit into the carefully curated still life I am sitting inside. But that is not what happened. I haven't seen Simone since I was nineteen and she was twenty-four, that summer on the island. I have no idea why Simone has done this, how she found me, why she's given me this.

'Something like that,' I say. I can feel the lie clunking around inside me. My phone buzzes and so does my relief. 'Sorry, it's an international number. It must be the lawyer calling, about the will.'

'Go, go,' Petra says warmly, and I hate that I've lied to her. She's my internal compass, the only one I trust to guide me.

The man's voice is a mixture of French and British English. Highly educated. 'Hello, am I speaking to Madame Wyle?'

'Yes, speaking.' My voice is calm; it does not betray my erratic heart.

'*Enchanté.* Nice to meet you. My name is Monsieur Rombard from Rombard et Associates in Paris. Thank you for your email. You have received the letter about the terms of Madame Durant's will?'

'Yes, I received it yesterday, thank you.' I sound so awkward. As though I'm thanking him for a food delivery, not someone's last will and testament.

'And you noted that Madame Durant has made some specifications that you need to sign the paperwork for the ... how do you say, release of the property in person, along with a Monsieur Félix Allard?'

'Yes, I saw that.' I feel something uncomfortable shift inside me, like a loose stone working free from a cliff face. Félix Allard.

'Madame Durant has made you joint recipients of her property.'

There are so many questions that I find I can't ask any of them. *Why has Simone done this? How did she die? Was it the thing that haunted her, even at twenty-four?* There is nothing on Wikipedia, not even an acknowledgement of her death, and nothing in the French news. Perhaps no one has been told about her passing except those close to her. *Those close to her.* I feel like a fraud. *Who am I kidding? I* am *a fraud.* I need to know why she's made this strange request that forces me to cross the bridge to that island I severed twenty-six years ago. But I'm afraid this lawyer will discover that Simone and I haven't spoken since we were young, that I'm not, in fact, deserving of this at all. And it will be taken away from me, this strange, improbable fissure in my life.

'Is it really necessary for me to travel to France to sign?' I ask, trying to make my voice sound calmer, more measured than I feel.

'That is what Madame Durant has written into her will. Mr Allard is currently residing on Île de Ré.'

I must pause for a long time because Mr Rombard clears his throat. 'Madame, I am not sure whether you are aware of how much this property is worth. Even in its slightly dilapidated state … even dividing it with Monsieur Allard …' He pauses pointedly. 'I think you may be able to afford a flight to France.'

CHAPTER 3

I had forgotten the liminal appeal of foreign airports. Almost but not quite in another land, almost but not quite the same as the one we've left in Sydney, twenty-four hours ago. As though my mind can't quite conceive that my body hurtled through the air in a decompressed cabin until it reached the other side of the globe.

An announcement comes over the loudspeaker, the words running together like a song I once knew, a song I've tried to forget, but which remains embedded stubbornly inside me. A woman in a dark red beret and matching lipstick rushes past us to embrace a man and I catch the emotion of her whispered words, as strong as the notes of her perfume. *Mon amour. Mon chou.*

I remember the first time I heard this language outside my own land. It was as though I'd stepped through a portal into another realm and understood finally that I did have the key. That through so many hours of work I'd unlocked the meaning of another culture – a place familiar and yet so foreign, so unlike my own small place in the world. And with that came wonder and delight, mixed with the trepidation of the complete and utter unknown.

I am suddenly aware of my heart beating in my chest, the stale metallic taste in my mouth, my body waking up. *Je suis revenue.* I have returned.

My daughters are like tiny stunned animals that have just stumbled out of hibernation onto a busy road, their eyes huge under the bright lights. They wrap themselves around both my arms and we plough through people, engulfed by the smell of coffee, fast food and aeroplane fuel. Dylan is up ahead with the luggage. He's always up ahead. He's not a particularly tall man but he walks like he is one, and as soon as he turns his attention on you it's hard not to notice his striking green eyes. It was the eyes that got me. He was a customer in the jazz bar where I was working. He was flirty the first time we met, and he came back alone without his mates the very next night. We made furtive eye contact across the smoky room and talked in fits and starts while I delivered food to tables. He stayed until closing and walked me to the bus stop. I felt safe, protected, at a time when I needed that more than anything.

We reach the car hire desk and there's a long line. Dylan walks right up to a counter without a line, even though it's clear you're meant to queue. I see the woman shake her head but then she smiles and types something into her computer. He's charmed her and he's waving us over, skipping us ahead of fifteen people.

'You really don't have to come,' I told him after the call from the lawyer. 'You're so busy with work. I'll just go over there and get the paperwork sorted, put the property on the market. The girls don't need to miss school.' As soon as I said it, I knew it was futile.

'Yeah, the girls don't want to stay in the French *villa* with a *pool* that Mum's inherited,' he said, prompting a flurry of begging from Dee and Lara. He raised his eyebrows for the win.

'Mum, can I buy new swimmers and summer clothes?' Dee gave me her best puppy dog look, her hands clasped in prayer under her chin. 'It's where the rich French people go for the summer and we'll be rich now, right, with this villa in our portfolio?'

I turned to Dylan to exchange a look, which said, *How the hell does our fourteen-year-old know about property portfolios?* But he was on his phone, and it occurred to me how much we missed each other's silent entreaties these days.

'And I want a donkey,' Lara chimed in. 'They have donkeys wearing trousers on the island! Do you think there'll be donkeys at the villa?'

My daughters were right on both accounts. Sometimes I marvel that there's only two years between them. Dee is fourteen going on twenty and Lara is twelve but still willingly plays the role of the baby of the family. 'We're not moving there,' I said. 'We're only going for a week.'

But as I lug our heavy suitcases now, filled with two new outfits for Dee and an Instax for Lara to take pictures of donkeys in trousers – all bought on the credit card Dylan doesn't know about – it feels like we're staying for a lot longer.

The warm Parisian air greets me softly, like its people's customary double kiss.

The mystery of how another country can feel more like home than your own.

I was so young, standing on the threshold of another life, another universe, with everything I owned on my back and my passport and a third of my money strapped to my front. Fear and excitement fused in my chest as I realised that for the first time in my small, myopic life, I was completely alone. No one knew where I existed in time or space, or whether I even existed at all. Everyone I had ever known was asleep. I was light-headed with possibility, reeling with freedom. Finally, I'd come to this country that had beguiled me from afar for reasons I didn't quite understand, and with a train ticket to a tiny island whose name I couldn't quite pronounce.

*

Le passé – the past
From the age of twenty-four she knew that she was cursed, that around every corner death might be waiting, just as it had been waiting for her parents.

Simone wound down the window in the back of the taxi and felt the salt air slap at her unslept face. Dawn was cracking the night open, a pale grey light leaking in at the horizon. She needed to smell the sea as she crossed the bridge to the island. She needed to see the place where they had left the earth, see if there might be some lingering feeling, some chink in the rail, some skid on the road. *N'importe quoi.* Anything. But no, for all their accomplishments, even though the world knew their names, the place where they had died was unmarked. There was only asphalt and concrete and bird droppings. There was no trace of the storm that had swept the island that night, leaving sheeting rain in its wake. The newspapers reported that the road on the bridge had been slippery, diabolical, that it had been her mother who was driving.

Simone closed her eyes as they left the bridge and the smell of pine needles reached her, and suddenly she was in the back of the old Renault, the radio playing the sentimental

French classics her parents were fond of, smoke from their Gitanes mingling with her mother's tanning oil, the scent of a whole summer stretching before them. When she opened her eyes, a low sun lit the smooth, flat contours of the island. Grassy paddocks trimmed with white stone cottages, sharp church spires piercing the horizon, pockets of pine forest that ran to the sea. It was their island. She had never been here without them.

She needed to be outside now, not in this airless car, and she asked the taxi driver to drop her at the beach. She could tell he was sorry for her, this girl with dark smudges of mascara under her eyes, a tight black dress hitched too high, carrying only a purse.

She had left the party at midnight. She had not known whose party it was, which arrondissement of Paris she was in, or how she had come to be there – she had taken too much wine. All she knew was that she could not be alone, on tonight of all nights, the first anniversary of their death. But the stranger who she had let kiss her in a dark hallway had left without saying goodbye. And then someone had asked if she was Simone Durant. She was just as beautiful as Hélène Durant, they said, it was like seeing a ghost. What a tragedy … No one had said her mother's name for so long and she must have had tears on her face because the people in the parlour parted as she moved through, as though they didn't want to catch what she had. She could feel their eyes on her. She was learning the difference between attention and love.

She picked up an abandoned glass of wine and drank it down. She had already had too much and she felt nauseous with it. She left the party and several men appeared at the front door, handing her slips of paper. It was always the same, this custom that was meant to be flattering. She took them, these numbers scrawled on napkins, on pages ripped from the corners of magazines, a business card, and she left alone. The Paris night was warm, but she found no comfort or romance in its embrace as she walked the quiet streets until she reached Gare Montparnasse. She had known she would end up here, eventually. She caught the next train south with only her purse and the clothes on her back.

She took off her heels and peeled the stockings from her legs until she felt bare in the sand, as she had when she was a child. She gazed out at the sea, calm and flat, lulled by the gentle hush of morning.

'I have come back, *Maman, Papa*,' she said to the wind, but no one replied.

She opened her bag to find nothing but the phone numbers of men she would never call. Only hunger made her move. She began to walk up the beach. She knew it by the scent of the oranges in the garden. She saw that the foliage had grown thick over the high stone wall and wondered who had tended this place for the past year. She left the beach, scrambling up the dune until she saw the gate in the wall. The rusted iron hinges creaked as she pushed it open. The garden was overgrown, birds nesting in the eaves. A flutter of wings startled her as she walked up the path.

She found the key inside the pot full of white pebbles and shells collected over a lifetime of trips to the beach. She held a shell between her palms and wondered how she was the only one left to know the stories within these smooth memory tokens. She tucked the pot under her arm and opened the front door.

The smell of dust and salt-encrusted rust and trapped sunshine was like walking into their embrace, and Simone felt so tired suddenly, and cold, so very cold. She took the shell pot and climbed the stairs until she reached their bedroom. The bed was made. Who had made it after they never returned that night, she wondered? Her mother had never been one for made beds. Simone fell into the sheets and wrapped them around her, scooping out a fistful of shells and holding them tightly until she felt the sleep-tug pull her under.

*

She must have slept for the whole day and through the night, because she awoke dazed, in a dreamscape, unsure of where she was in time and space. Her eyelids fluttered against the light, like insects at once repelled and attracted. She felt the crunch of sand and shell and she winced, finding tiny sea things pressed into her skin. She brushed the sheets and stripped off her dress to wrap herself in the gown that hung over the mirror. It was infused with memories of her mother.

Her hunger had turned fierce, and she followed its pull downstairs. The villa was cooler down here, with its high ceilings and thick stone walls, like going from the sunny surface into the depths. But it was also a reprieve from the midday heat. She remembered sunburned bodies spread out on the lounges for siesta, or cross-legged on the soft grass under the trees by the pool. Her parents had loved to throw long summertime lunches and *des petites soirées*.

Simone found coffee in the cupboard and lit the coffee pot on the stove. It smelled a little burned, and suddenly she could see her mother standing there making breakfast on hot summer mornings. Her mother had liked everything a little burned – her coffee, her baguette, her skin from the sun. It was why she loved this place. It was as though she wanted to feel and taste the crisp edges of things. Perhaps it was a foil to Simone's father, who was doughy and comforting and hid under broad-brimmed hats. He would eat her burned toast, drink her bitter coffee and sit under the blazing sun without remark, and from a young age Simone understood that this was what love was. But now, all that remained were the uneaten breakfasts on the old table under the kitchen window that never closed properly. The window that her father insisted every summer on fixing but that her mother had liked to keep broken because it allowed the smell of oranges to seep in from the garden.

There was no food in the cupboards, and Simone couldn't remember the last time she'd eaten. She didn't care that she was dressed only in a robe, her face still creased from sleep, her hair a mess, feet bare. She went outside to the shed, dusted off cobwebs and a thin layer of sand and took out a bicycle. The sun was soft on her skin, so she knew it was early, and the shutters of the village houses were still closed like eyes stuck shut. She bought a baguette and a stick of butter at the *boulangerie* and ripped off the end of the bread with her teeth then swallowed it down as she rode.

Back at the villa she put slices of bread in the toaster and watched as they singed at the edges and blackened all the way to the centre. She sat down at the place where her parents had taken their last meal and ate the toast, the charcoal and the black coffee burning the back of her throat. When she had finished, she went into the lounge and found the thin book of poetry her mother had written and a fat philosophy tome her father had edited and placed their comforting weights against her chest.

Simone closed her eyes, the scent of dusty pages and burning surrounding her like her parents' embrace.

'*Maman*, why were you driving that night?' she whispered. 'How could you leave me here alone?'

CHAPTER 4

We're on the outskirts of Paris. Every city has its ugly parts, its malls and industry, its concrete overpasses and grey apartment blocks, even Paris. But the ugliness is beautiful to me in its novelty – the impenetrable signage, the cars parked on the street touching hood to tail, people on the sidewalks carrying groceries with strange logos.

A woman on a bike sails by with a baguette under her arm; a man in a black beret walks a black dog; a flower stall erupts colour onto a tired street corner; patrons sip coffee outside a small café. And suddenly I want to taste the fresh bread, *du pain frais*, smell *les fleurs*, hear the man admonish his *chien* in French. It feels like a switch has been flicked inside me. Suddenly, I remember how the taste of coffee changes when it's taken *en plein air*, outside, watching the world pass by.

Je suis en France.

From the very first words learned at school, the language felt sensual in my mouth, mysterious, but also known. I could pronounce the words and they sounded somehow familiar, as though my mind had only been waiting for another way to make sense of the world. But it wasn't just the words, the lilt and jolt of them on my tongue, it was something else.

Something indelible, that made me feel this was a place that would have meaning in my life. That one day I would go there and find something I couldn't find at home.

We leave Paris behind and now there's only the autoroute, boring in any language. I crane my neck for the occasional flash of countryside in the distance.

'Could you drive any faster?' I ask, stupidly, because Dylan takes it as an invitation and puts his foot down. The girls squeal in the back of the car and that makes him go even faster. Adrenalin throttles through me and I grip the Jesus handle and swear, but I'm laughing. 'You do realise there's a hundred-and-thirty-kilometre-an-hour speed limit.' I'd forgotten I knew that.

'The French don't care about stuff like that.'

He's kind of right but I don't give him the satisfaction of saying so. I feel a strange sense of ownership over the entire French people and their culture, as though because I came here first, because I know the language, it is all mine and not his.

'So, are you going to elaborate on who this Félix Allard is, who's getting the other half of our villa?' Dylan's voice is deliberately casual but his eyes are locked on the road, his speed still excessive.

Blood throbs at my temples and my body stiffens. It's not a coincidence, the speed and his mention of Félix.

'Can you please slow down?'

He doesn't slow. 'Is he going to give us any grief in signing off on this thing?'

I knew this was coming. It was only a matter of time before he dug deeper than my offhand explanation. Maybe he was too excited about the money to drill me initially. I've probably made it worse by avoiding it. I don't know what I was thinking, I just didn't want to have this conversation.

I try to keep my voice light. 'As I said, he was just a mutual friend of Simone's and mine. He lives on the island … He's quite well known.' I don't know why I add this last part. It's only going to make it worse. But I feel a strange frisson admitting this.

'In what sense?' Dylan glances at me. The car slows a tad.

I couldn't say exactly when I knew Félix had become famous. *Célèbre*. It happened gradually, like a sun slowly rising until it was at its zenith in the sky. It was the same way I once acquired his language, by a slow osmosis. 'He's an actor. Just in French films.' I wave my hand dismissively. 'No one Hollywood would have heard of.'

'Have you watched them? The films? Did you have something with this guy back in the day or something?' he asks, his voice laced with amusement, but I feel a tiny twinge of power at the insecurity I hear in his voice.

'Never watched them,' I say. That's the truth. I've never been able to bring myself to, even though I have always loved French films. Perhaps *because* I have always loved French films.

'So, he's obviously got his own money. Great news.' Dylan slaps my leg playfully and keeps his hand resting there in a proprietorial fashion.

He asks nothing more and I breathe a sigh of relief and close my eyes.

*

I must have slept because it's early evening now. The ancient fort of La Rochelle is lit up against a still blue sea. It stirs in me a feeling. Cobwebs and old cobblestone streets. And I know that a part of me has remained here, always. I was on the precipice, on the very edge of my own life, just coming into being. The feeling of possibility. *L'espoir.* Hope. I crack the window to smell the salt air. Then that other feeling. *La peur.* Fear. How can I be back here?

Dylan is hungry but the girls are still passed out in the back of the car from exhaustion, so we stop by the port in front of a fish and chip shop called *Bouteille à la mer* – message in a bottle. The meaning is there in my mind, as though it has just been biding its time. The smell of hot oil and salt rouses the girls and we eat chips from newspaper wrapping, the car doors open to the balmy evening, the clang of sails from the boats in the harbour.

The word for gull is suddenly in my mind like a bright white dot in the sky. *La mouette.*

'Maybe we should stay here tonight?' I suggest. 'The girls are tired, and it'll be dark by the time we arrive at the villa.' I don't tell him that I'm not ready to cross that long arched bridge to the island, to my past, especially at night.

'No, we'll keep going. I want to see this place. If it's even fucking real …'

He doesn't try to hide the scepticism in his voice. The idea of Félix has upset him. He doesn't like that this is my place, my country, my past, before I needed him. It unsettles him nearly as much as it unsettles me.

'You think I'm making it all up?'

He laughs. 'Well, you've got to admit your grasp on reality is pretty flimsy sometimes, Saskia.' He pulls me towards him but I resist.

'What's that supposed to mean?'

'Oh, I don't know, you cut out little bits of paper for a job, and you're on meds. Come on, you know this about yourself, babe.'

27

He says it in a joking tone, his arm around my shoulder, but I feel myself redden, feel shame descend. He's right. I'm flimsy. I don't know what I was thinking, toying with him like that, telling him how famous Félix is.

It's this place. It's already making me reckless, reminding me of her, the girl I used to be.

*

Le passé

Simone awoke feeling again as though she had surfaced from a deep dream. The light here was different from the light in Paris. She could no longer hide from it in the way she could in the city — it found ways to get through the cracks in the shutters. She went downstairs. It was still early and a bird was calling from the fruit trees. She made herself the same burned toast and coffee, wrapped in her mother's gown. She had been running from this feeling for a year, numbing herself so as not to feel the depths of her own grief. But she knew she must face it, that there was nothing of any meaning left for her in Paris.

She took her coffee into the lounge and ran her fingers along the spines of the books that lined the wall. She slipped one book out and then another, and another until there were piles of them on the floor. *What am I doing?* she thought, but she couldn't seem to stop. She stood on a stool to reach the highest shelves, her nose itching with the dust. Her parents had spent so much of their time here reading, stretched out on the lounges, drinking the apricot wine her father made each summer and put away for the following one. Maybe if she read every one of their books she might find among these pages the parts of her parents that were missing. The parts she never understood, the answers as to why, on the night they died, it was her mother who had been at the wheel of the car.

Simone had never seen her mother drive. Hélène had grown up being chauffeured around Paris by drivers whose only job was to wait until one of the Durant family needed to be taken somewhere. But as a teenager Hélène would cycle everywhere, from the family's grand apartment in Saint-Germain-des-Prés to the cafes along the river where she would meet friends to smoke cigarettes and drink coffee late into the night. This was where she met Simone's father, Stéphane, a philosophy student, and it was as though she purposely chose a man who showed his devotion through quiet acts of service, such as driving his girlfriend and then wife. And he was dedicated to no one more than Hélène.

The first time Simone knew the power her mother had over other people she was very small. She must have been only four or five years old. They were in the salon of the apartment, the long windows open to the balcony, the light filtering through the poplar trees outside. There were mothers and their children everywhere. It must have been a mothers' group she had invited for tea. Simone remembered because of the cake. So much cake. Hélène was wearing her hair pinned half-up and half-down in the style she would later become known for. She drifted through the other mothers like a beautiful spectre, and Simone understood somehow, even at that young age, that she was adored simply for existing. That the other mothers were not like her mother, but they wanted to be. Or perhaps it was simply because she had the housekeeper buy so much cake for everyone. It was something Simone discovered much later, when she was twelve or thirteen and started seeing her place in the world more objectively. She saw that her family's money was a filter through which everything passed and that she, like her mother, could never be known or loved without its influence.

*

It took her most of the day, but by the time the shadows were falling through the windows, every book sat on the floor in the loungeroom. She didn't know what it meant or why she had felt compelled to do it, only that it had to be done. And now she was hungry for more than burned toast and coffee, and the two oranges she had eaten for lunch. She showered the dust from her skin and dressed in jean shorts and a white shirt with sandals – clothes that had remained in her cupboard from previous summers.

She got on her bicycle, not knowing where she was heading, just riding, feeling the chill on her bare legs. She reached Saint-Martin as twilight billowed over the port and diners spilled onto the streets under striped awnings. Late summer on the island had always been her parents' favourite time. The tourists were dwindling, the buzz of their mopeds along the laneways fading along with their tans. Simone slowed her bicycle and considered turning back. She was alone and did not fit into this festive scenario.

But she could see the bistro her parents favoured, the one that served the best *moules frites*, mussels and fries, on the island. Where they would drink cold beer and watch the fishermen coming into port with their fresh catches. To be raised by a philosopher and a poet was to grow up talking about life and death and the meaning of both in the same way other families might talk about sports, and she knew instinctively her parents would want her to sit in the bistro and take a glass of wine rather than return home to the empty house filled with piles of dusty books.

There was a slice of soft sunlight falling onto one of the outside tables and Simone sat down there. She could almost hear her mother whisper to her that there was still magic in the world, and she felt her eyes fill with tears, which she brushed away, mortified, and pretended to study the menu. She felt she was being watched, and she looked up to find a girl staring. The girl had large, worried eyes and pale red hair. She approached the table tentatively.

'I'm sorry, I don't speak much French. Are you okay?' she asked in English.

Her voice was soft, gentle, and Simone realised that since the funeral no one had asked her this. Or maybe they had, but they hadn't really wanted to know. There had been many questions about how her parents had died, morbid curiosity about her family's curse, flowers and gifts and condolences, yes, but no one had simply asked her if she was okay.

'I'm sorry to intrude, you just looked sad and alone, and I'm alone and a little, not sad, but ...' She shook her head. 'I'm sorry, do you even understand me?'

'Philosophical,' Simone said in English, with a small smile.

The girl returned the smile. 'Yes, philosophical.' She brought her small carafe from the adjacent table. 'Would you like some of my wine?' She poured Simone a glass.

Simone collected herself and took a sip of the wine, which tasted delicious and made her feel a little better. 'So, what has brought you here to find the only crying French girl on Île de Ré?'

31

The girl laughed. 'Oh, I'm the sort of person who will always find the crying French girl in any situation, and probably draw a picture of her.'

Simone noticed the girl had a beautiful leather-bound notebook on the table.

'You're an artist. May I?'

The girl opened the notebook and goosebumps erupted over Simone's bare arms, despite the heat. It was full of sketches. People in cafes, boats in the harbour, architectural details. 'You are in art school, *non?*'

The girl shook her head. 'I've deferred my second year studying law.' She must have seen the question in Simone's eyes because she went on. 'My parents ... they ... We don't have a lot of money, so when I got the marks for law, they wanted the best for me, the job security. There's no money in art.'

'It seems such a shame. You are so talented. Are you British?'

The girl shook her head.

'Australian?'

She nodded. 'It's nowhere near as romantic when we cry in cafes.'

Simone laughed. '*Non?* Where is your preferred place to weep then?'

'I grew up by the beach. There's a bench I go to overlooking the sea.'

'Ah, yes, I have one of these. It's on Le Bois-Plage, a little way from here.'

The girl raised her glass. 'To thinking spots on beaches.' They clinked glasses. 'I'd love to know the best beaches. I'm an au pair, so I'll be spending a lot of time at the beach I imagine.'

'On the island? Who are the family?'

'The Bisettes. They own a restaurant here in Saint-Martin-de-Ré and they need some help with their little girl.'

'So, you will be their au pair? You must like children then?'

'Yes, I mean, I think so. I feel a bit nervous. I start tomorrow.'

Simone felt suddenly protective of this sweet stranger. She did know of the Bisettes and their hatted bar and restaurant of the same name, but she didn't want to say so for fear of putting some sort of expectation in the girl's mind. They were quite a wealthy, powerful family on the island.

'I could help you,' Simone said, surprising herself.

'Oh, it's only the one child,' the girl said, smiling in an overly polite way that suggested she was perhaps starting to think Simone was a little strange now.

But I am strange, Simone thought. *I just spent the whole day taking books out of their shelves. I have a purse full of phone numbers and no one to call.* The words left her lips before she even realised. 'When you asked before if I was okay, did you mean it?'

The girl's hand stilled as she was sipping her wine, but her eyes said that she did mean it.

'My parents died a year ago,' Simone said. 'That's why I wasn't okay.'

The girl did not speak or fill the sad, awkward air with the empty sympathy Simone had become accustomed to. She just put her hand over Simone's, and it was only then that Simone realised they had become friends without even knowing each other's names.

CHAPTER 5

The bridge between La Rochelle and Île de Ré skims the darkening water, a long ribbon of light against a purpling sky. The island is so low it's barely an afterthought, as though the ocean will subsume it at any time, an Atlantis waiting in the depths of my mind. We pay the toll and cross the bridge and it feels like I'm crossing a threshold from one part of myself to another. I told myself I'd never return to this island, to that girl I was, but here she is, her pulse racing in her wrists, the wind in her hair. I gulp down the smell of salt marshes and seaweed.

'Can you shut the window?' Dylan asks. 'It stinks.'

I feel myself zipping closed again, as though there's a seam down my middle that I'd forgotten was there to be opened. But I obediently raise the window and the sterile smell of the hire car returns. Dylan's breathing, the agitated tap of his fingers on the steering wheel.

The bridge ends and we're on the island now. A bright, low moon rises over the ocean. We pass open fields, the conical roofs of windmills, vines bowing under clusters of grapes. I wonder if there are donkeys. I look into the back, but the girls have fallen asleep again. They would be mortified if they could see themselves, their bodies collapsed together like when they were little, when they loved each other unselfconsciously.

Out the window, low white houses with green shutters huddle together like roosting gulls.

'All the houses look the same,' Dylan says.

'The island's heritage-listed. You can only paint your shutters in certain colours. Green or blue or white.'

'Seems a bit boring.'

'It's beautiful.' My voice is strangely defiant, and I brace to be undercut but he doesn't reply. He's too focused on getting to this house.

The sat nav tells us we're minutes from the address, from Simone's villa. I feel it again – a ripple that runs through me. *L'anticipation.*

'So the key will be there?' Dylan asks, punching the sat nav with his finger.

'Yes, in an envelope in the letterbox.'

'This can't be it,' he says, slowing the car at the end of a small lane.

There's an arched timber gate bolted into a stone wall. In truth, I can't remember. I know he's thinking it's not grand enough for his vision of a French villa. But I remember the secret wonders of this country, the hidden homes behind humble walls. The soaring ceilings concealed by simple shuttered doors. This is what I loved about this place, this people. The simplicity and the subtlety. *Le mystère.*

Dylan cuts the engine and I get out. I want to see it before him. *This place is mine. She left it to me.* I find the handle of the gate under a tangle of vines. The Australian in me thinks this will be locked. But I'm on a tiny island in the Atlantic and so of course it is not. The gate creaks open and the dark bones of the house emerge. I smell the oranges first.

I remember lights strung through trees, smoke curling from slow-burning cigarettes, dipping my finger into candle wax pooling on the table, enjoying the soft sting of the shell forming over my skin. Félix peels the wax off and it feels like he's peeling me back to the bone, but I remain, astoundingly, intact.

You shouldn't be here, a voice inside me says. *It's not safe.* But there's something else stirring inside me, the thing I have ignored, the part of myself that I have allowed to grow over, like the weeds webbing the cobblestone path towards the house.

Dylan is beside me, shining his iPhone light around. 'Bit overgrown and crumbling.'

I can hear my girls getting out of the car, their sleep-husked voices in the dark, and I know I must do this, face this. Dee grabs me and I jump.

'I'm so glad I bought new clothes. This place is freaking amazing,' she says, suddenly wide awake. I feel her bony body nestle into me, and I wrap my fingers around her upper arm. It is so thin. I look at her face — there are shadows under her cheekbones, and I wonder, *When did you get so thin?*

I feel right into the corners of the letterbox. The key is not in there as the lawyer promised. My thoughts begin to spin. *What will we do now? Where have I brought us? Dylan's right. I am flimsy. Is this real? Have I mistranslated something?* I can feel Dylan's frustration building behind his calm facade — it's like smelling a storm before you see dark cloud. I'm a meteorologist attuned to his weather.

'It's not there. I knew we should've stayed in La Rochelle and waited till morning,' I say, then regret it.

Dylan sighs. 'It was your responsibility, Saskia. This is what I'm talking about. Fucking hopeless.'

'Language,' I say, though I couldn't count how many times they've heard their father swear, frequently at me.

'Come on girls, search the bushes. We're in France, no deadly insects here,' he says.

The girls look at me, unconvinced.

'Let's try under the doormat,' I suggest, even though I just want to go and stay in a local hotel and return in the morning under the bright reassurance of the sun.

We pass the dark reflection of the pool and an umbrella closed like a flower over an outdoor table. We find ourselves at the end of the path, at the front door. The paint is peeling off in strips.

I lift the doormat and look under a dying pot plant. Dylan is running his fingers along a window ledge, as though he's some sort of expert cat burglar.

He's found an open window. He pulls one of the rusty garden chairs over and tests it before stepping up.

'Dad, we can't just break in,' says Lara, her eyes huge, the bunny she still carries when confronted with new experiences, such as breaking into French villas in the middle of the night, clutched to her chest.

'It's our house, La-La. Daddy's got this,' Dylan says, using all his strength to push the window until something splinters and flakes of old paint rain down. I feel uncomfortable with his arrogance in breaking in, and yet his kindness to our children always undoes me.

He slings a leg over the windowsill and slips in and there's a thump as he reaches the floor. And then he's opening the front door as though it's his house, and I feel something ignite inside me. I quickly hug the girls to extinguish it.

'It's okay,' I say. I'm always saying the opposite of what I feel. There is a dull thud of anxiety at the back of my head.

Dylan has turned on the light in the foyer and we step over the threshold. I'm nineteen again and walking into Simone's house for the first time. There's a large white sculpture of a man in the entrance hall. The effect is one of drama and elegance, like walking into an art gallery rather than a home. The lounge is to the left – high ceilings, period furniture, a grand piano and a wall of books. It hasn't changed much, if at all.

'Is this where you lived?' asks Dee, her eyes wide. She's too old to hide things from now. She looks for the double meaning in everything. It has dawned on her that adults don't always say what they mean.

'No, I was friends with the girl who lived here, Simone,' I say, 'but I didn't live here.'

'Where did you live?'

A place with whitewashed walls and green shutters, the smell of flowers blooming in bright window boxes and of the morning loaves baking in the *boulangerie* below. An apartment above the most exclusive hotel on the island. Views of the port from every window. Waking to the soft clang of sails.

'I was an au pair,' I say. 'I lived with a family in Saint-Martin.'

'Is an au pair the same as a nanny?' Dee is scrunching up her nose. 'Why didn't I know this?'

'I was a lot of things before I was your mother, you know.'

'Yeah, like friends with really rich French people.'

'When did you get so sarcastic?' *And so thin.*

Dee shrugs and runs a finger along the sideboard. 'Not that dusty. So, did she die here? The woman who left you the house. Simone?'

Lara looks stricken and I put my arm around her. 'Dee,' I say, giving her a warning look.

'Well, did she?' Dylan is standing at the piano. 'You've been cagey about this whole thing.' He hits a single note and it echoes around the room.

'I'm not cagey, it's just that I know about as much as you. It was twenty-six years ago. This is a shock to me, too. We were meant to be doing parent-teacher night at the school tonight, not breaking into a French villa.'

'Fair,' says Dee, shrugging. 'So, where do we sleep? This place looks like it has about twenty bedrooms.'

'Mum, I'm hungry,' says Lara, looking up at me with tired eyes.

I pull her towards me, and for a moment wish she was little enough for me to pick her up, have her bury her head into my neck. How did that time pass without me noticing?

'Sorry, honey, we didn't have much of a dinner, did we? And I don't have anything.'

Instinctively, I find myself in the kitchen. It's a French-provincial style, the kind people try to replicate in Australia but never quite manage. A rustic timber dining table sits under the window. There are wide floorboards, long wooden benchtops, deep farmhouse sinks, and the copper pots I now know cost an absolute fortune, hanging over the stove. One wall is a built-in cabinet filled with stacks of crockery in the same muted creams and greys as the kitchen.

Dylan opens a double-fronted fridge. It's empty, save for some condiments in the side door.

'They must have let this out as an Airbnb or something. If we can find the keys, there might be a locked pantry.' Dylan is already opening kitchen drawers. It feels wrong, invasive. *Mauvaise.*

39

Dee is standing in front of me with a bunch of keys dangling casually from her index finger. Trust a fourteen-year-old to find the hidden keys.

'Where did you—'

'Same place we hang our spares. On the key rack in the laundry.'

'Now to find the locked cupboard with all the loot.' Dylan takes the keys from Dee and strides around the kitchen. This can't be what Simone wanted. Someone breaking into her house looking for food. I feel my cheeks flush.

'Stop,' I scream, and they all look at me, their eyes wide. I never raise my voice. 'Don't just go digging about. It's bad enough we broke in in the middle of the night.'

'It's our damn house now,' says Dylan, and I bite the inside of my lip to stop myself from exploding again. *What's wrong with you?* I don't know if I'm asking this of myself or Dylan.

'Mum, calm your farm,' says Dee. 'We're just trying to find food for Lara.'

I make my voice more measured. 'Stop. Just stop, please. Wait here.' I can feel their eyes on me as I open the French doors that lead into the courtyard. The orange trees are heavy with fruit, their scent infusing the warm night air. I twist an orange and hold it to my nose.

The memory trickles into my mind, like juice sluicing down my wrists as I squeeze the pulp in my palms. The taste of citrus is a pungent jump in my mouth. We've been up all night, drinking wine and talking about the beginning of our lives and the end of the world, and now we need something fresh, alive, to rouse us to this new day. I take the juice and the toast – burned from the overzealous toaster, out into the courtyard. Félix is lying on his back on the table reading a novel and Simone is floating on the surface of the pool, both gazing skyward.

I bring all the oranges I can carry into the kitchen. Dylan has gone, no doubt still trying to find a locked cupboard to ravage. I'm past caring. I'm too tired. I find a wooden chopping board and a knife and begin to segment the fruit and place it on a plate. The girls suck the flesh out of the oranges and toss the peels in the sink. Their lips are red, and their cheeks flushed with exhaustion. I feel it close over me too, and I lead them wordlessly into the loungeroom. We all find cushions and curl up together on the lounge. The sweet smell of my girls' hair pressed to my cheek, their long, restless legs touching mine.

'Mum, can you cut me a story?' asks Lara. She is so close to sleep but I acquiesce. It's our night-time ritual. Some mothers tell stories, I fashion them from paper. I go into the kitchen and find a pair of scissors in a drawer and rip a page out of a magazine from a stack in the corner.

Lara snuggles into me, her lids heavy as she watches the smooth movement of the scissors. I don't always know exactly what will come out when Lara doesn't give me a brief. I open the paper and the image arrives. A little girl under a full moon, looking up. I feel a shiver run through me and look to Lara. She's asleep, so I carefully crumple it into a ball.

*

Le passé
'Bisette' bar and restaurant was by the harbour, where the well-heeled liked to visit on oppressive afternoons when the sea breeze died in the sails outside. Saskia was standing at the bar, wearing a cream-coloured cotton sundress, her hair pulled off

her face. Simone felt a rush of warmth for this girl she had only met once but whose phone number, scribbled on a napkin, she had actually called.

She kissed Saskia four times in greeting, as she would an old friend.

Simone wanted to tell her she'd thought several times of trying to find her and the little girl at the beach, but she knew this was probably strange and intrusive. Possessive. And it had dawned on her that these were probably some of her mother's defining characteristics. Hélène would take up new friends and draw them into her life completely for months on end, taking them to events, gifting them books and presents, until the obsession dwindled and suddenly that friend wouldn't be around anymore, and Simone would wonder where they had gone.

'Island life suits you,' Simone said in English, threading her arm through Saskia's.

Saskia laughed. 'Everyone's so tanned and dark and slim, and I just feel pale and sunburned.'

'*Non, pas du tout.* Your pretty hair and pale skin, *c'est très exotique.* And you have effortless style.'

'Really?'

'*Ah, oui,* I am an expert in such things, believe me. My mother was considered very stylish. She still is. There is nothing like death to make an icon out of someone.'

'Was your mother famous?'

Simone smiled but said nothing more. Saskia did not know of her money, or her lineage, and Simone felt for the first time in her life the lightness and innocence of being free of these complicated burdens.

'Let's sit down and I will tell you the story of my life, but first, the important thing – what will you take to drink?' The bar was sumptuous and sensual with dark green leather booths, venetian shutters, tropical palms, and fans moving the heavy air over sun-slicked bodies.

'What do you suggest?'

'Have you tried pastis? You must.' Simone ordered and they took a seat in the corner of the room where the sun fell in long slats through the blinds. She lit a cigarette and drew the smoke into her lungs.

'You make smoking a cigarette look like art, you're so pretty,' Saskia said shyly.

Simone laughed and shook her head. 'Thank you, but it takes nothing for me to look the way I do – sorry if it sounds arrogant like this, but it's no real effort on my part. It is only the genes my mother gave me. Why do we all want the thing we cannot have? I don't want to be a model like my mother, scribbling poetry in her spare time between fashion shoots. I want to be a writer like my father.'

'What did he write?'

'He founded a very famous French literary journal in the seventies and eighties. He published some of the great thinkers, and he was a critic and wrote many books himself – philosophy, some novels. He was the smartest person I knew. My mother, she was beautiful, but she was smart too. I fear I only got the looks, not the brains.'

'That can't be true. You must be good at something.'

I am good at spending money, Simone thought. *And making people like me.* 'I have been trying to write. Perhaps something about my parents, a memoir of some kind, I don't know.'

'Would the memoir be about your glamorous mother, the model?'

Simone felt a seam of resentment open inside her. Was she destined always to be the muse rather than the artist? Was the most interesting thing about her always going to be her beautiful dead mother? After what Saskia had shared about her parents the first night they'd met, Simone didn't want to say that her mother was the daughter of the founder of Durant, the famous French cosmetics company, the root of her family's money and its notoriety. That her grandmother was one of the richest women in France.

Instead she said, 'Enough about me. How are the Bisettes treating you?'

'They're nice.' Saskia's eyes darted around the room.

Simone narrowed hers. 'You don't seem sure about that.'

Saskia waved a hand. 'No, Juliette is so sweet and Camille and Henri are being really nice to me. The house is incredible. They've got a housekeeper, so I don't have to do housework, and I only have to look after Juliette during the day. I take her to preschool, bring her home for some lunch — they're very particular that she has a proper lunch.'

Simone smiled. 'Oh yes, lunch … food … it is everything to the French, as you are discovering.'

'They're very interested in Australia. They take nannies from all over the world so Juliette learns lots of different languages and about different cultures.'

Simone wondered whether they were introducing their child to different cultures or just trying to find a nanny who would stick around, but she didn't want to spoil Saskia's tentative happiness. Everyone knew this family who owned the most prestigious bar and restaurant on the island, and especially Henri Bisette, the only Michelin-starred chef on the island. Saskia would be able to make her own judgement soon enough. 'And you get some time to yourself?'

'Juliette goes to her grandparents at the weekends, so yes.'

An image arrived in Simone's head of the two of them sunbathing by the pool at the villa, sketching and writing under the shade of the orange trees. 'You will have to visit my villa. We can swim and drink wine.'

Saskia smiled. 'I'd love that.'

A waiter arrived and placed the pastis and a jug of water on the table. He hovered a moment too long, holding the empty tray. Simone noticed his hands first — they were a worker's hands, browned by the sun. But he had a fine-boned face, almost beautiful, with wavy hair that fell into his dark eyes and a mole on his left cheek that gave him a distinguished air. He looked a similar age to her.

Simone felt her pulse race, wondering if he recognised her somehow, if the ruse was up, but instead he addressed Saskia.

'I've seen you around,' he said in English.

'I'm the Bisettes' au pair,' she said, her cheeks colouring.

'Félix,' a voice called.

They all looked up and Simone saw Camille Bisette approach. She was tall, with light hair swept up into a tight chignon. Her face was bare of make-up, but she wore red on her lips. 'We don't pay you to stand chatting with the customers.'

Félix looked chastised. '*Désolé*, Madame Bisette.'

Simone shifted uncomfortably under the woman's gaze. She felt strangely compelled to use her power to protect this boy, even if it did expose her.

'Oh, not just customers, we're friends. I'm sorry, it's my fault Félix is chatting,' Simone said in French, standing and kissing

Camille twice. She wore an overpowering scent. 'Simone Durant. *Enchantée*. I don't think we've had the pleasure. Saskia was just telling me about your charming little girl.'

Simone thought she felt Camille's body stiffen very slightly, and she wondered if she'd recognised her name, but when she pulled back her mouth softened into a smile.

'Oh yes, it has been lovely to have Saskia with us. She is very good with Juliette.'

'*Merci*, Madame Bisette,' Saskia said, and Simone was shocked at how formal her tone was.

Camille Bisette was perhaps in her mid to late thirties. The smile remained on her lips but there was something cold in her eyes, and Simone felt suddenly sorry for her, this woman who conducted herself like someone much older than she was.

Félix wiped the table nervously.

'Well, enjoy your evening off,' Camille said to Saskia, her eyes flicking pointedly to Félix.

'What time do you finish?' Simone asked him in French, enjoying the fact that she was the only one here not in Camille's employment.

He looked nervous and rubbed at the table's surface again. 'Two more hours.'

'I am having *un petit dîner* at my place tonight with some friends.' It was not true, she didn't even have food in the house. 'Come after work. Saskia is coming, yes?'

Saskia looked surprised but nodded.

'Okay.' Félix smiled.

Simone looked to Camille, who was still standing there, and saw something flash in her eyes – resentment, longing, both? But she turned abruptly and walked away.

*

As afternoon slipped into evening, the bar became quieter rather than busier as a similar establishment would have done in Paris. It was the sun in this place. It seeped into you and drugged you during its day-long embrace.

Simone had stopped coming here in her teens while her parents returned each summer. She supposed she thought of it as her childhood holiday place, not as sophisticated as the Côte D'Azur with her friends. But now, sitting here with Saskia, learning about her life and culture on the other side of the world, Simone realised she had been living in a vacuum. All her friends came from the same small Parisian world she inhabited, a world in which money never factored, was never mentioned, because it did not in any way negatively impact their lives. But for Saskia, clearly everything depended on it, from having another drink – which Simone insisted on paying for – to whether she would follow her dream of going to art school rather than what her parents wanted. Simone found she had to fight the urge to fix everything, to offer up her most powerful currency to save Saskia, and perhaps ensure that she liked her even more. For some reason it felt like her connection with Saskia was the only pure one she had ever had.

They were on their third drink by the time Félix pulled up a chair at their table, turning it around and straddling it backwards. He lit a cigarette and blew the smoke out from the corner of his mouth.

'So, where is this party?' he asked through smoke-narrowed eyes, grinning.

There was a playfulness about him that Simone hadn't seen when they'd met under Camille's watchful eye, and it disarmed

47

her. Of course, she had been following his movements around the bar, his confident manner with customers, the way women flirted with him a little. She didn't know why he was so fascinating. He was handsome, yes, but there had been so many handsome men over the years who had not moved her.

She felt Saskia's eyes on her, and for a moment she considered admitting that there was no party, but the words were out of her mouth before she could stop them. 'The party's at my place,' she said, responding to his challenge, draining the last of her drink and standing, a little unsteady on her feet.

As the three of them walked towards the door, Simone found herself looking back over her shoulder for Camille's tall figure, but she was nowhere to be seen.

The air was still warm and it smelled of fish. Boats were coming into port with their catches, carrying great containers flashing with silver scales in the blue evening light.

'So, you have a summer place on the island?' Félix asked, his hands in his pockets. There was that glimmer in his eye again, as though he was daring her, testing her.

Simone had said her name in front of Camille, but it didn't seem like Félix had recognised it. Or perhaps as an island resident he was simply immune to the influx of wealthy Parisians visiting for the summer. Either way, being with him felt freeing in the same way as with Saskia, and Simone found herself running towards the bicycles. 'I'll race you.'

Félix laughed and grabbed his bike then they took off, with Saskia a little behind.

'Hey, wait up,' she called.

The wine and the warm air streamed through Simone, and she felt a ripple of elation as she headed away from the port into the open poppy fields, their dark heads drooping under a slip of a moon. The muscles in her legs burned as she tried to stay in front of Félix, but he was fast, having grown up riding the paths that ran like veins through the long arm of the island. He would know these routes even better than her.

They followed the path that skimmed the beach and the pine forest, and the scent of crushed pine needles filled the air. Félix overtook her and she yelled out for him to stop. He did, and they bent over, breathless, laughing, their handlebars touching.

They were alone in the dark with the sound of the sea and the wind in the pine trees. Simone felt heady with something she could not name, and she felt herself move towards Félix. Her arms were around his back, his T-shirt damp with sweat, and she was kissing him. He tasted like the sea and the forest, mixed with smoke.

He pulled away from her and got off his bike, creating a barrier between them, and she saw confusion in his dark eyes. She realised she didn't know anything about him beyond him being a handsome barman, and she realised in that moment that she had misjudged him – that he was not like the men she knew in Paris.

'Sorry, I—' She stepped back, her hand on her forehead.

He ran a hand through his hair, suddenly awkward. 'So, you're up in the expensive part of the island?' He gestured towards the lights along the shoreline.

She shrugged but felt uneasiness scuttle through her.

'Where's Saskia?' He squinted into the dark path behind them.

'Saskia!' Simone called, but there was no answer.

Félix got back on his bike. 'She won't know which way we went,' he said, and Simone felt guilt twist in her stomach, for kissing Félix and abandoning Saskia. How had she just left her friend when she knew nothing of the island? Kissed a man she barely knew? And the thought came to her then. *I am just like my mother.*

'We need to find her,' Félix said.

'Yes, sorry,' she said, but Félix was already riding back the way they'd come.

The paths seemed darker now, the shadows more ominous, and Simone shivered. There were any number of paths Saskia could have taken. They reached a fork in the path and Simone took one way and Félix the other.

As she rode, she called Saskia's name, wondering how they would ever find each other again on these dark paths, and if, just as simply as the three of them had come together, they would now come apart. But then she heard Félix call out and Saskia and Félix were there. Saskia was pale, even paler than before, her eyes huge in the dark, and Simone dropped her bike and ran to her, drawing her into a hug.

'I'm so sorry.'

Saskia's face crumpled and Simone saw that she had been afraid.

Saskia wiped the tears from her eyes with shaking fingers, clearly embarrassed. 'Sorry, it's just, I'm so far from home, and a little drunk, and the island is so big ... Thank God I heard Félix.'

He hung his head. 'Sorry, I got carried away trying to race Simone.'

Saskia laughed through her tears. 'So, who won?' she asked, and Simone felt the tension between them ease.

'I did,' Félix said. 'But I get the feeling Simone is the kind of person used to winning,' he added wryly.

Simone felt chastised under his steady gaze. She knew she had gone too far in kissing him, and saw that Félix understood her, quite clearly.

'There is no party,' she said, shivering with the rawness of her own honesty.

Silence fell between them, only punctuated by the soft sounds of owls in the trees.

'Well, that's killed the mood,' said Félix.

Saskia laughed and Simone felt her shoulders drop in relief. 'I mean, there still can be one, but it will only be us,' she said, feeling too vulnerable, too open to their rejection. 'I don't know why I said it.'

'To be honest, I expected more from Simone Durant,' Félix said, not without warmth, but Simone felt a chill run down her spine. Why hadn't he said anything? She felt sad that the innocence of their connection was over. How long would it be until Saskia knew too?

'I have no food in the house. Maybe wine though,' she said.

'Saskia, what do you think?' There was an intimacy in his voice, and Simone wondered what had happened between them when he found her.

'I think we can make that work,' Saskia said, and Simone squeezed her hand.

They rode in formation like a flock of birds so no one would get lost. The windows of the villa were dark as they leaned their bikes against the stone wall.

'It's a mansion,' said Saskia.

'*Mon Dieu*, you live here, just you?' asked Félix.

'Just me,' Simone said, feeling the full impact of those words, and also wishing, for perhaps the first time in her life, that she lived in a normal house.

She led the way inside, avoiding the lounge full of books, and took them through to the kitchen. She pulled a bottle of red wine out of the cupboard and found glasses filmy with dust, which she rinsed in the sink. Saskia and Félix hovered. Simone could feel the gulf that had opened between them.

'Sit, sit down,' she said, gesturing to the bar stools at the island bench. She poured the wine and handed it to them.

Félix drummed his fingers on the bench. 'Okay, show me the food you have. I will make something for our party of three.' He got up and opened the pantry. 'Hmm, you really don't have food. How do you survive, Simone Durant?'

She shrugged and laughed awkwardly at his use of her full name. She wondered if Saskia, who had no idea of her heritage, thought it strange.

'Bread, oranges and black coffee.'

'That sounds like the perfect diet,' said Saskia reassuringly.

'I'm sorry, I know it's late, and I don't even have anything to feed you ...' Simone said, putting her wine down. She wanted to apologise for bringing them here under false pretences, for not being honest about who she was.

'You do have food!' said Félix, holding up a packet of spaghetti that he must have found in the back of the pantry. 'We will ignore the use-by date. Pasta never goes off.'

She was going to protest but he was already filling a pot with water at the sink. He found the slab of butter in the dish by the bread bin and a salt grinder.

'All we need for a meal.' He raised a sceptical brow. 'I hope this is my salt ... Île de Ré salt.'

'Oh, I'm not sure,' Simone said, confused.

'You can't ask a *saunier* to eat his pasta without good salt.'

'What's a *saunier*?' asked Saskia.

'A salt farmer,' Simone said, understanding now the deep brown of his skin, his rough worker's hands.

Simone would see the *sauniers* on hot afternoons in their brimmed hats, scraping the salt that would rise to the surface of the shallow seawater pools, like men collecting the earth's dried tears. White piles lined up like hourglasses measuring out the hours.

Félix ground the salt granules onto the benchtop, licked his finger and placed it on his tongue. He shook his head. 'No, no, no, this will not do at all. We need real salt. *Fleur de sel.* Come, I'm taking you both to my salt marshes.'

CHAPTER 6

The girls find the old stone pool first. The heat rises from
the overgrown lawn even at this early hour and Dee strips to
her underwear and hovers on the edge, her skin pale against
purple wildflowers. Dylan is still asleep and I feel as though
we've stepped into a secret garden, just the three of us. The
yard is ringed by a high stone wall where climbing vines and
ivy stretch out curious tendrils.

I close my eyes against the gentle sun and feel my senses
awakening. Bird calls in the fruit trees, the lazy buzz of bees
in the lavender. I feel the grip of hunger in my belly and my
fingertips still smell like citrus from last night. My eyes spring
open. Everything is in sharp relief. The blades of grass under my
feet are like cut glass. I realise I have not taken my tiny white
pills. My routine has been lost in the crossing of time zones, in
the sleeping on couches, the eating of oranges for dinner. I feel
it already, that familiar clench in my gut. My body waking up,
tuning in.

'Mum, it's all green and murky, Dee can't go in,' shouts
Lara, her small face lined with worry.

She's right, the pool is a luminous green, tinged by an algal
bloom. Dee dives in anyway and it takes my breath away,

her defiance, and the shock of the strength of my emotion, as though that cold water has sucked the air out of my own lungs.

She surfaces, gasping and floats on her back. Lara grabs handfuls of the purple flowers and throws them into the pool with a nervous energy I completely understand. Anxiety is a physical sensation, a prickling to alertness. It is a hair trigger.

'She's okay La-La, everything's okay,' I say as much for myself as for her. Dee looks like a nymph floating there in the green, with the flowers surrounding her long limbs, her upturned palms. I want to dive in, feel the cool surround me too, but I know I must go inside to find towels and my medicine.

A woman's head pops up above the fence. She has dark hair and a round, friendly face. Very fast French issues from her mouth.

'*Je suis désolée, madame, je ne comprends pas.*' The words spool out of me, my apology for not understanding what she's said. It's happened without engaging my conscious mind and I feel both my children's eyes on me, no doubt as shocked as I am that another language has flowed so effortlessly from my mouth.

'Oh, you are English? American?' she asks in stilted English.

I'm nervous suddenly that she's seen us for the intruders that we are, who broke in last night and gorged ourselves on ripe fruit. 'Australian,' I say.

'Hello, welcome. It is so nice to see the villa with some people in her. *Je suis Madame Gardner.* I am pleased to meet you.'

'*Bonjour,*' I say, realising with relief that she must think we're legitimate Airbnb visitors. Introducing ourselves, I say, '*Je m'appelle Saskia et voici Dee et Lara.*' The girls wave.

'Oh, *mignonnes,*' she says. 'You have a nice accent. You have lived in France, *non?*'

I feel my cheeks flush. For many years, I have not felt the chronic blushing I used to suffer. I realise, with a hot jolt, that I may have skipped more than one of my white pills.

'*Oui*,' I say. I do not say I lived on the island. That would invite too many questions. 'But my vocabulary is not so good anymore.'

She makes a tutting noise to argue otherwise, and I smile.

'Is there a *boulangerie* close by?' I ask to change the subject.

'We had to eat oranges for dinner,' says Lara with painful honesty, and I silently implore her not to mention breaking the window open.

'Oh, I have baguette, croissant, the fresh butter, and … how do you say? *La confiture*.'

'Jam,' I say.

'I have the jam from my own fruit. Do you have *du lait? Le café? Restez là*. I will bring *le petit déjeuner*.'

'Oh, *merci*, but bringing us breakfast is really not necessary.'

But she's disappeared behind the wall. My hunger almost but not quite outweighs my wariness. How well did she know Simone? Will I have to divulge that I own half this house? Where are my white pills? I'm aware that my thoughts and my heart are beginning to race faster than I've felt them do for as long as I can remember.

I manage to find a linen cupboard and wrap Dee in a towel then wipe down the table in the courtyard before Madame Gardner returns with a tray full of breakfast. I thank her profusely, but she waves me away, and I find I don't know where to put this gratitude welling inside me. She's set out bowls of hot chocolate for the girls and she shows them how to dip the flaky croissants in them. I eat fresh baguette with slabs of yellow butter and raspberry jam, washed down with strong black coffee.

'Where's Dad?' Dee asks between mouthfuls.

'Oh, you are four? I should have brought more food, you were all so hungry,' Madame Gardner says.

'We got in late. No time for grocery shopping,' I say.

'Ah, the *supermarché* is close, I will show you. There are *les vélos* – how do you say, bicycles? – in the shed.' She points to a corrugated-iron structure covered with ivy. The girls get up from the table and pick their way through the overgrown garden.

'Simone, the owner, she loved to ride everywhere.' A shadow passes over her face, and I know then that Madame Gardner is mourning her death. Perhaps that is why she's sitting here with us, perfect strangers, eating breakfast, imagining the two of them once taking a meal together. I'm desperate to ask her what Simone was like at fifty. How she died.

Dee and Lara emerge from the shed. I gasp when I see the pale, rusted green metal and the cobwebbed basket at the front. I can picture Simone, with her long bare legs pedalling fast, the wind in her hair.

'I hope you left some for me.' Dylan greets Madame Gardner with a double kiss, which surprises me, and also doesn't. Of course he has learned the polite custom of this country. Now he's complimenting her jam, saying '*très bon*' in a terrible accent, which she clearly thinks is adorable.

A feeling like electricity is buzzing through my brain and I press my fingertips to my temples. I leave the girls brushing cobwebs off the bikes and excuse myself then go into the house. I find my cosmetics bag in my suitcase and rifle through it for my pills. I know what's happening: the brain zaps, the racing heart and mind. I'm going back to my natural state. My body is on edge, poised to respond to something, anything. I find my pills. Pain lances through my chest, an old feeling. But I'm also aware of another emotion. *Relief.* To feel so keenly. I had forgotten.

I pop the two pills I've missed into my palm. Part of me longs for the numb, silent space in my mind, the place I've existed in, unquestioning, for so long. The other wants to let the feelings come, even the hard ones, even the terrifying ones. I know there are things here I must face. I want to be brave, but I'm not stupid. I know I can't go cold turkey. I split one pill with my nail and put half on my tongue. The smallest amount I've had in more than a decade. Trepidation and exhilaration trill inside me.

Dee comes into the lounge, brushing cobwebs from her hands. 'So, I told Madame Gardner that we own half the villa. She thought we were just holiday rentals, and she wants to know … how do we know Simone Durant again?'

My gut shifts as though it's made of sand. This feeling again. I'd almost forgotten the shifting desert of anxiety that once took up every plain in my body. So strange and yet so familiar, like this place.

I follow Dee outside. Madame Gardner is sitting in the sunny courtyard with a cheery, expectant look on her face. She stands, and her eyes are shining with emotion when she kisses me four times on alternate cheeks.

'You are like family then. You were Simone's dear friend. Please, you should have said. And I was treating you like the strangers.'

Dylan says what I'm thinking. 'If that's how you treat strangers, God, what sort of spread do you put out for friends?'

She points her finger in the air and there's a twinkle in her eye. 'Ah, you must come to lunch *chez moi*. I make for you the traditional French lunch.' Her English has disintegrated with the strength of her emotion.

'Invitation accepted, Madame Gardner.' Dylan pronounces her name with a flourish, rubs his stomach and stretches. '*Merci* for le breakfast. Dee, what's the water like?'

The girls have brushed the sand and dust off the old bikes and are riding them in circles around the paved area of the garden. The wheels crunch on the gravel.

'It's nice,' says Dee, extending a bare foot to ground herself and leaning down to pick a flower and thread it behind her ear. For a second her beauty startles me, and I see that she's almost a woman and I wonder how I hadn't noticed that until this moment. She has my pale red hair but Dylan's Mediterranean skin and green eyes.

'Well, I might go for a quick run on the beach then do some laps.' Dylan slaps his thighs, stands and goes inside.

Madame Gardner is sitting with her hands clasped together in front of her, clearly ready to hear about my life story with Simone. My mouth goes dry and all I can taste is stale coffee and the slight chemical tang of my pill.

She must interpret my silence for grief, because she pats my hand, her brows pulled together in sympathy. Her hand is rough and comforting, like a woollen jumper. She pours me more coffee and I wonder if she has children, such is her capacity for nurture.

'It's very difficult to talk about a friend dying, *non*?'

My heart scrunches inside my chest. I feel a cold guilt then, that I am taking this woman's home when I don't even know how she died. But I cannot ask for fear of giving myself away.

'How long did you know her?' I ask, deflecting.

Madame Gardner sits back, her arms folded against her chest. Under her linen pinafore she has the short but strong body of a woman who has worked outside for many days of her life.

'Simone's family came here to this house every summer since she was a child. Myself and Jean-Marc, *mon mari*, my husband, only moved next door ten years ago, when we got too old to work on the farm. Now we just work in the garden. God bless him, he thinks he's working.' She rolls her eyes. 'But his knees are not so much working anymore.' She shakes her head and takes a thoughtful sip from her cup. 'I met her only a few times as a neighbour. She did not like to return to the island.' Her voice lowers to a hush. 'Because of what happened to her parents here, you understand. The family was cursed. I'm sure you know the story … Sad, sad for that poor girl. But she returned not so long ago, just for a few weeks. She was very private, but she did say she was writing something.'

I smile. 'She was writing a book?'

'As I'm sure you know, she came from a very famous line of French writers. Such a shame she did not have children, pass on her family's gifts.' Madame Gardner looks towards my girls who are still cycling in circles, an indulgent smile on her lips. 'Your children are *très belles*.'

'Thank you. Do you have children?' I'm keen to steer the topic away from Simone, but at the same time I want to know how the last twenty-six years of her life played out, beyond what I can read on Wikipedia.

'Yes, a boy and a girl. They both live on the mainland. I am lucky, they are quite close by, so I can see my grandchildren.'

'That must be special.'

'It gives me something to look forward to. We have them here for Sunday lunch once a month.'

'Oh, lovely.'

Madame Gardner leans forward and touches my arm. 'Do you know what happened, in the end? The newspapers do not report it. I only know because a gentleman was at the house, perhaps, how do you say, the real estate person, and he told me the owner had passed away and he was making a value for the house. I am shocked, very sad not to know how she died. I think that maybe she did not want everyone to know because of that curse.'

My skin ripples despite the warm sun on my face. 'I only received a letter, about the house,' I venture. 'There was no mention of her death and ...' I can feel my pulse at my temples. 'I had not spoken to her in quite a while.'

'You have not told me how you two met.'

I swallow and lick my lips, which feel dry and chapped. 'We met at an art gallery, in Paris.' The lie slides off my tongue so easily it startles me. Petra's fantasy that she made up over the phone. It makes so much sense to steal it. 'I'm an artist,' I add. I feel so bad lying to this lovely woman, but how can I tell her the truth? That our bond was inexplicable, immediate. That everything came together as easily as it fell apart.

'Oh, an artist. *Naturellement.* Simone was always surrounding herself with *les créatifs*. The beautiful people always were attracted to Simone. She was a beauty, like her mother.'

'See, Mum, I told you the beautiful people come here for the summer,' Dee calls. She has been listening to everything.

'Oh yes, the Parisians come for the summer. *Les vacanciers.*' Madame Gardner clicks her tongue and her face darkens. 'But this island, it is the place the beautiful people visit, but it has had the tragedy over the years. The Durant curse, their car accident on the bridge, I'm sure Simone told you. So tragic.

61

And the little girl who went missing here, what was it now? More than twenty years ago.'

I feel the sands shift again, my blood rush through my veins as though they have been newly opened. My body is no longer under my command and I realise my story – this island, our joint history – is no longer mine to control.

*

Le passé

The salt marshes were mirrors of moonlight, as though the night sky was gazing at its own reflection. Simone had seen the marshes under a hot sun, the salt being scraped from the water's surface with wooden rakes, but this looked different, other-worldly. It smelled briny, but underneath there lingered a scent of rot, and as she got off her bicycle she felt a shiver down her spine. They were all alone, with only the sound of lapping water and the calls of shelducks, white stilts and owls.

They might have found a late-night supermarket and bought *la fleur de sel* for their pasta over the counter, but she knew this was not the point. The point was the thing she had glimpsed in Félix when they took off on their bikes into the dark. He wanted adventure, not supermarkets. And she understood that this was her discovery of Félix, the *saunier*.

They slipped off their shoes and followed him to the edge of the shallow basins. The water was still warm around their ankles from baking under the late summer sun. Félix trailed his fingers through it. 'We gather salt by hand. The island is famous for it – for *la fleur de sel*, the most expensive salt in the world.'

'Flower of salt. Salt flower,' Saskia said.

'Yes. It is rare and delicate and flaky, perhaps a little like a flower. There's a special process to harvest it, which is almost sacred. It dates back to the twelfth century, when it was introduced by Cistercian monks. My family has worked the marshes for generations.'

'That sounds romantic,' Saskia said.

'Spoken like someone who has never worked on the land.' Félix smiled.

'But you work at the bar too?'

'I work the marshes during the day and the bar at night.'

'You must be exhausted.'

He shrugged. 'You get used to it, but one time I did fall asleep at the bar after a shift.'

'Camille Bisette would not have liked that,' Simone said.

'I think this is why she is always watching me now. It is perhaps why I got into trouble for speaking to you. Thank you for rescuing me, by the way. With the invitation to a party that was not a party.'

Simone smiled, understanding that he was telling her that everything was okay after the kiss and Saskia being lost.

They tiptoed along the thin ridges that separated the basins, and two egrets rose into the sky, startling them, making them laugh uneasily. It felt as though they were breaking the stillness that lay over this land, breaking the code of the ancient salt men, Félix's ancestors.

'Are you sure it's okay for us to walk through this?' Saskia asked.

'Are you worried about dirty feet in people's salt?' Félix grinned.

'A bit. Why are there piles of salt?'

'It's the harvest. That is why we have the pyramids waiting to be collected. The coarse salt is collected first and then the very special salt crystals, the *fleur de sel*, are picked from the surface of the water with a special tool.'

'And your family taught you this when you were how old?' Saskia asked.

'I have been playing in these marshes, learning the ways since I was three years old.' He bent and ran his hand through the water with a slow reverence, and Simone remembered running her fingertips along the leather spines in her father's library, the crack of a book opening, her own apprenticeship of sorts.

Her father had been the kind of man for whom knowledge was power. From a very young age he had taught her that her brain was her most powerful asset – that the world could be accessed through books, through words. And her mother, for all her beauty, knew that her real power, her real intrigue, lay in the power of her mind. There was an age gap of a decade between her parents, and Simone came to understand that her mother was attracted to men of a certain age and a certain intelligence. She could have had anyone, and she'd chosen a man who valued her for more than her beauty.

'It's very special, I think, this knowledge that you have, the care of these ancient techniques,' she said.

'It is special, this place,' said Félix, crouching to pick up a handful of salt. 'What it gives, what it takes. The fine balance that exists in the natural world. One storm can ruin months of work. That is why we must know how to read the weather. It is almost my family's religion. I grew up expecting always that I would carry on the tradition but ...' He shook his head and then gazed out past the marshes to the dark horizon of the sea beyond.

None of them spoke, there was only the soft lap of water, and Simone understood the thing that inexplicably bound the three of them.

'You want something different from your life,' she said, guessing that the spark she had glimpsed in him was a force that was destined for things beyond this tiny island.

He rubbed the granules between his palms. 'My family expect me to never leave the island, to spend my life here harvesting the salt as they did. And you see how it is difficult for me to leave behind this knowledge. It feels like I am letting my family down.'

'I let my mother down,' said Saskia, her voice soft. 'I left when I should have been going into my second year studying law. It's all she ever wanted for me. She spent everything on a private education for me, and worked so hard, struggling as a seamstress. We never had any money, and I abandoned it all and came here to chase my dreams of being an artist.'

It felt like the salt was drawing out impurities, their fears and truths, as though by osmosis.

Simone wanted to say, *I want something different from my life, too.* But how could she, when all Saskia and Félix would see was her privilege? *I don't know if anyone truly loves me for who I am*, she thought. *I want my life to mean more than my family's money. I want my parents back. I fear that my mother left me, and she took my father with her.* Standing there, she was forced to face the fact that, deep down, she knew her mother had done something destructive the night her parents had died. For all her charm and beauty and warmth, her mother was also something else, something Simone and her father had always forgiven – the flip side, the shadow. The days of locking herself in her study, the unwashed hair and unmade face, when only days before she had been polished, perfect. She would tell them she was immersed in her work, but Simone had always known it was more than that. It had always felt like the thing her mother was hiding from them, the part of herself she did not want to be seen.

I fear she was a bad person, and that I am a bad person.

'And what do you want from your life, Simone Durant? What are your dreams?' Félix asked, leading them deeper into the salt pans. The water was becoming cooler. It was the first time someone had ever asked her that and she felt a wave of gratitude mixed with sadness wash through her. How could you want for anything when you had everything?

'People think I have everything,' she said simply.

'But you don't have your parents,' said Saskia, her voice soft, and Simone felt the ache of tears building.

'But you do have friends who cook for your dinner parties where there is no food and no dinner party,' said Félix, and Simone laughed and felt that she was being seen for who rather than what she was.

'Okay, who's coming in?' he asked, as the water reached his thighs.

'No! It's too cold,' said Saskia, her arms crossed over her chest.

'Come, *la fleur de sel* traditionally was used as a healing ointment for wounds. My family believe salt purifies and heals, and we are all a little bit broken, *non*?' Félix lowered himself into the water, hooting with the cold.

'I'm coming in,' Simone said, feeling once again the wild invisible force that had propelled her and Félix to race their bicycles, that had made her kiss him. She eased her body in, gasping.

Saskia hung back but Félix reached for her and took her hand. Simone noticed the tenderness with which he drew Saskia down beside him and Simone felt a small, uncomfortable snare in her chest. Was she imagining her connection with Félix?

Her insecurity made her bold. She held her breath and went under. Her eyes and nostrils stung but it felt good, purifying. And then she was breaking the surface and gasping for air and Félix and Saskia were laughing, and she remembered how her mother used to make her gargle saltwater when she had a sore throat and how sweet the tap water would taste afterwards. That's how the air tasted afterwards – sweet. And her body felt light, buoyant, as though there was nothing tying her to the earth anymore.

She looked over, and Félix and Saskia were floating on their backs as if they were bathing in the holy pools of the sky. They were still holding hands and Simone felt a jolt of jealousy, but Félix reached for her and pulled her between them, and Saskia took her other hand. They lay like that, linked together, watching a flock of white stilts rise into the night sky.

CHAPTER 7

Anxiety has been my constant companion, a needy thing tugging at me from the inside. I didn't have a name for it when I was Lara's age. I'd see my mother return late from working at the drycleaners, sewing hems and attaching missing buttons, with dark circles under her eyes. Or there would be no milk in the fridge and the bread would be stale and I would feel it coil like a snake in my belly, ready to strike. I thought it was normal to have a constant sense of impending doom. That dark brewing, as an instinct, disconnected from thought. The feeling always came first, before it dawned on me why I was feeling scared. Was Mum unhappy? Would we have enough food for the week?

But I know now why worry is pooling inside me, flooding me, as I sit opposite Madame Gardner in the sun in this villa that is not yet mine. *The little girl whose face appears in my papercut pictures.*

'What happened?' asks Dee, who has stopped cycling. She steadies herself with a bare foot on the chair next to me. She has chipped blue toenails. She is always half-listening to the conversations of adults. Lara is squatting by a pot of rosemary, watching ants, picking at flowers.

Madame Gardner waves her hand dismissively. She is a mother, a grandmother. I can see she will handle it sensitively, that she doesn't want to upset Dee and I'm so grateful for that. 'It was a long time ago. A little girl went missing on the island. Very sad. Her grandmother still lives here. She is hoping always that her granddaughter will come home, they say. Always waiting. Always hoping. Very sad. ' She shakes her head.

The pool of dread deepens inside me.

'How old was she?' asks Dee and I wish I could protect her from all the hard, bad things in the world.

Madame Gardner squints her eyes in thought. 'She must have been, oh, what was it now? Three or four. So young.'

Un, deux, trois. *One, two, three. I count on my fingers and Juliette counts on her tiny ones. We are learning each other's language, by bird, by flower, by whale, by sun, by grass. There are too many words and not enough to express the delight a child takes in learning to name the world.*

Regret wrings my insides and I close my eyes and force air into my lungs. I was meant to protect her. I cannot do this. I cannot be here.

'That's so sad,' I hear myself say.

'Mum, are you okay?' Lara is here in front of me, her eyes searching mine. She has dirt under her fingernails. My sensitive daughter is so attuned to my emotions.

'Jet lag,' I say, rising and steadying myself on the back of the chair. 'I think I just need a Panadol.' I need my pills. I'm not accustomed to feeling this much. It's drowning me.

'Oh, forgive me, forgive … I have stayed too long talking, talking, talking. My husband, he is always telling me this and I am never listening.' Madame Gardner laughs and stands and puts the remains of our breakfast onto her tray.

'No, I'm sorry,' I say, brushing crumbs from the table, but my hands are shaking and a cup clatters in its saucer. 'I think I'm just exhausted. You've been very kind.'

Dylan comes out of the villa with his running outfit on. Madame Gardner disappears through the gate. The knot in my gut loosens. Lara stands on the edge of the pool, dipping a toe in, and I give her a quick hug. It's strange that my youngest child is the only one who understands what it's like to be inside my jittering body.

'I'm going inside for a shower,' I say.

'Did you ask her about Félix Allard? She seems like the town gossip,' Dylan says.

My eyes flick to the fence line and embarrassment flushes through me. 'Dylan,' I say, incredulous, 'she just fed us breakfast.'

He widens his eyes. 'She can't hear. Well, did you?'

'No. I'll check my emails. There might be one from Monsieur Rombard about setting up a meeting.'

'Well, if you don't, I will. I want to get this place on the market ASAP.'

'It's not your place to sell.' I realise I've just said out loud what I'm thinking. I rarely say out loud what I'm thinking. But something runs up my spine, some feeling I can't quite articulate.

Dylan is tying a shoelace on his running shoe, and he looks up. 'What was that?' His voice is strangely neutral but his expression is not.

When I say nothing, he laughs. 'Sorry, but it's just I thought you were making some claim over this place, as though my family's money doesn't prop up your studio.' He shakes his head.

He's right. Shame shimmies through me. It is a familiar dance, but without the buffer of my pills it has become a boisterous thing, doing a crude cha-cha in my gut.

'Mum, can we *all* go exploring on our bikes?' Lara asks.

Her forehead is creased in worry, and I'm taken back to myself, age eleven, when my parents were still together. All those times I tried to ease the tension between them, distract and fix, distract and fix. I know exactly how my youngest daughter is feeling right now and why she said 'all'. She wants us to be a family, to do things together. It's her only power, the only way for her to try to stem the undercurrent of resentment she senses.

'Just let Dad go for his run. I'll take a quick shower and then we'll go for a ride.'

I kiss her hair and walk into the villa. It's cooler inside and I feel dizzy suddenly going from the bright outside to the dim interior. I steady myself on the dining room table. I'm finally alone. I can't hide from the pain of the past anymore. I need my pills. Our luggage is spilling in the middle of the loungeroom, as though we've been here for days instead of hours. I gather my bag, and the timber is rough and dusty on my bare feet as I climb the staircase that leads to the bedrooms.

I realise as I reach the first floor that this house has never left me. It has been in my dreams. The hallway is long, with a bank of windows along the right side where muted sunlight filters through. I look out and see the ocean painted pale against a watercolour sky. There are three bedrooms leading off the hall and two glass chandeliers hanging from an ornate ceiling. Dust motes and cobwebs glint in the morning light.

I find myself in front of the first bedroom. Dylan has staked his claim on the master suite, Simone's bedroom. He's one of those people who take from life without apology. There is part of me that's in awe of such confidence. I think that's what attracted me to him in the first place. It's what made me think it was a good idea to spend my life with him.

We were walking through the Botanic Gardens one humid afternoon after he had taken me to lunch. It wasn't for any special occasion, but it was at a very nice restaurant by the water. From the very start we shared an appreciation of beautiful things, fine food and wine. I had, after all, lived in France. But I had no money, had dropped out of uni, and was working in a bar while I tried to make sense of my life. He always insisted on treating me and I suppose it felt like being looked after.

'Toss a coin in for luck,' he said, handing me a shiny dollar. We were by a stone fountain, surrounded by nymphs and mermaids. His hands were in his pockets, face and forearms tanned against the crisp white of his shirt. The sun was sheeting off the water and I squinted and tossed the coin into this mirror pool.

'What did you wish for?'

I smiled. Even back then, even after dating for nearly a year, I had secrets. There were things I kept from him, pain I kept from him, but ours was never a relationship founded on deep emotional connection. We liked doing the same things together. His certainty eased my insecurity, the surety that infused everything he did.

'Saskia, what's that shiny thing? Just there?'

I sat on the mossy stone and dipped my hand into the cool water and gasped.

His face, my heart, full of hope as I lifted the ring from the fountain. And as he put it on my finger and kissed me in the bright sunlight, the smell of grass and flowers infusing the air, a blanket of calm descended and all the dark corners of my mind lit up. I felt, perhaps for the very first time since everything that had happened, safe.

I step inside Simone's bedroom now and feel a rush of longing. I take in the wide, bleached wooden floors, the long, shuttered windows and the arched mirror propped in the corner. The writer's desk is still there in the place where the sun falls in long lines through the window. *Why have you brought me back here, Simone? Why have you given this place to me? I don't deserve it. Why have you made me face this? Why have you made me face myself?*

I'm going to have to see Félix again very soon. I'm stumbling around blindly in a crumbling marriage. I tell myself it must be the jet lag. I tell myself I won't cry. I can't. I haven't, not for years. I touch my fingers to my face and find it wet. *Mouillé.* Tears. *Les larmes.*

*

Le passé
The wind set the salt to her skin as they rode from the marshes back to the villa. Simone was acutely aware of the others as they glided silently through the night in single file, careful that Saskia didn't get left behind, and attuned to Félix when he drifted close and then swerved away. It felt beautiful and rare, this strange connection the three of them had, but it also prickled, like salt on skin. Her hair was stiff with it and she put the ends in her mouth and sucked, feeling her belly growl with hunger.

Back at the villa, Félix put the salt granules he had collected into the boiling water for the pasta and they ate the spaghetti directly from the pot, sitting around the kitchen table, salt flakes and butter piquant on their tongues.

'You see? The salt makes the dish,' said Félix, grinning.

'It's good.' Simone elbowed him. 'Even if we had to cross the island and swim in cold water to get it.'

'Come on, you loved it.' His eyes flashed.

'Is this some special French tradition I'm being initiated into?' Saskia asked, twirling her fork and leaning over, strands of her long hair falling into the pot.

Simone scooped Saskia's hair back. It was stiff with salt like her own.

'*Oui, oui.* This is how all French people eat their meals.' Félix sucked spaghetti into his mouth and winked. 'It is not quite like the lunch you take with the Bisettes, is it? We know not to disturb Henri or Camille for that hour and that the service and food must be *parfait*. Perfect. It is how I knew you were the Bisettes' new nanny.'

Félix caught Simone's eye. 'It is a little strange, I think, even for the French? This fancy lunch Saskia takes with the Bisettes in the restaurant each day?'

Simone raised an eyebrow.

'Yes, I have to dress Juliette very nicely, a little bow in her hair – it's quite formal,' said Saskia.

'Henri Bisette is, how do you say ... a little bit eccentric. A genius in the kitchen, so people expect this kind of thing. You take the same menu every day, *non*?' asked Félix.

Saskia nodded. 'It's always five courses. Onion soup, followed by charcuterie, then the *plat du jour* – chicken, fish on Fridays – then green salad and cheese, and finishing with a tarte.' She looked confused suddenly. 'I've been wondering if all French people eat the same food every day for lunch.'

Félix's eyes met Simone's and they laughed. 'Only the strange ones.' He nudged her playfully and she felt a lingering warmth where their shoulders had touched. 'Like Simone and her bread, coffee and oranges for breakfast, lunch and dinner.'

She stuck out her tongue. She could not tell them that she hadn't felt hungry for a year. That it felt like her stomach was filled with stones. 'No, but five courses, *c'est normal* for the French. You do not take much for lunch in Australia?' Simone asked, genuinely intrigued.

'Coffee and raisin toast, or a sandwich if I'm splashing out.'

'With, how do you say ... Vegemite?' Félix asked.

Saskia laughed. 'Yes, we eat Vegemite sandwiches *en Australie*! It's salt! You'd love it, Félix.'

He looked scandalised and got up as though to walk out. Simone and Saskia laughed.

'This is not right at all,' said Simone. 'There are no bistros offering a *plat du jour* where you can sit with a little wine and discuss ideas with the people in your university courses?'

'No. Maybe a beer and hot chips at the bar,' Saskia said. 'The student bar is where everyone goes and it's dark and smells like beer and cigarettes. Sometimes a band is playing so you can't hear anyone. And I didn't have many friends at uni anyway. First-year law was too big. The lectures were massive.' She laughed nervously. 'Why are you both staring at me?'

'It's no wonder you wanted to escape to France,' said Félix, pouring her more wine.

'*Non, non, non*. This is not what university is like in France at all,' Simone said.

'What did you study?' Félix asked.

'French. I wanted to be a writer, but I didn't finish my course.' Simone shrugged, affecting indifference.

Her university years were a source of discomfort, shame. She had studied language, French and English at the Sorbonne in Paris. She had done well in high school and earned the grades to get in, but she was always in her father's shadow. She was always the daughter of Stéphane Chevalier, head of the philosophy department. The granddaughter of the Durant dynasty. And she did not do her best work. She was caught up in going to parties and having dalliances and drinking too much wine and smoking too many cigarettes at lunch, just like many other first-year students.

Yet she wasn't like the other students. When she didn't hand in her assignments, her lecturers were more forgiving than they ought to have been, and so no one pulled her into line. Her father humoured her in the same way he did her mother, telling her to enjoy her first year of studies, no doubt expecting her genius would soon assert itself. And he knew her – he knew she had her heart set on being a writer, rather than a fashion model or a society princess. But his faith in her was unfounded. She dropped out before finishing her second year, seduced more by the image of being a writer than the idea of doing the work, and instead meeting her friends in cafés, discussing their works, discussing books over coffee and wine. Her father had made her promise that one day she would finish, but now he was gone.

'You still can be,' said Saskia. 'A writer. I've never studied art and that doesn't stop me from making it. I think there must be somewhere in this house for a writing room?'

'Yes, but you have talent.' She was about to ask if Félix had seen Saskia's sketches, but something made her stop.

'As for me, I spend my life harvesting salt in daylight and picking up beer bottles at night and I have these crazy, stupid dreams of being an actor, even though I have never done it.'

'Look at the three of us. *Les bohémiens*,' said Simone. 'Anyway, it's not a stupid dream. You have the looks, the charisma. Saskia, what do you think?'

Félix rubbed his jaw awkwardly and Saskia's face flushed.

'And you know,' Simone continued, 'you have just met someone who may have some film contacts in Paris. You are sharing your meal with her in fact.'

He smiled. 'Really?'

'Look at that smile. Hollywood is calling.' Simone placed her hand on her chest. 'It's making me swoon.'

He gave her a shove.

'Can you join a theatre troupe perhaps, in the meantime? I mean before you become a Hollywood heart-throb,' Simone said.

Félix gave her a withering look and laughed. 'There are no theatre troupes on Île de Ré.'

'How about on the mainland? La Rochelle?'

Félix shrugged. 'It's only a stupid dream. I'm embarrassed that I even said it out loud. *Non*, I will just keep on watching French films on my television.'

'Do you like the classics? The old ones in black and white?' Saskia asked. 'Every lunchtime at uni I would take my muffin, or Vegemite sandwich' – she rolled her eyes – 'and go and sit in the video laboratories and watch old French films.'

'You like French films? I love them! Especially the old ones.' Félix's eyes lit up. 'Jean-Luc Godard. *À Bout de Souffle. Breathless*, I think it is called in English.'

'*Bien sûr*, of course. A classic,' Saskia said.

'Nineteen-sixty. The New Wave. I did not realise you were … how do you say it in English?'

77

'A film buff? It's why I came to France. I took French as one of my subjects, and watching those films made me feel like there was a more exciting life out there for me. A life with more feeling, more passion ... less Vegemite sandwiches for lunch, more five course *plat du jour*.' She scratched her head. 'Or something.' She looked shy suddenly, as though she'd just allowed her passion to show.

'Perhaps like sharing pasta from a pot with two crazy French people you just met and bathing in salt?' asked Félix.

'And *Jules et Jim*. Did you watch this one?' Simone raised her eyebrows suggestively.

She saw by the deep flush in Saskia's cheeks that she knew this classic film about a love triangle of two men falling in love with the same woman. A charged silence opened up between them and Simone felt heady with it. She had pushed things too far, as usual.

Félix broke the tension with a loud laugh. 'You are suggesting that the French are obsessed with sex and food.'

'Well, aren't we?' Simone replied and they all laughed again, and she felt the tension ease.

'*C'est normal*,' said Saskia, shrugging nonchalantly, and Simone and Félix both laughed, because that is exactly what a French person would have said. 'Oh, and you forgot wine,' said Saskia, picking up the bottle and filling their glasses.

'And literature,' said Simone, lifting her glass. 'Come and see.' She grabbed her packet of cigarettes and led the way into the loungeroom where the floor was strewn with piles and piles of books. '*Voilà!*'

'*Oh, mon Dieu*,' said Félix. 'What are you doing in here?'

Simone lit her cigarette then put Nina Simone on the old

record player, and the music was like a long sigh falling over them, mingling with the dust in the air.

'I am reading all of my parents' books,' she said simply.

Saskia, perhaps loosened by the wine and talk of freedom and sex, came and drew her into an embrace. She smelled of salt and wine and something sweet, and for a moment Simone wondered if Saskia was attracted to her, if the *Jules et Jim* prediction would come true. But then Saskia drew away and Simone saw that she had sympathy in her eyes, and she berated herself for always thinking that intimacy was tied to sex. She understood in some essential way that this was not her only currency with these new friends and an expansive feeling filled her.

She was so accustomed to trading in this currency, to taking lovers, yearning for physical affection, but she knew she had never been in love, never felt beholden to or bewitched or truly connected to any one person. Perhaps she was measuring everyone against her parents' relationship.

She had asked her mother once what it felt like to be in love. She'd said that love was like a tree. The first flush of young love was the green buds, the new leaves in the canopy unfurling, stretching for the sun. But that after that initial excited growth, the branches solidified, thickened. And that with time, you saw that new love, as sweet and green as it had been, was bendy and soft, and now love became the low branches, the trunk of the tree, round and solid. She said the love between her and Simone's father had become the roots that reached down into soil and sustained her whole ecosystem.

Simone lay down amid the piles of books, and Saskia and Félix each took their own lounge, like little boats floating in an ocean of words. The room was filled with music and suddenly she was very tired. And when the music finished Félix got up and found one of her mother's poetry books and one of her father's philosophy books, and began to read aloud.

His voice was deep and rich, a voice that would carry over salt flats under a low sun, and belonged to sun-browned skin. A voice that sounded like it could be in films. And she felt cocooned and safe and warm, and it was like this that she fell asleep.

CHAPTER 8

I dry my tears with my sleeve and find my medicine pouch again then sit on the bed that used to be Simone's. She still has linen sheets, but they've softened with age, like skin. I stare at the pills that have kept me buffered against my emotions for so long. There is no doubt in my mind that they saved my life when my doctor sent me home with a six-week-old baby and a diagnosis of postpartum depression and acute anxiety. As soon as I started taking them, I began to wake in the morning without a pall of dread over me. I was no longer afraid of my own child and the fact that I was the only thing that stood between her and death. I was no longer afraid of myself.

I was in wonder at this new existence unmarked by rivulets of fear. Was this how normal people lived? These pills have kept me on an even keel ever since. They have allowed me to function day after day, to raise two children. To run an art studio. But sitting here in this light-filled room in France, with the smell of citrus sharpening the air, the breeze from the open window in my hair and the hammering of my heart, I must concede that they have also numbed me. I've been watching my life play out from behind a screen. It's made me safer, but it feels like I haven't been emotionally present. I've been adrift in my own existence, but at least I have been alive. I remember conversations over the years with my GP about cutting down my dose, but I also remember how I no longer trusted the person I'd been before my body knew that sweet chemical ease. And how the me who had coped without the pills had never been a mother.

The ping of my phone startles me. I'm definitely more jumpy. It's Petra texting.

Are you there? Send pictures of your castle. I want to see goddamn turrets.

I smile. I miss her already. She's worth the pain of the rest of her family. I think back to the last time we were all together, for her husband Mark's fiftieth. Petra had wanted to have it at a restaurant, make things simple, but her parents, Sal and Eric, had insisted it be at the big house. We all call it 'the big house' because it's enormous as the name would suggest, but also to differentiate it from the other houses – the little house being their holiday house on the north coast, and the medium house being any number of properties in their portfolio.

It had been a cool day for spring and at the last minute my mother-in-law, Sal, had insisted on getting a fire pit and heaters for the garden. Despite everyone's protestations that it wasn't really that cold, it had ended up being Petra and me standing on the delivery dock outside Bunnings a few hours before the party was to start.

'How the actual did we get roped into this?' Petra asked as we hoisted one of several fire pits into the back of her Audi wagon.

'Sal always gets what Sal wants,' I said, knowing we could talk freely about her mother. I'm well aware that I've blamed

Sal for the hurt her son has caused me over the years, and Petra is acutely aware that her mother is a narcissist.

'But why aren't our husbands doing this?'

'Well, it's Mark's birthday, so we'll excuse him,' I said.

'Dylan, though. What's he doing right now?'

'Shopping for his brother-in-law's birthday present.'

Petra rolled her eyes. 'That boy.' She always refers to Dylan as a boy, despite her being only three years older. She's protective of him, probably because so much of his care fell to her during their childhood. She resents her mother for this, but perhaps it's made her blind to Dylan's faults, as though she still sees him as the mischievous seven-year-old, as though she can't see that he and their mother are made of the same stuff.

Sal greeted us at the door a few hours later with her hair like a frothy silver cloud around her head and dressed in a flowing moss-green pantsuit. Petra and I have long joked that she is perpetually dressed as mother of the bride.

'Oh Dylan, what are you wearing? And you need a haircut,' Sal said, her eyes appraising his perfectly acceptable jeans and navy button-up shirt, the slight wave growing into his hair. 'You look lovely, Saskia, as always, and the girls.'

That's the thing about people, they're not all good, or all bad. Sal is the sole reason I have a studio, that I'm a working artist. She saw some of my papercut works, and maybe she wanted to be able to say her daughter-in-law was an artist, so she hired me a studio space and connected me with her artistic friends. Sal is the type of person who owns everyone and everything in her orbit. She sees herself as the epicentre of existence, and she rules over us all and we allow it. She owns me, and so, by extension, does her son. I always feel sorry for Dylan. His faults are understandable, almost justifiable, when I see his confidence quashed so brutally, so often, by Sal. And so I've probably repressed my anger at my own husband and taken it out on his mother.

The party was a success. It was freezing, of course, and the fire pits made the night, guests huddling around them like rich homeless people around burning bins.

'God, I hate it when she's right,' said Petra, spearing a marshmallow with a stick and shoving it into the flames. 'I mean, bloody marshmallows.'

'Mark's having a great time, and it wasn't too hard picking up the stuff. Click and collect!'

Petra took a sip of my wine. 'You always make excuses for her. I mean, I know she's your mother-in-law so you probably feel like you can't be too rude, but honestly, why do you do that?'

I felt hot suddenly, the heat of the fire cloying. *Because it's what I do every day of my life with her son, your brother*, I wanted to say. Because that afternoon I had come home from Bunnings and walked into the kitchen to find every utensil laid out on the kitchen bench. I had felt myself shrink.

'You did it again,' Dylan said. I knew not to interrupt, it only made things worse. He had, after all, told me the way the dishwasher was meant to be stacked many, many times before. I was usually so careful, but I'd been distracted with work and with the party and …

'Sorry,' I said. Sometimes if I said it nicely enough he dropped it.

'How many bloody times do I have to show you how to do this? Why is it so fucking hard to stack a dishwasher?'

'I had to meet Petra, I was in a rush.' I hated the pleading in my voice.

'So, your time is more important than mine? Is that what you're saying? Now I have to go through the knives and see which ones are still dirty.'

'Sorry, I—'

'You're always sorry, but it doesn't change anything does it?' His voice was rising. I felt my temples throb. 'Just get it right the first time. You're not a child.'

That was always our dynamic, from the very start.

My phone pings again, bringing me back to Simone's room. It's Petra again. It must be the middle of the night in Australia.

I haven't heard from you, are you ok? Did you arrive safely? Worried x

My chest aches with love for this woman, her brittle edges and soft inside. What would I do without her? She is the only emotional scaffolding in my life.

I pick up my phone and walk to the window. Down below through the trees, Dylan and Dee are in the pool and Lara is sitting on the edge, picking the wildflowers that ring the sandstone rim and floating them on the surface. I take a photo.

No turrets, I caption the photo and send it to Petra. It occurs to me that this photo, this text message, sums up my entire life. Disingenuous. A fractured fairytale. A lie. Even my best friend is not immune to my deception. She is part of it. All my energy has been honed into making sure there are *goddamn turrets*, so that no one would suspect what is going on beneath the surface.

The phone vibrates, likely with her reply, but I ignore it. I empty my pill pouch onto the bed and scoop up the small plastic containers filled with white tablets. One blue container for the pills that tamper down my anxiety long term, one green container for a more immediate blanket of calm. I am like a Pavlovian dog, such is the positive reinforcement of just looking at them as I run my fingers over their smooth, plastic surface. I crave that sweet blanket of calm.

I look down at Petra's message. *You have such a perfect life.*

I find myself gathering up the plastic containers, standing and walking over to Simone's writing desk. I sit down and smooth my hands over the sun-warmed wood. It's a real writer's desk, mahogany timber with a rolltop. It smells of furniture polish. It was her father's. She told me she never dared to write here, such was the weight of expectation, and, yes, it does look like the desk that once belonged to a French philosopher. There are tiny drawers with brass handles and shelves filled with the yellowing pages of well-thumbed novels. I pull out a drawer and find it empty. I put my pill pouch inside and shut it. I slide each drawer out, feeling the same anticipation as opening an advent calendar at Christmas.

It's not until I pull out the drawer directly under the desktop that I see it – a thick pile of paper. I know immediately what it is – a manuscript.

Fleur de Sel
by Simone Durant

*

Le passé
Simone awoke to the sound of a man singing and the smell of coffee. She was completely disorientated, and the base of her skull ached. The coffee and the sore head were echoes of her life in Paris, when she'd rouse late in her hotel suite to find coffee already prepared for her and the spoils of the

previous night making themselves slowly known in her body. But the singing ... She remembered the same voice reading poetry to her last night and felt herself flush with the warmth of anticipation. She looked over to see Saskia still asleep, a pale arm thrown over her face, the blanket Simone had draped over her kicked off. Simone pulled herself from the lounge and went into the kitchen.

'You have a very nice voice,' she said, yawning and helping herself to the coffee he had made in the old Italian percolator on the stove. He was washing up the pot they had abandoned on the table last night and she thought how practical this was, so unlike the men she knew in Paris. And it occurred to her how rare it was that a beautiful man was in her house before 10 am and she had not slept with him.

'I'm actually glad we didn't all have a *ménage à trois* last night,' she said, allowing her thoughts to float to the surface, this time in French. Félix stopped singing and she remembered suddenly by the look on his face that he was the son of *sauniers*, and not *un type* from Paris. 'Well, because of *Jules et Jim*,' she added innocently.

He cocked his head, his mouth transforming into a mischievous smile. 'You're used to getting what you want, aren't you, Simone Durant?'

She couldn't tell if he was flirting with her or reproaching her – it was disarming. 'You can just call me Simone, you know.'

'Haven't you noticed that famous people must be called by their full name? It doesn't seem right to just call you Simone.'

'In that case I will call you Félix Allard, soon-to-be film star.' She spoke with the same mixture of flirtation, but with a tinge of the mockery she suspected she could hear in his voice.

'Fine, good practice for when I'm famous,' he said, his dark eyes a challenge, and she realised that in French, and without Saskia, Félix was a different beast, more forthright. Bolder.

'Maybe I am used to getting what I want.' There was defiance in her voice too, but deep down she respected him for calling her out on it.

'Is it true you live in the Paris Ritz like Coco Chanel?'

'Why, would it change your opinion of me?'

'No, I'm just curious.' He shrugged and took a sip of his coffee.

'I moved there after my parents died. The photographers outside my door, the memories, it was too much to stay at the apartment ... and I just never left. It has security. It never felt like home though, not like this.' She caught herself, surprised at her own admission. But it was true. The villa felt like it belonged to more innocent times, her childhood, before she understood her place in the world. Before she felt the world of expectations.

'You inhabit a completely different world from us, don't you?'

She knew he was talking about himself and Saskia, and she felt her stomach twist at this division.

'Is that what you want? Riches? People to know you by both your names? Do you think it will make you happy?' There was more defiance in her voice than she intended.

He put his coffee down. 'Must I stay on the island and scrape salt and pick up empty beer glasses for the rest of my life? I have only ever seen Paris once, as a child.'

She felt her face flush and she shook her head. 'Of course not, but maybe what you seek is not the answer to all of your problems. You have a family here ... deep roots.'

She saw understanding cross his face, which softened. 'This is quite an intense conversation to be having before breakfast, but you are, after all, the daughter of a poet and a philosopher.'

She laughed, remembering the way he had spoken their words the previous night.

'What about your grandmother?' he asked.

'We have a complicated relationship,' Simone said.

Sophia Durant had an almost godlike presence in her life. She seemed unreal. Even her mother had not been close to her. Perhaps one could not be one of the wealthiest women in the world, a woman before her time in business, and an accessible and loving parent.

Saskia came into the kitchen then, her hair messy and her eyes a little puffy, and the atmosphere in the room changed. The charge that had been running between Simone and Félix fell away.

'Ah, here she is, sleepyhead,' Félix said, back in English now.

He sounded sweeter, more naïve or innocent, and Simone wondered how much of a person was lost in translation. Was she a softer, simpler version of herself in English too? Had she and Félix reverted to more complex versions of themselves when they'd spoken in their mother tongue, or was there something more complicated between them that was yet to show itself?

'I had too much wine last night.' Saskia pushed her hair back from her face. 'How do you say it in French? In English we say we're hungover or "dusty".'

'*Avoir mal aux cheveux*,' Félix and Simone both said in unison and their eyes met.

'To have sore hair?' Saskia laughed.

'It's like saying, "Even my hair hurts",' Simone said.

'And do you have an equivalent of "hair of the dog"?'

'I do not know this one,' said Félix.

'It means taking another drink to cure the hangover.'

'*Soigner le mal par le mal*,' Simone said. 'Shall we? Take another drink? Let's cycle to the Saturday markets in La Flotte. We'll pick up food for lunch and some bottles of rosé and then take a picnic and a swim.'

There was silence and Félix and Saskia looked at each other, perhaps surprised at the level of detail in this plan. Simone cringed, hating again how desperate she sounded. Félix probably had his family's thousand-year-old tradition to uphold, and Saskia had a small child to look after. They had lives, purpose.

'If you don't have other plans,' she added, flicking her hair.

'Hmm, let me think … that depends – do we get to have an afternoon siesta after the swim?' asked Félix.

Simone wasn't sure whether he was teasing her about the idea of them all sleeping together, or making an innocent remark, but there seemed to be a current of communication between them that Saskia wasn't aware of. It occurred to her then that there was both a perfect symmetry and an eternal awkwardness in the number three, perhaps the reason for it being so compelling in design.

'I have the whole weekend off,' said Saskia, filling a large glass with water from the tap. 'Juliette spends time with her grandparents.'

'Ah yes, so you are free!' exclaimed Simone.

'But don't you want a break from us hanging around?' Saskia looked to Félix.

'We might eat all your oranges and drink all your coffee,' he said.

'I might make you cook and read me poetry again,' Simone said, hoping she didn't sound too possessive, but Félix bowed elaborately, and she saw again the part of him perhaps destined for the stage. '*Mi casa es su casa.* My house is your house. Take a shower if you like. There are five bedrooms and three bathrooms upstairs. Saskia, you can borrow some of my clothes.'

Saskia drained her glass. 'I'd love to have a shower. I still smell like salt.'

'*Bien. C'est le plan.* Help yourself to anything. There's a big cupboard in the hall by the stairs with towels and things. I'm going to take a bath.'

'Do you mind if I go for a swim?' Félix asked.

'No, go ahead. I got all the leaves and flowers out of the pool a few days ago.'

'How domestic of you,' he said, and she poked her tongue out at him, noting that he still hadn't outed the extent of her family's wealth to Saskia.

The bathtub was her favourite place in the villa. It was claw-footed and overlooked the garden from beneath a long, arched window. Her mother had written poetry in the bath, scribbling her thoughts while leaning on a little wooden stool. The ink would run, as though the words were crying black tears, and Simone would find sheets of paper stuck to the bathroom tiles.

She craned her neck to see the pool, watching as Félix dived naked into the deep end before surfacing. He looked up towards the house and she ducked her head, unsure if he'd seen her watching him.

CHAPTER 9

I pull the manuscript from the drawer. It must be two hundred pages, unbound and written in French. The words are typed and the paper is fresh, unmarked. This is a relatively new work. Has it been published? Is this what Simone was working on when she spent time here recently? I imagine her eating Madame Gardner's neighbourly gifts and writing.

I place the pages on the desk. I notice the pound of my heart as I gently peel back the title page. *From the age of twenty-four I knew that I was cursed, that around every corner death might be waiting, just as it had been waiting for my parents …*

I sit back. Everything is tingling. Is it anticipation? Fear? I can't tell anymore.

'Mum, what's taking you so long?'

I swing around, press my hands to my face, startled. 'Girls, you scared me.'

'You haven't even had a shower yet and Dad's already back from his run and had a swim.' Lara pouts.

I can see from the sheen on their skin that Dylan has probably reminded them to wear sunscreen. He's told them to wear sneakers, when no doubt they would have opted for bare feet or thongs. He is far more practical than me, the better parent.

He has always enforced things. His world is one of order and security. I know deep down he probably doesn't trust me as a parent, sees me as flaky, a dreamy creative, and he would be right. I have never fully trusted myself.

'Sorry, sorry, I just got distracted.' It's something that has defined my life. Walking into rooms and forgetting why I'm there. Running late for appointments. I shove the manuscript back into the drawer. 'I'll just put some fresh clothes on and come down.'

The girls don't look convinced. I wonder if they resent me for all the time I spend in the studio. I wonder if I would be a better parent if I didn't have the need to create, the necessary release of my art vying for my attention. But I want to spend time with them, I do.

'Promise,' I say, rifling through my bag for a pair of shorts and a shirt.

They flop on the bed dramatically. Dee is wearing a white floral dress, with gold hoops in her ears and slick still-wet hair. She looks like she's twenty. Lara is in short denim overalls, her loose curls around her shoulders. My surge of love for them is so strong that I collapse onto the bed, pulling their long limbs to me. They both fight me off but we're laughing.

I dress quickly and pull my greasy hair into a bun, wash my face in the ensuite and smear on some sunscreen and tinted moisturiser. I've never in my life been so desperate for a shower. I haven't had one since I left Sydney, but I don't want to disappoint my children.

We go downstairs and I grab a broad-brimmed hat from the hook at the entrance and shove it on my head.

'Check your emails?' asks Dylan, balancing on a bike, his hair still wet from the pool. 'Did the lawyer write?'

'No,' I lie. I haven't checked my emails.

Dylan sighs.

We set off on our bikes through the quiet streets of Saint-Martin. It's lunchtime now and everyone is *à table*, the streets deserted as the French take their main meal of the day. I can smell the salt air from the harbour, but it's mixed with the scent of flowers and home cooking rising from behind bleached stone walls. Wild lavender and hollyhocks line the cobblestone lanes and above the sky is a wash of powder blue. We pass through the town and the landscape opens up into wide paddocks of long grasses, a windmill turning languidly in the breeze.

Lara and Dylan are out front. Dee meanders behind, her long red hair streaming behind her, and for a second, out of my peripheral vision, it's like seeing a ghost. It takes my breath away and I gasp, my lungs aching for more air.

'Cows,' shouts Lara, and I'm thankful for the distraction. We laugh at their indifferent brown faces. 'Mum, where are the donkeys?'

'I'm sure we'll see some, La-La.'

'Where are the people? It's deserted,' Dylan says.

'Everyone's having lunch.'

'I mean, where are all the tourists? I thought it was going to be overrun.'

'It's late in the season, French school must be back. They must have all returned to Paris.'

'What are we having for lunch?' Lara asks, as though she hasn't just consumed a croissant and baguette an hour ago.

'We'll pick up some supplies soon,' I call.

I don't know where we're headed but it doesn't seem to matter; we could ride from one end of the island to the other. I remember it only takes two hours because the terrain is entirely flat. We pass a field of poppies, red dabs in a blanket of green, the sharp spire of a church spearing the sky. It feels like we're riding through a living painting. The sky is lower and the saturation of colour is softer here, unlike home, where the colours are brilliant, jewel-like. I recall that this change in light was the first thing I noticed when I arrived aged nineteen. It had seemed impossible that the quality of the light could be so different on opposite sides of the earth. This was what had made me realise how small my world had been until I had left the place where I was born.

We continue on through wheatfields, their golden fingers swaying in the breeze, past vineyards heavy with grapes, until we come to a forest that ushers in the smell of pine needles and the ocean. I hear a soft whisper on the breeze, and I shiver.

'Let's get ice cream,' I say to distract myself, ground myself in the present.

A whitewashed café with blue-and-white umbrellas sits on the shoreline, an idyllic seaside tableau. It sells coffee and handmade ice cream, and Dylan tries to order from the woman behind the counter. She's having trouble understanding his English and I can see his jaw working to contain his frustration.

Before I even register what I'm doing, I'm stepping forward and ordering *un citron pressé et une glace*. The names of the different flavours of ice cream are there, as though they have formed on my tongue many times before. *Chocolat, fraise, vanille, framboise.* Dylan looks at me with an expression I haven't seen before. I can't tell if it's respect or fear — perhaps it's both.

We sit in the shade of an umbrella. The skin on my chest has begun to burn from the sun despite the sunscreen I hastily applied. The ice cream is served in delicate glass bowls. I close my eyes, listen to the sounds of the gulls, the wash of the shoreline, taste cool sweetness in my mouth, feel the heat buzzing on my skin, and I remember the feeling – *joie de vivre*.

I recall Simone explaining to me that the French are sensualists, that they are taught from a very young age to enjoy the small things in life: the breaking of fresh bread, a glass of wine with lunch, sunshine on an outside table at a well-loved café, good conversation with friends, a favourite scent dabbed on a wrist, a walk around your neighbourhood after a meal. They were entrenched in their culture, these small reverences. I was entranced, and greedy for this same simple worship. I saw how this beauty could enrich a life. Félix and Simone were my teachers.

My mind returns to Simone's manuscript in the desk drawer, excitement and trepidation mingling inside me.

Dylan's cool hand on my shoulder breaks my reverie. 'Can you check your emails?'

I find my phone in my bag and get up, flash the screen at him. 'Just need to find a good spot for reception.' I walk onto a boardwalk that stretches along the length of the beach, dunes to my left and mangroves to my right. The beach is scattered with pale, sand-coloured stones and I suddenly want to feel their cool smoothness beneath my toes. The sea is the same soft, pale blue as the sky. The Atlantic has a different feel from the Pacific. It's a tamer kind of animal.

Monsieur Rombard has written.

Dear Madame Wyle,
I hope you are finding the villa satisfactory. I took the liberty
of making the employ of a cleaner before you arrived and
instructed her to leave the key in the letterbox when she left, but
I believe there was a misunderstanding and she left it in a safe

box around the side of the house where she has left the keys for Madame Durant in the past. There is no code on the box, but I apologise and do hope you were able to find the key without troubling yourself too much.

I am making contact with Mr Allard but he is not returning our calls and emails at present and so I have not yet been able to set up a meeting as per Madame Durant's wishes. I am sending you his street address in La Flotte in the hope you might be able to contact him directly on the island and arrange a time for us to sign the paperwork together.

As executor of Madame Durant's estate, I will do everything in my power to oversee the matter on the island in person once a meeting time is appointed.

All kind wishes,

M. Rombard.

I squint into the sun and feel sweat bead on my brow. I'd anticipated that this very proper and formal lawyer from Paris would arrange everything and I'd just need to turn up and sign some papers on a large desk, with glasses of still water in front of us. Perhaps I'd make polite conversation with Félix as we waited for Monsieur Rombard to formalise things with expensive fountain pens, and then we would both go back to our vastly different lives.

But is this really what I need to do? Hunt down a French film star and stalk him at his house? If he won't respond to a lawyer offering him free property, why would he respond to me, a girl he knew twenty-six years ago, before he became famous?

And yet, there is part of me that needs to see how his face has aged, what life has given him, what it has taken.

I copy the address into my maps app – *19 bis, Cours Félix Faure, 17630 LA FLOTTE* – then close the email.

I'm momentarily confused, but then realise that Félix must be living on a street that bears his first name. Is his ego so large that he chose the street for that reason? Or is it a simple coincidence? The Félix I once knew would think this pompous, ridiculous. But I correct myself – I no longer know this man.

I walk back to my family, who look as spent as the puddles of ice cream remaining in their glasses. Even Lara looks tired.

'Monsieur Rombard's still trying to set up a meeting,' I tell Dylan. I can't bring myself to say Félix's name.

Dylan rolls his eyes and pushes himself to standing, stretches. 'These bloody French take their sweet time, don't they?'

I recall how a party invitation for 8 pm would mean everyone would turn up at nine, that running late for something was not considered rude but *ordinaire*.

'Let's go back to the village and pick up some things for lunch. We can eat outside, by the pool,' I say, hoping to distract and placate Dylan.

'I'd die for a swim right now,' says Dee, peering over her 1940s-style film star sunglasses and wiping the back of her neck.

I let Dylan guide us, because he always knows the way back from places, whereas I am perpetually lost without my phone. We return to Saint-Martin, spotting a *supermarché* on the outskirts.

'Can we see if they have Tim Tams?' asks Lara.

'They better have decent fruit and veg,' says Dee. She has recently informed me that she's a vegetarian with vegan tendencies, though she seems to have conveniently forgotten this with her ice-cream selection.

'We do need basics. Do you want to take the girls inside?' I ask Dylan. 'I'll go to the *boulangerie*. We can't have supermarket bread in France – Madame Gardner would be horrified.'

As I say it, I know I won't go to the *boulangerie*. I'll ride past the local shops, into the port and out towards Félix's house in La Flotte. There's no other way to do this. I feel a sharp reminder needle through me that I am tapering off my meds.

'Don't be long, babe. You're already getting burned,' Dylan says protectively, but I wonder if he's sensing that the fragile autocracy he's built is on shaky ground.

I wave to the girls and take off towards the charming shops lining the cobblestone street. There's *une boulangerie* with flour-dusted loaves in the window, *un boucher* with fat sausages on shiny silver trays, *une fromagerie* with waxy wheels of stacked raclette, and *un café* with green shutters and bright pansies in the window. I actually feel the perfection of this scene as a warm longing in my chest. It's a new feeling, or maybe an old one I haven't felt in a long time – when something is so beautiful it aches.

As I pass the *boulangerie* I smell fresh bread, sweet and yeasty. I have always been at the mercy of my olfactory senses, even on my pills. My heart is racing, and my legs burning as I try to outrun the aroma, but it's like trying to outrun a memory. *The bread is scratchy under the soft skin of my arm, and I imagine the way the crust will taste, with the creamy butter, sprinkled in salt the way Félix has taught me. I hear a giggle from behind and her chubby fingers grip the end of the baguette then she bites into it and I laugh.*

The nostalgia is sickly sweet, like too much patisserie, and laced with pain. I don't slow, I can't. I ride until I am gasping for air, until the port is far behind and all I can see is open fields. And all I can hear is her name whispered on the wind: *Juliette.*

*

Le passé

The sun was already hot as they cycled to La Flotte. Simone's hair was damp, drying to her back in the breeze. They followed the curve of the ocean, the tang of salt mingling with the cool antiseptic scent of the forest that edged it, the fragrant pine needles crackling beneath their wheels. Félix rode out front, sometimes disappearing from view before returning, like a loyal dog. Saskia rode between them, acknowledging an unspoken agreement that they would not allow her to get lost again. Simone had never had siblings, but could suddenly imagine the feeling, the type of easy companionship they might inspire.

The Saturday markets spilled through the port, the clang of sails mixing with the calls of the *vendeurs* announcing their daily specials and the dings of bicycle bells as riders threaded through the stalls. The air smelled of crustaceans freshly pulled from the ocean, coffee, and roasting nuts. Fishermen laid out their sea treasures – orange crabs, briny oysters, silver fish. There were baskets of fresh produce – silky black eggplants, bright lemons, glossy apples, potatoes still dusted with earth.

They parked their bikes and meandered through the market, holding melons to their noses, passing each other thick slices of brie on toothpicks and eating strawberries from a paper bag. Félix stood in front of a farmer's stall and quizzed Saskia on the French words for the various vegetables. She got all of them right, except *l'épinard* – spinach.

Strangely, Simone found herself continuing to address Félix in English. She had never experienced this with another French person. She knew why – Saskia would be left out if they spoke only in French, and Simone sensed that Saskia was the epicentre of their little group, like the hub in the middle of a bicycle wheel around which everything turned ... though she couldn't say exactly why, and the feeling made her both happy and unsettled at the same time.

Simone knew that the dynamic between her and Félix altered when they spoke in French. Words, after all, affected and shaped reality. She had studied linguistics at university and had written a paper and discussed the concept of linguistic relativity with her father.

He spoke about the idea that language didn't just express ideas, it actively shaped them, determining how one saw and understood the world. He cited a study where Greek and English people were shown two hues of blue in the Aegean Sea. The English only had the word 'blue' to describe them, but the Greeks had *ghalazio* for the lighter shade and *ble* for the darker hue. The Greeks perceived a greater difference between the shades of blue than the English. Did a different language influence how people viewed the two colours? Were she and Félix seeing each other through a lens that made things simpler, showed only naïve versions of themselves?

Saskia spotted Camille and Juliette by the cheese stall and called out to them. Juliette was holding an ice-cream cone, which was dripping down her tiny wrist in ribbons of bright, raspberry pink. Camille was holding her daughter's hand but seemed oblivious to the sticky mess, absorbed as she was in inspecting cheeses from under her white hat. Her whole outfit was white – slim jeans and a gauzy shirt – and Simone wondered with almost gleeful anticipation what a streak of wet pink ice cream would look like down the side of her pristine leg.

Juliette let go of her mother's hand and ran towards her nanny, her hands splayed wide in delight. Saskia squealed in surprise as the little girl reached her, the ball of her ice cream lost on the cobblestones. She picked the child up, even though raspberry ice cream smeared her dress.

'*Ma poulette*,' Saskia said, kissing her sticky cheeks. It surprised Simone to see her using French so naturally with the little girl when she was normally so shy to speak it, but then it occurred to her that Saskia was probably at a similar stage of language acquisition to the three-year-old.

Camille was smiling, immaculate, not a mark on her, as Saskia pulled Juliette's sticky fingers from her hair. Simone thought, *You are the kind of woman who goes through life without the smear and grit. Nothing sticks to you.*

Camille turned back to the *vendeur*, placing a wheel of cheese into her basket. Meanwhile Félix and Saskia had somehow managed to wipe Juliette down with a napkin and she was chasing a gull, her hands outstretched in delight, squealing, '*Coucou, je vais t'attraper!*' – 'I'm going to get you!' – which made them all laugh.

Finally, Camille seemed to have made her cheese selection. She paid for it, then approached them. '*Nounou* Saskia is a favourite already,' she said with a close-lipped smile, her English accent almost perfect. She was obviously highly educated. She didn't remark on the state of Saskia's dress, which was actually Simone's, borrowed from her wardrobe that morning. Nevertheless she was just as aloof as when they'd first met, though she seemed somehow more fragile out in the hum of real life, without the buffer of her beautiful bar and restaurant.

'*Elle est si adorable*,' Saskia said. 'I actually missed her.'

'Well, you're welcome to take her now,' Camille said, with no hint of irony.

'We're getting some lunch and then going to the beach,'

Simone said, in an attempt to save Saskia from the responsibility of a child on her free day.

'That would be perfect. Her grandparents could not take her this morning and I have so much to do. Juliette loves the beach, don't you, *ma chérie? Tu aimes beaucoup la plage.*'

'*La plage, la plage, allons nager!*' Juliette sang, her blonde curls bobbing as she clapped with excitement.

Saskia laughed and picked her up again. 'You want to go swimming with us?'

Juliette nodded.

'I can collect her a little later in the afternoon. I just have some errands to run for Henri,' Camille said, indicating the basket in her hands. 'Which beach will you visit?'

'Le Bois-Plage,' Simone said. 'It is near my house.'

It was only after Camille had kissed her child's head and been absorbed into the crowd that Simone realised they didn't have any of the things she imagined one would need for a small child's trip to the beach. 'What about her bathing costume and sunscreen? And will she need lunch?'

Saskia smoothed Juliette's hair absentmindedly. 'Hmm, yes, I didn't really think about any of that.'

'And neither did her mother.' Simone scanned the market-goers for the large white hat but Camille had disappeared.

'Oh no, don't eat that.' Félix pried half-eaten *frites* from the pavement out of Juliette's little fist. 'She does seem hungry,' he said, as though he were observing a small animal instead of a child.

'We can make a little picnic and eat it on the pier,' Simone suggested. 'We already have strawberries and blueberries, and we know *you* like berries very much.' She pointed to Juliette's soiled dress and the others laughed.

'I'll grab some cheese and bread and meet you on the pier,' said Félix.

'And how about some rosé from the winemaker. The local wine is very good,' Simone said, thrusting a bunch of notes into Félix's hand. It wasn't exactly the lunch she had planned but they could at least have good wine.

'And orange juice for Juju,' Saskia called to Félix.

'*Merci, Nounou Sass Sass. J'aime beaucoup le jus d'orange*,' said Juliette politely.

'Oh, *mon Dieu, si mignonne*, so cute. *Juju et Sass Sass*,' Simone said.

'*Et là, c'est Nounou Si Si*,' said Saskia, pointing to Simone.

'*Coucou, Nounou Si Si*,' said Juliette, taking her hand. It was so tiny and warm and the little girl looked up at her with such big blue, trusting eyes, that the momentary hesitation Simone had felt for having a child dumped on them quickly dissolved.

They left the market and walked towards a wide jetty, its ancient pylons covered in white gull droppings. There were teenage boys fishing, and the slap of freshly caught fish in buckets fascinated Juliette. The boys laughed as she bravely reached out and touched the scales of a fish, and then squealed and ran into Saskia's arms.

They sat down and the wood was warm beneath Simone's bare legs. Félix returned with a tray of fresh oysters, lemon, sliced ham, cheese and a baguette, which he laid out on butcher's paper. They sat under the midday sun and shared lunch, Juliette sucking the oysters from their shells like a child who had grown up the daughter of a chef. She took bites of her sandwich between tentative visits to the buckets of fish. The wine was sweet and cold, and they passed the bottle between them, taking sips and pressing the cool glass to the backs of their necks. Félix had also bought an apple tart, which they pulled apart and ate with their fingers.

Simone lay down, sated, closing her eyes against the bright sky and feeling the knotty grain of the wood against her bare shoulders. She listened to the sea lap against the pier, the whirr of lines being drawn in and Juliette's laugh, and smelled the Gitanes the boys were smoking. She could have been a child again, there with her parents. And she wondered if this was the closest to having a family she would ever come again.

CHAPTER 10

I cannot outrun the past. It's everywhere and nowhere. Memories rising to the surface and bursting like tiny bubbles I've been swallowing down my whole life. My belly feels full of their air and yet I'm breathless, my lungs burning by the time I reach Félix's address. It's at the very tip of the port, behind an ancient sea wall pounded by the Atlantic. The house is three storeys and rendered in the island's classic whitewashed stone. A rusty anchor sits above the front door, and I wonder about the building's history, whether it once belonged to sailors or seamen, or whether it was an artisan's home. But there is no mistaking that this is a grand villa beyond the sea-weathered facade.

I don't stop but instead pull my hat low and cycle around the block, so as not to look conspicuous. It's early afternoon now and people are out walking their dogs, taking coffee in the small cafes that overlook the port. The sun is bright and insistent, and I sit under the shade of a lemon-yellow umbrella. When I order a *café au lait* in French and remark on the heat, the waiter, like Madame Gardner, tells me I have a nice accent, and I smile. He doesn't realise that like a long-ago song, the sound and rhythm of the words have never left me.

I have a perfect view of Félix's house from here. There's a balcony at the rear and it must overlook a backyard or courtyard because the branches of a cypress tree reach over the high stone wall that surrounds the property. A woman comes onto the balcony, wearing a robe, a white towel wrapped around her head and the same retro-style sunglasses Dee is partial to. The effect is pure film star. She sits down at a small table, picks up a magazine and sips from a wineglass. Is this his wife? There's no denying she's impossibly glamorous but at this distance, of indeterminate age. I feel it then, a spike of jealousy, even after all these years, even after all the hurt and the pain. There's another feeling too – frustration, and it rattles through me like a freight train. I open my phone. I am not in the habit of googling Félix Allard. For the sake of my own sanity, I've only allowed myself to do that a handful of times over the years when my resolve has crumbled, and then I've been angry with myself.

Apprehension mingles with something else, something I haven't felt for so long. *La nostalgie.* I find myself looking up Félix Allard's Wikipedia page on my phone. I need to know what I'm about to face. The photo they've used is one where he's older than when I knew him, but likely younger than the forty-seven years he must be now. Félix has the kind of classic bone structure that holds its beauty. There are lines around his eyes and over his forehead, etched in by his youth under the glare of salt flats and a hot island sun. His hair is longer and there are threads of grey at his temples. He's the kind of man old age will make distinguished.

The list of Félix Allard's films is long. He won a César Award for his most recent, with an acclaimed French director, Jean-Marie Martin, about a man struggling after the death of his wife. It was shot on a farm in the south-east of France, with the mountains on the horizon a metaphor for the man facing his internal pain. The man leaves the village where he's spent his whole life and walks into the wilderness. It was a film of long shots and sparse dialogue, a triumph of cinematography and restraint. His performance was 'raw and magnetic'. *Le Chagrin des Montagnes*, translated as *The Grief of Mountains*, was critically as well as commercially successful and proved him to be 'a leading man who has substance as well as the style for which he has become known', according to one critic.

Before the win, he'd appeared mostly in films as a typical charming leading man. It seemed he was viewed as an object of beauty but without much gumption. The Félix I knew would have hated this.

I feel an awakening of that old pain inside me. *I never really knew him.*

I scroll down. It seems he hasn't made any films since the mountain film. That was two years ago. Why would he stop when he was just starting to find critical success? And why has he come back here, the place he was once so desperate to escape?

I look up. The woman is still there, but the magazine has been put aside and it looks as if she's on her phone. I scan down for Félix's personal information, which I'm pretty sure the last time I checked did not say he was married. Now it says he's wedded to an actress who looks like a Gallic version of Marylin Monroe. Bobbed white-blonde hair, cleavage, but with dark eyes. Her name is Renée Allard. I scroll through photos of her. She was an ordinary-looking English girl named Ruth when she started out at a London acting school, her eyes and hair the same dark brown. There was no contrast, no drama. She is a woman who has fashioned herself into something that she wasn't before, an English woman masquerading as a French one. I feel the spike of envy sharpen.

I look up. She's unravelling her hair from her towel now. It's a startling chemical red. She tips the rest of her wine into her mouth, stands and goes inside. Is this the same woman? It's impossible to tell from here. I'm suddenly aware of my greasy hair and red face. How am I ever going to knock on Félix Allard's door? I feel a surge of anger now at Simone, for the feelings that I've just been made to face, for the uncomfortable hope that has lodged just under my rib cage, like a bird trying to stretch its wings in a confined space.

My phone buzzes. It's Dylan.

Where are you?

My time has run out. I'm going to have to say I got lost. I pay for my coffee and cycle back to the *boulangerie* with haste, buy two loaves of bread. I look at the *pain au chocolat* behind the glass, nestled between glossy eclairs and bright peach tarts. I hear my voice ordering one of the square pastries with the strip of bitter chocolate down the centre. The words are there on the tip of my tongue, as though they never left. All I have to do is turn off my conscious mind and my memory will find them, like fingers running over the keys of a piano, playing a tune learned long ago. I am barely out of the *boulangerie* when I take a bite. It tastes as bittersweet as the memory.

We are sitting by the port, spotting gulls. We sit here every day for our afternoon snack – le goûter – including Juliette's favourite, pain au chocolat. *She licks the icing sugar from her fingers and we throw pastry flakes to the wind until the birds have gobbled every last crumb.*

I stuff the pastry into my mouth, gulping it down until there is nothing left.

＊

I return to the villa to find Dee swimming again, her skin luminous against the dark green of the mossy stone. She's doing laps now, her body moving rhythmically, breathing and gliding. Lara's sitting cross-legged by the side of the pool, a pile of rocks, flowers and sticks beside her. I sit down on the hot stone, take off my hat and put it on her head, then dip my hand in the cool water and wipe it over my brow, behind my neck.

'Don't want you getting sunburned, little bird,' I say.

'All Dee wants to do is swim. I want to go exploring in the villa or the garden, but she said she has to wear off all the ice cream and jam and bread. She said France is making her fat.'

Anxiety twinges inside me. 'How long has she been swimming?'

Lara rolls her eyes. 'Since we got back. Dad's on the phone. They didn't have Tim Tams at the shops, but we found a French version. Nowhere near as nice.'

I give her a reassuring hug. I try to think, but it's too hot, the sun too insistent. How long has Dee been like this? The thinness of her arms, the vegetarian diet. When did that start exactly? Why haven't I been paying more attention? All the times I rose early to work before the girls woke. And for what? Tiny pieces of paper, strung up for finite amounts of time. Dylan has always been the one with the flexibility, working from home with his own marketing business. He packs their lunchboxes and does the school run in the morning while I try to do the afternoon pick-up as often as I can. But sometimes he does both. It's a guilt I bear low in my gut. He works hard but has the eternal security of his family's money, the beautiful house his parents all but paid for.

The cool shadow of Dylan's body looms over us. I shield my eyes and look up.

'I've just had the lawyer on the phone. He says he sent you an email with Félix Allard's address.'

I can feel the sweat oozing from my pores. I'm parched, so thirsty suddenly. I don't want to do this. I'm not ready to face it. 'Oh,' I say, squinting up at him.

'He says we should try to contact him, arrange a time to sign the papers. Their office has tried to contact him by email and phone, but he doesn't respond. He sounds like an arsehole. Who ignores being given millions of euros?'

I arrange my face into mild passive surprise. 'I think he has a lot of money.'

'He sounds like an arrogant French twat.'

I snicker despite myself. I can't be sure that's not exactly what he is.

'Language, Dad,' Lara says.

'Sorry, but we need to go over there and just knock on his damn door. He lives in La Flotte. Rombard said it's not far from here.'

The guilt of my earlier deception shimmies through me, alongside the flutter of my newly winged anxiety. 'Surely they don't just expect us to turn up on the doorstep of a famous French actor and start demanding things that lawyers are meant to be taking care of.'

'You said he wasn't that famous.'

I'm caught out. I shrug, try to appear indifferent, pick up one of Lara's flowers and remove its petals one by one.

'It's not like he's a complete stranger, you're sharing an estate with him. You knew him.' There's more than a little accusation and wariness in his voice, and it gives me a juvenile rush.

'Twenty-six years ago,' I say.

'As much as we'd all like to stay here eating bread and swimming in the pool, we're here to get that money.'

I feel it then, like the sting of the sun on my scalp. He's taken over again, reduced me back to my pathetic self. I want to stand up, shout at him as he's so often shouted at me. Belittle him as he's so often belittled me. But instead, I find myself jumping into the pool. I fling myself towards Dee.

'That's enough,' I say, lunging for her body, pulling her head out of the water.

'Mum, what the hell?' She's spluttering, confused, blinking the water from her eyes. Her eyelashes are beaded, black, her eyes the same green as the algae. The same green as her father's. I hug her fiercely to me. 'That's enough. That's enough exercise.'

Our eyes meet and I see that she sees that I know what she's doing. We hover there a moment but then she pushes me away, hard, and disappears below the surface.

'Mum! Mum.'

I swing around to see Lara standing next to Madame Gardner on the side of the pool. She's holding a tray with a jug and glasses. Pushing the wet hair out of my face, I try to compose myself, look as though it's normal to jump into a pool with your clothes on. 'Teenagers,' I say weakly.

Madame Gardner smiles. I see sympathy in her eyes. It's Dylan who saves me, thanking her for making us lemonade, pouring himself a glass at her insistence. She's baked cookies too.

Dylan takes the tray from Madame Gardner, puts it on the weathered chaise longue. 'We've just been talking about Félix Allard, this stuck-up French actor who lives on the island.'

I feel like putting my head underwater and disappearing. Dee is still swimming.

Madame Gardner's face lights up. 'Oh, Félix Allard. Yes, he is very famous in France. Did you know he grew up on the island? He's famous for his summer parties. The locals complain every year. All that noise. The cars parked in the streets. But he keeps to himself. No one sees him. We just hear the parties, always the parties.'

'So, he's *really* rich? And *really* famous.' Dylan's eyes meet mine.

'We try not to make a fuss on the island. All the famous French ones come here. It's natural, normal for us. Not like the American fans. No fuss.'

'How do you think he'd go with a couple of Australians turning up on his doorstep?' Dylan asks, his face twisting into a grin.

Madame Gardner looks confused. 'You know Félix Allard?'

'Saskia knows *all* the rich, famous French people apparently,' says Dylan, cocking his head, a saccharine smile plastered on his mouth.

'A long time ago, before he was famous,' I say, realising I'm still standing in the pool, feeling a body brush past me underwater. I'm suddenly suspended between two worlds that have been getting closer, unsure if it's my daughter beneath the surface, or the boy I once swam here with.

*

Le passé

The early afternoon sun was hot across Simone's shoulders as they rode, and she could feel perspiration prickling her back despite the gentle breeze. Simone worried about Juliette's skin burning as she sat perched behind Saskia in her child seat, but maybe she would be okay. While she had her mother's fine blonde hair, her unusual, striking *mélange* of olive skin and blue eyes was more like her father.

By the time they reached the hotel to pick up Juliette's and Saskia's bathing costumes for the beach, patrons were sipping from sweating cocktail glasses and hiding behind their shades. The ride in the hot sun had sapped their energy. Even Juliette's curls were plastered flat to her little forehead. The Bisettes' home was an expansive apartment with pale blue shutters above the bar and restaurant. They left their bikes and followed Saskia through a blue door, for which she produced a key from the leather satchel she wore across her body. The cool, dark interior was a welcome relief and they climbed a flight of narrow stairs towards a large stained-glass window, which split the sun into strips of blue and yellow light.

Simone was curious to see inside the Bisettes' house, but Saskia slowed in front of her on the stairs and put a finger to her lips. The muffled sound of a man yelling from behind a closed door caused goosebumps to spread along Simone's arms. It was followed by the higher pitch of a woman shouting. She couldn't make out the words, but the meaning of the exchange was clear. A door slammed, hard. Félix and Saskia shared worried glances. Juliette crouched down on the step, her little hands over her ears, and the sight of her tiny cowering body made a lump form in Simone's throat.

Another door slammed and Saskia jumped, grabbing Simone's shoulder in fright. Saskia scooped the little girl into her arms and they hurried back down the steps. Simone felt guilt surge through her, as though she had stolen something she wasn't meant to have. Her eyes stung from the assault of bright light.

'It's okay, honey.' Saskia smoothed the damp hair out of Juliette's eyes.

The little girl was trembling. Félix picked some of the pink hollyhocks that grew up the wall and gave them to her.

'Was that Camille and Henri, do you think?' Simone asked quietly, leaning against the blinding white wall.

Saskia shook her head. 'I don't know. I've never heard them fight before.'

They were all silent, the unspoken weight of what they'd witnessed as hot and stifling as the air around them.

'So, what do we do now?' asked Félix, wiping the sweat from his forehead. Simone and Saskia exchanged helpless glances.

'Let's just go back to the villa and swim in the pool so she doesn't need a swimming suit,' said Simone.

They rode in tired silence back across the island, snatching reprieve in the shade of overhanging trees. When they reached the villa, Simone dropped her bike on the grass and pulled her T-shirt over her head.

'I'm going in, it's so hot,' she said, remembering Félix had swum naked that morning. She stripped down to her underwear and dived in.

The water was startling, and she imagined her skin hissed as it met the cold. She took off her bra and flung it onto the grass. The heat had made her reckless. She usually wore a bathing suit that covered her torso. She was not accustomed to bathing topless, unlike her mother. Hélène had always told her that the constellation of moles that covered her back, chest and breasts were beautiful – *les grains de beauté* – but she had far more, Simone realised as a teenager, than other girls, with their creamy clear skin or light sprinkling of freckles. It was what had stopped her aspiring to model when everyone said she was destined for it, like her mother. In her figure, her face, she took after Hélène. But the pale skin and *les grains de beauté*, which she had learned to camouflage so well, came from her father.

It had made her shy with lovers, prone to making love by candlelight. But it had also made her needy and an expert in concealment.

Félix and Saskia followed her into the water. Félix kept his shorts on, but his torso was bare and a deep brown that told her he worked shirtless in the salt marshes. Saskia tucked her dress chastely into her underwear and stayed in the shallow end with a delightedly nude Juliette.

Simone stayed in the water until her skin pruned, suddenly self-conscious of getting out of the pool, of revealing her naked body to Félix.

She covered her breasts with her arms and got out, picking up her bra from the grass, turning away and slipping it back on. She could feel Félix's eyes on her, and when she looked back, he was staring. He must have read her shame because he pulled himself out of the pool and as he passed her she caught his small, quick smile. His words were so quiet she wondered if she'd imagined them.

'*Tu es belle.*'

She tried to catch his eye, but he shook his hair, scattering droplets over her, making her gasp and run away. He grabbed a handful of soil from the flowerbed. 'You have good soil here, you know that? You could plant vegetables. Grow your own food. I don't know, maybe so you have more than cigarettes, coffee and oranges in your diet?'

Simone squatted on her haunches in front of the flowerbed, showing him her pale hands, her clean fingernails. 'You want me on my knees, weeding plants and gardening, Félix Allard?' She didn't try to hide the sexual innuendo.

He nudged her with his leg and laughed. 'Well, the grass needs to be cut for a start.' He went into the shed, pulled out a mower and coaxed it into life, motor oil mingling with the scent of fruit and flowers.

She watched him and the satisfying movements of the mower cutting through the long grass. She had never known a man like this. The men she had dated were in their heads, combative. They smoked with nervous fingers and drank too much. This salt farmer had a different energy, as though he was connected to something other than his own fragile ego. But at the same time this frightened her, because of what he had said when he saw her naked in the pool. Because of what she had, inexplicably, been able to show him.

The afternoon sun had softened, and Félix put them to work in the garden. He waved away Simone's protestations, her promises that she could probably have her parents' old gardener, Bertrand, there the next day. He found gardening tools and gloves and showed them how to pull weeds from the soil in the garden beds. Simone had never done such a thing, and found a strange satisfaction in gripping a plant by the base and pulling, feeling the slight resistance give way to reveal a network of fine roots.

Juliette sat beside them, making piles of dirt and sprinkling them with flower petals.

'*Tu fais une tarte aux fleurs?*' Simone asked, and she nodded.

'Do you want flower cake, *Nounou Si Si?*' Juliette asked in perfect English.

Simone laughed and nodded, touched by Juliette's continued use of a nickname for her. She pretended to eat the pile of mud she was offered.

Juliette was smeared with soil, but Simone hadn't seen her as happy as this all day. They had gone all the way to the Bisettes to get her bathers and now the little girl was frolicking naked in the garden like a nymph. Only Saskia was fully dressed, the bottom of her dress merely damp. She was peeling an orange in the shade of the trees, putting the segments onto a plate, and feeding Juliette small pieces.

The mower cut out suddenly, and Simone turned to see Camille Bisette standing in the garden in her perfect white outfit. Her brows were knitted, her mouth slightly agape. Simone looked at Juliette and realised what Camille was seeing – her small, naked child covered in dirt.

'What are you doing in the dirt?' Camille's voice had lost the measured tone Simone had heard in the bar and in the market. She bent down to Juliette and then thought better of touching the child. She straightened, a huff of frustration issuing from her mouth.

'*Désolée*, Madame Bisette.' Saskia picked up Juliette, swung her onto her hip and attempted to brush the dirt from her sticky skin but only managed to smear it further.

'I went to Le Bois-Plage to find you. It's her dinnertime. You can imagine how worried I was. You said you were taking her to the beach for a few hours, not to play in the dirt without clothes. Do you know how late it is?'

Simone's eyes met Saskia's. She could tell Saskia was unsure how to proceed, how much to defend herself when the explanation involved what they had witnessed at the top of those stairs.

'Sorry, we lost track of time,' Simone said. 'And we didn't have a bathing suit for her, so we brought her for a swim in the pool instead.'

Camille still hadn't moved to take her daughter. She was trying to contain her rage, biting her lips, her arms crossed tightly across her thin chest. 'You don't just take other people's children and do whatever you like with them. If you say you're going to do something, that's what you do. You could have come back to the house.'

'We did.' Simone was surprised by the strength and measure in her own voice. Camille froze, glared down at her. Simone found herself standing. She was nearly level with her eyeline, almost as tall as her. 'We weren't able to come up to get Juliette's things.'

The weight of her words filled the air like the smell of the rotting fruit under the trees. Simone saw it then – Camille's fear – and a part of her contracted on sensing the other woman's pain. But then Camille lunged forward and grabbed Juliette from Saskia's arms. The little girl's fists were still full of soil, and Simone felt a rush of satisfaction as it smeared over the perfect white of Camille's shirt. She physically recoiled but she held the child firmly and Juliette began to fuss.

'Sass Sass,' Juliette said, her whole body pitching forward, reaching for Saskia. Saskia froze, her eyes wide, unsure.

Camille ignored her daughter's pleas for her nanny and moved towards the gate. She stopped and turned. 'Saskia, I would be wary of who you surround yourself with. This is still a superstitious island. People listen to rumours ... You don't want to be making enemies too early on.'

Her eyes met Camille's and Simone felt dread drop into her gut. *So you do know who I am, and you know where I live.*

CHAPTER 11

The white stone facade glows against a darkening sky. The weather has turned, the searing heat replaced by a biting Atlantic gale that grasps at my back as I get out of the car. I had forgotten how quickly the winds rise from the cold ocean currents here, how quickly the hot days edge into frigid nights. I am breathless, buffered, standing in front of Félix Allard's house with the wind in my hair. Dylan has insisted on the girls coming with us. Who can turn away a family with kids on their doorstep? But then a man who can turn away millions can turn away anything.

My protestations were met only by Dylan digging in his heels harder. My husband is a puzzle my mind is addicted to trying to solve. And Dee, angry with me and aloof after our moment in the pool, is taking his side. She understands that this is the best way to punish me. It's Dee who reaches the door first. It, like the rest of the house, is salt-stung, rustic. A kind of beautiful decay. She raps using the knocker in the shape of an anchor.

Almost immediately the door swings open and the woman with the red hair I saw earlier on the balcony is standing there. Up close her bone structure is a study in oblique angles. Ruth, who became Renée. His wife. A sweep of mortification comes over me that I know this and that we're here, at his front door.

'*Bonjour!* We're just on our way out to beat the storm, aren't we?' she says in French, her accent unable to disguise the clipped British underneath. She has two tiny dogs on leads and the girls immediately rush to pat them.

'They love cuddles,' she coos, squatting down. She seems completely unfazed that strangers have appeared at her door.

'Is Félix Allard here? Your husband?' Dylan asks, uncertain because he can't speak French and possibly because this woman is so glamorous. He looks to me and I gaze back blankly. He's on his own.

She shrugs, replies, this time in English. 'He's here somewhere.' Her eyes widen but her voice is exaggerated. 'The master at work and all that. We can't disturb Daddy, can we?' She shakes her head at the dogs who are still bouncing around Dee's and Lara's knees.

My curiosity is piqued. She hasn't bothered to disguise the thin strand of resentment in her comment.

'Oh, they're so cute. What are their names?' Lara asks.

'Queenie and Pooch,' she says. 'Are you ... not British ... Australian?' she asks.

Dylan clears his throat – this is not what he'd been expecting. 'Yes, hi, Australian. I'm Dylan, this is my wife, Saskia. We're actually here to get some legal papers signed. Your husband has co-inherited a villa on the island, and we just need his signature, so we can put it on the market and maybe all make some money.' He splays his hands out and grins as though he's a children's entertainer, cajoling with exaggerated gestures.

'Oh Australia. My sister lives there. She's always posting pictures of the beach. I've always wanted to go. You know, the British dream and all that? Okay, girls, it's time to calm down.'

Dylan tries again. He's not used to being brushed off. 'Our lawyer tried to contact your husband via email, mail and phone, but hasn't been able to.'

'Your lawyer and all the others. Take a ticket and get in line.'

I like Renée. She's put Dylan in his place in one French manicured swoop.

At that moment a van pulls up at the front door and two men get out. 'We've got an order for Renée Allard,' one of them says in French.

'Oh, yes, for the party. There's a garage around the corner where you can unload.'

'I love parties,' says Lara, who has picked up Queenie or Pooch and is nuzzling into its fur.

'Oh, you must come then. It's our end of summer bash, before everyone heads home to Paris for winter. Félix may be there. Who knows? And then you can ask about your lawyers.'

'It might just be easier if we can have a quick word now,' says Dylan. 'Just get it done, seeing as we're here.'

He hasn't been listening to a word she's said. This woman has no interest in money; money is all she has. It's worthless to her because of its abundance, I can see that so clearly. What's not as clear to me is why she's so indifferent to, and distant from, her husband.

I find myself stepping forward, propelled by the same force that drove me here earlier today.

'Thanks, we'd love to come,' I say. 'When is it? What time?'

'Tomorrow night,' Renée says, sweeping out the door with her dogs. 'I don't know. In the afternoon some time.' She waves her hand vaguely. 'You'll know. Just follow the music.'

We watch her disappear around the corner of the house, trying to keep up with the dogs.

'What the hell is wrong with these people?' asks Dylan, running his hands over the back of his head and down his face. 'We're trying to give them free money.'

I have an almost gleeful appreciation of Dylan's frustration. Doesn't he know that this is how things are done in France? Everything can wait. Nothing is what it seems, layer upon delicious layer, like *un millefeuille*, which must be eaten, savoured, before business can be done.

Dee makes a clicking noise with her tongue. 'Dad, you don't get it. They're so rich. Didn't you see? She was wearing YSL runners. The dogs had Chanel collars.' Her eyes widen suddenly. 'Okay, so we are *sooo* going to this party with the French celebs.'

'And the dogs,' says Lara.

And the man who has eluded me for twenty-six years.

*

It's raining by the time we get back to the villa. Dylan's in a mood because a glamorous dog-wielding woman has put him in his place. I can feel the grumble of his anger roll over my skin, which feels as thin as the rain-spotted windowpanes. Everything is fast, sharp, too immediate. I'm relieved when he says he's taking a shower and the girls go on their devices. I climb the stairs, listen for the sound of the water running and find my pills hidden in the desk drawer. I split one down the middle, but I can't bring myself to put it in my mouth. I can't go back to the thick silence of my mind, even though things are too loud, too close. I shut one drawer and open the other one.

Simone's manuscript. I read the first page. It's as though I've just heard her voice in the room and I shiver and turn to look behind me. There is nothing but rain-grey light and dusty floorboards.

I'm shocked at the easy meaning of her words in my mind, as if she's speaking just to me. But perhaps it was studying French literature at university. Perhaps I've not entirely forgotten. My reading has always been better than my speaking and writing. I used to read French novels – Albert Camus's *L'Étranger*. Marguerite Duras's *L'Amant*. Can I possibly read this entire manuscript in French? It will take me so long, but I need to know what she is telling me, because surely she knew I would find this.

I take the manuscript downstairs into the lounge and hide it under a stack of books. I'll have to read it while Dylan is asleep. This fills me with a strange, collusive energy.

I pull together a simple dinner – tomato, fetta and red onion salad and some cold meats and bread. Dylan comes down from his shower, his hair wet and his skin darkened by a day in the sun. I can see the pale shadow his sunglasses have made over his nose. He is handsome in this moment. His beautiful Mediterranean colouring set against his green eyes still moves me. Dee's skin has also tanned from our bike ride, but her face is flushed. The sun has just left Lara and me slightly pink. I touch the sprinkling of freckles scattered across her nose like cinnamon.

'What's this?' Dylan asks, joining us at the kitchen table where I've laid out the food.

'Dinner,' I say, feeling my pulse lift slightly at his tone.

'We bought steaks and chicken at the supermarket while you were off riding God knows where. We haven't eaten a proper meal in days.'

My shoulders drop. I'm trying to cater for everyone, for Dylan who prefers meat and Dee who doesn't, but I know there's no point in saying any of this. It's not actually about the food, it's his frustration over Félix and the elusive signature. It's his insecurity in the face of a French film star. Maybe I took too long on my solo bike ride and it's aroused his suspicion. I try to swallow the burning in my throat, but I can't.

I take a breath. 'We're all tired, I just thought something simple—'

Dylan stands abruptly, and we all start. Lara's eyes lock with mine and I feel her worry needle into me.

'I'm not hungry anyway,' Dee says, also rising, her chair scraping across the floor. She leaves the room.

My insides are churning. It's as though I'm looking at myself from outside my own body. I stand and open the fridge. I hear my own calm voice. I hate the slightly upbeat sound of it. 'Here, I could fry up some chicken.' I hate myself in this moment.

Dylan grabs the bottle of wine on the kitchen counter, opens it and pours himself a glass. He takes a long sip. He's watching me as I find a saucepan.

'You know what, Saskia, don't worry about it.' He drains his glass, picks up the car keys from the bench and walks out the door.

I look over to see Lara's face drop. She can't understand the subtext of our exchange, that it wasn't about chicken or steak, but she can feel it. I wait a beat to make sure he's gone then go to her, pull her into a hug.

'Come on, let's have a picnic in the loungeroom. We can watch French TV.'

Her face brightens and we take the food into the lounge and turn on the enormous flat-screen TV on the wall. We flick through the French news, game shows, a soap opera. We stop when we find *Tom and Jerry* cartoons in French.

'Can you understand what they're saying, Mum?'

'Some of it … *Ça revient doucement.* It's coming back slowly.'

'You seem different when you talk in French.'

'Do I?'

'Why was Daddy so angry with you about dinner?'

Her eyes are so sad, it feels like all my organs have been hollowed out of my body. *I don't know*, I want to say. *Maybe because I deserve it.* Instead, I smile reassuringly. 'He's just tired is all. Jet lag and a long day in the sun. You know how grumpy he gets sometimes.'

Lara snuggles under my arm. I hate myself for shutting down her natural instincts. *Why do you excuse him?* I feel a surge of self-loathing. Lara's body has gone limp with exhaustion. I help her onto the lounge, pull a blanket over her and kiss her cheek. I'm about to ask if she wants me to make a paper animal, but she's already asleep.

I arrange some bread, cheese and salad on a plate and take it up to Dee, but she's asleep too, her phone on her stomach. A surge of love renders me immobile, and I hover there, mesmerised by the rise and fall of her chest, the soft movement of her eyes beneath her lids. All those years I watched them sleep, as though the mere act of watching would protect them. But now I don't know what I'm protecting her from. Herself? Am I imagining her subtle fading away? Her slow erasure? How do I find a way to talk to her without her getting angry, punishing me? Perhaps she has learned this from her father. I pick up her phone and wonder if breaking into it would help me understand her, but I don't. I can't bring myself to betray her trust like that.

I go downstairs and walk outside. The night rain has gone and a half-moon has risen. I can hear the waves beyond the high stone wall, and the smell of salt mingles with the damp heat rising from the soil. The car is not there. He's gone and I'm glad. I return to the loungeroom and find Simone's manuscript. Reading another language is like moving underwater, the meaning liquid, mutable. But she is writing about the summer we met on the island. She is laying it out like a towel on soft sand and I find myself lying down, allowing the nostalgia to blanket me, sweet but burning, like sunlight. I pick up the scissors I left on the coffee table last night. I find myself fashioning the front page of the manuscript, and I'm so tired, so wrung out, my defences so down, that as I unfold it, I find that there are three figures and a little girl.

*

Le passé

Simone was suddenly very aware of how naked she was, sitting in the garden, her fingernails black with dirt, her skin stinging from a day in the sun. This was not who she was. Why had she even come here? She should be in Paris, her skin still alabaster, taking a drink at her favourite bistro by the river with people who found her intriguing and seductive instead of cursed, dangerous.

Saskia stood very still, her eyes on the gate through which Camille and Juliette had just disappeared. Simone was filled with a crushing shame. 'You should go with them,' she said, unable to look Saskia in the eye. 'I do not want you to lose your position because of me.'

'What's she talking about?' Saskia asked.

Félix came over and sat down cross-legged in the dirt beside Simone. 'Don't listen to that woman. The truth is that people on the island, we don't care about anything. We're relaxed here.' He put a piece of orange that Juliette had half-eaten and left in the dirt in his mouth and chewed.

Simone laughed. She wanted to hug this man, or maybe she wanted to kiss him again. Saskia looked confused and Simone realised she owed her an explanation, that she had to tell her the truth and lose the innocence of their connection.

'Camille is talking about my parents. The way they died. It is why I never drive a car.' *It was why my mother and her mother never drove a car.* 'For all our fortune we also have *l'infortune* ... misfortune. Three generations have been killed in tragic accidents. My parents died in a car accident on the island, in the same way my great-uncle died, and my great-grandfather died in a boating accident. My grandmother is one of the richest women in France, but she has lost her father, brother and her daughter prematurely.'

'Oh no,' said Saskia, her face taking on that same expression that had haunted Simone for a year – pity mixed with something else, maybe fear.

'People are always thinking, "When will Simone be next?" Or they think that it is romantic to be cursed, like Romeo and Juliet or something. But they do not realise that it is they who cursed us. If we had no money, if we were not in the papers, we would just be another unlucky family, *non*?'

Simone stood up and went inside. She knew it was rude to abandon Saskia and Félix, but she couldn't be under anyone's scrutiny any longer. She had been silly to think she could escape it on this island, the very place they'd died. She was just starting to let her guard down, to feel like she belonged somewhere. Camille's comment had stung more than she'd expected.

Her feet were still covered in soil, but she didn't care. She walked through the house and climbed to the first floor. She stopped at the bottom of the stairs that led to the second level — a garret that housed her parents' studies. She had avoided this part of the house so far, just as she'd closed up their Paris apartment and left to live in a hotel.

She went up the stairs and passed her father's office. She'd known her father. He'd been a transparent, clear force in her life. They were made of the same thing. Of course her mind was not brilliant like his, but when he'd spoken she'd understood his meaning, his intention, and communication was always smooth, simple. Perhaps they were in some ways united in their grappling to understand her mother. She was the force, the energy, the person they both loved most.

Simone stood at the entrance to her mother's studio. It was a small tower on the side of the villa that caught the light from all angles, like a prism. Hélène would never have been able to work in a dark corner. She had taken the most magical place in the house, unapologetically, as she'd taken most things in life. She had been in this room the last time they'd spoken. The phone was on the floor in the corner. Simone knelt and placed the receiver to her ear. The line was dead. There was no longer a phone call she could make when she needed to talk to her father about a book she'd just read, or when she needed her mother's advice about what dress she should wear to an event. Or when she just needed to call for no reason at all. To be in the world without your parents felt like a taste of what the loneliness of death would feel like. She replaced the receiver. She sat down at the desk. There was a small ceramic bowl and inside it was a pair of earrings. Simone couldn't remember her mother wearing these – two small gold cats with sapphire eyes. She threaded them through her earlobes.

Camille's comment had stirred something inside her that Simone had been trying to ignore. Was that what everyone thought? That she was a bad omen? She felt defensive of her parents, of their reputations among the island people, people they had once welcomed into their home each summer. And she supposed that Camille had once been here, probably for a party. That must have been how she knew where to find Juliette.

Her parents had been going to a party in La Rochelle the night they died. But they were always going to parties. Her mother had not mentioned it the afternoon they spoke, but maybe somewhere there was *un journal intime* – a diary, something that held a glimpse into the final days or hours of her life. Hélène had always kept one – she'd had piles of them sitting around the apartment over the years. She'd called them her *chouchoux*, her pets. She never tried to hide or secrete them. Simone had been tempted to open the pages of these books, their covers stained with wine, their insides spilling with words but also pieces of fabric Hélène had collected, articles she'd been inspired by, feathers, dried flowers. She'd wanted to glimpse the private woman, the person her mother was outside of being a mother and the person other people expected her to be. But a part of Simone was scared, too. As though intuiting this temptation, Hélène had once told her and her father, *You can look at what I write, but be warned I am honest about my feelings and you might not like what you find.*

She watched the dust motes play in the last light sifting through the window. It was getting cold and that lonely feeling of the past year spread inside her like the spiderwebs that stretched across the corners of the room. She had found nothing, no diaries, no secret notes. The house was quiet, and she went downstairs, expecting it to be empty, expecting Saskia and Félix to have left, spooked by Camille's superstitious warning and her own petulance when all they were doing was helping. But she heard voices from the courtyard as she descended the stairs.

The evening was still, and they had set the outside table with candles, and hollyhocks picked from the newly pruned garden beds. The table was laid with crockery and cutlery that she had no recollection of ever seeing before, and glasses were filled with red wine. There was an empty place setting.

They both looked up and saw her at the same time, and their smiles were shy because of what they'd done, because of what it meant. Simone felt her throat constrict and her smile wavered, and she felt the hollowness inside fill up. This was the second meal they had conjured for her from nothing.

Félix stood and pulled the chair out and she sat. Saskia poured wine into her glass.

He disappeared into the kitchen, and she shot Saskia a questioning look. Saskia laughed and shook her head. 'It wasn't my idea.'

Simone took a sip of the full-bodied red, woody and old — it was like drinking history — and she knew it was from her parents' cellar. She thought how much they would have liked this scene, that their wine was being drunk here at this table where they had shared so many meals with friends.

'What about your job? What about what Camille said?' Simone asked.

Saskia put her chin in her hands. 'I think she was just upset about how dirty Juliette was. That family needs me so badly and, besides, Juliette loves me too much.'

'Maybe a little too much,' Simone said. 'I was so happy watching Camille's white clothes finally get dirty.'

Saskia laughed. 'It felt like it was happening in slow motion. I was entranced. I couldn't look away.'

'And the way she held Juliette out from her body. Oh my God, it was so tragic. And then Juliette calling for you, not her mother.'

Saskia winced. 'I know. And I've only been here a little over a week.'

'Has it really only been that long? It feels like a month.'

Félix arrived with three plates balanced expertly on his arms.

'Madame.' He placed the plate in front of her as so many fine waiters had over the years, and then topped up her wine. 'Organic tomatoes from the corner of the garden and basil pulled from under a bush, with olive oil hidden in the back of a dusty cupboard.'

Simone felt a lump in her throat and laughed to dislodge it. 'And what are the origins of the wine, *monsieur*?'

'Stolen from the cellar,' Félix said, straight-faced.

She locked eyes with Saskia and they giggled. It felt like they were children at a tea party fashioned from flowers and sticks and soil from the garden, like Juliette's *tarte aux fleurs*. They all played along, sitting up straight carefully cutting small segments of tomato flesh and chewing thoughtfully. The fruit was ripe and good, and tasted sweet, like sunshine. And salt. Félix had, of course, sprinkled it with *fleur de sel*.

Simone sat back and dabbed at her mouth overzealously with her napkin. 'My grandmother is one of the richest women in the world. I have inherited more money than I can ever spend and dined in some of the most famous restaurants in

France, and this is the most beautiful dinner anyone has ever served me.'

Saskia pursed her lips, her gaze soft, and Félix nodded solemnly and then laughed under his breath. 'You know that's it? There is no second course.'

Simone felt tears prick her eyes. She thought about her friendships. Beatrice, a childhood friend, whom she had always trusted because they were on an equal footing – both from wealthy Parisian families, both only children with preoccupied parents. But she had pushed her away this past year, unable to be the fun person Beatrice probably expected. And there was Lucian, her hilarious cousin from her father's side whose company she really liked. He had come to visit from Provence, and she had dragged him to different parties around the city. But he had been worried about her and had tried to stop her going out, smoking and drinking too much and spending time with men who didn't care about her. She had eventually pushed him away too.

And her school friends, who went skiing together in Chamonix for several winters after school finished. What had happened to them? Why had it taken these two strangers who had fallen randomly into her life to make her feel that she was not alone anymore? Perhaps she had spun a tight cocoon of grief, tighter and more impenetrable than she had realised.

She took the tobacco pouch she had found at the back of her mother's desk drawer out of her pocket. There were two joints inside, which she had rolled while sitting at the desk. She placed them on the table, with the same reverent ceremony with which she had eaten her tomatoes.

'We are going to smoke some hashish, and then I am taking you both to dinner at the most expensive restaurant on the island.'

They looked at her questioningly, and she raised an eyebrow and smiled wryly.

'You don't mean Bisette?' Saskia straightened the cutlery on her plate and chewed her lip.

'Shall we order everything on the menu?' Simone shrugged innocently.

Félix picked up the joints, lit the tips in the candle flame and handed them round. Saskia looked a little nervous but took a small puff. Simone inhaled deeply and felt the drug loosen her. She stretched and flicked a leaf from her tongue.

Félix blew smoke out his mouth and propped his bare feet on the table. 'I think this is a fucking brilliant idea. I might get fired, but I don't even care.'

Simone laughed. She could tell he was excited by all this, that she was conjuring the wildness, the daring in him. She reached over and patted his hand. 'It's okay, *chéri*. I'll hook you up with my people in Paris, *darling*. It's about time you started on that acting career.'

He leaned forward intently then shook his head vigorously and sat back and laughed. '*Bien, bien*, do you want to see my *impression* of an Australian accent? I have been studying Saskia very closely, practising.' He stared at her intensely until she giggled.

'*Oh, mon Dieu, oui,*' said Saskia.

He rose, affecting a kind of relaxed swagger and stuck out his hand to her. 'Hey mate, how the hell are you? Are you ladies in the mood for a night out at a fancy restaurant?'

Saskia and Simone collapsed in laughter.

'Wow, you are good,' said Simone.

'*Vous êtes tous les deux de mauvaise influence, mais oui, allons-y,*' said Saskia.

'I'm not the bad influence, it's her.' Félix pointed at Simone, his face full of mock outrage and she poked out her tongue at him.

'Okay, yes, let's find some nice clothes and go to a fancy dinner,' said Simone, linking her arm through Saskia's and realising they were all speaking in French.

CHAPTER 12

I had pale red hair that hung long at my back. I'd never felt beautiful in my country but in France I was considered a novelty, and I allowed myself for the first time in my life to feel alluring.

Now my hair sits neatly at my shoulder blades, cut and dyed into middle-aged submission. I don't feel alluring anymore. I think I'm probably tasteful but invisible.

'That dress makes your arse look good, but your knees look a bit bony,' Dylan says, patting me on the bum. A compliment wrapped in something I don't know where to put. Because of this, I laugh.

I'm in my 'going out for a nice dinner' black shift dress, not having anticipated we'd be attending a French *soirée*.

He leaves the room and I take off the dress. Usually I'd just wear it, and his backhanded compliment.

My daughters, it seems, always anticipated a French party and they swan into the room giving me a fashion show.

Dee's wearing a sorbet-orange mini dress with puffed shoulders, demure sandshoes and ankle socks. It's a dress she wore years ago that she's obviously dug out of a drawer and repurposed to look like it might be a study in sartorial irony from the pages of *Vogue*. Lara's in her favourite denim overalls, but any utilitarian vibe is quashed by her colourful accessories. I always knew my daughters had a strong sense of their own style – Dee refused to wear shorts as soon as she could vocalise this pressing need, and Lara was always partial to colourful accessories, preferably involving animals. But there's some new bar being set here, and I wonder if it's because they're in another country. They sense the freedom that comes from being in a foreign place – being able to remake oneself because the codes are different. There are no rules to abide by because you don't understand the rules anyway.

I go to the wardrobe in the corner of the room. Simone's wardrobe. I haven't dared open it but now I do. It smells a little musty, but it's filled with filmy dresses in the lightest silk and a cream pantsuit, tiny spots of yellow the only hint that it's been here forever. I remember the time I wore one of these dresses.

I choose a dress now that feels like liquid, still black, but it's floor-length and skims my hips. It's not the sort of thing I wear these days. This is a dress that draws attention to itself, to the body. But I remind myself that there are no rules to abide by here. My daughters insist I look glamorous, and I let myself believe them.

We go downstairs. Dylan has dressed casually in jeans and a black T-shirt. It's his protest at not being in control of this situation. He's not going to give this party the dignity of his effort.

'You've changed,' he says, his eyes on me.

'It hides my knees,' I say.

His right eye twitches. He opens his mouth and then shuts it. He was going to say I should go upstairs and change, that it's a ridiculous dress to wear to a party with people we don't know. I can see it all cross his face. But he purses his lips. He's still doing penance for his behaviour last night. He turns and grabs the car keys.

Driving through the sleepy early evening streets too fast with his sunglasses on, he says, 'This Félix Allard bloody better be there this time. It's ridiculous that we have to do this. The lawyer should be handling this.'

'You said it yourself, the French do things differently. The rules are not the same. They're more elastic.'

'At this point there are no rules,' he says.

'Frankly, I think the rules went out the window as soon as I inherited a French villa,' I say, some small, loudening part of me enjoying the power of ownership, that same power I felt at the ice-cream shop when I spoke in a language that excluded him. When he could see that I was something else, something he couldn't quite understand. The feeling ripples under my skin and my lips slip into a secret smile.

'Well, inheriting a villa isn't much good if we can't actually get the money from it, is it?'

I let his words wash over me. It's something I've learned to do. We've hardly spoken since he left last night to take himself to a local bistro for dinner. He returned late and slept late. The girls and I woke early, and Lara and I spent the morning collecting pebbles and shells at the beach. Dee spent the morning swimming in the pool, and we returned to find her sunbaking. In the afternoon we sought the shade of the orange trees before getting ready for the party.

I hear the music first. It's a song by Serge Gainsbourg. Its melancholy notes float on the warm evening air, issuing through the open windows and doors. It's his famous duet with

Brigitte Bardot, the song that made them lovers. 'Bonnie and Clyde'.

And suddenly I'm sitting in Simone's salon on the green velvet lounge and she's plaiting my hair. Félix is singing the Gainsbourg part and Simone is singing Brigitte Bardot. Félix has a beautiful singing voice, deep and as easy as talking. He's sprawled on the lounge, feet bare, with a book, sipping apricot wine. Simone's wearing winged eyeliner, a cigarette between her lips, and she could be Bardot. On weekends we retreat here from the hot afternoon sun, to nap and read and play cards. I feel my eyelids grow heavy, the light hazy, the feeling like slipping in and out of a dream.

'Cool song,' says Dee as we get out of the car.

The front door is open and the music swells as we walk up the front steps and enter the house. I can feel Dylan tense beside me, but the music feels like it's invading my cells, taking me over. I grip Lara's hand and hope the day will never come when she no longer seeks comfort in my touch, and the comfort goes both ways. We step into a room with looming arched windows overlooking the port, and polished parquet floors. It opens onto a terrace strung with lights. Salt and perfume scent the air, mingling with the smell of baking pastry. The room is filled with people. Some are standing by a trolley bar, pouring drinks; others have gathered around a grand piano and there are bodies reclining on lounges. But the only person I'm looking for is a boy with sun-browned skin and dark eyes.

Renée is over by the piano, and so are the dogs. The girls and the dogs see each other and there is a commotion of mutual affection. Renée is in a figure-hugging silver dress and smoking a cigarette, but she's wearing pale blue sneakers. She's a 1950s siren from the ankles up. She's talking to a man with a shiny bald head wearing a colourful scarf around his neck, and a petite woman in a pantsuit. On her other side a woman in a flowing kaftan is sipping from a cocktail glass. Sitting on a lounge nearby there are two men who look like they've just stepped off the beach. It's an eclectic crowd, which puts me at ease a little.

'Ah, the Australians. You came.' Renée's words are languorous. She's already drunk. 'You're in luck, he's skulking around here somewhere.'

It's a strange way to describe your husband, but I smile warmly. 'You have a beautiful home, thanks for inviting us.'

'Oh, here he is.' Renée grabs a man.

From behind, he could be any one of the dark-haired French men in the room. The first thing I notice is his suit. It's slightly too big for his frame. He's thin, thinner than he was as a young man. And he holds an elegant cane topped with a silver lion's head. He turns and I know even before I see his face that it was a mistake to come here. I'm aware of the ache in my chest, the shallowness of my breath. Age has deepened the lines around his eyes, salted his hair, but the same mix of depth and mischief is still there. He looks at me and I feel it in my core. But his face remains blank. He hasn't recognised me. Of course he hasn't. Why would he?

'I'm sorry, I've forgotten your names,' says Renée. She takes his arm. 'And was it something about a house? *Mon chou*, they need to talk to you about a house.'

'We need to talk to a man about a dog,' says Dylan, laughing, his feet shifting nervously on the spot. It's rare to see him this uncomfortable, this out of his depth. No one says anything. They have no idea what he's talking about. I want to disappear.

A man comes up and whispers something in Félix's ear and he nods. 'I'm sorry, excuse me,' he says in English, and then he's gone. Renée shoots us a look that says *Sorry, but I told you so.*

Disappointment and relief are like oil and water inside me. I grab a glass of champagne from a passing waiter to feel the cool liquid ease down my throat. Dylan is beside me. 'Where's he gone? I'll go find him. Bloody hell, what's with the cane?'

I know the cane has made Dylan less intimidated by Félix. He's perhaps not the Gallic heart-throb he'd feared. 'I have no idea. Maybe he has an injured leg,' I shoot back. 'No, I'll go. Can you keep an eye on the girls?'

'Fine.' Dylan scans the room, evidently looking for Renée.

I'm so relieved to be free of him that it feels like I've shed a layer of clothing. I walk onto the terrace, feeling the warm air caress my bare arms. The lights of the restaurants wink along the port. It reminds me of Van Gogh's *Café Terrace at Night*, the evening painted in blues and yellows. The voices of the guests float around me, mellifluous, sensual. I catch snippets of conversations, words I understand, others I don't. I could be anyone. I could be anywhere. A French woman, a stranger.

I close my eyes and feel a sensation well from deep inside me. I want to be anonymous, lost. Free. I want to be nineteen again.

'*Je te connais.*'

I turn and Félix is there. He tilts his head to one side, his eyes narrowing. I feel pinned in place, I can't move or speak, such is the gravity of his full attention.

'I know you.' He says it again, this time in English, and steps towards me. The tip of his cane taps against the stone, an echo of my loud heart. 'Your hair. It is no longer red.'

I touch my hair, and the intimacy with which he has spoken fills me with a longing that feels too expansive to fit inside my body. I shake my head. 'I'm sorry,' I say. I don't know why.

'Saskia, the Australian artist.'

'Félix, *le saunier*.' I have spoken it without thinking and see a shadow pass over his face, fleeting as the movement of the clouds over this windswept island. I try again, grasping hold of the thin line of recognition that has threaded between us. 'Or should I say Félix, the film star?'

He smiles and looks down at his feet, which I notice are bare. 'Retired.'

'You still don't like shoes.' I am shocked by my own audacity.

He shakes his head. 'It has been, how long?'

I arrange my face into the shape of uncertainty, even though I know full well how long it's been.

'The years go faster the older you get, *non*?'

'They seem to,' I say, though I'm not sure if they've sped up or slowed down, such is the cocoon I have woven around myself.

'And you have a family?'

I nod. 'Yes, my daughters. They love your dogs.' I'm suddenly back to myself. 'I'm sorry, you're probably wondering why we're all here.'

'You're not here for my summer party?' He raises an eyebrow, amused. 'Renée, she loves it. The parties, the summertime. It is all to make her happy.' He has a habit of tapping his cane. Quick taps, like full stops at the end of sentences.

There is affection in his voice but also something else. *This is not what makes you happy*, I think. *You thought that this was what you wanted when you were twenty-one.*

'Yes, sorry, she's the one who invited us to the party.'

'*Bien sûr.* Of course. She invites everyone. The man on the street, he will be here also.'

I sink inside at his implication. 'Sorry, we just turned up on your doorstep and she—'

'You say a lot of sorry. This was not the girl I used to know.'

I feel shocking, inexplicable tears gather behind my eyes. I want to say sorry. I want to slap him. I feel myself burn under the intensity of his gaze.

'I did not think you would ever return here, to the island,' he says.

Our eyes meet, and I feel the skin on the back of my neck prickle, feel our history crystallised beneath the surface, like the minerals in the briny water in those shallow salt pools we bathed in the night we met. This strange intimacy – so unexpected, yet not surprising – must be emboldening me, cutting through the shame his comment has induced, because I say, 'The same could be said of you.' I hold his eye. But what I don't say out loud is: *After everything that happened.*

He looks away and taps his cane three times. A man appears beside him and whispers in his ear.

Félix bows his head. His eyes flick to me and then away. 'You must excuse me for a moment, I need to attend to something.'

And with that, as quickly as he has reappeared in my life, Félix Allard is gone from it.

*

Le passé
The restaurant was full of the wealthy island people who had once inhabited her parents' outer social circle. They would soon be migrating back to Paris like a flock of restless birds, back to their opulent apartments with views over parks and

squares, back to their city lives – galleries, theatre, *apéritifs* in cafes – until they would move again en masse to the French Alps for the winter. Always the same group, always speaking of the same politics, the same art. The men wore pressed trousers and boat shoes, and the women wore summer knits and nude lipstick. If she was going to be recognised anywhere on the island it would be here, but Simone found that the only thing she cared about was making Saskia and Félix happy. She felt like a child who had done something naughty and was waiting for her punishment. She scanned the room for Camille, and felt a rush of adrenalin through her veins.

The air was laced with aromas of spices, frying meats, sweet wine. The hashish had made them ravenous. They had washed away the dirt and sweat from the garden and dressed for a formal meal. She and Saskia wore silk dresses from Hélène's wardrobe. Félix had borrowed her father's dinner jacket and it hung too large over his bony frame. It gave him the air of an eccentric poet and Simone found herself stealing glances at him. Only their hair, wind-tousled from the ride across the island, gave away their true state.

They waited at the entrance to be seated. 'No laughing,' she said, holding up a warning finger too close to their faces until they laughed.

Félix straightened and formed his face into a picture of seriousness. 'Terrible service here,' he said, affecting a refined British accent.

'Oh, you're British now, are you?' asked Saskia, poking him in the ribs.

The drug had stripped her of her inhibitions. She had become more tactile, more sensual. Everything felt soft and easy and cushioned, so much so that Simone hadn't thought about how they would actually get a table at Bisette without a reservation, beyond shamelessly using the social cachet she had been so studiously avoiding.

'No, seriously, we have to be serious now,' Saskia said, seeing a *serveur* approach.

'*Bonsoir, Saskia, ça va?*' The *serveur* greeted her then they exchanged *bisous* and Simone realised that Saskia was in fact the one who had the power there, that the staff knew her because of the family's daily lunches in the restaurant.

'*Avez-vous une table pour trois?*' She had a charming accent that sounded more British than Australian. It was as though another part of her had slipped out, a mirror girl, almost but not quite the same.

Simone felt the *serveur's* eyes on her, felt her skin grow warm. She wondered if he recognised her.

'*Attendez.*' He left and returned with the corner of his mouth screwed up.

'*Je vous donnerai un pourboire de cinq cent francs,*' Simone said before he could announce that there were no tables.

His eyes widened just enough for her to see that he would find a table. Simone felt a rush of satisfaction when she looked at her friends' faces.

'Did you just say you'd tip him an insane amount of money?' Saskia gripped her arm.

'*Bien sûr.* What's the point of having money if I can't use it to treat *mes amis?*'

Félix tugged at his shirt sleeves and slicked his hair back with mock affectation. 'I could get used to being rich and famous.'

Simone sighed. 'Oh, the places I could take you two in Paris.'

She knew she was being over the top, incorrigible really, revelling in her wealth and bringing them here when Camille had so clearly expressed her disdain. But it had felt from the start, since their midnight trip to the salt flats, like they were in collusion, like there was some extra part of life that none of them had accessed until they had found each other.

There was a story her mother had told her as a child about a magic tree that was a portal into other lands. She would describe in great detail what it was like to climb this tree, and then when she reached the top she would ask which land Simone wanted to visit. The land of all the flavours of ice cream, or the land of never having to stop playing. Or the land of being and saying and doing exactly as you pleased. And this was the feeling she had with Saskia and Félix, that they opened up another world to her.

The *serveur* led them to a corner of the room where he had managed to squeeze a small table between two large groups. They sat down with their knees touching.

'Not quite what I was picturing,' Félix said, elbowing them, mock-vying for table space.

'I'm still ordering the whole menu,' Simone said, picking it up with a flourish.

Her parents had taken her to the finest restaurants in Paris as soon as she could walk. She was expected to try new foods and talk about sensible and interesting things and even take small sips of wine. This was almost the sole occupation of her adolescence and adult years. She would join her friends at chic new restaurants and bars that everyone was talking about, and drink the cocktails everyone was drinking and take the meals everyone was eating, and then drink espresso and smoke cigarettes over empty plates. But now Simone wondered if she had *enjoyed* the experience. Or had she always been trying to impress her parents and then her friends with her maturity, her sophisticated palate?

'Oh my God, you can't order too much, there's no room on the table,' Saskia said. She looked around the restaurant, clearly scanning for Camille. 'I really am going to lose my job.'

Simone touched her hand lightly. 'No, you won't.'

Saskia grimaced.

'And if you do, you stay with me at the villa. *Simple.*'

Saskia looked reproachful, but Simone nudged her reassuringly.

She caught a different *serveur's* eye and he approached cautiously, obviously slightly confused about the impromptu table.

'We'll take a bottle of Cristal champagne and three glasses,' she said in French. 'And what do you recommend? Can we smoke in here?'

'*Bien sûr, mademoiselle,*' he said, scribbling in his notepad.

He reeled off a list of house specials while she lit a cigarette and inhaled.

'We'll take one of each.'

His arms dropped by his side. '*Excusez-moi.* One of each dish, *mademoiselle?*'

'*Oui.*'

He raised his eyebrows as he wrote down the order. As he walked away he looked back, suspicious, and they began to laugh.

'Ouch,' Simone said as someone kicked her under the table.

'We are going to get thrown out, and I am going lose my bar job and have to go back to scraping salt for the rest of my life,' said Félix, squeezing his eyes shut and putting his face in his hands.

'*Oh mon Dieu, merde.*' Saskia's hands went to her cheeks as a silver ice bucket with a bottle of champagne was placed on the table.

'But it is going to be worth it,' said Félix.

'Swearing in French, Saskia. This means you are truly assimilating the language into your heart,' Simone said.

Félix stood and poured the champagne with the same flourish he had used at the garden table. 'It might be the last time I pour a drink here.'

The food began to arrive. It was comical really, as Simone knew it would be. They started with *les huîtres*, which were briny and fresh and which Félix said were grown on the local oyster farms. They threw them down their necks to make room for the rest. The specials were seafood pulled from the local waters – a whole fish, a seafood platter, a fish pie, crab linguini, and, *naturellement*, lobster bisque. The *plats* were piled onto the tiny table, the bottle of champagne relegated to an ice bucket on the floor. The *serveurs* used pizza stands to tier the food so that it sat in precariously balanced towers.

It was as excessive and ridiculous as Simone had hoped. They were all a little drunk and still a little stoned and talking and laughing too much, and she could feel the eyes of the other diners on them, but she didn't care because Saskia and Félix had already told her several times that this was the best night of their lives. They lolled back in their seats, rubbing their aching stomachs, but she couldn't tell if it was from the laughter or from the excessive food.

Simone saw Saskia's face blanch and wondered if they had gone too far, whether she was actually feeling sick, and then she followed her line of sight.

Camille approached the table, and Simone felt a surge of energy that eclipsed her intoxication. This was what she had wanted, after all. She straightened and met the other woman's eye.

'I trust you are enjoying your evening?' Her smile was impeccable. Simone could not even tell if it was fake. Camille bent down and picked up the bottle of champagne on the floor and topped up their glasses, like a perfect hostess. She was in white again, this time in a shirt with an exaggerated collar, paired with flowing culottes. Her hair was pulled into her signature low bun. Nowhere in her deportment was the woman who had threatened Simone in the garden.

It was completely disconcerting, and Simone felt a seam of guilt open inside her. Maybe she had been childish coming here and endangering Félix's and Saskia's jobs just for this power trip. She realised suddenly that she was behaving exactly like her mother, whose generosity seemed always tied to some other more subtle design, like the excessive cakes at the mothers' group. Like the time she turned up at school with designer handbags for Simone's friends when she had been struggling with friendship dynamics. Always in the service of obtaining love.

Was this what she was doing now? Using her money and power to secure the love of Félix and Saskia? Or was it Camille she was here for? To show her that in the end she would always win, because, as Camille's gracious, deferential demeanour now showed, money always did.

Saskia was mute, on alert, unsure of what to do, where to look. Félix was trying to tidy the ruins of their meal, stacking plates, clearly on edge. Simone knew she had to say something. She spoke in English, perhaps as a way of distancing herself from Camille a little.

'The food has been beautiful. I have always wanted to eat here. Henri's reputation is certainly deserved,' she said, trying to sound genuine.

Something flicked across Camille's face, a tiny spasm of her lipsticked mouth. 'Well, I hope you have an appetite, there's more to come. I heard you ordered all the specials.'

Simone felt her cheeks grow hot with embarrassment and she lowered her eyes and exchanged furtive, chastened glances with Saskia and Félix.

'I think our eyes have been too large for our stomachs. I apologise. Charge it to my bill, but I am happy to feed your staff tonight with what we cannot eat.'

Simone hoped Camille understood the underlying meaning – a concession in a way, that Félix and Saskia were hers.

Camille stood there a moment, blinking rapidly, as though to stem a flow of tears. Simone wondered if she was wrestling with some emotion and what it might be. Whether perhaps all she was doing this afternoon was trying to keep her child safe, and maybe she had really been scared about where she was, and it was for that reason that she had lashed out.

At that moment, Henri arrived beside his wife. He was an imposing figure, tall and lean, with a mop of grey hair and a wiry frenetic energy. He wiped his hands on his apron before leaning in to kiss Simone's cheeks. She hid her surprise at this warm greeting, so different from his wife's. He smelled of garlic and red wine mixed with something earthy, like rosemary.

'I heard there was a Durant in the restaurant ordering all of our beautiful seafood specials and felt it was only polite to personally greet our special guest. Please, all my condolences for the loss of your parents. I did not know them well, but of course our paths crossed over the summers.' He pressed his hand to his chest, and Simone felt a bolt of unexpected emotion at his honesty. 'And I see you are entertaining some of our best employees. Saskia and Félix are like family.'

Simone struggled to marry this warm, welcoming man with the scene they had overheard from the stairwell. She tried to catch Saskia's eye, but she was looking nervous, wringing her serviette in her lap.

A *serveur* arrived and placed three small glasses of liqueur and a tiny plate of something cheesy and gelatinous in front of them.

'An amuse-bouche from the chef's kitchen,' he said, rearranging Simone's plate carefully in front of her.

She tried to hide her horror at the thought of one more morsel of food crossing her lips and thanked him profusely, doubly chastened now.

He excused himself and went back to the kitchen.

'Enjoy the rest of your meal,' said Camille with a serene smile, but Simone couldn't help but notice how tightly her hands were clasped in front of her. There was no way they could refuse this food now after her husband's generosity.

And when Simone looked into her eyes, which were as dark as her hair was pale, Simone saw that Camille knew she had won.

CHAPTER 13

I stand on the terrace and draw my arms close. A sea breeze makes the small hairs on my arms shift, and I can hear it rattle the rigging in the port below. I'm frustrated, unsure whether I should wait here for Félix to return from whatever urgent business was whispered in his ear, or go back to my family. What is his business anyway, given it seems like he's stopped making films? I feel a surge of anger now, hot and unruly. I waited once for him for three days, in a city I didn't know, and he never came. I remember that warm Spanish air, the hope I had that we could leave behind the pain of what we'd just been through, that everything would be okay. I knew I had to leave the island, escape all the questions I couldn't answer. I wanted to be anywhere but France. Barcelona was his idea. I thought he was protecting me, but he didn't come, and I didn't ever escape, not really. Why should this be any different? He still feels like quicksilver running through my fingers, only now he can disappear with three taps of a cane. Perhaps I scared him away. But no, it was he who started it, he who conjured up the past.

I won't wait for him again. I take a glass from a passing waiter and drink it all. I go inside and feel the alcohol hit my veins and my vision swims a little. My body feels like a crude experiment. I don't know what's going to happen after two days without my little white pills. I only know that my emotions feel close, immediate, bubbling on the surface. It's as though someone has pressed play on my insides after years of being on mute. My thoughts race. *Yes*, I think. *This is how it used to feel.* Out of control. Dangerous. But also, it feels like waking up. It's bright and startling and yet I feel alive, awake, more present.

I go inside. The lights have dimmed and the music is no longer French love songs but a kind of sensual French house, with a deep bass that reverberates through me. The music feels like a slow heartbeat, and I feel my body loosen. My girls are still over by the piano with the dogs. Lara is holding both of them, one under each arm and Dee is trying to prise one out of her grasp.

'You guys okay? Have you found some food?'

'Mum, can we get a dog when we get home?' asks Lara, her eyes pure.

'How do you know we won't just live in the French villa from now on?' I ask, just to see their reaction.

'Really? Can our friends come to visit? Can we have pool parties,' asks Dee, her eyes huge.

'What about Tiger?' asks Lara, putting the dogs down. Her allegiance will always be to our cat.

'I thought Dad wanted to sell anyway. Doesn't Félix Allard want to give up his half?' asks Dee, picking up a dog and squishing it to her face, and I'm struck again by how she knows exactly what's going on.

'I'm having trouble finding Félix Allard.' I scan the room. Dylan is standing by the bar, drinking a cocktail and talking to Renée, naturally.

'Girls, go and get some food. There's a huge plate of cheese over there and macarons.'

'Oh, macarons,' says Lara. Dee shrugs but they both make a beeline for the food.

I walk over to Dylan and Renée. My husband is in full flirtation mode. He's listening intently to what she's saying, rubbing his chin in an expression I haven't seen for a while.

As I approach, she laughs and puts her hand on his arm. 'Oh, your husband is funny. He's telling me about Australia. All the crazy insects and deadly animals. Crocodiles in the sea! I'm terrified to go there. I grew up in the English countryside where you can roll in the grass without getting bitten by a snake.'

I smile indulgently. 'How long have you been in France?'

She shakes her head. 'Too long. It's beautiful but ...' She shakes her head. 'I mean I *adore* Paris and I love coming here for the summer, but ...'

'You miss home?' I offer.

She nods and seems very young all of a sudden.

'How did you and Félix meet?' I ask.

Renée waves a hand. 'Oh, it's boring really. He was doing an acting masterclass in Paris and I was one of his students, and I pursued him, relentlessly.' She laughs. 'I didn't move to France, change my name and lose fifteen kilos to end up married to some schmuck. No, I wanted *the* Félix Allard, didn't I?' She tips the dregs of her cocktail into her bright mouth and indicates for Dylan to pass her another from the bar. 'Would you be a darling?'

Dylan obediently takes her empty glass and trots off to the bar. If only I had him on such a tight leash. I move closer to Renée and she leans into me conspiratorially.

'You are so nice, you and your husband. Australians are so nice. The French can be so … honest. Brutal sometimes. Don't you find?'

'I know what you mean,' I say. It's true. There's a forthrightness that is both refreshing and unnerving. I think of Félix, challenging me about returning to the island, escaping when he couldn't answer the same question.

Dylan returns with two martinis and hands them to us.

'You're a darling. Your husband, he's quite charismatic,' Renée says, as Dylan returns to the bar for his own drink.

Before I can answer, an older woman approaches and covers Renée's cheeks in kisses, speaking in rapid-fire French. She tries to drag her away to another group but Renée resists. She touches my arm.

'We're taking the boat out tomorrow, one more time before I go back to Paris. Will you come? It feels like you're family. Brits and Aussies stick together, right? The girls would like it. The dogs come on board, of course.' She winks.

I laugh and look to Dylan. He shrugs and nods. 'It's one of those big ones moored at the port, is it?'

She's got him. He's always loved sailing. '*Bien sûr*,' she says, flashing a smile. 'Only the biggest and the best.' And I think I catch a note of sadness in her voice.

Dylan graciously accepts. She has thoroughly charmed him. And I must admit I like her too. She gives us a little wave before being absorbed into a group of people.

'What a character,' says Dylan with a small shake of his head. 'You say she's famous in France, too?'

'I presume so.'

'Anyway, did you find Félix Allard?'

I hesitate. I want to play my cards right here. 'I saw him briefly. He got pulled away, but he remembers me. I think I can get him to sign.'

'Do you think he's going back to Paris, like Renée?'

Dylan uses her name so casually, it amuses me. 'I don't know. I get the feeling he stays here and she's the one who flits between their houses.'

He takes a sip of my cocktail. 'Who would have thought two weeks ago we'd be in France stalking French movie stars, going to parties, invited on boats, eh? Maybe we could get used to this after all.'

He puts his arm around my waist. He can be utterly disarming when his ego is stroked. There's a reason I fell in love with him.

I raise an eyebrow. 'That's a bit of a turnaround from how you felt an hour ago.'

'Well, maybe the French *je ne sais quoi* is rubbing off on me a bit. You know, I've been so busy with work, with life. I've been running on empty. That's why I just wanted a nice meal last night.' He looks at the ground and then up at me. He has that look in his eyes. He's imploring me to let him off the hook. 'I'll take you and the girls to this little bistro I found tomorrow night. The manager, Fred, lovely guy. Great food and wine. It'll be nice. You'll love it. You shouldn't have to cook all the time. Remember when we used to go to a new restaurant every week?'

He has framed it so beautifully, so innocently, and with a little nod to our happy past, as though it was always his intention to discover a charming restaurant for his family to enjoy. He kisses me on the cheek and takes my hand and I'm left doubting my feelings from last night, wondering if the silent punishment I felt was real after all. I force a smile onto my lips. Did I imagine the hurt? Was I overreacting?

I feel a hand tap me on the shoulder and I turn to see the same man Félix summoned with his cane. He's dressed in a suit, with grey hair and thick black glasses.

'*Excusez-moi, madame.* Monsieur Allard apologises for being called away. Would you like to follow me?'

I share a look with Dylan, and he squeezes my hand and nods for me to go. It feels like I'm being summoned by royalty, perhaps to some grand room in this incredible home. I suddenly feel self-conscious and smooth my now dull hair, wishing it was long and red and full of salt. I laugh under my breath. I feel too old to be here. Félix Allard shattered my heart at nineteen. I'm delusional to think he'll somehow be seduced by the middle-aged, mentally unstable woman I have become. No, all I need from him is half the villa. All I need is his signature on a piece of paper and I will be free. Finally, I will be free.

*

Le passé

Simone could see Saskia at the far end of the beach, her hair bright under the afternoon sun. She was on her hands and knees building sandcastles with Juliette. The little girl ran back and forth between the shoreline and her nanny as though an invisible string connected them, and Simone thought what a good mother Saskia would make one day. She was so gentle and patient with the girl, it was no wonder the Bisettes adored her.

They had been meeting most afternoons on the beach for weeks now. Simone looked forward to it in a way she would never admit to anyone. It was her reason for rising in the morning; it gave purpose and certainty to her days.

Camille seemed to have mellowed towards Simone since the night of excess at the restaurant. She wasn't sure exactly what had transpired between them, only that there now seemed to be a mutual understanding that Camille would tolerate Simone coming in and out of her life. She still felt a little uneasy joining Saskia and Juliette at the beach every afternoon, wary that a woman dressed in white might turn up to accuse her of being cursed. But Henri had been so welcoming that Simone was sure Camille hadn't meant what she'd said that day in the garden – she had just been worried about her little girl. Saskia had even mentioned that Camille had asked several times after Simone's health.

'*Salut, mes chères,*' Simone said as she reached them.

Saskia looked up and smiled, and Juliette ran to her shouting, '*Nounou Si Si,*' and it felt as warm and welcoming as the sunshine on her skin.

'*Salut, Juju.* I have brought *un petit pique-nique* today.'

She set down the basket and took out a cloth, which Juliette helped lay carefully over the sand. Every day Simone went to the market to buy food for the house, another ritual that anchored her, made her content. She was determined never to have the villa bare for her friends again. But she knew she was a little extravagant. The cupboards were filled with biscuits and sweets, rice and pasta and cereals, and condiments of every kind, and her fridge was overflowing with fresh produce and the best cuts of meat. Every day she rode to the *boulangerie* for fresh bread. And she was hungry, too. She didn't know how she had survived on so little food for so long. It was as though the dinner at Bisette had reset her appetite. Or perhaps it was Saskia and Félix who had given her back her *joie de vivre*. It finally felt like life had been restored to the villa of her childhood.

She set out strawberries and grapes and crackers with *fromage de chèvre* and slices of *tarte aux pommes* and *pain au chocolat*. She had brought a thermos of tea and a juice box for Juliette. Saskia had explained how grapes were a choking hazard, so now Simone cut them in halves. Juliette ate them with sandy fingers, her little face upturned, sticky and grinning. She didn't want the juice box but insisted on sipping their tea, like *les filles adultes* – the big girls.

They watched Juliette take up her spade again, digging and piling sand into wet mounds.

'You are so good with her. Do you want children?'

Saskia leaned back on her elbows, eyes squinted against the sun, legs crossed at the ankles. 'I think so. I mean, not for quite a while. It's nice to give her back on weekends.'

Simone laughed. '*Oui. Exact.*'

'What about you?'

Simone shook her head. 'I don't know if I'll have children. I don't think my parents were that suited to it. And I've heard you actually have to find a nice man to have babies with.'

A silence fell between them, not awkward exactly, but a little charged, and Simone wondered whether they were both thinking of Félix. She still wasn't sure how Saskia felt about him, or him about her. She only knew this energy she felt running between her and Félix, but she didn't know if he felt it too. She quickly changed the subject.

'My parents were artists, creatives. I grew up competing with their books, their work. If I was going to have children, I'd have three or four so they could occupy themselves while I worked.'

Saskia laughed. 'You try looking after one. I don't know about four kids …'

They both looked at Juliette, who was patting her sandcastle lovingly.

'I don't know, it seems pretty easy,' said Simone. 'No, I know, I know four is not a good idea, but I am a person of extremes. I take after my mother.'

'What was she like? I mean, apart from her beauty.'

'I don't think she can be separated from her beauty. It was her defining factor, whether she liked it or not. That and her money.'

Saskia hesitated. 'You are very similar to her it seems. Is that how it feels for you?'

Simone laughed under her breath and put a finger to her lips. 'These are not things one can ever make a complaint about.'

'Yes, but I imagine they can make you lonely.'

Simone felt tears prick her eyes and she swiped them away and linked her arm through Saskia's, leaning her head briefly on her shoulder. 'I'm not lonely anymore.'

Juliette came towards them, plopped herself on Simone's lap and started playing with her hair. Simone closed her eyes, feeling sleepy and peaceful under the little girl's soft touch.

Juliette reached up, her fingers finding Simone's earlobes. '*Le chat, miaou miaou,*' said Juliette.

Simone touched her cat earrings. '*Tu aimes les chats, mon chou?*'

'Cats make different sounds in English, you know. In French they *ronron*, in English they purr,' said Saskia, and Juliette copied the word.

Simone gave Juliette a tight hug. '*Oh, tu es si mignonne,* too cute.' She touched her earrings. 'These earrings were my *maman's*. She loved cats, too.'

'We have Bobo,' Juliette said.

'That's your cat's name? I love it!'

Juliette nodded and pretended she was a cat, purring and licking her paws.

Simone tickled Juliette under the chin. The little girl laughed and got up then ran to the shoreline.

'To answer your question, my mother was a complicated person.'

Simone was tempted to confide in Saskia, to tell her about Hélène driving the car the night they died, what it meant. To spill the burden, calm the uncomfortable feeling that had sat within her for a year, but she decided against it. She had not found any evidence to explain it, or even anything to suggest that her mother had been in one of her darker moods.

'She had ... I don't know how to explain it exactly – when I was a girl I just thought this was what mothers did – but she had times when she was so bright, so happy, so generous, it made up for it, you understand? She would be doing photo shoots, seeing friends, going to parties. And then other times when she wasn't available to me or my father for days on end and she would lock herself in her study. She would blame the writing, her work, but I came to understand as I grew older that it was more than that. It was like a switch would flick, and she'd go dark. My father and I never talked about it, we just gave her space, and she would always come back.'

'Do you think she had depression, or something like that?'

'Maybe. I don't know. She was a very passionate person. There was some pain in her family. She had a terrible relationship with her mother, my grandmother. I don't think she ever forgave her for devoting her life to her business. My mother was raised by nannies, and her father, who was a very kind, patient man. But, you know, my grandmother had lost her father and her brother in tragic accidents. She threw herself into her work, maybe to cope with the pain. She was a woman before her time. Look at what she achieved. Durant is one of the biggest cosmetic companies in the world. It has made our family one of the richest. Can you be a good mother and also a pioneering businesswoman? No one ever asks this about the man.'

'True,' said Saskia. 'It's like Henri and Camille. Henri is the great chef, but he doesn't have to think about Juliette, about being there for her. He's always in the kitchen. But Camille, she's the restaurant manager and that's maybe even more work, but she's also expected to be the perfect mother.'

'It's lucky that she has you,' Simone said.

'What's your relationship like with your grandmother?'

Simone shrugged. 'You know, I respect her more than anyone at all. She is so smart and just very honest, and I like her a lot. But I don't know if I love her, not in the way of family. Which is odd, and I feel quite bad about that. But she did not have much time for me either, growing up. She was running her empire from *la forteresse*. That's what we call it. The fortress. And she is quite a hard person, not much emotion, and I don't think it was a good combination with my mother, who was all emotion.'

'What about your father? Did he get on with Sophia?'

'Sophia wanted Hélène to marry someone she thought worthy of the empire she had built. She grew to like my father, maybe after he had a lot of success with his books. But at first she was against the match. I think a family never really recovers from that.'

'And can I ask how she's been since they passed away?'

Simone remembered that phone call the day they died. The slight waver in her grandmother's normally deep voice. The way she spoke only of the practicalities. Had the lawyers been engaged? Did Simone have access to the bank accounts? Was she managing the press? *Non? I will send Robert. Don't say anything to the newspapers.*

And Simone had asked, *Why, Mémé, why? Why are they gone? And what will I do?* She hadn't called her grandmother *Mémé* since she was a little girl, but at that moment she'd felt so small.

And her grandmother's voice had cracked, and she'd said, *Silly girl, what was she thinking, driving that car?* Then she had composed herself and continued to speak about lawyers and funerals and flower arrangements.

But Simone couldn't take any of it in. All she could think was, *No, Mémé, you haven't understood. I mean, what will I do with my heart?*

'She calls me every now and again. She asks me if I have been taking care of my skin,' Simone said.

Saskia laughed loudly. 'No!'

'*Oui, oui*, she's very strict about such things. *Naturellement*, the Durants must have perfect complexions. We are all dead, but our skin is perfect.'

Saskia laughed, covering her mouth. 'Sorry.'

'No, it's true. Crazy, *non*? But enough about my insane family. What about your parents?'

Saskia picked up a handful of sand and let it run through her fingers. 'My parents are divorced. My mother works as a seamstress. She's a talented sewer but … she takes up hems and sews on buttons for a dry-cleaning company. She's paid a minimum wage. She works too much for too little.'

'What about your dad?'

'He also worked at the dry-cleaning company, that's how they met. Now he works in sales. But I don't see him much. It's just me and Mum.'

'Are you close?'

'Yes and no. She wants so much for me to be a lawyer, to have what she hasn't had — money and security. But that's not the path I want, it's not the path I've taken coming here. I don't know if she'll support me if I decide to study fine art instead of law.'

'She must miss you though.'

Saskia frowned. 'She does. We write airmails to each other. She can't afford the calls. She worries.'

'You know you can call her from my phone whenever you like. You can come and stay with me any time you like.'

'*Merci*,' said Saskia, resting her head on Simone's shoulder, and Simone wished for a second that it was just the two of them in the friendship, and that they had never met a boy with dark eyes and sun-browned skin.

CHAPTER 14

I expect the man to take me upstairs into the depths of this grand mansion, where I picture Félix standing by a window in his study with his cane, looking out to sea, like the captain of a ship. But instead, I'm led outside. The breeze is brisk – it has that Atlantic bite to it, and I wish I'd brought a coat. I brace myself and look around, but Félix is nowhere to be seen. It strikes me as strange that he would meet me outside, given he seems to have been painted as somewhat of a recluse and given his apparent physical frailty.

The man stops at a small door built into the stone wall that surrounds the back half of the villa and asks me to wait. He disappears inside a small workshop of some kind and comes out with two bikes.

I laugh, because it is such an odd sight – a dapper old man in a suit holding two bicycles. I shake my head in confusion. 'Can Félix still—'

'Ride a bike?'

The voice comes from behind me, and I swing around. Félix is standing there in the half-light. He runs a hand through his hair and smiles that lopsided grin that is seared into me, and I feel my body react to him.

'You mean this?' He holds out his cane. 'I injured myself on the set of my last film, that's what brought me back here, to the island, to make a recovery. I don't need it anymore, but I bring it out in public, so that the media thinks I am still making my recovery, so they leave the injured recluse alone. No one asks when I will return to Paris, to films. And besides, I like the drama.'

The honesty of his confession shocks me, but then I remember this other part of him, the showman, the chameleon, the actor. And I'm forced to wonder whether he was acting the whole time. Was any of it real? I watch, speechless, as he hands his cane to the man and throws his leg over the seat of the bike.

'Well, are you coming?' he asks, and I am reminded of the boy he was, his startling spontaneity, his wild energy.

He takes off and I stand there for a second, stunned, wondering if I should just follow him into the night when my family is inside.

'Where are we going?' I call. But he's gone and I'm reminded of that night we met, when I got lost on these dark paths and he found me.

Damn you, Félix Allard. I hitch up my long dress, get on the bike and follow him into the dark. My muscles are sore from the previous day's riding, but I push through and catch him.

'Where are we going?' My voice is breathless, lost.

'I needed a break from all those people. Talking, talking, talking. Always wanting things. This is what I do. I ride at night. Never in the day. I prefer the silence.'

I want to indulge him, I really do. It's entirely in my nature to indulge, inevitably to my own detriment, but the reality is that I don't know where he's taking me, I've left my children behind in a strange house, and he's the type of man who's spent his life being indulged by sycophants. I don't trust him.

I stop my bike.

It takes him a moment to realise, and he doubles back. He puts a foot down for balance and he could be twenty-one again, and I am back there, dinking behind him, feeling the heat of his body through his thin cotton shirt as we ride into the night. The air still, sultry, fragrant with summer, but all I can smell is him – tobacco mixed with too-strong cheap cologne, the salt from his sweat.

'Forgive me, Saskia. I just wanted to take you somewhere quieter for a drink.' He points ahead. 'It is not far. Will you humour me?'

The look he gives me, it's the same look, the same eyes, slightly downturned at the corners, giving him an air that toys between seduction and melancholy.

I smile despite myself. 'Fine,' I say and follow him past the brightly lit restaurants full of patrons until we reach a small café right on the outskirts of the port. It's clearly not a place tourists come to. The plastic awning flaps loose in the breeze and the tables and chairs carry the rust stains of too many sea storms. There's no one here.

'This is where I come at night. I take a *digestif* and look out at the water. Sit, sit. Do you still smoke?'

It's that same easy intimacy, like he's telling me his secrets. I shiver and it's not from the cold. It feels dangerous, thrilling. I lean my bike against a pole and take a seat beside him. We're sheltered from the wind, which has picked up outside, turning the horizon into a Turner painting.

An old woman brings us drinks on a tray. She speaks a few words to Félix, but I don't understand. Perhaps it's not French.

'Cognac. I hope it's okay.' He raises his glass. 'To old friends.'

I smile. '*Santé. Aux vieux amis.*' The drink is smooth and warms me.

'So, you still remember some French?'

I shrug. 'Your English is excellent, still.'

'I have an English wife, so ...'

'Yes, she's very charming. And what does she think of this café? I can't imagine—' I stop myself. The alcohol has made me more forthright. Or maybe it's Félix.

'You can't imagine it would be to her taste?' He rocks back on his chair and once again, it's as though twenty-one-year-old Félix is back. 'Well, you are correct. She has never been here.'

I feel something stir in me, some shameful satisfaction that I'm here instead of her.

I make light of his admission, pick up a limp, stained menu then raise an eyebrow. 'But you've given me the honour.'

He laughs. 'To be fair, I only come for one drink. And one cigarette.' He lights it and blows the smoke out of the corner of his mouth, just as I remember him doing.

He hands it to me, and I'm aware of our fingers almost but not quite touching. I know I should resist but I can't. I want my lips where his have been. I draw the smoke into my lungs. I can feel him watching me. It makes me even more breathless than the smoke curling from my mouth.

'Tell me, did you become the artist you dreamed of at nineteen? You are not on the social media.'

I feel colour creep up my neck. He has tried to find me.

I press the back of my hand to my cheek, take a breath, try to play it cool. 'I did become an artist. I make paper art. I'm on Instagram, just not under my old name.'

'What is your artist name then?'

'Papier Rose is my business.'

'French then.'

'*Bien sûr.*'

'Paper art. What do you make? Will you show me?'

I take my phone out and find some of my recent works on Instagram.

'This is incredible work. So fine and delicate. It suits you.'

I laugh at his intimacy, the way it borders on arrogance, but I'm flattered by his compliment. 'Thanks.'

We're quiet for a second. I can almost feel the past settling around us. 'What about you, Félix Allard?' I have used his full name to effect. He knows I'm asking about it all. The fame, what he has become.

He shrugs and takes his cigarette packet out of his pocket. 'I have resisted having more than one for so long and then you turn up, Saskia Wyle, and I want two.'

I put my hand up, refuse to share another cigarette, as though this is going to keep me safe from his charms, his familiar tone.

'I didn't recognise you at first, but now I see that you are not so different. Unlike me. With my hair turning grey like an old man.'

'It's very debonair.' I affect a French accent. 'Very *sérieux* French film star.'

He laughs. 'I'm glad you like it. I'm not sure it makes the ladies swoon in quite the same way as when I was young.'

'It seems like you're above that now. You've won important awards. For your last film.'

'So, you too? Internet stalking?'

The heat of his insinuation hits my face.

'And you still blush.'

My cheeks are on fire. 'I haven't watched it, if that's what you're thinking.'

He shoots me a mock-hurt look and I stifle the urge to kick him under the table. 'You've stopped making films though. Or is Wikipedia wrong?'

He shakes his head and breathes deeply. I can sense his frustration. 'I'm taking a break. After the accident ... I broke my ankle badly. We were doing a lot of filming in the wilderness. I returned here, to reassess my life, I guess. The warm weather helped with the recovery and I have not had the desire to return to Paris.'

'Well, you've conquered the world, Félix. You can retire knowing you achieved what you dreamed of doing at twenty-one. I remember. Look at what you've become. You've done it all.'

He shoots me a reproachful look. 'Have I? Is this conquering the world?'

'You have a huge house and a man who arrives at your side when you tap your cane — which is purely for show, to keep the press at bay.'

Félix laughs and shakes his head. 'Saskia Wyle, you realise no one would dare say this to me?'

I smile. I love that he makes me bold, and I make him humble. It's as though we turn each other inside out. I don't try to hide the warmth, the nostalgia in my voice. 'All I can see when I look at you is a boy with a bad Australian accent.'

He laughs. '*Non, non, non*, you cannot say this. I practised for hours to impress you. I stupidly thought this would make you fall for me.'

So I wasn't dreaming. Maybe it *was* real. 'I did fall for you.' The words slip out before I can stop them. I silently curse this open line of communication between us.

His drink pauses midway to his lips.

My breath is so shallow it comes out as a whisper. 'That's why I never understood … why you didn't …' I can't even say it out loud I'm so ashamed. *Why it ended, why you didn't come.* His eyes meet mine and I feel the undercurrent of our connection surge. It is still there. I can't breathe with its intensity.

'Saskia, I …' His head drops. The old woman comes to the table and clears our glasses. Puts down a fresh ashtray.

'Can I tell you why I come to this place every night?'

I nod, swallow. Feel something inside me shift. I can't tell if it's fear or excitement. Maybe it's both.

He smiles, sadly I think. 'Josie.' He gestures towards the old woman who has just gone inside the café. She is Juliette's grandmother.'

I feel blood rush to my head and my throat swells. I knew there was a risk that we would come to this place eventually, but now that we're here I don't want to be here.

'She's ninety. Her husband is gone, all her friends. But she says she cannot die until her granddaughter is found, and …' He shakes his head and looks out at the water. 'I come to see her every day because of this.'

I feel my chin tremble and I swallow hard to try to dampen the emotion building behind my eyes. It feels like a hot wave, and I'm not used to the struggle of having to control it. Tears spill down my face.

'Sorry, I—' I lunge for the serviettes on a nearby table and try to compose myself. I curse myself for not taking my pills, for my lack of control. What am I even doing here reliving a past that I've spent a lifetime trying to forget? 'I should get back. My girls. It's late.' My words are mumbled, I can't look him in the eye.

I get up and grab my bike. My hands are trembling. I realise my whole body is shaking. I'm freezing.

'Saskia, wait.' Félix is taking notes out of his pocket, putting them under the ashtray.

But I don't wait for him. I can't. *This is why he didn't come.* My guilt feels like it's strangling me. I can't breathe. I need to get away. I look behind and he calls out again, but I ride away without looking back.

*

Le passé

The morning sun was warm on her bare shoulders as she rode. Her skin had browned a little in the months she had been on the island, and she thought about how her grandmother would not approve of the sunburn that had turned her face and neck red as she worked in the garden, pulling up weeds as Félix had shown her. She wanted it to look beautiful for Saskia and Félix's weekend visits, when they would meet at the markets for coffee, cycle back to the villa to prepare lunch, then eat it at a table covered in white linen, under the dappled light of the trees. They'd have pasta with fresh herbs from the garden, or pan-fried fish, or mussels cooked in white wine, followed by a crisp salad and cheeses. After their meal they would spend hours lying by the pool, drinking wine and swimming. Saskia would sketch, Simone would write in the shade of the orange trees and Félix would read plays, interrupting their quiet reverie occasionally with a soliloquy that would make them roll their eyes and laugh.

It felt like the villa was transforming, coming back to life. For the first time in as long as Simone could remember, she had a purpose, modest as it was. And one she knew would have made her parents happy, one that connected them to her in simple ways. After she had returned all the books to their shelves in the loungeroom and filled the pantry with food, she had begun to attend to the care of the house. She swept the cobwebs from the corners, wiped sea salt from the windows, vacuumed and washed the floors and set to cleaning up the garden. This work was so foreign to her – it was work she had always assumed was terrible and boring and to be delegated to others, but she found a strange peace and pleasure in it.

That morning she had found herself wanting to ask Félix about planting some flowers in the beds around the house that she had cleared of weeds, and the idea had come to her that she should ride out to see him at the salt marshes. She felt a little rush of excitement as she thought of the picnic basket on the back of her bike filled with a surprise lunch. He had cooked for her many times now, and she wanted to repay the favour.

The salt marshes were bright under the late morning sun, edged by mangroves, glasswort and sea lavender. Simone squinted and shielded her eyes, searching for Félix's tall frame among the basins. She saw other *sauniers*, scraping the water's surface with their long sticks. They were hidden under broad-brimmed hats, and she wondered how she would find him. But then she saw his mop of hair. He was wearing sunglasses and an old T-shirt over shorts. She stopped the bike and watched him for a little while, mesmerised by the slow sweeping movement of his arms as he raked the salt. It was a kind of alchemy, almost religious to behold, and she wondered how he would ever leave this island when its ways were so strong in him.

He stopped and straightened, and she waved until he saw her. He put the rake down and walked over, pushing his sunglasses back onto his head.

'Simone. What are you doing here?' He kissed her cheeks in greeting but his tone was not particularly warm.

Her heart sank a little. She had expected a warm welcome. She realised he had addressed her in English, as he often did when Saskia was around. She responded in French. 'I was in my garden thinking that I needed to ask you what type of flowers to plant around the villa, and then I thought I'd come and ask you in person and bring you this.' She took the basket off the back of her bike. 'Lunch.'

He rubbed at the back of his head and scrunched up his mouth. She knew him well enough by now to know that this meant he was uncomfortable, and she shuffled her feet to hide her hurt. 'If you don't take a lunchbreak, it's cool,' she said in English, laughing, trying to hide the disappointment in her voice.

He leaned to the right and then the left, looking behind him, and she marvelled at how awkward he was, but somehow this was part of his charm. He answered in French, making their conversation feel like a strange dance between intimacy and formality. 'Believe me, I would love a lunchbreak, but I have so much to do before my bar shift this afternoon. I really don't have time to stop.'

She felt pathetic, desperate again, the same feeling as when she had kissed him and he had pulled away. She chastised herself for her privilege. Of course, he had to work. He didn't have time to talk about flowers for a garden bed and take a picnic. She went to put the basket back on the bike and he took it from her hands.

'Okay, but I will have to eat quickly.'

They sat in the shade of a timber hut and looked over the salt fields, the marshes beyond.

She handed him a baguette and he looked chastened. 'I'm sorry if I was rude. It was very kind of you to ride all this way. It's just, my brothers are working on the fields over there and they're already giving me a hard time about working at the bar and not being serious about the salt. If they see me eating lunch with a pretty girl, I'll never hear the end of it.'

Simone felt her cheeks colour. She was already so hot from the ride, now her skin was burning. 'So, I take it they don't know about your aspirations to be an actor?'

He laughed. 'No one knows about that silly little dream except you and Saskia. I don't even know why I said it. It's never going to happen. If I feel guilty having lunch, how could I ever leave?'

'I feel guilty about not having a job, a purpose. I feel guilty about coming here and distracting you. Too much guilt!'

He put his hand on her shoulder. 'It sounds like you're doing great things with the garden. That's something worthwhile. Anything in nature is worthwhile. It's a means unto itself. It's what makes us happy, I really believe that. And it's why I'm not sure I can ever leave here.'

They gazed out onto the hot bright landscape and watched a flock of egrets soar across the sky. The only sounds were the slosh of the saltwater and the soft movement of the wind in the low shrubs that edged the flats.

'Oh no, here come my brothers.' Félix stuffed the remainder of his baguette into his mouth and dusted his hands on his shirt.

'Do you want me to go?' Simone shoved her own sandwich back into the basket.

'Too late. Just ignore them.'

'Hey, we have a visitor!' the taller one called. He was huge, built like a wrestler, with arms like tree trunks. The other brother was more like Félix, tall but wiry. They all had the same sun-darkened skin and Simone found herself wondering which was the eldest.

They kissed her cheeks in greeting and sat down in the shade of the hut, taking off their hats. Félix introduced them as Ludo and Christian.

'Félix, why didn't you tell us about your beautiful friend?' Ludo asked. 'And what's this? A little lunch?'

Simone opened the basket. 'You're welcome to have some.' She handed out fruit and sandwiches, glad she had packed more than they could eat.

'So, you live on the island, Simone?' Christian asked.

'Yes, over by Le Bois-Plage. It's a summer house, very neglected, and Félix is helping me with the garden.'

'I'm sure he is,' said Ludo suggestively and Félix punched him on the arm. 'Anyway, we're having a party tomorrow night. You'll have to come,' Ludo added.

Simone smiled. 'I'd love to.' She wondered suddenly if Saskia would come to the party too, and felt bad that a small part of her hoped she wouldn't, that she'd get Félix and his family all to herself.

Félix rolled his eyes. 'Not one of Arno's parties.'

'I think we're going to the beach bar. But Arno throws the best parties. His parents have one of those huge villas on the island by the beach. Paris types.'

Félix and Simone exchanged a look and she silently implored him not to make a big deal out of her own house, even though he had the opportunity to trump his brother and it was clear the two were competitive.

'Fine. We'll ask Saskia if she can come too,' said Félix, and Simone felt a little drop of disappointment in her stomach and hated herself for it.

Ludo laughed. 'How many girlfriends do you have exactly?'

Félix shook his head. 'None. She is a friend from the bar. I have friends, which is more than I can say for you.'

Ludo leaped up and grabbed Félix in a headlock and Simone understood from the exasperated look on Christian's face that he was the eldest brother.

'Come on, you two, back to work,' he said. 'Thanks for the sandwich.' Christian stood and stretched then put his hat back on his head. Ludo slapped Félix on the back and waved to Simone then followed his brother into the marshes.

Félix sat down. 'So that's my idiot brother, Ludo.'

'They seem nice. Christian is more like you. Ludo is obviously the ladies' man.'

Félix laughed and feigned hurt. 'You mean I'm not a ladies' man?'

Simone shot him a suggestive look. 'I'm not sure, you tell me?' She wasn't imagining it. It was there again, this tension between them, a flirtation, a playfulness.

'No, he's way better looking than me, he's built like a truck,' Félix said. 'Anyway, Saskia and I were talking about going to see a film in La Rochelle some time. You should come. It's the new film about Rimbaud. I can't guarantee it will be any good. The Americans are making a film about a French poet, what could go wrong?'

Simone laughed but felt that same unease rattle through her. Of course, Félix and Saskia saw each other at the bar and around Bisette. And Félix was inviting Simone along, not leaving her out. But it still felt like an afterthought.

'Yes, I'd love to come.' She tried to sound upbeat.

'And we didn't get to talk about your garden, but I know we'll be back at the villa on the weekend, you know, cooking for you, making sure you have food in the house.' He nudged her playfully.

She laughed but couldn't help feeling despondent. Was she still his charity case, or did he really want to spend time with her? 'Hey, I've cooked for you many times, and you know I always have food in the house now.'

'I'm just teasing. And I'm glad to see you looking after yourself.' He kissed her on each cheek, thanked her again and said goodbye.

As she packed up the picnic basket and watched Félix head out again into the salt, she reassured herself that she had a party and a movie to look forward to, and both involved Félix and Saskia.

CHAPTER 15

I'm sweating despite the cold wind nipping at my back. I've ridden as fast as my legs will allow, away from Félix, away from the past. My mind knows I can't outrun it, but I'm not operating rationally anymore. I'm past that. My body has become pure feeling, emotion, instinct, as though I'm an animal woken from a long hibernation, trying to stay alive in the wild. The light and the music and the sound of joyful voices from the terrace reach me on the street and I feel nauseous as Félix's mansion comes into view. I don't want to go back in, but I need to find my family.

I'm dizzy with exertion as I lean my bike against the outside wall. I look behind me as I climb the stairs to the entrance, but Félix is nowhere to be seen. I'll need to be quick.

The party has shifted into another gear, like an expensive car rounding a mountain. Johnny Hallyday croons into air thick with cigarette smoke and perfume. I chastise myself for letting my asthmatic daughter breathe in this air, and move through the crowd looking for small dogs and my daughters. My own lungs feel tight and it's hard to get air in. I feel the room begin to spin and I'm sure I'm going to faint, right here in the middle of this beautiful salon.

And then suddenly Félix is in front of me, grabbing my arm. He's saying my name, but I wrench out of his grip. I mumble something about needing to find the ladies. I can't breathe. It feels like my heart is about to burst out of my body. I clutch at my throat, willing the air to go in. Why can't I breathe? What's happening to me?

I rush towards what might be a bathroom and to my utter relief, is. I lock the door, lean against it and press my hand to my chest. I wonder if I'm having a heart attack. How stupid I've been to think my body would be okay left to its own devices. My anxiety feels like a black horse rearing up, exposing the whites of its eyes. Someone is banging on the door now and I yell for them to wait. And then I realise who it is. I open the door and Dee falls into my arms.

'Mum. Are you okay?' Her face is pale with worry.

I shake my head and then nod, not wanting to scare her. 'I'm okay.'

'You're shaking,' she says, pulling me into a hug, and I smell the sweet, familiar scent of her, and it calms me. 'Maybe you're having a panic attack. Hannah had one after her boyfriend broke up with her via text at school – so not cool – and she looked exactly the same. She thought she was going to die.'

That's exactly how I feel. Shame washes through me, thick and sickening, that my daughter has to see me like this. But I think she's right. Knowing that I'm not having a heart attack, and that it's probably my recently uncaged anxiety, makes sense.

'Good. Take some deep breaths. It's okay, panic attacks are very common.'

Something about the way she's talking to me, her startling maturity, her having to look after me, when it should be the other way around, undoes me and I begin to cry softly. I sink to the floor and cling to her as I force air into my lungs, try to claw back to the surface, to equilibrium.

The door opens and Dylan comes in. I can see Lara hanging back, her face scrunched, and I hate myself for causing it. One of the dogs runs in and licks my leg. I pat it absentmindedly.

'What's going on?' he asks.

'She's having a panic attack,' says Dee and her tone suggests that she's only just stopped herself from finishing the sentence with 'you moron'. I want to cheer her for standing up to her father when so often she has witnessed me unable to. He disappears and returns with a glass of water. I take a sip and it helps.

'It's okay. I'm okay,' I say, pulling myself off the very expensive-looking tiles and sitting on the edge of the enormous bath.

Dylan ushers Dee out. 'Okay, go and say goodbye to the dogs, and grab a macaron for the road. I think it's time we called it a night.' He crouches next to me, his forehead creased. 'What's going on, Saskia? I'm worried about you.' His tone is gentle, his hand on my arm solid, steadying, warm. He's always responded like this when I'm physically weak or injured. It's when he's at his best. The saviour.

I squeeze his arm. 'I'm okay. Too much to drink, not enough food. I just need a minute. I'll meet you and the girls in the car.'

He fills up the glass again. 'Here, have some more water, it'll make you feel better,' he says, rubbing my back. 'You sure you're okay to get to the car by yourself? I can wait.'

His eyes search mine and I smile reassuringly. He leaves and I breathe a sigh of relief, steady myself against the basin. I look terrible. My cheeks are flushed, and my hair is flattened to my head with sweat. I don't want Félix to see me like this. I run my fingers through my hair, splash my face with water, and apply some fresh lipstick from my small crossbody bag. I find two Panadol and swallow them. Now that the rest of my body has stilled, my head is thumping.

I step out of the bathroom tentatively, but there's no one around and I almost weep with relief. As I'm crossing the lounge to the front door, I see Félix in my peripheral vision. I feel his eyes on me and I will him not to follow me. I walk fast towards the front door. He doesn't try to follow and a strange combination of relief and disappointment flows through me.

The air outside is fresh and clean, and the car is waiting out the front with the engine running. The girls look exhausted, and we drive across the island in silence. The thump in my head begins to ease.

Dylan takes my hand, presses my fingers to his lips. 'You okay now?' His tone is still soft. 'What brought that on?' He knows it's more than being tipsy. 'Do I want to know what happened with Félix Allard?'

'I'm fine. Not now, we'll—'

'Talk about it later,' he finishes, entirely reasonable and understanding.

I shut my eyes in relief, lean my head against the window and drift off.

The slam of the car door jolts me awake. I have no idea what's going on with my body. I can't anticipate its reactions, I don't trust it. We go inside the villa, Lara's arms a warm circle around my waist.

I take the girls straight up to their bedrooms. Dee kisses me on the cheek and I pull her into a hug.

'I'm so proud of you,' I say, and she rolls her eyes, my petulant teenager back.

'Night, Mum.'

I help Lara out of her clothes and into her pjs. As she snuggles beneath the doona she says, 'That was a fun party. I hope Daddy didn't make you sad again.'

My heart squeezes and I kiss her forehead. 'No, no, I just felt a bit sick. You know the worried feelings you get in your tummy? They just got a bit big.'

'You should have done our breathing exercises.'

'I know. I should have. Luckily your sister reminded me. And now I feel okay.'

'When can we see the dogs again?'

I think about Renée's invitation to go on the boat and my stomach squirms. 'I'm not sure, honey. Hopefully we'll see them again.'

'I miss Tiger.'

'I know you do. We'll be home before you know it.'

She closes her eyes and I want to curl up next to her and avoid Dylan, who'll be waiting downstairs for an explanation I can't give him.

'Stay,' she says, and I capitulate and lie down. *I'll just stay for a few minutes*, I think.

The next thing I know, Dylan is shaking my shoulder gently. I rub my eyes and get up. Lara is asleep with her thumb in her mouth.

'Feeling any better? You should probably eat something, get your blood sugar back to normal. Have you checked your emails?' he whispers.

'No, I fell asleep.'

'Well, whatever you said to Félix Allard worked. Monsieur Rombard emailed. I asked him to keep me in the loop after we spoke on the phone. Allard finally responded to the emails and they're setting up a meeting. Rombard will be here in the next day or two so we can get this thing signed off.'

I try to look as though I'm not shocked. Did Félix already know about the email from Simone's lawyer? Why didn't he mention it? Or mention Simone? The villa? Why didn't I? Deep down I know the answer, of course. Simone is like a rift running through the middle of everything. The fault line waiting to split and rumble the earth beneath our feet.

'That's great news,' I manage. 'You go to bed. I'm just going to get a glass of water and, yeah, I should make some toast or something.' I indicate down the stairs.

'Do you want me to make you cinnamon toast?'

It's always been my comfort food. Dylan knows just how to make it, with too much butter and cinnamon. For all his faults, he knows I like my coffee strong and black and my tea weak and white. He pulls me into a hug, and I feel my body relax into the warm familiarity of his chest. We stay like that for a long time, and I wonder why it can't always be like this.

'It's okay, you go to bed,' I whisper.

'Okay, don't stay up too late,' he says, kissing the top of my head and disappearing into the bedroom.

I go downstairs and pour myself a glass of milk and then realise I'm starving and pour some cereal into the glass. It's called Chocapic and it looks like a sugary Coco Pops–style breakfast – no doubt Lara's choice. I eat from the glass with a spoon and open my email to find Monsieur Rombard's correspondence. He'll be on the island as soon as he can manage, at which time we'll all meet to sign the paperwork.

I feel a shiver along the back of my neck and turn. Of course there's no one there. *What do you want, Simone?*

I find myself in the lounge and retrieve Simone's manuscript from under the pile of books where I've hidden it. I pull a throw over myself and sink into the nearest lounge. I open Google Translate on my phone. This is the only way to find out.

*

Le passé

The bar was at the tip of the island, right on the beach and the lights of the mainland shimmered across the water. Coloured lanterns were strung through the pine trees and long tables sat on the sand. A man strummed a guitar and a woman sang softly into the summer air, her voice mingling with the wash of the shore. Groups of people drank cocktails and beer and the air smelled of fish cooking and something spicy.

There was a relaxed party atmosphere and Simone wondered why she had avoided the island in her teens when it looked like so much fun. It was different from the parties she frequented in Paris, with their wine sipped inside chic apartments, rooms filled with smoke and serious conversation. But she supposed she had thought the island *gauche*, almost childish. Her parents had always begged her to spend the summer with them, but she'd always had what she imagined were more sophisticated plans in the city.

She took Saskia by the arm, glad to be arriving with her and Félix. Christian had insisted on picking them all up in his car – an old Peugeot that looked like it had been left in the salt air too long. Ludo was apparently already there, having been drinking in the sun with the party boy, Arno, since lunchtime.

As they approached the table, Simone felt suddenly shy. She hadn't been in a group of people since the party in Paris weeks back. Ludo made a loud noise in greeting and got up from the table to kiss them. They all wished Arno *bon anniversaire* and took their places at the end of the table.

Félix fetched them beer and Simone enjoyed the cool bitter drink, wondering why she didn't drink it more often. She and Saskia had spent another afternoon at Le Bois-Plage with Juliette, swimming in the clear aquamarine water. This seemed like the perfect end to a day at the beach and the delicious barbecue smells wafting across the sand made her hungry. Christian was on her right and Saskia on her left, with Félix sitting across from them. He was wearing a white fedora hat, smoking a cigarette, and she saw at that moment the man he would become, and a longing moved through her. He had never looked so beautiful, with his tan deep against the white of his shirt, open at the collar, and his artisan hands holding his glass of beer.

She couldn't explain it, this feeling she had. She had never felt this way about any other man. Did attraction need an explanation? Or was it simply chemicals being released in a brain? And why had it taken her so long to feel this? Her mother had met and married her father by the time she was her age, twenty-four. Why this boy, in this place, at this time? And why, of all the men she had known, all the men who had desired her, was his affection for her so uncertain?

A hand on her arm interrupted her thoughts. Christian had brought her another glass of beer and she thanked him.

'So, you live in Paris normally?' he asked.

He had the same bone structure as his brother, the same deeply suntanned skin, though his face was more symmetrical than Félix's. He was traditionally more handsome, but he lacked the charisma, the pathos of his younger brother.

'Yes, I haven't been on the island since I was, well, a child really.'

'Félix told me your parents have a summer villa.'

A bolt of tension went through her, making her square her shoulders in anticipation for what was coming – some enquiry about her parents' death.

'Near Le Bois-Plage? He told me about this beautiful old villa, with only a packet of pasta in the cupboards.'

She breathed out and laughed with relief. He didn't say this in a judgemental tone, but it told her that he and Félix were close. She sensed Félix had more of an emotional connection with Christian than with Ludo.

'Yes, we went on an adventure to get *fleur de sel* for the pasta, to the salt marshes.'

Christian's brow creased. 'My little brother did not tell me about that bit. I hope you didn't steal salt from our harvest.'

He was teasing, but Simone recognised that he was a rule-follower, unlike his brother.

Food was set down in the centre of the table. Spanish rice and fish tacos and foods with spice and soul, and Simone found herself eating with her fingers.

She stole looks at Félix across the table. He was talking to Saskia and she longed to be part of their conversation, but Christian was telling her about the salt marshes and his family's history on the island. He was clearly passionate about his *metier*, but Simone found herself only half-listening to him so that she could catch snatches of what Félix was saying, his head bent towards Saskia's. Her hair fell over her face and something he said made her laugh and throw her head back and she tucked her hair behind her ears.

They did not talk about Félix at all when they were alone on the beach with Juliette, their toes dug into the sand, the sun in their eyes. It was as though he didn't even exist. There were so many other things to discuss. Simone found herself telling Saskia more about her family than she had ever told anyone. Saskia had a way of listening without judgement, something Simone had not really encountered before. All her Paris friends had so many opinions on everything, from politics to fashion to family, and were willing and able to debate them. Simone wondered if it was something about the Australian versus the French temperament, but she found Saskia's non-combative way in the world soothing. And in turn Saskia shared things about her own life back home, her family. Perhaps it was the fact that they came from such different places that allowed them to connect; their conversation was easy, just as it had been that first evening they'd met at the café. Sometimes they just sat in companionable silence watching Juju pat sandcastles into shape.

Simone was just about to ask Saskia if she wanted to dance – the music had become louder and more vibrant, the guitar player standing and the singer swaying her hips to the Latino-style music. Bodies were already moving under the lights on the sand, and the beer and the warm night and the delicious food had worked their way into Simone, loosened her. She allowed the rhythm of the music to move over her. She loved to dance but usually to electronic music in nightclubs – small dark, sweaty places below street level, where she could forget herself, often with the help of a pill placed on her tongue by a friend or a friend of a friend.

Before she could pull a clearly hesitant Saskia to her feet, she felt a hand on her back.

'You move so well,' Christian said. 'Shall we?'

He took her hand and led her into the mass of bodies. She closed her eyes and let her body find the beat. Christian kept his eyes fixed on her. He had good rhythm and she wondered if it had something to do with the way he used his body at work, the way he scraped the salt rhythmically, like a caress. But her awareness was still at the table, where she could see Félix pulling Saskia up and twirling her around. Simone felt dizzy and light-headed imagining it was her in Félix's arms and envy prickled over her skin. She pretended not to watch them move to the dance floor and join her and Christian.

Saskia reached for her and they twirled each other around, laughing, and Simone thought maybe her jealousy was unfounded as they danced in a platonic group, Félix doing daggy moves and making them roll their eyes and laugh. This, she realised was the thing that Christian lacked. He was serious, earnest even when he danced, and she found it annoying. Some small part of her wanted to tease him to see if she could shock him.

The music changed, the pace slowing and the woman's voice growing mournful. Christian drew her to him suddenly, his arm around her waist. She looked over to see Félix pulling Saskia into his arms and her heart felt like a wet towel wrung out. No, she hadn't been imagining it. The way he lowered his gaze, his hand brushing Saskia's hair from her shoulder. How had she been so blind? It was Saskia he felt something for. The beautiful stranger. So kind and sweet and nurturing, yet with a brilliant artistic talent, something Simone would never have. Something she had envied in her parents her whole life.

Simone felt suddenly as though she was back in Paris, at one of the parties. Her insides felt hollow as Christian pressed his hand into the small of her back and drew her closer still. He moved his pelvis against her, as so many strangers had in dark clubs. She could smell his cologne, strong and overpowering, and she couldn't help comparing it to Félix's scent when he'd passed her on his bike and they'd shared lunch side by side looking over the salt flats. When she had kissed his lips. He had tasted somehow known to her, not like Christian, who was another stranger who wanted her without knowing her. She felt her throat ache with unexpressed sadness.

She glanced furtively at Félix and Saskia, their foreheads pressed together, and in that moment she knew he was lost to her. Every molecule of her body wanted to run but instead she felt herself lifting her chin for the kiss she knew Christian was waiting for. And when it came it was wet and somehow adolescent and she felt nothing. But she knew that Félix had seen it, and some small part of her hoped it might arouse in him some jealousy, that it might make him want her more.

She and Christian stayed on the dance floor long into the night. He brought her rum and cola and it sloshed over the sides of her glass as she danced. She didn't know where Félix and Saskia had gone, but she didn't care. She laughed and felt the music dig deep into her bones and she kissed Christian passionately, trying to bury the pain, returning so easily to her old familiar ways. But he was serious and chivalrous and not drinking as much as everyone else on account of driving, so he steered her away from the dance floor when she could hardly hold her head up.

Saskia and Félix were there now at the table. Saskia pulled Simone's hair off her face and Félix gave her water, telling her to drink and taking the glass of rum out of her hand, and it almost felt like it was back to normal, back to just the three of them, and no one kissing anyone.

Félix said it was time to go and they got in the car. Saskia was smoothing her hair and all Simone could think was, *I could never hate you*, even when she saw Saskia and Félix exchange a look, and she knew they both pitied her. She was the same girl who had come here from Paris alone and piteous.

Christian stopped at her house and offered to stay with her, and she wished she could say what she was thinking. *No, I only want Félix. Or Saskia.* But they weren't making any signs of getting out of the car and so she said that she was fine. Christian found a pen in the glove box and scribbled his phone number on a piece of paper then handed it to her.

As she pulled herself from the car and watched them drive away, she looked down at the piece of paper and wondered, *How have I ended up back where I began?*

CHAPTER 16

I wake and sleep in fits and starts, reading snippets of Simone's manuscript before descending once more into the depths of slumber. Her words merge with my dreams, and my memories fuse with the language I once knew, so that I don't know if I've read, or remembered or dreamed things, whether they're in English or in French. I see Félix on a bike riding through a tunnel of trees, the bright white of the salt flats under a low, hot sky. I awake with an image of the perfect symmetry of Simone's cheekbones, her chin in her hands. I open my eyes. A pale light filters through the sheer curtains and I'm suspended between waking and sleep, past and present. Perhaps it's the withdrawal from my pills that's making reality so nebulous, so slippery. Perhaps it's knowing that I will likely see Félix Allard again today.

I pick up my phone, which is about to die, and google Simone Durant. There is still no mention of her death. I find a recent photograph, and those cheekbones are the same, though the skin is thinner, the angles sharper. If anything, age has made her more beautiful, starker. She never published any work despite all those dreams she had of being a writer, of being like her father. I look down at the pile of paper on the floor beside me, the corners already dog-eared. Is this her only novel? And another thought occurs to me. Is this the only copy?

All these questions I want to ask Monsieur Rombard, but I am still guilt-ridden. Her fondness for Félix and me, for the island of her childhood, is evident in these pages, but there must be another reason, there must be more. I pick up a page to keep reading but there is movement in the kitchen, and I push the manuscript under the chaise longue.

In the kitchen I find Dee in her bathing suit eating from the box of Chocapic that I left on the benchtop. She jumps when she hears me behind her.

'God, Mum, you scared me.'

'Sorry. You're up early.'

'I'm going for a swim.'

'I can see that.'

'What is this sugary shit Lara bought? '

'Language ...'

'Would it help if I said *merde* instead?' She arches a brow.

'Ha ha, very funny. Fine, you can swear, but only in French.' She shrugs. 'Deal.'

'Let me guess: you know all the swear words already.'

She flashes me a cheeky smile and I'm reminded of the easy bond we used to share. I want to hug her. I want to talk to her about last night, thank her for being so strong, but she grabs her towel from the bench and moves past me.

I reach for her, catch the end of her ponytail, which slips from my hands like a ribbon. 'Sit down, pour yourself a bowl. I'm making tea if you want one?'

She turns, her face a picture of exasperation, the wall between us back. 'There's no chai.'

'We'll have to pick some up at the supermarket ... Dee ... you can have breakfast. You know you don't have to do laps after eating some sugary cereal. We're doing so much bike riding ...'

Her eyes narrow. Her voice is cold. 'Really? Are *you* really in a position to be giving *me* health advice?'

'Don't you dare talk to me like that,' I snap, shocked at the barely repressed anger in my voice.

'You don't seem to have a problem with other people talking to you like that.'

And before I can stop myself, I've closed the gap between us and slapped her cheek. My palm stings and shame crashes through me as my hand flies to my mouth.

Dee's eyes are wild with hurt and I reach for her, to apologise, to draw her near, but she pushes me away and runs out the door. I watch as she goes to the pool and dives in.

I squeeze my fists into tight balls to stop myself from screaming. I can't believe I've just punished my daughter for the sins of her father. I hate myself more in this single moment than at perhaps any other time in my life. *Almost any other time.* There was one other time, and it feels so close, its guilt still cloying and sticky. I feel so raw, so utterly surrounded by my demons that the feeling of last night takes hold of me again.

I find my phone on the side table in the loungeroom. I don't know what time it is, and I don't care.

I am a terrible mother. I just slapped Dee on the face after a fight, I'm so ashamed, I write.

I wait for the dots to appear, to show me Petra is reading, wait for her absolution, but nothing happens. And I know there's only one way out now.

The shutters are closed, and Dylan is still asleep in the dim light as I tiptoe past the bed. I find the pills in the desk drawer and take out one of each and swallow them down without water. Their taste is acidic and comforting at the same time, and I'm sure I can already feel the edge coming off. *Enough.* I cannot be in this world without a buffer, the cost is too great. I crawl into bed beside my husband. He rouses slightly and pulls me into his body, which is warm and familiar and everything is okay. I'm safe now. Everything will just go back to the way it was.

I feel his morning erection press against my back, and he runs his hand over my stomach, my breasts. My breath catches and I push his hand between my legs, feel myself responding. His skin smells like home, the soap we use. His breath quickens, which makes mine quicken too. He kisses my shoulder and then bites it.

'You looked hot last night,' he mumbles into my hair as he hitches my dress up – the one I'm still wearing from last night – removes my underwear and pushes inside me. It hurts but I enjoy the shock of it, the stolen pleasure of it. We move slowly, drugged by the ease of early morning. He makes a strangled sound as he comes. I don't, but some need in me is met.

He wraps his arms around me. 'That was very nice. You know I love you.' He kisses the back of my neck.

I am safe. I am numb. I am safe.

We doze for a while but are roused by the sound of a text message coming in and I grab my phone expecting to find Petra's reply, but it's out of battery.

I pick up Dylan's phone and see a message from a number without a name. *Hi Aussies, We're leaving from the jetty just down from the house at 11 am. Doggies on board! Hope to see you then. Renée x*

He's given her his mobile number. It's his way of clawing back the power that Félix Allard has stolen from him.

'I see you've got the French actress on speed dial,' I say, keeping my voice light, playful. 'Renée's texted about the boat trip today.'

'Oh, so … are we playing *this* game? Okay, fine. Are you going to tell me where you went last night with Félix Allard then? You were gone for quite a while … I did notice.'

My hand flutters at my throat. 'We just … He wanted to get away from the noise so we could discuss the villa properly. We just walked outside so we could hear each other talk. And … it obviously worked.' I make my voice upbeat.

'You seemed pretty emotional afterwards, in that bathroom.'

I swallow and lick my lips, trying to stay calm under the scrutiny of his gaze.

'I think I was having a bit of anxiety. You know I don't like parties. And the pressure to, you know, get him to agree about the villa. And I missed a few of my pills, with the flights and the time difference.'

He draws me to him, tenderly smooths my hair off my face. 'Well, that makes sense. You know you shouldn't be messing with your meds, Saskia, that's a recipe for disaster.'

'I know.' I stay in his arms, which are wrapped tightly around me. He must believe me about Félix because he takes the phone from my hand and smiles.

'Can you imagine what this fucking boat is going to be like?' He pats me on the bum. 'Come on, we should get up. Thanks for that nice morning wake up.'

I smile back and kiss him. I feel like I'm floating. It feels like relief.

Lara comes down to the kitchen shortly after I've cut up fruit and put on coffee. I wrap my arms around her and offer to make her jam on toast. Dee is nowhere to be seen, but I can see from the wet towel on the back of a chair that she's come inside. I put fruit salad in a bowl with coconut yogurt – her usual breakfast – and take it up to her room. She's showered and dressed and is lying on the bed, on her phone.

As soon as she senses me at the door she turns over, away from me.

'Dee, I'm so sorry. I shouldn't have slapped you. I'm feeling very emotional at the moment. But of course, that's no excuse.'

She doesn't respond. I know this will be my punishment for the next day or two and I can hardly blame her, it's the way I punish as well. I've modelled it to her. Shutting down after Dylan's hurtful words, until he slowly coaxes me back into the land of the living.

'I've got some fruit salad here if you want it.' I put the bowl on the bedside table. 'You know, I just want to look after you.' I pause, watching the slow movement of her breathing, the way the skin on the back of her neck is darker from the sun. 'Thank you for looking after me last night, and' – I feel tears prick my eyes and I bite the inside of my lip until I taste blood – 'I'm sorry that I'm not stronger.'

She says nothing and I leave the room. At least she heard me, even if she didn't acknowledge me. I know she just needs time. After showering I dress carefully. I wear white linen pants and a navy singlet top. I think about Félix's loose suit jacket, his bare feet and his cane, and wonder what he would wear on a boat. I'm torn between wanting to see him and feigning a migraine after my spell last night. I could stay home and read

Simone's manuscript and drink the bottle of white wine in the fridge, lying by the pool.

But some instinctual part of me knows he will be there. There's unfinished business between us, and there's an undeniable pull, the exact same feeling from twenty-six years ago.

*

It's already hot when we reach the port at La Flotte. The sun has cast jewels over the water and there's a light, cool breeze coming in off the Atlantic. I know nothing about sailing, but I can sense it's a perfect day to be on the water. The girls spot Renée and the dogs on a jetty near Félix's house. The dogs are dressed in navy and white outfits and Renée is wearing a broad-brimmed black hat and a flowing black and white floral kaftan. Coupled with her bright red hair, the effect is dramatic. She waves as she sees us and the dogs race towards the girls.

I laugh as my daughters pick up the dogs and let them cover their faces in kisses. It's good to see Dee happy, though I don't expect her to acknowledge me for at least another twelve hours. I see him then. He's standing on the bow of a luxury yacht, the kind that media moguls and French film stars evidently own. The kind that has bedrooms, a bar, cream leather seating and polished timber decks. He's wearing a captain's hat, but at an angle that makes it look ironic. A polo shirt, shorts and bare feet complete the look. I notice he doesn't have his cane.

'Oh, I'm so glad you came, Australians!' Renée says, kissing us, her heady perfume competing with the sea breeze. 'Welcome to *Happy Hours*.' She points to the name painted on the hull and I realise that this is definitely her boat.

'This is amazing,' I say. Dylan is mute with shock at the beauty of this vessel.

I notice there are a few others already on board. We walk across a short gangplank to be greeted by a man who is presumably the real captain, dressed in sailor white with socks pulled up to his knees. Renée introduces us to two other couples, both already seated at the rear of the boat, nursing glasses of wine. They don't speak much English and I try to remark on the lovely weather in French and they smile, no doubt humouring me.

The boat has begun to pull away from the jetty and the wind picks up. Félix is with the captain at the wheel. He's pointing at something up ahead as the captain manoeuvres us through the port out onto open waters. The long arm of a sandy white beach appears to our left and in the distance is the mainland, shrouded in a heat haze. Félix still hasn't greeted us, but that seems to be his elusive way. There is charisma in mystery after all, and he had it as a twenty-one-year-old too.

'This is the life,' says Dylan, helping himself to a beer from an esky. He's clearly more relaxed now that he knows the paperwork is in order. The sex this morning probably helped too. We used to have a more adventurous sex life; now we just have variations of what occurred this morning – trying to sneak it in in stolen moments, hoping a child won't walk in. I've always thought of it as a symptom of middle age and two decades of marriage, but there's usually a measure of intimacy afterwards, and that's a symptom of our chemistry – a literal push and pull. A casting out and reeling back in.

I find orange juice and pour the girls drinks. They're at the front of the boat, where there's space to sit against the curve of the cabin's windows and catch the sun, playing with the dogs.

I wonder how on earth the animals don't fall in but they're racing around, obviously delighted to be on board. As though answering my question, Lara tells me they're sea dogs, that they love the boat and the water.

'Renée says Queenie was scared at first, but Pooch loves it and now Queenie does too.'

'You disappeared very fast last night.' I turn around to see Félix behind me. He kisses me on both cheeks in greeting, and I feel blood rush to my head. Clearly my meds haven't taken the edge off completely.

'The dogs love you,' he says to the girls. 'Sorry, I didn't introduce myself last night. I'm Félix.' He takes his hat off, bows, and then puts it on Lara's head. 'Do you want to drive the boat?'

Lara nods shyly and Dee takes the hat and puts it on her own head. 'Yep.' She gives a salute and Félix returns it and winks. I can see that she's charmed.

'Philippe will let you steer.' He waves to the captain and the girls pick up the dogs and go inside the cabin.

'They're great,' he says. He isn't facing me, he's looking out onto the smooth blue surface of the water, the endless line of the horizon. 'I'm glad you came today. I see your husband is enjoying happy hour on *Happy Hours*.'

I laugh. 'Thanks for the invite,' I say, my tone light, staying on the surface. 'Dylan loves boats. He's in heaven.' He's at the back of the boat with the others, drinking, and flirting with Renée.

'And what about you? What do you love these days?'

Again, I'm taken aback by his directness, and I steady myself on the handrail. I can feel his eyes on me. It's been so long since someone asked me such a thing. 'Um, time to myself.' His forthrightness has made me honest in turn. 'I must admit I nearly pretended to be sick today just so I could stay at the villa alone by the pool with a bottle of wine.'

'Like old times.'

He tasted like oranges, lips cool and sweet as we lay under the fruit trees, our hair still wet.

I laugh awkwardly and he looks at his feet, shifts his body weight. I'm not imagining it, the taut line between us, threading together the present and the past, hovering over all the things left unsaid, the things I can't face.

'I'm sorry I left you last night,' I say, glad of the steadying line of the horizon, avoiding his eyes. 'It's hard for me to talk about ... When you mentioned Juliette ...'

'No, it's me who is sorry. I know it must be hard being back here after everything that happened.'

'It was Simone's doing.' There, I've said it, introduced her name, the reason for being here.

He is silent and I wonder what he's thinking behind those dark eyes.

'I saw you responded to her lawyer's email,' I venture.

'I don't know how I missed it. I have a – how do you say? – an assistant in Paris, and she hadn't opened it – the first correspondence, the letter. And the emails, I am terrible with such things. The practicalities.' He throws his hands up.

I don't respond. I don't know how to. We're entering uncharted territory.

'I would say that I'm sorry you had to come to my party, on account of my lazy administration, but ... that would not be entirely true.' He shoots me a lopsided smile and I feel my body respond. I look at his hand on the rail in front of me. The skin is weathered and rough and I wonder what it would feel like on my neck.

'And it seems this' – he indicates between us – 'is what Simone wanted. And Simone always got what Simone wanted,' he says.

The hairs on the back of my neck lift. *What does that mean? She wanted you. It's littered through her manuscript. Did she get you, in the end?* I brace my arms across my body. The wind is picking up and a sail clangs in the wind. The boat lurches and I'm thrown against him. He grips me with a fierceness that doesn't feel like it's merely to protect me from slipping off the side of the boat.

His lips are close to my ear. 'Saskia, I ...'

I push myself upright, away from his frightening intimacy. I realise he's still holding my wrist and I break from his touch. 'Well, we can say what we like, but Simone was nothing if not generous,' I say.

'Was she? Maybe I remember her differently. To bring you back here, after everything that happened?'

I feel a twinge of annoyance. 'But she's left me half her villa,' I counter. 'Three million euros may be nothing to Félix Allard, but it will change my life,' I say, my voice verging on defiant.

He shakes his head. 'Do you remember? What money was to her?'

'All she wanted was for people to see her for who she was beyond her money,' I say with an intensity that surprises me.

He laughs, sadly, I think, and shakes his head and I realise that he is silently expressing the irony in this. That people cannot see him beyond his wealth, his name. I look towards Renée, ensconced on the back of her cruiser, and understand that this is also the currency of his marriage.

'Is it possible, do you think,' I ask, gentler now, 'to see beyond the money?'

He looks thoughtful. 'Only for those who knew me beforehand,' he says, and the way he looks at me it's as if he is looking right through me to the girl I used to be. I feel engulfed by the past, by him, and I want to fall into him again, be embraced by the strange familiarity of his scent. *How can someone still smell the same after half a lifetime?*

I'm acutely aware that everyone can see us, and I compose myself.

'Is that why you've returned here? Is your family still on the island?'

'My brothers are – you remember Ludo and Christian? Both still working the salt. They have families. They never left the island, and my father is still alive. I have him in a very nice home in Ars-en-Ré. He's very old now and not well.'

Not well. I think of Simone. I have to know. 'Félix, I'm ashamed to say I don't know how Simone died. I couldn't find anything about it online.'

He looks out to sea. We're further out now and the wind rips the tops off the waves, turning them white. 'Neither do I. Until I received that email, I had no idea.'

This tells me he hasn't been in contact with her for a while, perhaps a long time.

As though reading my mind he says, 'There was a retrospective of her mother's work a few years ago, in Paris. Hélène Durant, you remember? She invited me to that. That was the last I heard.'

'Did you go?'

'No, I was on location.'

'For the film that won all the awards?'

He faces me now, puts his hand over mine on the rail and looks into my eyes. 'I thought of you while I was making that film.'

My mouth goes dry, but I don't move my hand. It's his eyes: in this light, with the sun shining on them, they are amber. I can see the tiny lines that the years away from me have mapped onto his face and I want to reach out and trace every one, know the laughter and sorrow behind each flesh-etching.

I pull myself together and move my hand away. I try to remember what the film was about … a man climbing a mountain … a man grieving the loss of his wife.

'You thought of me?' I manage, but it's lost on the wind ripping around us, through us.

He is very close to me now. I can't tell if it's his breath or the wind on my cheeks I feel. 'Yes, you. Why do you think Simone has done this? Why do you think she has brought you back?'

I don't know, I want to scream, *but you abandoned me when I needed you, and I never heard from either of you again, so I don't know who to trust.* My head is spinning, and the boat crests a wave before dipping down the other side and we both grab at the rail, our bodies thrust together. I feel the tightness close around my throat again, the same feeling as last night.

And then Dylan and Renée are beside us, holding onto their hats and laughing at the size of the swell. The girls and the dogs race out and squeal as a wave sprays us and we all cower. I meet Félix's eye and he holds it. It's me who looks away.

Philippe joins us and suggests we retreat to the back of the boat. He's going to try to steer us into calmer waters for lunch. His wife, Frida, has prepared a meal of salads, prawns, oysters and fresh baguettes at the polished timber table inside. I spend the rest of the afternoon trying not to look at Félix. Trying not to feel his eyes on me. Dylan is attentive, topping up my wineglass, a stray hand on my hip, and I wonder if this is just an overflow of our dynamic of the past few hours, or whether he can sense it, this energy running between Félix and me.

We turn back to port after lunch. There's an ominous strip of navy cloud in the distance, a dark rip in the seam of the horizon.

'There'll be a storm tonight,' Philippe says. He speaks in a dialect I'm not familiar with, so I'm not sure exactly what his next words mean, but I think they roughly translate as 'You don't want to mess with an island storm.'

When we disembark, I ask the girls to thank Renée for lunch, and for the unfettered access to her pets. She kisses us and tells us that if we're ever on the island again to come and pay her a visit. I look back to see Félix still on the boat. He's looking towards the horizon, the amassing storm clouds. He turns and waves. It is not his way to say a gushing goodbye like his wife. In any case, he has already said what he needed to say. He grabbed me by the elbow as I was leaving. 'Will you meet me? Tonight. At the bar we rode to? After nine. I will wait for you.'

I can still feel the imprint of his fingers on my skin.

*

Le passé
Félix and Saskia were already sitting in the back of Christian's car when he picked her up the following afternoon. Saskia leaned out her window and kissed Simone, and Christian came and opened the front passenger door for her with much ceremony. Her stomach churned. He was very chivalrous, and handsome in his crisp white button-down and loafers, but she couldn't help but feel like she had won the consolation prize. It was very clearly a double date, and she wondered why she hadn't been properly consulted – it had been just the three of

them planning on going to the film, and she hadn't called the number on the piece of paper. Somehow it was worse that it was the number for Félix's home as well.

She tried to comfort herself with the thought that his car was being used as an excuse, a convenience. It was a long way to ride their bikes into La Rochelle and Christian had probably offered to take them, as though there was no ulterior motive on his part. Simone wished she could have refused, talked to Saskia about her feelings for Christian – or her lack of them – but she could not, because that would lead naturally to talk about Saskia and Félix and she wasn't sure this was something either of them could face. She turned around to smile at Saskia and Félix in the back seat, her gaze landing on the way their legs touched, and she wished they had all just got the bus. But she supposed it was better than having to go out with Christian alone, with all his earnest attention.

They drove with the windows down, the smell of manure and cut grass lifting off the fields. The others were chatting, about their days, about their excitement for the film, but Simone wasn't really listening. She felt set apart, other. And as they crossed the bridge to the mainland, Simone said a silent prayer to her parents.

The film, *Total Eclipse*, was an American version of nineteenth-century literary France, and she found it ironic that they were reading subtitles in a film about a French poet. But the main actor, a new talent called Leonardo DiCaprio, was mesmerising. Simone wondered if there wasn't something about him – a boy on the cusp of manhood, passionate and wild – that reminded her of Félix. She was acutely aware of his body beside her in the cinema. On the other side was Christian, offering her popcorn and Coke and whispering comments in her ear. She couldn't stand it – she wanted to swipe him away like a mosquito, and she felt awful.

She excused herself and left the cinema halfway through. In the bathroom she splashed water on her face and considered leaving. But leaving was what she always did. She thought back to that last party in Paris when she'd left and got on a train to come to Île de Ré. It was her only way of coping with pain, her only way of surviving. She thought of her mother, escaping to her studio and locking herself away for days on end. Perhaps this was where she had learned this coping mechanism.

Saskia came into the bathroom. She stood at the sink and their eyes met in the mirror. 'Are you okay?' she asked.

Simone's heart began to race. She wanted to tell Saskia that no, she wasn't okay, that until last night at the beach bar, things had been good. She had felt what happiness was, what true friendship was. It had felt like the three of them against the world. But now the happiness felt like it was slipping, and those who had given it to her were taking it away.

But she couldn't say any of this. She knew it wasn't Saskia's and Félix's intention to hurt her. Just as it wasn't Christian's intention to annoy her. Perhaps she was the one with something wrong. Perhaps the person she was beyond the money, the reputation, wasn't actually very nice, wasn't someone to fall in love with.

'I'm just tired. I drank too much last night,' she said.

'You looked like you were having fun with Christian.' Saskia shot her a playful look and Simone smiled thinly. 'Oh, you don't like him?' Saskia's brows creased.

She wanted to say, *No, I'm falling in love with the same man you are.* But instead, she shrugged. 'He's nice, I guess.'

'Sorry, I just … the way you guys were kissing, I thought you were pretty into him.'

'That's just the way I behave with every man who gives me attention,' she snapped, and Saskia's face went blank and then flashed with hurt, or shock, Simone wasn't sure.

An uncomfortable silence fell between them. 'Are you enjoying the film? Do you want to go? We can just go,' Saskia said.

'No, no, let's go back in.'

As Simone left the bathroom, Saskia caught her arm. 'We'll have a secret code if you want to leave. Félix wants to get dinner after the movie. But if you're uncomfortable you can' – she thought for a moment – 'wink at me.'

Simone felt waves of both affection and sadness wash through her. Saskia didn't realise it wasn't just about escaping Christian. He was the symptom, but what she was having to witness blossom between Saskia and Félix, that was the disease.

Simone sat through the rest of the film, which was about a man tortured, divided between dutiful love for his wife and the passion he felt for Rimbaud, his soul, his very being, and all she could think was how Christian was like the wife, and Félix was like the French poet who was doomed to torment and break her.

Afterwards the four of them sat on the pier eating croque monsieur bought from a street vendor. Christian pressed his thigh up against Simone's, his oily fingers brushing her skin. Saskia kept looking at her, full of anticipation, waiting for the wink. But Simone found she couldn't engage their secret code, and she knew that the thing that had bound them since that first night at the café was gone.

*

Simone was glad to be leaving La Rochelle and going home. It wasn't late but she just wanted to sleep. She felt so tired having to pretend, having to witness the easy flow of the conversation, Félix and Saskia quoting lines from other films, laughing. She leaned her head on the cool window and let it all wash over her as they drove back onto the island, and she wondered how she had had the energy to do this for so long, when perhaps she was always destined to be on the outside looking in.

They reached the lane leading to the villa and the headlights flashed over a bike rider. The night was moonless, the heat of the day lay like a blanket, thickening the air, and Simone wondered who would ride on such a night. Christian pulled up outside her gate, and she turned and gave a wave to Saskia and Félix in the back seat. Saskia's leg was thrown casually over Félix's and they were holding hands. It felt like someone had punched her in the stomach.

Simone was about to get out when Saskia said, 'Wait,' and disentangled herself from Félix. She got out of the car and Simone felt a little rush of hope, that maybe Saskia and Félix would come inside and Christian would finally get the message and leave, and the three of them would make food and bathe in salt flowers and be happy, like before.

But when Simone got out of the car, she saw what had drawn Saskia's attention. Camille was standing next to her bike in front of the gate.

'Is everything okay?' Saskia asked, approaching Camille, her voice breathless with worry.

It was then that Simone saw Juliette on the back of the bike. Camille's face looked gaunt and pale in the harsh light of the headlights. Simone sensed that this was not just an offhand visit and a needle of anxiety worked through her as she remembered Camille's cruel words the last time she was there.

'I thought you might be here, Saskia. Juliette, she … I … ' Her voice broke and the fluttering nerves in Simone's stomach took flight as Camille's face collapsed. Juliette began to cry. Saskia rushed to the little girl, took her from the bike seat and cuddled her. Camille seemed stunned, unable to function or to comfort her child.

'I'm sorry to just turn up here,' she said as she got off her bike, smoothed her hair and brushed the front of her dress. Simone saw that she was barefoot.

'No, no, don't worry, come in,' she said, opening the gate. 'I'll make us tea.'

Christian had cut the engine and he and Félix got out of the car. Simone shot Félix a pleading look that she hoped he'd understand: it didn't feel right for Christian to be there, and she wanted him gone. But Félix didn't get the message, and so when she caught Saskia's eye, she winked.

Saskia nodded in understanding and went to Félix, whispered something in his ear.

'We'd better get going,' he said to Christian.

'Sure, yes, it will be a busy day in the marshes tomorrow. Bye, Simone,' Christian said, his voice painfully hopeful, and she allowed him to kiss her cheeks, noticing the way he lingered with each one.

Simone led the way into the villa, switching on lights and gesturing to Saskia and Camille to follow her into the kitchen. She put the kettle on and busied herself with preparing tea and finding sweet biscuits for Juju. Saskia was making her laugh and the sound eased the sense of foreboding growing in Simone. It wasn't until she was placing the mug in front of Camille that she saw the bruises.

Simone gasped and hot tea sloshed over the side of the cup and scalded her hand.

'Are you okay?' Camille asked in French.

Simone shook her hand and her head. 'Sorry, yes, but your face ... Are *you* okay?'

Camille ducked her head and her hand flew to her cheek. There was a moment when Simone thought she could see the inner workings of the other woman's mind, deciding whether or not to tell the full truth. Given the Camille she had encountered so far, Simone expected her to dismiss it, to blame it on a door, on a cupboard corner. Instead she said, 'I didn't know where else to come.'

'Did Henri do this?' Simone asked, emboldened by Camille's honesty.

'Things were very difficult at the restaurant tonight,' she said.

Simone thought how completely charming Henri Bisette had been when he'd introduced himself to her at the restaurant table, and it sent shivers through her.

Simone and Saskia exchanged a knowing look. Silence fell between them, and Camille took a sip of tea. 'Thank you. For the tea, and the biscuits.'

Juliette was chewing on a *galette*. Her tears had dried but whereas she normally might be chatting or looking for the grey cat that thought this was its second home, she was quiet. Simone found herself sitting down next to her and smoothing her blonde curls, offering her another *galette*. Juliette nestled into her, and Simone's heart ached at this small gesture of trust, and for what this little girl might have witnessed between her parents.

'I know I probably shouldn't have come, and with Juliette on the bike. It's such a dark night. It's just …'

Simone put her hand on Camille's arm. Her skin was cold and clammy. 'It's okay. We won't say anything to anyone. You are always welcome here.'

Camille's face crumpled then. 'I'm sorry I was so rude to you when I first met you. Using your parents' death to shame you.' She shook her head. 'I am a horrible person.'

Simone felt a lump in her throat, and saw that perhaps Camille believed she deserved this. 'It's okay. Really, it's okay. I'm sorry for ordering everything on the menu in your restaurant.'

Camille laughed and wiped under her eyes.

'It was very arrogant of me. I was just showing off for my friends. Forgive me.' She squeezed Camille's hand and they shared a smile, and Simone realised how inaccurate her judgement of Camille had been. Her aloofness was fear; her brittleness, fragility.

'We fight,' Camille said. 'We always have. We're careful not to when the nanny is around.' She looked at Saskia sheepishly and Simone understood that the succession of nannies was probably Camille's shield.

'But tonight was different.' She stroked her daughter's cheek. 'He scared Juliette.'

Simone and Saskia shared another look, both wondering whether they should tell Camille about Juliette's reaction that day in the hallway when they'd happened upon the shouting.

'Why don't you stay here tonight?' Simone suggested. 'We can work out what to do in the morning. Juliette looks so tired.'

The little girl had hopped onto Saskia's lap and was twisting her long hair around her little fist and sucking her thumb. Her eyes were heavy, as though she was close to sleep. Simone wondered how Camille felt about their closeness, whether there was some part of her that was jealous or wondered why her child felt safer with Saskia than with her own mother.

Camille put her mug down, straightened, and pushed her hair behind her ears. 'Thank you, but we can't stay here.'

'It's too late and dark to ride all the way back to Saint-Martin and I don't have a car to drive you,' said Simone.

'We can leave our bike here. If I could use your phone, I'll call a taxi.' Camille had composed herself. It was as though her shell was growing back, her fragility turning brittle again.

'Camille, are you sure? Are you sure you should be going back there?'

She swallowed with difficulty but nodded calmly. 'He will have calmed down. Saskia will be with us.'

Saskia gave Camille a reassuring smile, but all Simone could see was worry written all over her face.

'But ... he'll do it again,' Simone said.

Camille stood then, the chair shrieking against the tiles. 'I can't. I know what you're asking me to do, but I can't.'

There was a tap on the French doors that led to the garden and Simone felt her pulse pound. But the face behind the glass was Félix. She let out the breath she had been holding in, then she opened the door and he stepped inside.

'Everything okay?' he asked, his brow heavy with worry, his skin slightly damp with sweat. She wondered if he had cycled all the way back, and thought at that moment that she had never loved a man more.

'We need to get going,' said Camille, peeling her daughter off Saskia, who looked at Simone helplessly.

'I can drive you. I have Christian's car,' said Félix.

Simone wanted to say no, that they should all stay in her huge empty house. She'd make them a supper of eggs on toast and put Juliette to bed, and they could take a *digestif* in the loungeroom and listen to some music, then wake in the morning and eat breakfast together outside in the soft morning light.

Juliette began to fuss in her mother's arms, having been woken, and before Simone thought about what she was doing, she was drawing close to the girl's scrunched-up face.

'*Voilà, mon chou*. You remember *les chats*? Your favourite.' Juliette reached out her little hand to touch the gold cat earrings in Simone's ears. 'Remember, *miaou miaou*?'

'*Miaou miaou*,' Juliette repeated, calming and jamming her thumb back into her mouth.

'Juju adores my cat earrings,' Simone said to Camille by way of explanation.

Camille's eyes were steady, and she nodded very slightly, almost imperceptibly. 'Yes, they were your mother's,' she said.

Simone's breath hitched in her throat and her hand found her lobes. She wanted to ask how Camille knew this, but she was struck dumb by her statement, as raw and unexpected as her comment about her family's curse.

Camille glanced back but was already following Félix and Saskia out the door, her back straight, her head high, as though she had never shown them her soft, vulnerable underbelly.

CHAPTER 17

The water lashes the windowpanes and I stuff a tea towel into the gap where the window won't quite close, where the sea air has swollen the wood. I wonder if Simone had to do this when it rained, whether her parents had to do it and the people who owned the villa before them. It occurs to me that houses are like people, with their idiosyncrasies and weak points, passed down through generations like stories. I remember the story behind this eternally broken window. Simone told me that first night I stayed here. She would never get it fixed because it reminded her of her mother, who liked it broken so the smell of the orange trees could seep through.

There's a distant roar, the sea thrashing the beach beyond the dry-stone wall. Streaks of lightning lance the darkness, illuminating the pool and garden outside in surreal vignettes. It's 8.45 pm. The girls are in their rooms reading in bed and Dylan is watching something on the iPad. Would they even notice if I went? Took the car just as Dylan did a couple of nights ago on the pretence of wanting a decent French meal? I look at the kitchen benchtop. I could leave a note, say I'd ducked out to get *chocolat chaud*, hot chocolate for everyone. There's an umbrella in the foyer. If I'm going to go, I need to go now. I remember the feeling of Félix's hand on my arm.

I thought of you while I was making that film.

I need to know what that meant, what that means. I walk into the kitchen and find a piece of paper and a pen in a drawer, but the words won't come. There's another crack of lightning and the whole room lights up, like a strange dream.

What are you thinking? He won't even be there.

I put down the pen. I couldn't bear for him to not be there again. I couldn't bear to face Juliette's grandmother serving me a drink in that run-down little bar with its sticky tabletops.

No. He can feel what it's like to wait and for no one to come.

*

I sat under a hot Spanish sun on blinding white steps, my skin already pink from the glare of sitting there the day before. I wanted to be in the shade, under a nearby tree or in the cool Colosseum-like structure at the top of the stairs, but there were so many people that I was afraid he wouldn't see me if I moved. And we'd said, very clearly, to meet on the white steps of Gaudí's Park Güell at midday, the ones with the lizard in the middle. We'd studied the picture in my *Lonely Planet* book. We'd chosen the youth hostel we'd stay at. It was called Kabul and it smelled like other people's socks, joss sticks and chai tea. I looked at the colourful reptile rendered in mosaic beside me. It was absurd but somehow still beautiful, like this whole fantastical park with its bright swirled tiles and organic shapes, and I wondered why we hadn't chosen somewhere else to meet? Somewhere discreet. Somewhere less like a strange dreamscape.

But what I was really asking was why he hadn't come. He'd promised. After the second day of waiting, I used the public phone in the hostel to ring the phone number of his house. It rang for a long time, the tone a flat line, so different from how it sounded calling home. I thought about his family out on their salt flats. They were not home. But eventually his father answered and I heard him hesitate when I told him who it was, and shame engulfed me.

'I do not know where he is' was all he said, in halting English.

'Will you tell him I called?' I asked, but his father had already hung up.

*

No. I will not ride into this raging storm to meet Félix Allard, I will see him tomorrow at the upmarket restaurant in Saint-Martin, just as Monsieur Rombard has arranged, just as Simone intended. We will sign the legal papers, and I will go back to my life three million euros richer.

Instead, I turn my attention to Petra's response to my admission about slapping Dee. *Hon, you have a 14yo girl. They're hard work and you're probably still jet-lagged. Don't be too hard on yourself. Mum washed my mouth out with soap when I was a teen. PS: Sorry to compare you with Sal. Haha xx*

I wish I could tell her about what I'm going through, about Félix and everything that coming back here is unearthing, the fault lines I can feel rumbling through my life, my marriage, my body, but I know in the end she would side with her brother. She loves him in a more elemental way than she loves me. Of course she does, he's family. What would she think of Félix?

217

She'd probably find him pretentious, with his bare feet and his enigmatic eyes and luxury homes and yachts, but she'd still admit to falling in love with him a little bit.

I sleep fitfully, dreaming that Félix is knocking at the window in the rain, trying to get in. At one point it feels so real that I get out of bed and look down into the wet garden, but there's no one there and I feel consumed with guilt that he's ridden in a storm to meet me and I didn't go.

The day slips between my sheets early. In my garden-gazing dream state, I've forgotten to close the shutters. I get up and close them so Dylan doesn't wake. I take my pills out of Simone's desk drawer and lay them in my palm. I'm going to be nervous today doing the paperwork with Félix. The largest part of me wants to swallow them all, give me a buffer, but there's a tiny part of me, the part that has been quiet for so long, the part that saw Félix in my dreams last night, that's screaming. That wants to be heard, present, alive, awake to life. I'm acutely aware that there is no easy solution here. Part of me needs this medication, part of me is blunted by it. And I know this on-off approach to my meds isn't ideal. It's probably what triggered my panic attack at the party. I should be tapering off slowly, not being extreme. I split one pill with my fingernail and put half on my tongue.

Downstairs the house is quiet, but I can still hear the sea surging beyond the stone walls. The storm has found its way into the kitchen. The tea towel I used to try to keep the water out is soaked through and the table below is covered with water. I clean it up and make coffee then sit with Simone's manuscript in the weak morning light.

She is describing the night we met Félix, the night he made the three of us ride to the salt flats for *fleur de sel* for our pasta and we bathed in salt. In her words it sounds like a religious experience, and I'm moved and humbled by her apparent reverence for us, her new friends. *His hand found mine as we floated, the sky a thick blanket of stars.*

I reread the passage. Have I mistranslated? I remember Félix holding my hand that night. It was the first time he did. I remember the soaring promise of it. Had he held Simone's hand too, under that shallow water? I feel the familiar slide in my gut. I remember the night vividly – the salt drying on my skin, in my hair. The strange excitement of it all. But it was also the night I got lost on the dark paths that crisscrossed the island after Simone dared Félix to race her. It was the night she kissed him.

I hear footsteps moving around above and hide the manuscript in a kitchen drawer. Dee comes down in her swimming costume and I greet her, perhaps a little more upbeat than is warranted, and she sees straight through me and grunts, walks out the door and dives into the pool. I try to remember whether she ate dinner last night. I was so consumed by Félix and whether I would meet him. Yes, I made salmon with roast potatoes and green beans, and she ate the potatoes and beans. I would usually offer to make her an egg, some extra protein, but I didn't push it. I knew she'd recently reduced her egg consumption and I couldn't help the twist of anxiety that triggered in me. There's something so instinctual and hardwired about my need to feed my children. But another more rational part of me comforts myself that she is, as Petra pointed out, in the most tumultuous and difficult teenage years. That flirting with veganism is her way of asserting control over her own life, and I know all about that.

On her way back through the kitchen, trailing a damp path, she fights me about coming along to the meeting with the lawyer in Saint-Martin, insisting that she's old enough to stay behind and look after Lara. And she is, but I can't explain it, I want them with me. I tell her they can walk along the port and buy ice cream, and she rolls her eyes and says she doesn't eat ice cream, despite the fact she did so only days ago. I tell her that they'll have non-dairy alternatives, and she raises her voice at me in frustration and storms out of the room.

There's a tap on the open door and Madame Gardner appears, looking cheerful. She's holding a basket with a muslin cloth over it. I feel a sudden surge of affection for this sweet, nurturing woman who has brought us food again, but it's mixed with apprehension. The last time we saw her she was quizzing me about Félix Allard. I hope she isn't here to ask more questions.

'*Bonjour*,' she says, kissing my cheeks. 'I have brought some fresh strawberry jam, for your breakfast.'

Under the cloth sit jars of homemade condiments and a freshly sliced baguette. 'You are too kind,' I say, 'bringing us food all the time.'

'I wanted to check you were all okay after the storm last night. Very strong wind.'

I point to the window that doesn't shut. 'Just a leak here. The window doesn't seem to close properly.'

Madame Gardner inspects the wood, running her fingers along the bottom of the warped frame. 'Ah *oui*, Simone always had trouble with this window. My husband offered to fix it for her, but she said it was part of the house's — how do you say? — charm. We told her that the wood would keep getting more and more wet, more and more swollen and hard to close the longer she left it, but she insisted she did not want it fixed.'

I feel a shiver across my shoulders, as though someone has traced their cold fingertips along my skin. It's not the first time that I've felt that Simone might be here, in her house. I know why she was attached to keeping this broken window, but I don't share it with Madame Gardner. I wring a wet tea towel into the sink. 'Well, I guess we should respect her wishes then' is all I say.

There's a long silence as we both think on this, and I'm aware of all the unanswered questions hovering between us. She probably wants to know how Félix Allard's party was. Why I spent time on the island in my youth.

'So, you have met Félix Allard?' she asks, reading my mind, and my stomach twists.

Dylan comes into the room then and throws up his hands in some kind of exaggerated greeting, as though he's known this woman his whole life. 'Ah, Madame Gardner, my favourite person. You have brought me *le petit déjeuner*. Did I say it right?'

Madame Gardner nods enthusiastically and she and Dylan kiss in greeting. She shakes her head fondly at him. 'Oh, I love that you appreciate my cooking, Dylan. I wish I had such a husband.'

'I wish I had such a wife,' Dylan exclaims, winking playfully, and Madame Gardner looks coy and shows him her basket of spoils.

My eyes roll so far back in my head I nearly fall over. But of course, this is what Dylan has always wanted, a traditional woman who makes him food and knows how to stack a dishwasher. 'Gee, that's so progressive of you, Dylan,' I mutter under my breath, my sarcasm undisguised.

Dylan has grabbed a slice of baguette from the basket and is very deliberately spreading jam on top. The sickly-sweet smell fills the damp air. 'My wife is an artist.' He looks into my eyes and bites into the bread. Chews and swallows. 'She likes to cultivate an air of bohemia and mystery. French villas popping up out of the blue, ex-boyfriends who are French movie stars, but, under it all, I know who she really is.'

I realise that he's not talking to Madame Gardner anymore. For all his flattery of moments ago, he doesn't give a damn what she thinks.

'She's just a scared, broken girl, prone to panic attacks, who I picked up working at a bar.'

The casualness of his cruelty has sucked the air from my lungs. My chest hurts as though he's physically punched me. But what did I expect? Wearing that dress. Disappearing with Félix at the party. Did I really think there'd be no repercussions? That his recent warmth and kindness would last?

I look at Madame Gardner, whose mouth is pursed in confusion. He's said this in company for a reason. I can't fight back. He sees this and goes on, his voice light.

'So, we went to Félix Allard's party and on his yacht yesterday. I've got to give the guy credit, he's got good taste,' he says, brushing the crumbs from his lap.

I can't tell if this is a reference to the house, the boat or me.

Madame Gardner looks to me and I smile awkwardly. It's easier for us both to ignore the tension in the room. She puts her hand over her heart and swoons. 'Did you know Félix Allard was a *saunier* in his youth? His is a salt family, part of the proud tradition of the island.'

'I'm sure Saskia knows all about it,' says Dylan, his lips lifting into a smile that doesn't reach his eyes.

They both look at me, expecting me to elaborate. The pain in my chest intensifies. I'm skirting too close to everything –

Dylan, the past, the truth. How long will it be until Madame Gardner puts everything together? She must have seen the media coverage at the time. We were all over the French news. I smile thinly and Dylan says, 'We're seeing him today actually. Simone Durant is making us split half the villa with him.'

I need to get away from his smirking mouth, from Madame Gardner's surprised face. I excuse myself to take a shower and get dressed, say that we have to be in Saint-Martin soon, even though it's not until after lunch. I look back to see her shock morph into something else, and fear that maybe it's understanding.

*

Le passé

The stone walls of Citadelle Vauban rose into a low sky. The water beyond the fort was the same steel grey, and a fine sea mist clung to the corners of the ancient walls. Simone felt it on her skin and she shivered. It wasn't exactly the perfect day for a visit to one of the island's most historic sites, but at least there weren't many tourists. On the phone that morning, Saskia had agreed without hesitation to meet her, expressing a tacit understanding that they needed to talk about Camille, about what she'd revealed the previous night.

Simone twisted one of her earrings. How had Camille known these were her mother's? Had they been friends? Why hadn't Camille revealed this, if they had? There had been times over the summer when she might have mentioned a connection, expanded on Henri's admission in the restaurant that he knew her parents. Instead, she had said nothing, remained always slightly aloof, always a little wary and hard to read.

She saw Saskia and Juliette by their bike, waiting for her on the overgrown green grass that rimmed the fort. An arched bridge and a grand entranceway loomed above them, but the ancient structure was slowly crumbling, greenery sprouting in unruly tufts from centuries-old stones and tree roots pushing through walls as though they were chalk.

They embraced in greeting, Juliette jumping into Simone's arms and pointing out the donkeys in the field with excitement. Simone felt relieved that she was okay after the upset of the previous night. Simone noticed that Saskia looked radiant, her cheeks flushed from the ride, or perhaps from what had happened. She remembered, with a twist in her stomach, Félix's and Saskia's fingers entwined in the back of Christian's car.

Simone took apples and carrots from her bag, and they walked over to the animals with Juliette, showing her how to feed them with the flat of her hand. The donkey lightly nipped Juliette's finger and she drew it away in fright.

'*Oh là là, tu es une vilaine mule!*' she cried, shaking her finger at the animal, a frown on her little face.

Simone and Saskia looked at each other, torn between laughing at this tiny outburst and feeling unsettled by her sudden and aggressive reaction. They covered her hand in kisses until she laughed again.

'*Ahh désolée*, sorry, I didn't realise about the naughty donkeys,' Simone said, as they watched Juliette pick wildflowers from the grass.

'Do you think she's okay?' she quietly asked Saskia, and she could see in her eyes that she understood the question wasn't about the donkey nip.

Saskia nodded but Simone wondered if she was imagining the slight tension between them. Did Saskia know how she really felt about Félix? Maybe he had told her about the stolen kiss now that they were clearly together. She felt pathetic, ashamed suddenly.

'What is this place? It's huge,' Saskia said, craning her neck towards the arched cobblestone bridge marking the citadel's entrance.

'It's very famous. It's a star-shaped fort made by a very well known designer, Vauban, to protect the island from invasion in the 1600s. It was a prison at one point in its very long history. Now there are just tourists and seagulls.'

'So much history. In Australia we have rocks that old, but not buildings.'

'When you've seen one Vauban fort, you've seen them all.' Simone laughed.

Saskia shrugged. 'At home when you've seen one sunny beach, you've seen them all.'

'I'd rather a sunny beach,' said Simone. 'The beaches here are grey half the time.'

'And I'd rather an ancient fort,' said Saskia, and Simone was reminded that they had only known each other for two months and came from vastly different backgrounds.

'So, what happened after you left last night?' Simone's voice dropped to a whisper. 'I mean, what Camille told us ...' She winced.

Saskia smoothed Juliette's hair as she ran back and forth between them and the naughty donkeys, fascinated but still a little frightened. 'Henri wasn't even there when we got back, thank God.'

'But, I mean, do you feel safe there? Knowing what we know?'

Saskia bit her lip. 'Camille said it was a one-off, that he's never done that before. And I feel like when I'm there, it's okay. I haven't even heard him raise his voice. And there are always people nearby, downstairs in the bar and restaurant.'

'You don't think Camille's ...'

Saskia's eyes narrowed. 'What, making it up?'

'No, no of course not, but ... I just can't read her. She seems so hot and cold, so ...' Simone wanted to tell Saskia what Camille had said about her mother's earrings, but something made her hesitate.

'I know what you mean. Sometimes she's so warm and other times she's distant. She acts the same way with Juliette.'

'Do you think she's a good mother?'

Saskia's face darkened and her voice was hushed. 'Are you asking if she would keep Juliette in a situation that's dangerous for her?'

Simone raised her eyebrows in question.

'No. She lives for Juliette, she loves her.'

Simone exhaled deeply and crouched down to Juliette. She spoke in English. 'You're doing so well. See? The donkeys aren't scary, they love you.'

Simone stood and Saskia looked awkward suddenly, crossing her arms against her chest. 'Simone, I wanted to ask. About me and Félix ... last night. Are you okay? I mean, I know we've been a bit of a threesome, I mean, not actually a threesome.' She shook her head and looked at her feet. 'But the three of us have been close as friends and now it's a bit ...'

'*Bien sûr*. Of course,' Simone waved her hand dismissively and focused on petting the donkey's soft nose, but her insides were churning.

'Christian won't stop talking about you,' said Saskia, her voice excruciating, hopeful. 'But I know you're not that interested—'

'You know what? Maybe we should go on a double date,' Simone said cheerfully, but the smell of manure and cut grass rose around her, making her feel sick. She took Juliette's hand, desperate for a distraction. 'Come on, *ma chérie*, let's take *une petite promenade*, a walk around the fort.'

'I think there's a storm coming,' Saskia said, looking at the clouds lumbering towards them from the horizon. A fine rain had begun to spit from the sky.

'I thought you liked our wild European weather better than boring Sydney sunshine?' Simone didn't try to hide the challenge in her voice.

'Here, I've got her raincoat,' Saskia said, pulling it out of her satchel and securing it around Juliette's body.

'Come on, it's a loop. It only takes a little while. We'll beat the storm.' Simone led the way across the bridge, enjoying the sting of the wind whipping her hair against her face, the haunting calls of gulls and the slap of the sea against stone. 'Oh, isn't this fun? An adventure,' she said to Juliette, who was in between them, holding both their hands.

They stopped at a lookout offering an uninterrupted view of the churning Atlantic. The drop over the side of the wall was sheer and fell to dark rocks below. Juliette scrambled onto a seat to see over the top of the wall, Saskia steadying her.

'Simone, are you sure? About the double date, I mean. I thought ... what you said at the movie ...'

'Well, he's very handsome, isn't he? Christian, I mean. He's actually objectively much better looking than Félix,' she said.

Saskia smiled weakly and Simone felt shallow and pathetic for trying to hurt her with this fickle observation.

Confusion or maybe hurt crossed Saskia's features but she made herself brighten. 'He is very good-looking and how perfect would it be if we went out with brothers!'

Simone bit her lip until she tasted blood.

'Félix was talking about a new bar that's opened in Ars-en-Ré. Maybe we could all go there after he finishes his shift one Saturday night.'

'Sounds great,' said Simone, plastering a smile onto her face.

Saskia grabbed her hand suddenly, her eyes searching. 'Félix told me you tried to kiss him. That night I got lost on the bike trails. I just ... I just wanted to check ...'

Simone felt her gut drop and she held back the hot humiliation that threatened behind her eyes. He had told Saskia. She had been imagining the secret language she'd hoped they'd spoken, that wild, silent connection. She was so stupid. She thought of the two of them laughing at her desperation, her pathetic neediness. She should have just stuck to the Paris *mecs*. They understood her and she understood them.

'Oh that. That was nothing. I was just playing, you know me. We'd had so much pastis. Félix takes things *far* too seriously.'

Saskia breathed out with evident relief. 'Oh, thank God. I've been so worried about talking to you about it. I don't want to lose what we have. Our friendship is so special to me, ever since that first night we met in the café, and I know how much you've been struggling with the loss of your parents. I don't want things to change between the three of us. Promise me it won't.'

Simone felt a choke of emotion close around her throat. *It already has*, she thought. But she shook her head and smiled weakly. *'Bien sûr que non.'*

Saskia smiled in relief.

They continued to follow the path along the top of the fort in silence, each holding one of Juliette's hands, the wind and rain making them run the last fifty metres. By the time they returned to their bikes there was lightning lancing the sky and the donkeys were gone.

Saskia put Juliette in the bike seat and fitted her little helmet to her head. She hesitated a moment. Usually Simone would invite them to the villa for a hot chocolate and biscuits, and Juliette might watch cartoons while she and Saskia had a glass of wine. But for the first time since she'd returned to the island, Simone just needed to be alone.

'Simone, last night, did Camille say something about your mother? I was just so tired, and everything felt so surreal. I wasn't sure if I heard it right?'

Simone hesitated. Saskia was so intuitive. It was what had brought them together in that café. Part of her wanted to confide everything to Saskia, explain to her the complicated relationship she had with her mother, the mysterious way she had died, the questions left haunting Simone, and now Camille making this strange mention of her mother, but her body was already moving away.

She slung her leg over the bike. 'Oh, I don't think so, *non*. I can't imagine why she would mention Hélène. Bye bye, *ciao. À tout à l'heure.*'

She rode away, wind and tears stinging her eyes.

CHAPTER 18

Dylan whistles along with a French tune on the radio as we drive to Saint-Martin. Annoyance skitters over my skin. I've managed to avoid him since this morning. I'm walking on eggshells with Dee, and I can't deal with his sharpness beneath my soles too. He's acting happy. He's about to get what he wants.

We arrive at the port. It's sun-flooded and sparkling, with no hint of last night's storm and I glimpse it through the rigging of the boats – Bisette. There are people sitting at tables under the awning and I swear I can see three young people there. For a moment, it's Félix and Simone and me taking our coffee and croissant on a weekend morning, Simone reading a novel, me sketching and Félix people-watching. Only no. As we get closer, I see the restaurant is no longer Bisette – now it has another name and the awning is a different colour. I shake my head, try to ground myself in the present. The slope into the past is getting steeper. I can feel myself slipping.

I feel the rattle of nervousness in my belly. I didn't meet him last night. Will he confront me? Will he punish me? Will he still sign the papers?

The sat nav announces we're outside the hotel but I know it without being told. It's a pale sandstone building with white shutters and beige awnings, discreet and elegant. It's Paris by the sea. I've dressed in anticipation of this in a cream linen dress, a white broad-brimmed hat and black sunglasses. I'm possibly channelling Emmanuelle Béart in *Une Femme Française*. It's a film Félix and I both admired when we were young. Only Félix would understand this obscure film reference. I don't know why I've done this. Maybe it's because I feel bad for not meeting him. Maybe I want to be beautiful for him. Maybe it's a reaction to Dylan's grappling for power. His eyes silently appraised my outfit, but he said nothing. Perhaps he understands, after the party and then the yacht, that this is the world we have entered.

Dee understood it all along and she glides ahead of us towards the hotel in her floral mini dress, downplayed by slip-on sandals and unbrushed hair. Dylan opens the heavy brass-handled door. He has always been chivalrous, never lacking in gallantry or social niceties, but a handsome French film star has him on his best behaviour. His hand rests on the small of my back.

Walking into the foyer makes me feel like I'm three million euros richer already. I feel like I'm floating, light-headed with nerves and anticipation. The decor is refined and classic – creamy marble with brass accents and hardwood floors. There are deep-set sofas, blue chinoiserie vases and opulent wallpaper. The air is fragrant with candles and with the fresh flowers that are placed on every surface. By the fireplace sits a sleek black cat and Lara is patting it before I can say, '*Regarde le chat.*' A staff member informs us that its name is César and that it's she who runs the place, and we all smile knowingly.

I imagine sinking into one of the cream sofas, kicking off my sandals and staring out at the sparkling blue of the harbour through the tall windows. There's a reception desk up ahead and a restaurant that overlooks the port. I spot the man I assume is Monsieur Rombard, sitting at a table with a jug of water in front of him. He's balder and rounder than I'd imagined from my cliched mental image of a Parisian solicitor. But he's wearing a navy suit, perfectly cut, and blending with the décor. As we move towards him, he rises and does the button of his suit jacket up. He shakes our hands, gestures for us to take a seat, and pours water into our glasses.

'Girls, do you want to get a soft drink here or go for a walk?' I don't mention the ice cream; it's already a sore point.

Dee shrugs. 'I guess we'll go for a walk.'

'Don't go far. Just stay by the port.' I pass my credit card to Lara. 'Here. Can you keep this safely in your pocket, in case you want pastries or ice cream,' I say, pointedly leaving Dee out of the ice-cream politics.

'Can I get three flavours?'

'Knock yourself out,' says Dylan, scruffing her hair.

He's in a good mood and I wonder if there's more to this than simply the money. I wonder, in the face of his parents' wealth and all that they've given us, if this is a matter of pride for him, that this money symbolises being independently wealthy of them for the first time in his life. He never discusses with me how much his business makes, but I know our mortgage is heavily propped up by his mother. Or maybe I'm reading into things. Maybe he just wants more money.

I watch the girls go and I scan the foyer for Félix. I notice my foot is tapping the floor nervously. Maybe he won't come. Maybe he'll make it hard for me to walk away with this. We have unfinished business, after all. My foot stills and I straighten when I see him enter. He's dressed in jeans and a white T-shirt, a suit jacket and black runners. He pushes his shades up. Now he looks like the manager of a European soccer team. He's a chameleon, but I guess that should be no surprise. He's an actor after all. A feeling of uncertainty worms in my gut and I shift uncomfortably. As soon as I feel like I have him figured out he slips through my fingers. Like sand. Like salt. He sees us and lifts his chin slightly in acknowledgement.

We all rise as he approaches and he kisses me, his hand on my wrist as he draws me in. It's an intimate gesture that makes my pulse sound in my ears, and I hope it means he's not upset about last night.

When we're all seated — Félix on my right, Dylan on my left and Rombard on the banquet seat opposite — the lawyer takes a folder of paperwork out of his leather briefcase. While he's arranging the paperwork in front of him, Félix gestures to a waiter and speaks very fast into the man's ear so that I don't catch his words. Several minutes later, an ice bucket containing a bottle of French champagne arrives. I know why he's done it. He's conjuring the night we all went to Bisette and ordered a bottle of their most expensive champagne and everything on the menu. Or maybe this is just what French heiresses and film stars do routinely.

Rombard's phone rings. He apologises profusely, tells us he must take the call then walks away. As he does so, Félix leans towards me on the pretence of steadying the stem of my glass while the waiter pours the champagne. It's the closest he's been to me. He smells like pine needles and salt.

'Well, you didn't meet me last night, so we will take our drink now.'

He has spoken in French, so Dylan can't understand, but I wonder if Félix knows that, and I feel a shiver rush up my spine at his audacity. I take a generous sip of the champagne. It's cool and delicious and I barely manage to resist pouring it all down my throat.

'Nice drop, mate,' says Dylan, drinking the champagne. 'I imagine you've got quite the wine cellar at home in that impressive place of yours. You'll have to try some Australian shiraz. It's our favourite wine.'

My innards feel as though they are being wrung out. *No*, I want to say, *shiraz is your favourite wine, but it's too heavy for me, it smothers me.*

Félix smiles and indulges Dylan in some wine talk. It's the first time they've spoken more than a few words to each other and, as I watch them, I feel as though all the paths in my life have led me to this one place, between these two men who could not be more opposite specimens of the male gender.

Dylan has requested the wine menu and is evidently thrilled that it features some Australian wines. He shows Félix, who nods politely. Then he's talking to the waiter about their selection, regaling the poor man with Australian wine regions. Sometimes Dylan is so transparent it almost makes me feel sorry for him. He's trying so hard to compete.

I hear my voice before computing I've even said it. 'I couldn't get away last night.'

'Saskia's been showing off, speaking in French,' Dylan says to Félix, as though now that they've exchanged wine knowledge, they're complicit in something I'm not party to.

'We're in France,' I say.

The waiter has brought out several bottles of red wine, which he's pouring into glasses for Dylan to sample. Dylan always asks to taste his wine in restaurants before he accepts it. It's the same characteristic, I realise, that echoes through almost every part of his life. Perhaps it was this self-assuredness, this hubris, that initially attracted me to him. How is it that the very thing that once attracted now repels?

'Your husband doesn't understand us, does he?' Félix asks.

I feel myself colour at the cheekiness in his voice. I would worry that Dylan has picked up on his familiar tone, but the whole of the French language sounds like a seduction.

Félix must read my face because he asks, 'Do you remember the first time we made love?'

I choke on the champagne and cough as though I'm dying. Dylan pats me on the back and Félix hands me a napkin.

'Saskia's a glass-and-a-half kind of girl,' Dylan says.

'Would you like some more?' Félix asks, his brow arched, a ghost of a smile on his lips.

'Yes,' I say, and I know that we're not speaking about wine.

'I want to reach out and touch you. But instead, I will tell you what I remember,' Félix says.

I squeeze the tops of my thighs, sit back in my chair and clear my throat, try to find enough breath so as not to appear as flustered as I feel.

'I remember your hair smelled like oranges. The first time, that secret kiss under the orange trees at the villa, do you remember?'

'Félix. My husband is here.'

Dylan is swirling a heavy-bodied red in a glass, telling the waiter about why Australian soils produce big, bold reds.

'We made love on the beach once. Was it that night of the beach party? We were both drunk but maybe that's what gave me the courage to finally be with you. Also, in my brother's car.'

The blush is creeping into my hairline. I feel desire throb through me and glance nervously at Dylan, but he's still engrossed in his wine talk.

'And tell me, do you love this man?' Félix doesn't look at Dylan, he's looking straight into my eyes now and I feel the line of energy between us finally connect, as though he's slipped his hand between my thighs. His hand is resting on the table so close to mine. It would be nothing at all to reach out and grasp it, but we may as well still be on different sides of the planet.

I lower my gaze and say nothing. I know my silence will speak volumes.

'That is what I thought.'

'What about Renée?' I ask, trying not to sound as defiant as I feel.

'I thought I'd made it clear that it is a marriage of convenience. We have an open marriage and only see each other in the summer. She lives in Paris. She's seeing a musician who flies in from Las Vegas. And I thought *she* made it very clear with her flirtation with your husband.'

'Isn't that what all married French men say?'

Félix looks hurt and I swallow.

'Saskia, is there any part of that girl left? The one I used to know?' he asks.

I feel a wave of grief wash over me, because he's right. I didn't just lose him, I lost myself. But I feel a surge of defiance. 'You never met me, so I had to leave that girl behind.'

Félix's eyes flash and he reaches for my hand, but I pull it away. And then Rombard has returned to the table, profusely apologetic again, and Dylan is pouring us all wine, insisting Félix and Rombard taste it, and I'm torn between being relieved and disappointed. I take a chaste sip of my sparkling water and smooth my hair down. I feel as though I've been rolling in the dunes with Félix, his words stuck to my skin like grains of sand, or salt.

Rombard smiles, humouring Dylan, and takes a sip of the wine, then slips the paperwork in front of Félix and me. I'm not sure what I'm expecting, perhaps some kind of letter or speech from Simone from beyond the grave, issued by Rombard's fleshy lips, or an explanation from Simone as to why she's left us the villa and required that we sign the papers together. But it's all very straightforward. Rombard shows us where to sign the contracts, each place marked with a yellow tag, and we do so. I watch Félix inscribe his signature below mine several times on the paperwork. The only sounds are the scratching of our pens, the soft clink of glasses and cutlery on nearby tables, the distant calls of gulls and the clanging of masts on the promenade outside. Félix doesn't demand anything of us or the lawyer, but I feel his eyes watching me.

Dylan's leg is jiggling next to mine, and he leans over periodically as though he can read the contract, written in French legal language, as though he has any kind of control over this, or me. I feel my blood zip through my veins.

'So how long until we can sell the villa and divide the profit?' Dylan asks.

Rombard looks over his glasses at Dylan and then at me. 'It will take a few weeks for the paperwork to be processed. Then that's up to your wife and Mr Allard to decide,' he says pointedly, and I put my hand over my mouth to hide my smile.

Dylan laughs nervously and I enjoy the brittleness of the sound. I can feel a subtle shift happening, as though someone has turned an hourglass on its head and the sand is flowing in the other direction now. This is the first time in my marriage that I have had money of my own. I feel light-headed, a little dizzy. It could just be the champagne, or the lingering feeling from Félix's intimate words. I press my palms to the cool tabletop, steady myself.

Rombard carefully returns the paperwork to his briefcase, and we all stand. It has all happened so quickly, so seamlessly, I'm in shock.

Dylan slaps both men on the back. 'Nice doing business with you.'

He's like a blunt instrument and I cringe and look away.

We're walking towards the foyer and part of me is panicking, wondering whether this is the last time I'll ever see Félix, when Lara comes running through the front door. Her little face is flushed and her eyes are terrified. A cold blade of fear cuts cleanly through my chest. It is the knife all mothers know is there, that we hope and pray we or our children will never feel.

'Mum, Mum. Dee fell over. Come quick.'

Adrenalin kicks through my body and I run. I see the huddle before I see her, and claw through the concerned strangers to find my little girl lying on her side on the pavement. Her eyes flutter open and she's six again and unsure and scared, as though she's walking through the school gate for the first time. I kneel next to her and smooth the hair from her sweaty brow. It's clammy and cold and she closes her eyes, relieved that I'm here.

'What happened?' I ask everyone and no one.

'She fell over,' a woman tells me. 'Or maybe collapsed.'

I quickly survey her body for injuries — her temple and elbows are grazed.

Félix and Dylan arrive.

'Come on, you're okay,' says Dylan, urging her to get up.

'Dylan, she can't. Look how weak she is,' I say.

Félix squats beside me. 'I've called the hotel medic. She is on her way.'

A woman arrives with a small medical kit and asks the onlookers to make some space. She places a blanket under Dee's head and takes her blood pressure.

'Her blood pressure is a little low. Has she been sick?' she asks me.

I shake my head, but deep down I know that she has not been healthy. 'She's recently become vegan,' I offer. 'She probably doesn't eat enough protein.'

The woman's eyes meet mine. 'That's something that could cause her body to become very weak, if she's not eating properly,' she says, her eyes running the length of my daughter's skinny limbs.

She asks Dee a few questions and shines a light in her eyes. 'I think she's okay now. I'll dress her wounds and give her some hydrolytes, but this is something you should speak to your doctor' – she pauses pointedly – 'or psychologist about.'

I nod and feel guilt clamp in my gut. I'm so dizzy that I have to press my palm into my forehead and steady myself on the ground with my other hand. I knew Dee was struggling, didn't I? Exercising too much, eating too little, and I excused it, blamed it on typical teenage behaviour ... Or did I not even see it because I was so numb to everything? Because numbing myself is what I do. The only way to avoid the guilt, to avoid the fear. I don't know how to talk to her about what she's doing to her body, what's causing it.

But some small part of me, the part that has recently awoken, the part that has shaken itself free from the numbness, the hibernation, is screaming in the recesses of my head.

Everything is too bright, too raw, the sun too hot on my scalp. The past is here now, and I have no defence against it, no escape. I look down at my slight daughter lying on the pavement with her long pale red hair spilling out from her body, and I know I did this to her. I am not to be trusted. I haven't been able to keep her safe.

I don't deserve to be a mother, I don't deserve anything, not after what I did to that little girl, not after what I did to Juliette.

CHAPTER 19

Le passé — Saskia

The wind whispers through the pines. Only the sea answers.
Félix rides behind me, the click-click of his bicycle wheels like
languid forest insects. It's hot and the sun slides slow light and
shadow along my arms as I ride. My skin is the colour of golden
syrup, flecked with tiny freckles from these long afternoons
with our bodies smoothed out on the sand by the sea. Juliette's
soft voice behind me, singing in French. We reach the beach,
and I lay our towels down and kick off my sandals, sweep the
hair off the back of my neck, pull off my dress. Juliette is already
squashing handfuls of damp sand through her fingers. The soft
curls of her hair cling to her cheeks.

'*Où est Nounou Si Si?*' she asks.

This is the place we always meet Simone. Juliette has become
accustomed to the easy ebb and flow of our talk, like the draw
and pull of the waves, sometimes in English, sometimes in
French.

'She's a little busy today,' I say, feeling a sticky guilt inside
me for wanting Félix all to myself.

Why didn't I invite her? It has always been the three of us.
But something has changed. I felt it when she rode away from

us at the fort, when she didn't call the next day, or the ones after.

I think about what Félix told me – how she kissed him that first night we met him. Maybe knowing that has changed everything, even though she denied feeling something for Félix. I think of everything Simone and I have told each other about our lives, perhaps more than we've told anyone, because we have been freed from the sometimes stifling context of our own cultures. Free from the expectations everyone else has of us. And yet the thing right in front of us both, the thing between us, has remained unsaid.

I look over at Félix, who's taking two bottles of beer out of his backpack, and feel my lips curl into a smile. I watch the precise movements of his hands opening the bottles. The flick of his hair from his face. He looks up. Makes a silly face. Smiles. He knows I'm watching him. He doesn't mind being watched – it's the performer in him. He's too playful, too magnetic not to be watched. I have tried to understand, to rationalise the appeal of him, because there are better-looking men. But it's not just his looks. He tends to skinny rather than muscular, and there's an awkwardness to him sometimes that's strange and disarming. Is it that he's part-boy, part-man? Is it his vulnerability coupled with his outgoingness, his desire to be seen?

He has asked me to draw him, and I've brought my sketchpad and pencils. He sits on the towel next to me, his leg pressed against my thigh, and rolls the cool glass of the bottle over my bare back until I shiver. He kisses my neck, his lips soft and ticklish, and I squirm, swinging around to kiss him hard. He falls backwards and I lie on top of him, our lips lingering, our breath quickening, until I compose myself and sit up. It feels as though my body has always belonged to him, as though he's an extension of me. It seems impossible now that we could have ever been just friends.

Will you come for a drive with me? I knew as soon as he'd asked me on the phone what would happen. We had begun to explore each other's bodies on the beach at the party, loosened by alcohol, by dancing, entangled on the sand. It had felt like a beautiful, badly kept secret. I didn't know who we were keeping it from, or maybe, deep down, I did. There was nowhere else for us to be alone – not in his house full of brothers, not at Camille and Henri's, full of unspoken tensions. Not at Simone's villa.

He picked me up at the apartment. It was late, but the evening was warm and the moon swollen, and I snuck quietly through the house and out into the night. We were both quiet, and I was feeling a mixture of nervousness and excitement, my body aching for him as we drove to a beach car park.

I can still feel the grip of his hand behind my neck as he drew me to him and kissed me hard. His hands over my body. There was a desperation between us that I had never felt in the lukewarm kisses with boys I'd liked over the years. It felt as though everything we had ever said to each other, every glance and touch, had been leading to this one moment.

The windows were open to the dark night and the sea roared. As he lifted my dress over my shoulders and looked me in the eyes, it seemed improbable that he should choose me, a shy girl from the Sydney suburbs, over someone like Simone Durant. I wanted to ask him why it was me and not her. She was rich and beautiful and confident. I was just a girl who was lost and trying to find her way in a world that felt too big and too small all at once.

But all I could feel then was the buzz of our bodies in the places they met – cheek, chest, lips. I lay down along the back seat and he pulled off my underwear. I was entirely naked, and he was suspended above me, his hair in his eyes. He put his finger in my mouth and it tasted like salt. He used the wet tip to touch me, while watching my face. When my mouth opened and my eyes closed in pleasure, he entered me. It was gentle and tender and aching and fierce, and the world disappeared.

'*Nounou Sass Sass! Regarde-moi!* Look at me.'

Juliette's voice pulls me back. Félix's hand on my leg, the cold beer in my mouth, the burning sun on my shoulders. Someone has made a huge sandcastle surrounded by a moat near the shoreline and Juliette is sitting in the deep hole of it, waving.

Félix and I go over and add shells to the castle and drape it with seaweed. Seawater has seeped up into the bottom of the moat, creating a shallow pool where Juliette splashes. I tell her she's a mermaid and that this is her castle. We swap the words as a little game. Mermaid. Castle. *Sirène. Château.*

'Imagine if this was our life,' says Félix patting the sand into shape earnestly. 'Our little family.'

I feel tingles all over my body, laugh. 'You want to be a famous actor in Paris, not a young father stuck on Île de Ré.'

Félix points to a couple sitting further down the beach. 'Oh yes, we live in Paris, naturally. We're just here on vacation for the summer. They're my fans, stalking me for autographs.'

I elbow him. 'And what about me?'

'You have a studio and are represented by one of Paris's top galleries. We can walk to the Louvre from our apartment.'

'And where do an impoverished artist – a uni drop-out – and a *saunier* get the money for a Paris apartment?'

'Our incredible talent,' he says, and I flick water from Juliette's bucket at him.

'Do you ever imagine what it would be like to be as rich as Simone?' I ask.

Félix sits back on his haunches. 'Yes, but she's so unhappy. Her money has become like a chain around her neck. She doesn't know who really loves her.'

I feel an uncomfortable twinge. Do I really love her? Does Félix? *Yes*, I think. I didn't know about her money when I met the crying girl in the café. 'But you have to admit, the money must make life so easy, in many ways,' I say.

'Are you jealous of Simone?' He grabs me, tickles me until I gasp.

'Well, she could give us a tiny little bit of her fortune, it would be nothing to her.' I laugh.

'See, even you have an agenda,' he says.

'No I don't, not really.'

'But part of you hopes ...'

'No, it doesn't.'

'Come on, you're only human.'

'Okay, maybe a tiny, tiny part, but I would never expect that. That's not why I'm friends with her. I feel sorry for her losing her parents like that, and I find her fascinating.'

'Because of her fortune.' He gives me a knowing look.

I punch him. 'No!'

'I don't believe you,' he says, but he's smiling.

'Are you sure it's not you who likes her? She's richer and more beautiful than me. And she likes you, she kissed you.'

'Did it seem like it was Simone I liked the other night?' He kisses my neck and I shiver, remembering what we did.

'No, but—'

'Back to our imaginary life. We have made our own money from our talents. We have a nanny, naturally, but never one as good as you.' He laughs. 'You would be a good mother.'

'Is that really what men are looking for? What about a great artist?'

'You can be both.'

I nudge him, feigning annoyance, and he puts a cold hand on my warm back, and I squeal.

Juliette, sensing a game, splashes us both, and Félix picks her up and races to the shoreline, zooming her through the air as though she's an aeroplane. He dips her into the sea and she squeals with delight. The water is as tepid as a bath and we luxuriate in the warm shallows, Juliette's little body safely between my legs, splashing and jumping over the tiny waves. Félix dives out deeper, his skin glistening, his head thrown back to the sky like an Adonis.

The low afternoon sun dries the salt on our skin and we sit on the towel, Juliette eating her snack of strawberries from a little tub. I take my sketchpad from my bag and begin to draw Félix. He's leaning back on his elbows, one leg bent, looking at the sea, but I know his form so well I could draw him with my eyes closed. I have felt the hardness of the sinew in his arms, the soft dip in the base of his neck.

'I feel like you're touching me,' he says. 'You know, like that nice, sleepy feeling when someone is playing with your hair.'

'I am in a way,' I say, 'touching you.'

He flicks me a suggestive look and I laugh. I work quickly, feeling the sun's cooling fingers ease along my back.

'Tell me more about our life,' I say, my mind emptying as I let the drawing take shape.

'We go to dinner parties with other artistic types. We read books and drink wine and take long strolls by the Seine after dinner.'

'It sounds like a French movie.'

'And we watch French films, with me in them, naturally.'

'How will you learn how to act? I've been practising drawing since I was, like, three.'

'And how do you know I haven't been acting since I was three also?' A mischievous smile haunts his lips.

That contradiction in him. The ambition that I can't entirely reconcile with the sweet, awkward *saunier*. But even so, I'm starting to learn that people can be two things at once.

'And what about your family?' I ask.

'They will hate me for leaving, but they will forgive me, and I will return to the island every summer.'

'With your fans stalking you for autographs,' I say, nodding towards the couple up the beach.

I show him my sketch and he kisses my cheek. 'I have never met anyone as naturally talented as you,' he says. 'I'm not just saying that. You are incredible, Saskia.'

'So are you ... I can't believe ...'

'What can't you believe?' It's like he's seeing straight through me, into a part of me that's never been seen.

'This. You. Us.'

'I think I can convince you.'

He touches my face, kisses me. He tastes like beer and salt. I could dissolve forever in him, and as our foreheads touch I close my eyes, feel myself start to disappear.

He pulls away reluctantly. He has to work tonight. I'm already thinking how I will sneak downstairs when he finishes his shift. He gets up, brushes the sand from his legs.

'Where's Juju?'

I look at the indent in the towel next to me where her little body was only a minute ago. The container of fruit is empty. I pick it up. It still smells like strawberries.

'She was just here,' I say, 'eating her fruit.'

I show him the container, as though it's some proof of her existence. I stand, shield my eyes against the low sun. I hear my voice call her name.

Félix is running to the shoreline, to our mermaid castle, and I follow. I feel relief. That's where she is, in the little moat, digging with her yellow spade.

But she's not there. The thud of my heart is loud in my ears.

I look back at our towels and up the beach, towards the couple that were there before, but they're gone. How are they gone? Wasn't it just moments ago that they were there? I look out at the water and feel sick and my head spins. No, she can't be in the water. She knows never to go in the water without me. She is a cautious child. Cheeky but obedient.

Félix is beside me. I can hear his breath — it's fast, he's been running. 'I can't see her on the beach. How long, Saskia? How long were you drawing me?'

I shake my head and tears sting my eyes. 'I don't know. I lose track of time when I'm drawing. I thought it was only a few minutes. I thought she was beside me.'

I want him to reassure me, but he squats down and then stands, runs his hands over his head, his eyes darting from me to the water. 'You don't think she went in the water?'

I shake my head. 'No, she knows not to go in without me.'

He nods but he walks into the water anyway, up to his thighs. He's calling her name. He dives under. I feel myself drop to the sand. It's cold now and the sun has sunk into a bank of clouds on the horizon. Long shadows are cast like ghosts along the sand. *No, no, no, no, no, this can't be happening.*

I get up and start to run along the beach in one direction but there's no one as far as I can see. A mist is rolling in, I can taste it in the back of my throat. I turn around and run back to our towels. My lungs are burning. Félix has run in the other direction but he's back, his face pale, paler than I've ever seen it. It says everything I need to know.

He grips me by the shoulders. 'We have to call someone. We have to call the police.'

I feel my body shaking but I tell myself it's from the cold. 'No. Not yet. It's okay, she's here somewhere, I know it. She can't have just disappeared. We would have noticed if she went into the water. And she knows not to. She knows. We come here every day.' My teeth are chattering now, my thoughts spinning so fast I feel dizzy.

But never with you, a voice deep inside me says. *Never with you here to distract me.*

He grips me, harder this time, makes me look him in the eyes. 'Saskia, listen to me. She's not here. Juliette is not here. And it's getting dark and she is just not here.'

It's as though I've separated from my body, like I'm floating above this scene, an observer. 'But she has to be here, Félix, she has to be. Please, can we just keep looking?'

His brow is knitted in doubt, but he nods. 'Okay. We haven't checked the bikes. She might be waiting there. Or the dunes. Let's check the dunes.'

We run up the beach and into the soft sand. It's so fine I struggle to get traction and I scramble on my hands and knees, the sand slipping through my fingers like time in an hourglass. How long? How long was I drawing? It could have been five minutes, it could have been twenty-five. Enough time for anything to happen.

I hear my voice call her name over and over, but it is distant, an echo, no longer my own. He takes my hand as we run, stumbling over tufts of coarse sea grass and pine cones shed from the trees that edge the beach. But there is no one in the dunes, only a still, hovering moon, and I know, in the same way the water knows the land, that she is gone, and that she is never coming back.

CHAPTER 20

I've pushed it down, deep into my depths for so long – the guilt, the pain, the anger at myself – but it's the sinkhole that I've grown up with, the stagnant, murky knowledge that I ruined a life, ruined lives. It has sat at the very centre of me my whole adult life. It's the story of my incompetence, my weakness, and it will never end.

I haven't picked up a pencil since the day it cost a little girl's life. For many years I gave up on art. I returned to Sydney, I forgot Île de Ré, Félix Allard and Simone Durant. They felt like they were all part of a strange dream I'd once had, so very bright yet so very dark, almost like a film negative I could only see, or remember, in outline, when the lights were out. It was something about the language. I went from speaking fluent French to never uttering it again, and the girl who had spoken those words seemed like another person entirely. I was able to leave her and her guilty words and actions behind, compartmentalised in my mind. Or so I thought.

I tried to finish my arts law degree, just as my mother wanted, just as I knew I should, but I couldn't. Because my mother was the only one who knew what I'd done, I pushed her away as I tried to push away my guilt. Maybe I left uni to hurt her, or maybe I finally realised it was her dream I was following, not my own. But I didn't dare go back to art. I got a job in a bar and told myself I just needed time to sort out my life. I had short affairs with barmen who weren't French. I didn't let anyone close. No one in Australia read the French news. I didn't read the French news. Back then the world was less connected. We didn't have international news feeds on our phones, we had newspapers with a small foreign section. If I heard that language float close to me, it felt like a dangerous caress, and I crossed the street. I threw away my sketchbooks with Félix Allard's face in them and his home number scribbled in the back.

Papercut art only came to me by accident. Dee was a tiny child. We were crafting and I picked up a pencil and immediately put it back down, a metallic taste flooding my mouth, like lead, like blood. She was the same age Juliette had been. By then I'd been medicating myself for three years. It was the only way to trust myself as a parent – to stay in the present, to not drift into the terrible past.

When Dee's body was pulled from my own, I didn't feel joy or relief, but dread. Dylan wanted two children. He made that very clear, and I wanted to make him happy, especially in those early years when things were good, when he felt like the safety, the surety I'd been craving. I convinced myself that I wanted a baby. I did want a baby. But being responsible for this tiny, helpless human was like being buried alive. How could I trust myself to protect this little girl when I had let another little girl disappear?

I googled it once in a moment of weakness. Ambiguous loss. The feeling when there's no resolution or closure in a missing person case. The feeling when you never know what happened to someone you loved. I had this with Juliette. And I had it with Félix.

But when I picked up a pair of scissors, it was as though there was something inside me that cut through my numbness, my ambiguous loss, something that, despite everything, was still alive and had found a way to get out. It sliced through the stupor, cut through the guilt and the grief. I taught myself papercut art watching YouTube videos while Dee's crude crayon drawings became legible words, while her stick people became beautiful, expressive faces. And eventually her teachers began asking me if there was an artist in the family.

It is as I always suspected – I don't deserve this beautiful daughter I've damaged, who is lying here broken on the ground. When was the last time she made her once beloved art instead of punishing and driving her body with exercise?

I feel my shoulders bunch to my neck and my hands curl into balls until my arms ache. I can't be here anymore, in front of Félix and Monsieur Rombard and the kind strangers who are still hovering about Dee as the medic plasters her grazes. Part of me wants to run, away from them all, away from everything that's crowding me. The past that's caught up with me, the future that's terrifying me. Right now, the loss is no longer ambiguous. I am losing my daughter. The very thing I feared the most is finally happening. She is disappearing before my eyes.

Panic grips my throat and I close my eyes and try to breathe. Everything in my body is telling me to run, to hide, to push down the pain as I've done for so long. My little white pills are no longer protecting me. I am not strong enough to protect her.

But she opens her eyes and the first thing she says is 'Mum'. It's barely audible, a whisper, but I would hear that word through a snowstorm. I would find her at the end of the earth. If she disappeared, I would never stop looking.

I do what I should have done despite all her protests, despite her rage and her pushing me away these past few days. I wrap my arms around Dee.

She whimpers in relief and my heart contracts.

'I'm here,' I say. And perhaps for the first time, I really am, here, present, alive.

We stay like that for a long while until she feels strong enough to move. Dylan and I help her stand. I thank everyone and Monsieur Rombard says he'll be in touch.

Félix hovers beside me. His face is pale, his expression worried, and I'm returned in a flash to his face that day on the beach when we lost Juliette. A confusing mixture of emotions rushes through me – guilt, resentment and, still, even now, desire.

'We need to discuss the real estate,' he says, and I know what he's really telling me. 'You have my number. I hope your daughter, I hope Dee is okay. If you need anything.' He touches my shoulder and I can't help it, I flinch, like the anticipation of an electric shock.

'Thank you,' I say and concentrate on getting Dee into the car, which Dylan has brought in front of the hotel. Her skin is clammy and cool. I remember all those times I felt her forehead for fevers. All those times I drew on her back to comfort her.

'Okay, kiddo?' asks Dylan as we get into the car.

'Yeah,' says Dee, slumping against the car door.

I see Lara reach out and take her hand and Dee lets her. I flash Lara a small smile of understanding. Dee's defences are down for both of us.

We travel back to the villa in silence. Once we're inside, Dee says she just wants to sleep. She hesitates on the staircase.

'Can you draw on my back?' she asks, and I feel gratitude and tears swell behind my eyes, which I quickly brush away in case she sees them and withdraws the offer.

She pulls the sheets up to her chin, curls into a foetal position and closes her eyes. I trace the protrusion of her spine with my finger. She is too thin, I can see that now. The shadows under her cheekbones, her tiny bird-like wrists, the soft down on her arms catching the light. Her body trying to retain heat, trying to keep her safe when no one else would. I feel sick that it has taken me until now to really see what is happening to her.

'When I was a little bit older than you, I did something terrible,' I hear myself say. It's strange. It's me speaking but I feel removed from the words forming in my mind, on my lips. It's the same feeling I had when Juliette disappeared, as though I was fracturing, becoming two different people. And perhaps I was. How could I ever be the same person carrying such a shameful secret at my core?

Dee rolls over and faces me, her eyes wide.

'It was an accident. I didn't mean to. It was all ...' I shake my head, freeing the memory to rise up from my gut where it's been festering for twenty-six years. 'I was a nanny to a little girl. Her name was Juliette. Juju.'

I take a breath but it's hard to get air in. It feels like there's something blocking my throat, stopping the words inside me like a corked bottle. I know I must tell someone. I think I've always known I must. I just didn't think it would be my daughter. But some small part of me knows that this is the only way, that this is the bridge that might connect us and open up her own pain to be lanced.

'We were playing on the beach, just like we did every afternoon. But on this particular day I was distracted. I was with

255

my boyfriend. I was drawing him, sketching him and … she just disappeared. We looked up and she was suddenly gone.'

Dee has propped herself onto an elbow. She is staring at me, waiting for the end of a story that has no end. 'What happened?' she asks, a soft desperation in her voice.

I bow my head. 'Nothing. Nothing happened. No one could find her. There was a massive police search. She was never found.'

I let the shame engulf me. It has always felt like drowning, and that's only fair because that's probably what happened to Juliette.

Dee grabs my hand and presses her cheek to it. 'Oh, Mum.'

I feel hot tears on my face. 'I've never told anyone, except your grandma – she knows.'

Dee's face is a reflection of the pain I feel in my chest. 'Mum, it wasn't your fault. Someone could have taken her.'

I shake my head. 'The police would have found them. There was a big search. No. It was my fault. If I hadn't been with Félix—'

'*The* Félix. Félix Allard?'

I nod.

'He was your boyfriend?' She's incredulous.

I laugh sadly. 'He wasn't always a famous actor. He was a simple salt worker. He was the first boy I ever loved.'

'What happened?' Dee is sitting up now, both hands grasping one of mine, her face flushed.

'Maybe we both blamed each other for what happened. We said we didn't, but deep down I think we did. Or maybe he was in love with Simone Durant, the woman who left us this house. She was very rich, very beautiful. And he probably went to Paris to be with her. Those two were better suited anyhow.'

Dee straightens and takes both my hands in hers, as though she's the parent trying to get something into a stubborn child's head. 'Mum, you were amazing. You came here when you were a teenager, not much older than me. But there were no mobile phones, no emails. You were all alone. You were so brave. I could never do that. And you were so beautiful, with your long red hair. Of course Félix Allard loved you.'

A breath escapes my lips.

'Why don't you wear it like that anymore? Your hair?'

I look at her, my daughter who's starving herself into some mould she feels she needs to fit, grappling for acceptance, for control, in this harsh and unforgiving world. I meet her eyes. 'Maybe it's hard to accept ourselves and our bodies as they are. To love ourselves.' I give her a pointed look and she looks away.

'Dee ...'

'I know I haven't been that honest with you. I've been ...' She picks at her nails. I wait. 'I've been ... I don't even know what I've been doing.' She throws her hands up. 'I just can't do this anymore.' She indicates to her own body.

I speak very quietly. 'You mean all the exercise?'

Her body is hunched over and her voice a whisper. 'And the food.'

I smooth her hair. 'I know. You must be so tired, so, so tired.'

She puts her head in my lap and curls her body into mine and I hold her, listen to the soft rhythm of her breath, as soft as the wash of the sea outside.

She rolls over, looks into my eyes. 'What about Dad? Does he know what happened? With the little girl?' she asks.

'God no,' I say.

Dee takes my hand very gently. 'Mum, you know you don't have to stay with Dad for us.'

I feel my body begin to shake before I realise that I'm crying. My little girl holds me as I sob into her beautiful red hair, the hair I gave her and took away from myself. She and Lara have known all along. How could they not? Guilt and shame boil inside me. How could I have modelled such a terrible relationship for my daughters? Why did I stay in this destructive, emotionally abusive marriage? Why have I been so damn blind, so damn weak?

I look at her and it could be me lying there, a fragile teenage girl, so young, so broken, and yet somehow strong, despite it all. I feel a rush of fierce, protective love for my daughter, but also for that girl I used to be. I hear Félix's voice in my head – *Est-ce qu'il reste quelque-chose de cette fille?* Is there any part of that girl left?

I eviscerated her – her strength, her love, her fearlessness. I was so weak, so full of guilt and regret. I was broken when I returned from France. I thought Dylan would help put me back together, but I let him destroy her and everything she stood for, once and for all.

I can't remember the first time I didn't live up to what he wanted – it was more subtle than that. It was a drip that turned into a flood. We'd been living together for a few months. I was in my mid-twenties and I was cleaning out my wardrobe. It was never said overtly, it was just an offhand suggestion at first. *You should wear more classic, simple clothing – you're not a uni student anymore. You'd look great with shorter, darker hair.*

When something is suggested so many times, it can feel like your own decision. I don't know why it was important for him to model me into this particular image, but I suppose I was complicit in forging the shimmering illusion of our lives.

For our wedding, he told me he didn't like me wearing too much make-up, and by then it was more overt. *You look better without all that crap on your face.* I wore a barely-there face with my darkened hair and a sleek contemporary dress with a boned bodice that made it difficult to breathe.

By the time of Dee's entry into the world, I'd forgotten that I loved to wear my hair long and loose and red, that I liked whimsical dresses and smoky eyes. I had fashioned myself into an image that was no longer my own, trying to curate the perfect life. Physical changes may seem benign, but they're the outer expression of an inner identity. This was the first, seemingly superficial step in my surrender of myself.

I don't know how much Lara's anxiety and Dee's early signs of an eating disorder can be blamed on the emotional abuse they witness day in, day out, but there's a pattern. I've been numbing myself, punishing myself by staying with their father. Dee can see how unhappy I am. How much I've let him make me small. Because small is all I deserved. *Small. Petite.* As small as a tiny girl who never came back.

I feel like I'm going to be sick and press my hand to my belly. I let him take control of every part of my life. Physical, emotional, financial.

But how to explain to your own daughters how little you believe in your own power, your own agency. When you're told how hopeless you are for so many years, you eventually internalise it. You're not able to question it because you don't trust yourself anymore. It is so gradual. All the tiny comments, all the subtle slights. It's like the sea chipping away at a rockface. So slow, so quotidian, but after years the erosion is a landslide. He has wiped me out. And maybe some part of me wanted, needed that obliteration. If Juliette disappeared, maybe I needed to as well.

Dee holds me until my body stills. She has seen the true me, seen the girl I used to be, and she still loves me, despite everything.

I kiss her softly on the cheek. 'Thank you,' I say, squeezing her hand. 'Rest now. Everything will be okay.' And for the first time in many, many years, I believe myself.

She closes her eyes, and I can feel her exhaustion, but also her relief.

I check on Lara, who's reading on her bed. I hug her tightly to me and go downstairs. Dylan is eating a sandwich in the kitchen, shovelling the food into his mouth. I feel revulsion course through me. I wonder how on earth I have let this man do what he's done to me for so long.

The words form very clearly on my tongue. 'You need to find a hotel to stay in tonight,' I say.

He looks at me quizzically and it's only then that I realise I have spoken these words to him in French.

*

Le passé

'Have you heard? A child has disappeared on Le Bois-Plage.'

Simone felt a strange sensation along the fine hairs of her arms at the shopkeeper's comment. Le Bois-Plage. How many afternoons had she spent there with Saskia and Juliette, playing in the water, taking their picnic? She looked at her wristwatch and her shoulders dropped in relief. No, it was far too late in the day. They would be home by now, Saskia giving Juliette her bath, washing the sand from her hair. Also, they had not been going to the beach these past few days, as she had not been invited.

But something, some ghost of a question floated through her, making her shiver. *Why hasn't she asked me to meet them there since that day at the fort?*

'This happened when? What time, do you know?' Simone asked.

'Not long ago. I saw so many police and fire engines, and I asked what was happening. They were all heading to Le Bois-Plage. There's a big search on the dunes and in the forest behind the beach.'

Simone thanked the woman and went outside. It was early evening and dusk had turned the sky deep blue and leached the heat from the air. It would be dark soon. She put her string shopping bag in the basket of her bike. *No*, she thought, *it could not be Juliette. There are many children playing on that beach every day. Saskia is so careful.*

But she knew that was not really true. There were not that many people on the beach now, this late in the summer. That is why they loved it. It felt like their own special place.

She found herself turning right instead of left at the bike path, and riding towards the beach.

The normally quiet stretch of sand was swarming with dark bodies, like ants, under two floodlights. The sight made fear grip her low in the belly. It did not look right, it did not look natural, all these men in uniforms, *les flics*, their leashed dogs scouring the sand where she and Saskia and Juliette had passed so many peaceful afternoons. A cold wind was coming in off the water, picking up sand, which stung her bare legs as she walked. The police had cordoned off the area with bright tape and a small crowd had gathered, their heads together in whispers, crossed arms bracing their bodies.

Simone saw Saskia and Félix before they saw her. They were sitting on the sand, huddled against the wind, surrounded by police. Félix had his arm around Saskia, and she was wrapped in a blanket. A feeling, like sliding down a sand dune too fast, moved through Simone and she felt her pulse thicken. She ducked under the tape and a policeman held up his hand.

She pointed. 'Please, please, they're my friends. Is it ... was it a little girl? Was it Juliette? Saskia's her nanny. My friend is her nanny.' As the words left her mouth it didn't feel real. *No, this could not be Juju. This could not be Nounou Sass Sass. I am Nounou Si Si!* she wanted to scream at the man. *I am responsible for her too. I love her too.*

The apology in the man's face told her everything she needed to know, and he let her pass. She could feel him watching her as she walked. She took off her shoes to better navigate through the thick sand and it felt like one of those dreams in which she was trying to move but going nowhere.

Saskia saw her and their eyes locked. Simone was sure she had never seen such sadness in a pair of eyes, and it opened something deep inside her – the well of her own grief, the well that would never empty, which she was always skating over, hoping not to fall into it.

When she reached them she sank onto her knees in front of them, gripping Saskia's hands. '*Non, non, mon Dieu, ce n'est pas Juliette, non, ce n'est pas possible.*'

'Yes,' said Félix, his eyes downcast.

'*Comment? Pourquoi? Non. Non.*' Simone felt tears slip down her face and she didn't try to brush them away. It felt like she was dissolving back into the place that had nearly drowned her, the place Saskia and Félix had saved her from.

Félix held his head in his hands. 'We don't know. She was there and then she was gone. We looked for so long. We looked everywhere.'

Simone got to her feet. 'Why aren't you searching?' Her voice was high, shrill. *Why didn't you invite me?* she thought. *I would never have let this happen to Juju. This would never have happened if it had just been me and Saskia and Juliette, as usual, as it was meant to be. This would never have happened if you two hadn't decided to leave me out.*

Saskia looked at her mutely and Simone realised she hadn't spoken a word, that she was suspended in some kind of blunt shock.

'The police won't let us go. They're interviewing us,' said Félix.

'But it wasn't your fault.' But even as Simone said it, something uncomfortable, a deep dread dropped inside her and she wrapped her arms about her body. *Maybe it* was *your fault.* 'Where is Camille?' she asked. 'Where is her mother?'

'The police are telling the Bisettes. I don't know where they are,' he said.

She needed to do something. 'I'm going to help them search,' she said, backing away, dizziness engulfing her so that she stumbled. 'It's getting dark.'

'I don't think the police are expecting to find her on the land,' said Félix quietly, and Simone looked towards the darkening water. It was only then she saw the flashing lights of two boats. Her mind reeled.

A policeman wearing a bright vest approached and asked her who she was. He didn't listen when she tried to answer, or maybe she didn't explain well enough, that she loved Juliette too and these were her friends. He asked her to get back behind the tape and when she didn't move, he pointed, his whole body a threat.

She beseeched Saskia and Félix with her eyes to tell the man that she needed to be there too, that she could help, that their unspoken bond remained, just the three of them, that it would never be broken, but they were mute. It felt like a slap in the face, the silent sting of their rejection, and she stumbled away from them down the beach, away from the harsh lights. She was dimly aware that she was suffering some kind of shock from what had happened, but also from the connection that so clearly bound Félix and Saskia. Félix's protective arm wrapped around her. Her head resting listlessly on his shoulder. Simone realised that whatever the three of them had was gone now.

The beach was dark once she left them behind. All she could see were the lights of houses in the distance. Why weren't the police searching further up the beach? She called Juliette's name, but her voice sounded so plaintive, so alone, that it terrified her. She imagined that tiny girl right now, so alone, without her mother. *I know how that feels.* Was she somewhere, lost and scared? Or had she already passed into the place where Simone's parents had gone? Simone squeezed her eyes shut at the thought.

She was breathless and light-headed by the time she reached the villa, scrambling over the dunes, slipping on the soft sand in the dark. She'd left her bike and all her food at the scene. *The crime scene. Is that what it was?* She found the key under the pot of shells and let herself in. A crushing loneliness clamped around her as she looked at those shells. She felt as though she was back where she started, a lonely girl climbing over deserted dunes to an empty house, with no one to care for, and no one caring for her.

She went to the kitchen sink and splashed her face with water. She pressed her cold hands to her cheeks, trying to shake herself out of her self-pity. This was not about her. How would Saskia, how would Camille be feeling right now? They must be so frightened. She went to the fridge and took out a bottle of wine. She needed to steady her nerves. There was a noise behind her, and she jumped. The bottle slipped from her fingers and shattered on the floor.

'Who's there?' Her voice was tiny, terrified. In the dim light coming from the open fridge she saw movement under the table. She yelped in pain as broken glass pierced her bare foot. Her whole body was primed to run, but she fought the urge and squatted down. *It's the cat who has slipped through the window, as he sometimes does. I'm just feeling on edge,* she thought.

'*Oh mon Dieu.*' All the air escaped her lungs. She couldn't breathe from the shock, but also the relief.

A tiny form under the table. Not a cat. 'Juju,' she cried but the little girl retreated further underneath. Simone lowered her voice to a whisper. '*It's me. It's Nounou Si Si.*'

She slowly tiptoed over, trying to avoid the glass, unable to bear weight where her foot was cut. She got down on her hands and knees under the table. She counselled herself to remain calm, not to convey in her voice the panic she was feeling. Was Juliette okay? Was she hurt? Why was she here?

'It's okay, *ma chérie.* You're safe here, you're safe. Sorry to scare you. I just got a fright. I thought it was the cat.'

Juliette didn't move. She was hugging her knees to her chest, obviously frightened. Simone wondered how on earth she had got there. It was such a long way for a little girl to walk. It was then she felt a cold breeze brush along the tops of her arms. She looked up at the window, the one that never closed properly, and saw that it had been pushed open just enough for a little body to slip through.

'You are so clever, such a brave girl. Coming all the way to the villa by yourself. You knew the way, didn't you, from when we walked with *Nounou Sass Sass*? And you used the secret entrance through the window where the neighbour's cat comes in, didn't you? I think maybe you wanted some of my special *galettes*? Or maybe to see my *miaou miaou* earrings?'

Juliette didn't move, didn't say a word. Simone knew what she had to do. She tiptoed over to the pantry and found the tin of biscuits. She switched on the lights over the bench, took a quick look at her foot and saw there was glass embedded inside. She'd have to see to that later.

She brought the biscuits under the table and Juliette slowly crawled towards her. Simone felt the knot in her stomach loosen and she sighed with relief when she saw that Juliette was not hurt. She offered her a biscuit and Juliette sat in her lap and nibbled it. Her skin was cold, her hair was stiff with sea salt, and she had bare feet and only her swimming costume on. A rush of gratitude filled Simone, and she hugged her tight, kissing her head and giving her more *galettes*. She realised Juliette was probably dehydrated and fetched a glass of milk and a blanket. Should she call the police? She remembered the harshness of the policeman ordering her back behind the tape. She picked Juliette up and sat her on the table, so she didn't leave her sight or cut herself on the glass.

'I'm just going to call *Maman*, okay, *ma chérie*?'

She picked up the phone on the far end of the kitchen bench and pressed the Bisettes' number, which was programmed in for her frequent calls to Saskia.

'*Oui?*' Camille answered very suddenly, breathless, desperate, as though she'd been waiting with the phone cradled in her lap.

'Camille. It's Simone. I have her. I have Juliette at the villa. She was here all along, I think. She must have walked up the beach.'

She heard a moan come out of the other woman, something like she'd never heard before. It was filled with a haunting anguish, but mixed with a bone-deep relief. The line was silent for a few beats and then she could hear Camille weeping.

Tears fell from her own eyes as Simone felt the same relief, mixed with the grief for a mother who had never returned home.

Eventually Camille spoke, her voice grave. 'Simone, thank you. Oh my God, please, I need her to stay right there. Do you hear me? Stay right where you are. I'm coming.'

'We're not going anywhere.' She shot Juliette a smile. 'Are we, Juju?'

'Have you told them? Have you told the police?' Camille asked, her voice suddenly icy, pitched higher in her throat.

Simone felt a chill run through her, as though she'd done something wrong, that same hot-cold feeling Camille had always given her. 'No, no, I just called you, straightaway. I knew you'd want to know.'

'Don't tell anyone she's there,' said Camille.

Simone heard a door slam and she jumped, looked around the kitchen, but there was no one there. 'But what about Saskia and Félix. They're at the beach with the police. They're devastated. Can I just—'

Camille's voice was more pleading, more urgent than she'd ever heard it. 'Please, I'm begging you, Simone. I'm coming now. Stay there and don't tell anyone.'

CHAPTER 21

Dylan stops chewing and laughs. 'You're speaking to me in French now, are you?' He wipes at the side of his mouth with his thumb and shakes his head. 'I think it's time to go home. *Home* home. We've got the villa now.'

'I can't do this anymore, Dylan.' The words are crisp, clear. In a language he can't fail to understand.

He snorts. 'Yeah, I'm just about over France, too. There's only so many French villas and film stars one can take, and God only knows the etiquette around how many kisses.'

You didn't seem to complain about this when you were on the French film star's boat, being kissed four times by his wife, I think but don't say.

'No, this.' I indicate between the two of us. 'I can't do *this* anymore.'

His brows are knitted, but he's smiling. 'You're tired. And worried about Dee. I get it.'

He rises to come to me. I know exactly what he'll do next. He'll place his hands on my shoulders, his fingers digging deep into the side of my neck where he knows I hold all my tension. He'll knead until he feels the knots release. That's the thing about toxic relationships like ours, he is enmeshed with me.

Dylan knows me better than I know myself – my body, my mind and all my mental and physical pressure points.

And yes, this is precisely what he does. I almost feel myself dissolving under his kneading touch. *This is how he gets me. This is how he gets to keep me.* This is how he makes me think that I'm imagining how I'm feeling. It's classic gaslighting, but the thing about it is that it's so endemic to our dynamic that it's been almost impossible for me to pinpoint, to understand, to face. But standing here, with my daughter's brave, wrenching words still ringing in my ears, I can. I can finally see it so clearly.

I shrug his hands from my shoulders, move away from his grip. 'No, it's not Dee I'm worried about actually. She's stronger than I realised. It's me.'

He laughs and cocks his head as though I'm a small funny dog that has done a trick.

'Why are you laughing?' I ask, my voice measured.

'You're just being overly dramatic, emotional.'

He turns back to his sandwich, and I want to grab it from his hands and throw it across the room. The familiar resentment courses up my arms and into my neck, and I find that I can't control it, this emotion. It feels too strong, too big for my body. The dulling safety net of my meds is no longer there. This terrifies me and empowers me in equal measure, and I watch with a sort of abject horror as literally I rip the sandwich out of his mouth and fling it across the room, my body making a sound that I don't recognise, part groan, part cry.

His eyes swivel towards me and I see the flash of his shock as we both watch the food spray over the floor.

'What the fuck?' he exclaims.

I feel years of resentment, of pushing down my feelings, blunting my emotions, galvanise deep inside me and I straighten and face him. 'I *am* emotional. I am an emotional woman. That's what I am. Why do you have such a problem with that? With me expressing anything, ever? Why do I have to hide, to change who I am for you?'

He takes a slow swig of his beer and places it on the table very deliberately, just to show me that he's not buying into my 'emotions', that he's bigger than that. He bends down and starts picking up the sandwich and putting it back on the plate very calmly.

'Jesus Christ, I was just joking. What's got into you? Don't be so sensitive. I just wanted to finish my goddamn sandwich.'

I've just proven to him that I'm insane. Pathetic. Unhinged. But I know what he's doing. Distraction, obscuration. He's trying to make me forget what it was that started this ... he's trying to make me forget that I want to leave him. But it won't work, not this time.

I nod my head very slowly and smile at him benignly. I speak very slowly. 'And *I* just want to finish this goddamn relationship. And then you can order as many sandwiches as you like in the *Formule 1* up the road.'

He laughs and slides the remnants of the food into the bin. 'We'll talk about this tomorrow when you've calmed down. Look how you're talking to me. I can't deal with this right now.'

It's my turn to laugh. 'There you go, dismissing me. You don't even have the decency to acknowledge my feelings when I tell you that I'm leaving you. And that's because what I want, what I feel, is irrelevant to you. It doesn't matter to you at all.'

'How can you say that, Saskia? After everything we've been through together.'

He looks hurt as he moves towards me, and looking into his apologetic eyes I feel myself waver, like a hologram, like an illusion. It's always been his eyes. I step back so he can't draw me to him, and remind myself that he's good at this, that he's pivoted, and this is the part where he starts to reel me back in.

'Dylan, please. Enough with the games. Enough with the emotional manipulation. It's not going to work. I've made up my mind. There's nowhere for us to go from here. You won't talk to me about our marriage, you won't address all the messed-up toxic things going on, so we can never fix it. This is the only way. Just leave, please.' I point to the door.

He finishes his beer and slams it down. 'I'm going to take a shower.'

I block him. I physically put my body in the path of the kitchen's exit. 'This is my villa, I own it and you're not sleeping here tonight. Find a hotel.'

His eyes blaze. 'What do you want me to say, Saskia? Do you want my sympathy? Is that it? I've given you everything, right from the moment I found you working in that dingy bar.'

I take a beat. Try to calm myself. He wants me to bite now. 'No, I don't want your sympathy, Dylan, because we both know you're not capable of that. I just want you to listen to me. All I've wanted is for you not to dismiss me. But when was the last time you listened to me? To what I'm really saying to you?'

'Oh come on, you're totally overreacting. I've spent my whole life listening to three women. I'm the only man in the house. We've had a big day. We're all tired but we've got a villa.'

'No, I've got a villa. Simone left it to me.'

His face darkens. 'So, you want to get into all that? You really want to go there? Okay.' He jabs my chest with his index finger. 'You have lived off my family's money for the past two decades.'

'And you've enjoyed that, haven't you, having all the power. You've made me so small. And maybe I've let you, but I'm not being the hopeless child to your abusive parent anymore.'

His eyes narrow and he shakes his head, a smile on his lips. 'What are you going to do, run off with your old boyfriend? Is that what this is really about?'

He knows more than he's let on. But a defiance rears inside me, quick and sharp. *Maybe. Yes, maybe I damn well will.* 'Well, I could have a conversation with him where we actually understand each other. I could speak bad French and he'd understand me better than you do.'

He stiffens as though he's a snake and for a second I think he's going to strike me. That's the thing – he has never laid a hand on me, never exhibited any physical violence and in part that has allowed me to excuse his behaviour as never *that* bad. To always wonder if it was all in my head, if I was just being overly emotional, overreacting.

We're at an impasse. I'm standing at the door of the kitchen; he's standing in front of me.

'Dylan,' I say, urging myself to stay calm. 'I don't know how to convey this to you any more clearly. I don't love you anymore. I don't want to be in this painful dynamic with you anymore. Please, just go, I need you to leave.'

His face crumples. His shoulders cave, as though he's been punched in the gut. He reaches for me, pulls me towards him, but I resist, push him back with a flat palm.

'I'm sorry,' he says, his eyes large. He brushes away tears with the heel of his hand, hangs his head. 'Please, you can't do this to me.'

I want to slap him. I should have known that this was next. The final manipulation.

'I *can* do this, and I have to. We'll both be happier in the end, Dylan. I think deep down you know that.'

'So, you've just used me, is that it? Stayed with me for my money until you got your own?'

'This is not about money. There was a small part of me that always hoped that I could please you enough. That I'd be what you wanted. That I could make you happy and that you'd see me and listen to me and hear me. That you'd love me. Like you used to. We did, we used to be in love.'

'I do love you, Saskia. I love you.'

'You have a messed-up way of showing it.'

'I'll do better. We could go to counselling. I know you've suggested it in the past.'

'No, Dylan, I can't, I'm done.'

He grabs my hand. 'Come on, come upstairs, and we'll address it all in the morning.'

I laugh a little maniacally now. I turn to him. I don't try to take my hand from his. My gaze is steady as I look him right in the eyes and nod very slowly. I know what needs to happen now.

'No, you know what? That's okay, Dylan. Yes, we'll talk in the morning. You go take your shower. Go on.' I indicate upstairs. I'm talking to him like he's a small child. Somehow the dynamic has changed — I am the adult now and he is the child. I feel light-headed with the control he has given over to me. The control I have taken.

His face registers dumb relief and I watch as he slowly ascends the stairs, his head hung. I hear the shower start. He takes long hot showers, especially when he's stressed. I know I have about ten to fifteen minutes.

My pulse is sprinting along my wrists and pounding in my ears. I rouse Dee who's fallen asleep in her bed and get

Lara, who's on her iPad. They're tired and probably hungry but they must sense my urgency. I'm not sure how much of our fight Lara heard. But they trust me, and Dee knows what's happening – I see it in the wary flick of her eyes. She helps Lara slip on some shoes and find the charger for her device. I thank her for looking after her sister and she nods, and I feel the quiet strength in our new connection. I still have them. I will always have them. Thank God.

We walk quickly, quietly through the house and into the early evening. There are lights on in Madame Gardner's house. I knock tentatively on the door. She appears with her hair in rollers, her eyes startled, glassy. But her face lights up as soon as she realises it's us. I tell her that Dylan and I have had a fight and ask if we can stay with her for the night. She grips my hands tightly and presses her lips together and I know by the way she scans the garden before shutting the door and locking it that we will be safe here. There is talk of *chocolat chaud* and sleeping in the spare bedroom where the sheets are always made up for her grandchildren.

Dee hugs Lara to her and I feel a burst of love for my daughters, pure and intense, and I know, *I know* I've done the right thing. I put my arms around both of them and we all stand there for a moment, hovering as though suspended between our old life and a new one. Madame Gardner ushers us into her kitchen and we sit at her table in the low warm light and watch as she turns on the stove to heat the milk.

I feel my phone vibrate in my pocket and I jump. I know it's Dylan. I don't want to look, but I do.

Saskia, how is Dee? I hope you're all ok. Please, I am asking again. I will beg. I am not ashamed to beg. Will you come and meet me. There is so much we still need to talk about.

274

Félix.

This time I know I must go.

I look at my daughters sipping their hot chocolate, watching something on the iPad. I know they'll be okay here for a little while. There's something I've got to do, I tell Madame Gardner, but I'll be back. She tells me where the spare key is and pats my hand reassuringly. If she thinks it's strange that I'm leaving my daughters with her, she doesn't say. She only smiles, with maybe a hint of understanding in her eyes.

I find my bike against the dry-stone wall. Evening is falling, the air cooling. I realise I'm barefoot but I don't care. I need to feel the burn in my legs, the salt air in my lungs. And as I'm riding away, I realise that, for the first time, Madame Gardner and I have conversed entirely in French.

*

Le passé

The sea wind roared behind the wall, raging through the tops of the orange trees as Simone listened through the open window for the sound of Camille's approach. She imagined she could hear the echo of loudspeakers in the distance, the police still searching for Juliette, but she didn't know if it was just her imagination. Would Camille drive or ride her bike?

Simone kept the house dark. It felt as though she was in some eerie wartime dream, as though she needed to conceal what was inside, pretend no one was home. She had wanted to run Juliette a bath, warm up her little body and comb the knots from her hair. Wrap her in a cashmere sweater. But she was hesitant to do anything other than put a blanket around the child and clean her face with a warm washcloth. She was now curled up on the chaise longue in the corner of the kitchen, her tummy full of biscuits and milk, exhausted and asleep.

Simone realised she was afraid of Camille, her unpredictability, her unreadability. She was fragile and restrained, and yet Simone sensed something fierce below the surface. She didn't know why Camille had insisted she stay quiet, secrete Juliette away. She only knew that her devastation, and then her relief, had been visceral. She had felt the other woman's pain so keenly, because her own had barely healed.

Simone had to fight her instinct to ride back to the beach, to alert Saskia and Félix. She imagined the relief flooding their pale, worried faces, the feeling of them embracing her, returning to her. That cold frightening distance between them, gone. They would fetch Simone's abandoned bike, laughing nervously at the drama of it all, because in hindsight they should have known that of course Juju was okay. They would come to the villa and Félix would make a late supper of their favourite comfort food – croque monsieur, the bread pan-fried with too much butter and salt – and they'd drink whisky to calm their nerves and Juliette would curl into her *nounou's* lap. And they would all recount how worried they had been, and in talking about it together they would rid their bodies and minds of their fears.

But Simone did not want to cross Camille. She sensed there was something else at play and needed to understand what it was. She heard the squeak in the swing of the gate and watched as the woman walked through the dark garden, her white dress luminous. She wondered why Camille always wore white. At first she had thought it was because she floated above the ordinary, the dirt not sticking to her, but now Simone knew enough to understand that this was an illusion. She opened the French doors and gestured to Camille to come through the courtyard into the kitchen rather than use the front door. She was not going to leave Juliette in a room alone for even a second.

Camille's skin was damp with sweat, her hair pulled off her face. She had obviously ridden her bike. As soon as she saw Juliette in the corner of the kitchen she rushed to her daughter, sinking to her knees and resting her head against her small sleeping body. Juliette stirred but did not wake. Wordlessly Simone filled a glass of water. Camille took it and drank. She then stood on unsteady legs, suddenly so fragile, so thin, and drew Simone into an embrace.

Her voice was muffled by Simone's hair. '*Oh mon Dieu*, thank you, thank you, thank you,' she said.

When she drew back, Simone could see the depth of Camille's grief, her red-ringed eyes, her sallow skin. She thought of those hours of terror she had endured.

'I didn't do anything except have a window that doesn't close properly.' She gestured to the window above the table.

'You think she climbed in there?' Camille asked.

Simone nodded. 'I think she must have. She knew the neighbour's cat gets in here sometimes. And that's where she was when I found her, just under the table.' She hesitated. 'But why would she have come here do you think? It's such a long way to walk from where we swim at Le Bois-Plage. I know we've walked here together, but for a child alone …'

Camille closed her eyes and when she opened them there were tears in them. Her voice was soft. 'I think she probably felt safe here … after we came here that night.'

Simone reached out and touched her shoulder, realising the gravity of what she'd just admitted.

Camille seemed to deflate then. She sank to the ground, her white dress a puddle around her. 'It's been bad. At home.' She put her face in her hands. Her voice was quiet, muffled. 'Worse than that night.'

Simone felt something sharp and dark move inside her. 'Where is Henri now?'

'He's with the police, searching. He thinks I'm still at home. He wouldn't let me leave. He wouldn't let me search for my baby girl.' She looked over at Juliette, who was still asleep with her thumb jammed in her mouth. 'He's so controlling. It's getting worse.' She shook her head. 'That's why, that's why I didn't want you to call the police.'

Camille stood and grabbed Simone's hands. Her grip was cool and her eyes fierce. 'This is it. Don't you see? This is our chance, Juliette and me. No one knows Juliette is here except you.'

Simone felt a twist of anguish in her stomach and she shook her head. 'What are you talking about, Camille? You can't just ... All those people out there searching for Juliette, the police ...' Her mind reeled. What was Camille suggesting? That she wanted to disappear with her daughter? It was impossible, insane, but when she looked into the other woman's eyes, she saw raw desperation.

'Please, Simone. Please, you must understand. We are trapped. I cannot just leave him. If only it was that simple. He will always find me. Juliette will always be in danger. And look at her ... How scared she must have been to have come all the way here.'

They both looked at Juliette sleeping peacefully, her beautiful little face so calm, so innocent, and Simone felt an uncomfortable sort of yielding sensation inside her, a slipping of her resolve.

'We heard you,' she said. 'We heard you fighting. That time we all met at the markets, and Saskia and Félix and I rode back to Bisette. Is that why you get so many nannies? To protect yourself?'

Camille wrung her hands in the fabric of her dress. 'You must understand, Henri is a very proud man. He would never display his temper in front of Saskia, in front of any of his staff. So yes, to a degree, that explains the nannies. Before, he never touched me, just yelled abuse,' She laughed at this, as though it was a sad, private joke. 'And so, I could always say to myself, *But he doesn't hit me*. And then one day, he hit me. And now that he does I can't say that to myself anymore.'

'I'm so sorry, Camille.'

'So am I. I never meant for this to be our life. I loved him once, of course.' She pushed her hair off her face, composing herself, almost painfully dignified. It broke Simone's heart to watch.

Camille pulled out a chair at the table and sat down, signalled to Simone to join her. Her fingers tapped nervously on the wood.

Simone slid into the chair opposite. 'Camille, I want to help you, but it's just ... what you're asking me to do ...'

'Simone, there is more to this story that I need you to know.'

She felt very cold suddenly. 'I don't understand.' She braced her arms against her chest.

'Your mother.'

Simone's fingers found the earrings in her lobe. It felt like all the air had been sucked from the room. She was breathless when she spoke. 'What about my mother?'

Camille's hands flattened on the tabletop. 'Oh Simone, your mother, she was' – she shook her head as a tiny smile played on her lips – 'remarkable.'

Confusion jostled with hope, and Simone found there was anger inside her too. 'You were friends, weren't you? The earrings. That's how you knew they were hers. Why didn't you tell me this from the start?'

Camille sat back in her chair and smoothed her palms over the top of the table. 'Friends, no. We were more than friends.'

Simone's heartbeat accelerated and her throat went dry. 'What does that mean? You were best friends? What are you telling me?'

'Can I tell you a story?' asked Camille, leaning towards Simone and tucking her hair behind her ears, as though they had all the time in the world, as though they were not hiding a little girl while all the island searched for her.

When Simone didn't respond she went on. 'I still remember very clearly the day I met Hélène. She was almost naked, sunning herself by a friend's pool. You know how she was, she always wanted to be topless in summer, to absorb every little bit of sunshine into every bit of her skin.' Camille gave an awkward laugh. 'She terrified me at first. She was so free. So spontaneous, so fearless. She was the opposite of me. She and I, we clashed at first. We didn't understand each other.' She looked sheepish. 'Maybe a little like you and me ... We found each other ... I don't know, I was too cold, she was too hot. But there was between us something we could not articulate. This tension ... And there was your father.'

Simone shook her head. It was as though everything was scrambled, upside down. She needed to make Camille understand. 'Camille, my mother wasn't … I think you have the wrong idea. She loved my father. She adored him. She wrote poems dedicated to him. A whole book. She described her love for him as being like a tree.' But even as the words left her mouth, some small part deep inside her was ringing, like the high note of an insistent insect in the dark. How had her mother described that tree? Their love?

The first flush of young love was the green buds, the new leaves in the canopy unfurling, stretching for the sun. But after that initial excited growth, the branches solidified, thickened.

She had always interpreted this simplistically, as her mother's deepening love for her father. But Hélène reached always for the sun. She craved its warmth, its heat. She craved newness. She craved excitement and growth.

It felt like a puzzle piece falling finally into place. All those friends who had come and gone over the years, the elaborate gifts Hélène had given them, the constant outings to parties, the searing intensity of those friendships. Then something would happen, the new friend would disappear and she would never see this woman who had so consumed her mother again. And all the while Simone's father was at home with his books, seemingly accepting of the simple notion that his wife was the social animal in the relationship. Of her need for constant company, excitement, novelty, admiration.

'Yes,' said Camille, looking Simone in the eye. 'She adored your father and he her. They were everything to each other. He gave her the security she craved. And they were a meeting of two brilliant minds. But, Hélène, she was a complicated woman. She also loved women.'

The words did not shock Simone as she would have imagined, but she shook her head regardless. 'No, I think I would have known this. My father would have known. He loved her passionately. I don't know that he would have been okay—'

Camille spoke very gently. 'I know this is very difficult, to find out things about your parents after they're gone, when they can't respond … but Stéphane, I am certain that he knew. He knew that Hélène was complicated, that she had two sides that both needed fulfilling. And he also knew that because of this Hélène would never leave him, or, more importantly, leave you.'

Simone felt tears on her cheeks and she brushed them away furiously. 'How dare you? You made me feel like my family was cursed, you judged me, and now you want me to believe that my mother was, what? Your lover? And that my father knew and somehow sanctioned it?'

Camille reached for her hand, but Simone withdrew it. 'I'm so sorry I judged you, that I said those terrible things to you. I don't know why I did it. You frightened me. You reminded me of her. Her energy, her beauty, her rawness. Of everything that I did wrong. Of the mistakes I made. I am hurting too, Simone. I'm in agony over losing her. More so because of the guilt, because of what happened.'

Simone felt as though someone had traced her spine with a sharp, icy fingernail. She shivered, both desperate for Camille to go on and paralysed with fear about what she would say. 'Were you there?' A stony realisation settled in her stomach when she looked at the sadness on the other woman's face. 'You were there. The night they died.'

Camille's eyes filled with tears and her mouth twisted in pain, which she fought, swallowing it back. It was a while before she could speak. 'Hélène was so afraid to drive, because of the Durant curse.'

Simone felt a strange sensation, like déjà vu. Hélène had never revealed this fear to anyone. She had always excused her inability to drive on her privileged upbringing, having been chauffeured around since she was a child. She laughed that she had just never got around to getting her licence because she had her bicycle. Only her father, Simone, and her own mother, Sophia, knew the real reason. Simone understood then that her mother had revealed her most vulnerable self to Camille and that she was telling the truth.

'You see, Hélène was driving that car because of me. It's because of me that she and Stéphane are gone.' Camille put her face in her hands.

Simone felt a darkness descend, like entering a tunnel. 'Camille, what are you saying? Why? Why was *Maman* driving? It's true, she couldn't drive.'

Camille looked up. Her eyes were red and she drew in a shaky breath. 'We were at a party on the mainland, in La Rochelle. Henri was not treating me well that night, and Hélène, you know how she could be. She'd had too much wine and she pulled me out into the garden, and she was begging me to leave him once and for all. But she didn't understand that I couldn't just leave him. Even with all her money, all her protection, he would always find us.' Camille looked over at her sleeping daughter and then back at Simone. 'He will never let me and Juliette be free. He has money, he has power, and he will use it. But Hélène didn't understand this. She was married to a good man, so she could not understand that a husband might threaten to kill his own daughter if his wife left him.'

Simone felt her body go cold. Camille looked hollowed out and she wanted to reach for her, but she didn't. She needed to hear how this ended.

'I thought she would never, ever leave your father to be with me. How could we openly be together anyway? And yet I understood that she did love me and could not stand to see me with Henri any longer. She wanted me to tell Henri about us, to break it off, but I was too scared. I told her no, I can't leave Henri. She told me she would protect us, but she didn't understand, not really, this power he had. She was so mad, she stormed out of the party. I saw her get into the car, into the driver's seat, and I ran after her. Maybe she just wanted to scare me at first, I don't know. But then Stéphane was there pleading with her to let him in, to let him drive. And then …'

Camille took a deep breath and closed her eyes. 'Then he said that he knew, about her and me. He knew that I was the love of her life, and it was okay, he wanted her to be happy, finally to just be herself, and be happy and free.'

Simone's face crumpled. '*Papa*,' she said, her voice a whisper, her heart squeezing at how truly this reflected her father's nature. She could almost hear his voice saying those words.

'Hélène looked at me, pleading, finally, if now I would leave Henri and we could be together. But she didn't realise that she was asking me to choose between her and Juliette. And I don't know, she must have seen my despair, my answer, because she unlocked the door and let Stéphane into the car. And then she drove away.'

Simone could feel Camille's eyes on her, wanting a response, a reaction, exoneration for what she'd done, but she was numb.

She couldn't move, she couldn't talk. They sat in silence, punctuated only by the small sounds of Juliette sleeping and the soft rain outside.

Finally, Simone felt herself standing and walking out into the rain-damp night. A night like the night her parents had died. Every surface, every leaf glistened. She also thought of Saskia and Félix, perhaps still searching for Juliette in the rain. Her emotions felt too large for her body, too overwhelming. The smell of the oranges mixed with the ocean, and she thought about how much her mother had loved coming to the villa in the last year of her life, how much time she had spent here, even without her father, and now Simone understood why.

She looked into the kitchen at Camille, who was sitting very still, very straight, at the kitchen table. Could Simone accept this version of her mother? She had always known Hélène was not entirely happy, always searching for more, but wasn't that the remit of the creative, of the artist? When you grew up with someone, you didn't expect them to ever be any different from how they were.

She could see Camille's despair, her impossible decision. She wanted to ask her about Hélène, who she had been with her. Had she been happy, happier than with her father? But was there a way to quantify happiness? Was there a way to quantify love?

Simone thought of Félix. Sometimes love just was. Sometimes it was indisputable.

There was hurt and anger, too, that everything had played out the way it had. That her mother had been so impulsive in getting behind the wheel of that car. That Camille hadn't been brave enough to take up her mother's offer and her father's sacrifice, to finally let themselves be happy, and to save herself and her child from a violent man.

What Camille was asking her to do now was impossible. But she looked at the woman through the window, her head cradled in her hands. Maybe, Simone thought, maybe this was her being brave now.

CHAPTER 22

The pine forest is dark and cool, and I negotiate my way through its paths by muscle memory. The heat of the day rises from the earth, the scent of damp soil under my tyres. It feels like I'm racing shadows. It feels like I have wings on my back and fire in my belly. My chest hurts like I've been punched in the solar plexus. I am flooded with feelings. I've just left my marriage, the only thing I've known for so long. Doubt and fear consume me. Even pain can be hard to give up when it's familiar, when you've internalised it as part of who you are, of what your life looks like.

But there's also a wrenching defiance inside me that feels like hope. I throw my head back and close my eyes for a second, feeling the bike wheel blindly forward. For the first time in so long, I don't know where my life is going, what I'm doing. I have nothing to buffer me anymore – I'm pressed up against the rawness of life, my own feelings. I don't know if I can do this.

And then the landscape opens up before me and the salt flats stretch out, vast and bright, like a blanched dreamscape.

And I see him.

It's been half a lifetime since I cycled here, but it might have been yesterday. I remember how free and hopeful I felt, meeting friends who seemed immediately to understand me, to accept me. The unspoken bond we all felt floating in these salt pools, the feeling of his hand finding mine.

He is waiting for me, as I knew he would be. He's standing very still, his back to me, silhouetted against the darkening basins like a lone night bird. He is a bird with a broken wing, one who has come home after the vast migration of life, and it makes me want to care for him, to gather him to me. I realise Félix always had this quality, even as a young man, a vulnerability that he's not afraid to show the world. It's what made him a great actor. It's something I've never experienced intimately with a man again. Perhaps it is simply emotional intelligence. I've longed so deeply, so viscerally for that connection, so far from what Dylan is capable of. To be listened to, to be heard, to be understood. How ironic that I had to come to the other side of the world, to find the words in another language, to realise this.

He hears me and turns. He doesn't smile, we don't greet with kisses. He must know why I'm here.

'Are you okay?'

His face is so soft, and his concern makes me want to reach for him. I stop myself, my body bracing, arms knitted to my chest.

'Not really.' I smile sadly. 'I just told my husband our marriage is over and discovered my daughter is sick.'

I'm not sure why we're speaking in French when Dylan is no longer here, but a door has been opened to intimacy, our barriers have dissolved, in his language, not mine. Like salt dissolving into water.

'Do you remember when we bathed here?' Félix asks, reading my mind, turning towards me. 'We were drunk on pastis and old red wine, and I made us ride all the way here for salt for our pasta?'

'I remember. All of it.' I pause. 'With Simone.' Her name rings out in the stillness. A bird cries mournfully somewhere in the marshes. I can hear my own breath loud in my ears, like being underwater. 'Félix, I need to know why you didn't meet me in Barcelona.'

He looks down, squats and scoops water into his palm, washes the back of his neck, his hands. A cleansing. I wait. I have waited twenty-six years already, and I can feel my heart thumping like a clenched fist.

He stands. 'I never loved Simone, if that's what you're wondering. It was always you, Saskia.'

I feel the knot of my heart release and something like elation soars through me. But then my throat constricts. 'Why then? Why didn't you meet me like we planned?'

'I was in Paris with Simone, it is true. But we were never lovers, I promise you that.'

Confusion and relief fuse in my chest and I press my palm against it. 'I waited for three days. I called your house, spoke to your father, but he hung up on me. I felt so ashamed, after what had happened with Juliette.'

'I tried to call you at the hostel, the one where we agreed to meet, Kabul. I promise you, I left messages with reception.' His voice has a pleading quality that doesn't suit him. 'It was a strange time, after everything that had happened. I was overwhelmed with it all, as though it was a bad dream, and I thought that maybe you didn't want to see me.'

I bite my lip, avoid his eyes. 'I never got any messages, Félix.'

He grabs my hands. 'But it was you I thought of when I made *The Mountain*. As though I was a man mourning for his dead lover. I thought of losing you, what it had done to my life, the wrong path it had sent me down. And then when I won the award I knew, I really knew. Because that was all I had ever wanted from life, the success, the accolades; I was no longer the simple boy from the salt marshes.' He gestures around him, and a breath of air escapes his lips. 'But really, we never leave who we are, the place that forms us. That's why I returned here. I was empty, I had no one to share the success with. I had let something very special go when I was too young to understand. I made a mistake, Saskia.'

I want to wrap my arms around him, but I resist. 'I know that what we had doesn't come along every day because I've never found it again. To talk like this with someone, so easily, so openly. To speak about our emotions.' I laugh, and it has a hysterical edge to it. The emotional connection I have with this man is stronger than the one I have with the man I've shared my bed with for nearly twenty years.

He pulls me close to him, so close I can smell his particular scent, one that has never changed. Salt and soil and sun. I close my eyes, feel myself dissolving. But no. I press him away from me. 'But you broke me. You broke me when I was already so broken from what had happened with Juliette.'

The weight of her name is heavy in the air. These ghosts, Juliette and Simone, surround us, like the lengthening shadows in the bracken rimming the marshes.

'Saskia, it wasn't your fault. We were so young. I was also messed up after what happened with Juliette.'

'I have punished myself for a lifetime. I thought that was why you never came. That it must have been why you never contacted me again. You once talked about having a family, what a good mother I'd be, that same day Juliette disappeared, and then I—' A sob escapes my lips and I cover my face with my hands. 'I lost her.'

Something painful crosses his face and he runs his hands through his hair. 'Saskia, you did nothing wrong. I was the selfish one. I distracted you that day on the beach. And then I ... You have to understand how much I wanted to escape this place, this life. And Simone got me an audition with a very well known director in Paris. Can you imagine, this *saunier* from Île de Ré going for the main role in an Arnold Bressel film? The main actor had to pull out sick and I was his replacement, and the filming was starting straightaway. It was the opportunity of a lifetime and I ...' He squeezes his eyes shut. 'Because of this, perhaps I did not try hard enough to contact you. There was no email, no social media. I couldn't go there, to meet you. And then I was so caught up in everything that my life had suddenly become. Some part of me hoped that maybe you would join me in Paris, as my messages suggested. But it is no excuse, I see that now ... I was so naïve. I made the wrong decision. My career over you.'

I can feel his regret, as bottomless as my own, and I smile sadly. 'But, Félix, you didn't make the wrong decision. Look at you now. One of the most famous men in France.'

He holds out his hands and in his eyes I see a whole ocean of sadness, the breadth and depth of his loneliness. I want to step into it, drown in it, but I stand very still so as not to sink. 'No, you made the right decision. What we had was just a long-ago summer romance.'

He smiles. 'Look at us, Saskia. Look at us right now. Look at where life has brought us. We have come full circle. Do you really believe that?'

I taste tears on my lips. *No, I don't. I never have, that's why you have always haunted me.* I find I have no resistance when he comes to me, when he draws my body to his and kisses my eyelids. His hands feel like rough sand on my wet cheek.

'It is not your fault,' he whispers in my ear, and I lean into him, wanting to believe this above all else, as though it is he who can absolve my guilt, yielding finally to the rip of him that I've felt tug at me since returning to his island. 'Forgive me,' he says into my neck, my hair.

And I find that I am kissing him. He tastes the same and our mouths find a rhythm that is both familiar and strange, awkward and yet somehow natural. The soft brushing of lips, dissolving into tongue over tongue, soft and rolling, rough and deep. I feel like I might never come up for air. He feels so different from Dylan's fleshy lips and body. Félix's shoulders and arms are strong, but he is thinner than my husband. Life has whittled him differently. I know I should not be doing this. We're both married to other people. The familiarity of those other bodies lingers, making each touch between us startling, new.

Félix still hasn't explained everything. I don't know if his answer as to why he never met me is enough, but I find I don't care anymore. I can't. I am no longer solid. I have liquified. I feel alive, and all I feel is him; I'm finally free from the pain in my chest, free from the demons that have haunted me, free from myself. Darkness has descended and fused with the salt mist so that the air has the hazy quality of a dream. There is no one else here except the egrets and herons.

Long reeds and bracken edge the salt flats and we fall into this humid marshland. He presses me down into the soft grasses and I pull my dress over my head. He traces a finger along my shoulder, down between my breasts, across my stomach and between my legs. I can only just make out his dark eyes. I close mine. It has been so long since I've felt my body so aroused. My medication dampened everything down, and I forgot years ago that there was a hum that could be coaxed with a single touch. I forgot that I was a sensual being. Perhaps, in hindsight, it made it easier to be with Dylan. To be numb, and passive. But the touch of Félix's bare skin to mine feels so charged, so erotic, that I feel as though I could climax. I shiver and pull him on top of me. Our kissing becomes more feverish, and I want to take our bodies where they're heading. I sigh as he puts the tip of his finger inside me. His tongue plays over my stomach, and my breath hitches higher in my throat.

He watches me as he touches me, reading my response. I have never felt so exposed, so seen, so raw. It excites me, and when his tongue finds my clitoris, I grip hold of reeds and grasses and let him urge me over a wave of pleasure. After, when he enters me, a groan comes from deep in my throat and I whisper in his ear, '*Ça fait du bien.*' That feels good. He cups my face gently in his palms and the tenderness of this one gesture while he is inside me undoes me. I have not felt such intimacy with a man since him. I've not been able to show myself entirely since then. Part of me was always hiding. Now I am split open. It's terrifying, it's beautiful. He gives himself to me wholly too, offering up his own vulnerability, crying out, shuddering against me.

We lie naked under the dark sky for a long time, holding each other. The sounds of night birds and the waves from the shore beyond the marshes wash over me, through me. I wish we could stay this way forever, hidden in the salt haze.

He kisses the palm of my hand. 'Thank you, for giving yourself to me,' he says, so simply, so authentically, as though he has thanked me for passing him the salt.

293

I close my eyes and smile, warmth spreading through me at the intimacy of his words.

'Thank you for seeing me,' I say, putting my ear to his chest, listening to his heart. Maybe what I really mean is thank you for freeing me.

'I don't think life has changed us as much as we think, you know. It feels the same between us. You still feel the same.'

'Just flabbier.'

'No, more beautiful.'

It has been so long since someone called me beautiful, I feel it as a pang, like longing. He must see this, because he says, 'Your husband, he is someone who skims the surface of life, am I right?'

I raise an eyebrow. 'I've never thought about it like that, but I suppose so.'

'Were you ever happy?'

I sigh, trace a finger along his collarbone. 'Yes, I think so, at the start. He gave me what I needed.' A breath escapes my lips. 'I thought it was security, now it's a dead weight holding me down.'

Félix nods. 'I too am suffocated, but in a different way. Renée is like a balloon, she floats on the surface also. Perhaps that is why my wife and your husband seemed to hit it off.'

I laugh. 'He's not rich and famous enough for her.'

'I see you have understood my wife's appetites.'

A moment of silence stretches between us, filled with all the complicated unsaid things about our marriages, our lives. It feels like we're floating beyond all that, cocooned in our salt haze dream.

'Do you know we have never made love in a bed?' Félix smooths a strand of hair behind my ear.

'You're right. In the car, on the beach. Now the salt marshes. You would think at our age we'd have grown out of it.'

'I would like to have you in my bed though,' he says, and I shiver at the implications of this. He must feel my hesitancy because he kisses my cheek, his lips lingering there a moment too long. 'I know you have your life back in Sydney, but now you have a villa on Île de Ré as well, *non*?'

'Félix, why do you think Simone left us the villa?' I feel a tiny drill of adrenalin, like I've put my finger on the invisible tension between us, but it is the last barrier between us and so I must ask it.

Félix goes quiet. I can almost feel him retreat into himself. He props himself onto an elbow so he's looking into my face. I can just make out the sharp planes of his cheekbones.

'Saskia, I need you to know something.' He shakes and then hangs his head and I feel anxiety skittle through me. Instinctively I sit up and pull my dress on.

'I have tried so hard to not tell you. To respect Simone's wishes, Camille's wishes, but Simone, she brought you back to me by giving you half of the villa. How can I not tell you?'

'Tell me what, Félix? You're scaring me a little.'

I can see the whites of his eyes in the dark. 'Saskia ... Juliette is alive.'

*

Le passé

Simone walked inside the villa, past Camille whose face was still buried in her hands at the kitchen table, past Juliette, who was still fast asleep. She switched on the kettle and made tea then took the cups to the table.

'Thank you,' Camille said, and Simone knew by the expression on her face that she wasn't thanking her for the tea but for what it represented – that Simone had heard the truth of what had happened to her mother that night and she was still here.

'Simone, I am so sorry for what happened ... Maybe now you can see why I cannot live with this guilt, why it has made me crazy, why it made me cruel.' Camille wrapped her hands around her mug. 'But I am not sorry for loving your mother. I will never apologise for what we had.'

Simone sat down and looked into the other woman's tortured eyes. 'My mother was never happy. She had everything in the whole world, but it was never enough. Maybe now I understand why. Maybe she wasn't able to be who she really was.'

Camille reached out and squeezed Simone's hand. 'You are just as remarkable as your mother. Do you know that? You have her compassion. Her deep understanding of life's complexities. She was a poet at heart. I see that in you too.'

Simone felt tears in her eyes. People had always compared her to her mother's beauty, but never to her brilliance, to her soul. She took a deep breath. 'Will you tell me? Who she was, really?'

Camille smiled and Simone saw a light coming out of her that she'd never seen before. 'She was my beautiful dream. I wish I could tell you we were great friends, but there was from the start an energy between us. I've never felt like this with any other person – man or woman. She was so full of contradictions. She fascinated me. She was so raw, so truthful that sometimes it hurt. There were times when your father was called back to Paris or at conferences and these were the times we were free to be together. I love to cook, but there has never been enough room in my marriage for two chefs, yet I cooked for her. She loved my pasta with burned butter sauce. My crispy fried fish. Anything cooked over charcoal. Food with spice.'

Simone smiled. Camille did know her mother.

'And we both loved to read. We would write each other letters when we were apart.'

'You weren't scared Henri would find out?'

'Henri is a jealous man but, perhaps because of this, his focus is narrow. He would never even imagine that I would not love men, but women instead.'

Simone nodded. 'Was my mother the same? But what about men? What about my father?'

Camille met her eyes, her gaze steady. 'One day it might be different, but for girls like me and your mother, we married men because it is what women did, what women do. You know your grandmother would not have abided knowing her daughter was gay. She struggled enough with your father, who was the perfect gentleman. Sophia would not even let Hélène or you take his surname, perhaps as a symbolic gesture of her fear that he would take her fortune.'

This had been a source of tension in their family over the years. Hélène had simply done what her mother had wanted, had kept the name Durant, and Stéphane had not had a say.

'If Sophia had known, she would have cut Hélène out of everything. And your mother did love your father, but it was a platonic love, in the end. And for him, I believe that was enough. Because really, just to be in her orbit was enough for any of us, wasn't it?' She smiled, a soft sigh escaping her lips.

'She did have an orbit,' Simone said.

'And after everything, your father was there for her in the end.'

Simone's eyes filled with tears again. 'I miss them so much.'

Camille took her hand and squeezed it. They sat together like this for a while, the only sound the wind whistling softly through the crack in the window. When Camille spoke her voice was soft, a new vulnerability there.

'Simone, can you help me?' She looked over at Juliette. 'I can never lose her like I did for those terrifying few hours today. I feared he'd done something to her, because he knew I was so close to leaving him this time.'

Simone felt anxiety stretch inside her. She knew it was what her mother would have wanted, to keep the woman she loved and her child safe from a terrible man. 'Camille, I know what you're asking me to do, but I don't ... I don't even know how that would work. The police ... everyone is searching for her.'

Camille straightened, her eyes fierce. 'We can hide her. Just while things die down, and then we can escape. Juliette and I can start again, somewhere small, in the countryside. I have an aunt in the Lot Valley. We'd be safe, we'd finally be free because he would not come looking for us.'

Simone felt panic course through her. 'We can't hide her here. The police might search the villa when they don't find her tonight. And we need to tell Saskia and Félix that Juliette is okay. They're devastated. They blame themselves.'

Camille's face was stony, the sharpness returning to her features. 'No, we cannot tell them. The police are interrogating them. They're our alibi.'

'Camille, what you're asking me to do ...' Simone pressed her palms to her eyes. 'They're my friends, the most real ones I've ever had. You don't understand. To grow up as I did, people don't see you for who you are. All they see is your money, what they can gain from you. To find something true and untainted by that is ...'

Camille reached out and squeezed her arm. 'Simone, I understand. I understand this more than you realise. It was your mother's struggle too.'

Simone softened at the love in the other woman's eyes. Of course, this would have been Hélène's cross to bear. But she thought about Saskia and Félix, collapsed in exhaustion and defeat on the beach. She couldn't betray them. She couldn't leave them blaming themselves for a little girl's disappearance. The heaviness of that burden would never leave them.

But she looked at Camille, this woman her mother had loved. The woman her father had sacrificed himself for. There was an uncomfortable feeling forming inside her. A tiny part of her, a terrible, sharp sliver that felt like revenge for Saskia stealing Félix from her. Simone pushed the feeling down, deeper inside, a crash of shame engulfing her.

'No, absolutely not, I can't do it to them. It is too much to ask, even for my own mother. Even for a little girl.'

'Please, Simone, please. I too would feel terrible for not telling them, but Saskia cannot know. She's Juliette's nanny, she is being interrogated by the police as the last one to have seen Juliette. She doesn't understand the language properly. She is too young, too naïve to be able to lie to the authorities, to keep a secret like that safe. Knowing would implicate her in a crime. Not telling her would keep her safe. It is the only way this could work.'

A crime. 'But I don't even know ... How do we get you and Juliette off the island? I can't drive her. I can't hide her here ...'

'Is there anywhere we could hide her, just for a few days? They won't search forever. They have police boats out, they think she drowned.'

The thought filled Simone with despair, the idea that everyone would eventually give up.

'Is there somewhere on the island the police would not think to look? Somewhere she could be safe, where you could stay with her? Would you do that for me? You are not involved in any way. They won't be looking for you. Just until I can leave the island without it seeming suspicious.'

Simone thought suddenly of the wide, deserted salt flats, and a tiny wooden cabin that housed the *saunier* tools. It was remote, on the other side of the island. *No*, she thought, *Félix would have to be involved then*. How could she tell Félix of their surreptitious plan and not Saskia? Pull him into this net of deception? It would drive a wedge between him and Saskia forever.

The sharp, shameful sliver of retribution twinged inside her again. But they were deceiving for a good reason, weren't they? Her mother's last wish. Keeping a little girl safe from a violent man. It was the right thing to do, wasn't it?

CHAPTER 23

Juliette is alive. The hairs on my arms stand and my whole body convulses, like I've been plunged into freezing water. I gasp. The little girl who has haunted my dreams, whose pale, dead, floating face has shadowed my nightmares – she's not dead, she's alive. I start to shake.

I know that on some level this news should fill me with joy, because I loved Juliette, I mourned her, and I hoped for her too, because the missing can never truly be mourned. But instead there's a sickening dread growing in my gut. I feel dizzy and scramble backwards, away from Félix, like an animal sensing threat. I've been deceived in some deep way I'm yet to fully understand, this I know. I can see it in the lines of regret etched deep into his face, the despondent hang of his head. My voice when I find it is small.

'What do you mean? I don't understand.'

Félix has pulled on his pants; the naked desire and intimacy we just shared feels like it never happened. He's on his knees, his eyes pleading.

'Saskia, I'm so sorry. I shouldn't be telling you this – for her safety, for your sanity – but I just can't have this secret between us. What we have is so real. Some connection that can't be

301

put into words, only expressed through our bodies. And my body is telling me that I can't keep this from you any longer. I should never have kept it from you. I understand that now, as a grown man with life experience. But I was young, I was reckless, ambitious, selfish. And please understand that Juliette, she was in grave danger. What we did was to keep her safe. To keep you safe.'

The grass and bracken scrape at my skin as I put more distance between us. I feel naked, ridiculous for giving myself to this man I don't really know at all, abandoning myself in this juvenile way.

'What do you mean, "we"? And what do you mean keep me safe? What are you talking about?' My voice has a hysterical edge to it, but I don't care. 'Juliette going missing destroyed me. The guilt ate me up from the inside. I could never trust myself because of what happened that day on the beach. I thought it was all my fault and that I was a bad person. It made me doubt my ability to be a mother. I've medicated myself against the pain for years. I had PTSD and then it gave me postnatal depression when I had my daughters. I didn't think I deserved to be a mother. I didn't think I could keep them safe.'

'No, no, no.' Félix is shaking his head, face creased with pity. He reaches for me but I shrink from his touch.

My voice is emotionless, direct. I don't want any more of his empty flattery. I just want the truth. 'When did they find her? When did they find Juliette? Why didn't anyone tell me? Don't you dare say it was before we had email. Or that you left messages that I never got.'

He puts his head in his hands. 'No, you don't understand. She never went missing. Not really. Not for more than a few hours.'

His words feel like a blow and I cower. It feels like everything that just opened and softened inside me has closed again. 'What does that mean? What are you telling me?' But even as I ask this, I know, deep down, I know what he's telling me.

'I'm so sorry, Saskia, I thought I was doing the right thing at the time, and they made me promise not to tell anyone, not to tell you. It was for your own protection – the police, they were interrogating you. We didn't want to risk ...'

They. Them. Everyone was in on this but me. *Simone, Camille, Félix.* He lied to me. It has all been lies. It wasn't the film role that stopped him from meeting me in Barcelona. It was some pact that I wasn't a part of. Barcelona was a way to get me off the island, get me out of the picture. I'm such a fool.

I pull myself to my feet. He's all over me, drying on my skin like salt. I shake myself but he won't come off. I stumble in the long grasses and fall, mangroves and saltbush scraping my bare legs.

'Saskia, wait,' He's pulling on his shirt. I can't believe I've just had my face pressed to his bare chest. I run towards my bike.

'Please, let me explain everything properly.' He's running after me. His body knows these marshes instinctively and he gains on me. He grabs my arm and I swing around, my teeth bared.

'Don't, Félix. I don't trust anything you say. You've made my whole life a lie.'

He must understand the gravity of this and see the coldness in my eyes because he lets me go.

I am in survival mode. It feels strikingly similar to those moments after I learned that Juliette had gone missing. Dread is seeping through me, and I know I can't outrun this new pain.

Not this time. I have to face it, I have to know the truth and Félix isn't the one who can give it to me.

I straddle my bike and ride into the dark woods and now the shadows have caught up with me. It feels like they're clawing at my back, dismantling the wings of hope I flew here on. I'm riding blindly through tears, my eyes stinging, muscles aching, but I push on. I can hardly see the way forward in the dark.

I have been so incredibly blind, so incredibly stupid. I need to get back to the villa – I don't even care that Dylan is still there. I have only one focus now and that is to read the end of the manuscript written in French.

*

Le passé

The smell of the salt came through the cracks in the thin timber walls, so that it was in their hair, on their skin. Juliette licked her palm and said '*salée*'. The food Félix had left for them under a cheesecloth in the shade – baguettes, apples, strawberries, Juliette's favourite *galette* biscuits – tasted briny with it. Simone would never again smell salt on the air without thinking of those strange days in the cabin by the edge of the marshes with Juliette.

It was hot and the days became fluid and ran into each other. They cooled themselves under the tap in the rusty sink and Simone read stories from the children's books they had brought from the villa, stories her own mother had once read her. They sorted the jars of seashells on the windowsill, arranging them by shape and size, and making them into houses for Juju's dolls, which she had fashioned from a salt and pepper shaker. They had brought very little with them. Juliette had only the clothes on her back and a few things that Simone had stuffed into a bag from the villa.

At first it was all a wonderful game. Camille had explained that they were playing *cache-cache*, hide and seek, Juliette's favourite. That Juju would be hiding with *Nounou Si Si* for a little while before *Maman* came to find them.

'Why is *Maman* taking so long?' Juliette asked, standing on tiptoe to look out the grimy window as the first day seeped into night, her voice full of exasperation. '*Maman* bad at *cache-cache*,' she said and burst into tears.

Simone drew her away from the window. She didn't dare put on the electric light. They had torches, candles, blankets and pillows, which at first had been so exciting – *le camping*. But now Simone saw that Juliette could tell that something wasn't right. Perhaps she was simply sensing Simone's own fear. The only thing that would calm her were Simone's cat earrings. She would cradle them in her tiny palm, stroking them as though they were real pets, whom she lovingly named Fifi and Bibi. It was as though the little girl knew how precious the earrings were to Simone, so being allowed to touch them, hold them and keep them safe made her feel safe. It was an uncanny connection, but it felt in these moments, rocking Juliette in her lap, that her own mother was there beside them. And that this was what she would have wanted.

The nights were even longer than the days. The heat would fade but Juju would sleep fitfully, waking in tears and calling for her mother and *Nounou Sass Sass*. It was impossible to explain to her and it broke Simone's heart.

It was like a fever dream, being trapped in her mind inside this tiny cabin for so long. All she had to keep track of time was a wristwatch and the slow slide of the sun through the sky. There was nowhere for Simone to hide from her demons. No parties, no cigarettes, no wine, no men. Only seashells and make-believe. But she found in the slowest hours just before dawn broke that she understood two things very clearly. Finally, she had found reprieve from the haunting questions of why her mother had been driving the night she died and why she had been such an enigma in life. Simone felt like everything made more sense now. Her mother made more sense. And she knew she was in love with Félix.

Félix came to the cabin on the third day as night was falling over the marshes and the calls of the birds in the low scrublands and mangroves grew loud.

He closed the door behind him then looked out the window, checking he hadn't been seen.

Juliette ran to him and he hoisted her into his arms. They were both excited just to see another human being, and Simone was desperate for news.

'Look what *Maman* sent.' He took a small teddy bear out of the bag he'd brought, and Juliette squealed and hugged it tightly before introducing it to her salt and pepper shaker dolls.

Simone and Félix exchanged a look. 'Have you been okay?' he asked.

She scratched her head. Her hair needed a wash, and she was sweaty and exhausted, her body sore from sleeping on the ground, but she nodded. 'I'm not sure how much longer we can be here but ... she's been very good, considering. What's happening out there?'

He put his hands on his head and sighed, and she saw the toll this was taking on him. 'Hang on, let me ...' He took fruit and a baguette from his bag and laid them on the table, and they settled Juliette there to eat. Simone was hungry and bit into an apple.

'They've suspended the search,' he said, his voice low, grave.

'Really?'

'It's past the time a small child could' – his face scrunched up – 'normally survive in the elements. They said it's reasonable to assume that she has drowned ... but they couldn't find anything in the water.' His face was pale, blanched with guilt, and she wanted to reach for him, draw him to her, but she resisted. 'The police have no more questions for me and I think that soon they will stop interrogating Saskia. I can probably drive Juliette off the island tomorrow.'

Simone sighed with relief. She felt it flood through her, cooling her sticky skin and calming her mind.

*

Simone had not expected Félix to agree to help them, to lend them his cabin, as readily as he did. All the emotions had crossed his face as they'd sat him down at the kitchen table at the villa and told him Juliette was safe. Relief, elation, but then confusion, uncertainty. There was also sheer exhaustion. He had been searching for hours, questioned for hours by the police, and then as soon as he'd returned home, he'd got the message to call Simone's villa.

She'd poured them whisky at the kitchen table and Camille had explained everything again to Félix. He sat with his elbows on the table, his hands raking through his hair, his eyes flicking towards a still-sleeping Juliette.

When Camille finished, he looked up, took a slug of his drink and closed his eyes for a beat. He put down his glass and steepled his fingers on the table.

'I understand, Camille, that you and Juliette need to escape Henri. He has a reputation. He's difficult, everyone knows that, yet he's so charming. I can't believe he—' Félix pursed his mouth. 'I know what it's like to live with a man with a temper.' He hung his head. 'My father has hit my mother twice. She defends him. I don't understand it, but then, somehow, I do. I know it's not the same with Henri, but what I'm saying is that I can see how a woman can be trapped. And I want to help, I do. I can hide Juliette in the salt cabin, but we have to tell Saskia that she's okay. She's devastated. She thinks it's her fault. She thinks Juliette is dead. She'll leave this place and never come back.'

Camille gripped both his hands and then pressed her palm to his cheek. 'Please, Félix, understand that this is bigger than Saskia. She is the one who is under the greatest pressure from the police. It's too much of a burden for her to keep this secret, and it would be unfair to make her lie to the police. And it would put her in danger if she were to somehow slip up. Right now, she has an alibi, she's innocent. She would not be if she knew.'

'Why did you tell me then? They're questioning me too.'

'Because you … you are an actor, right? You can lie convincingly. You have a confidence that Saskia does not. Her grasp of the language, of our culture, it's not enough. She's a foreigner after all,' Camille said.

'And we need you,' Simone said. 'I can't drive, and we'll need to get her off the island somehow.'

Félix put his head in his hands. His anguish was apparent. Simone felt in some strange way that he was choosing between her and Saskia and the guilt of that made her squirm. It was morally complicated. They were breaking the law, they were deceiving the authorities, but they were keeping a little girl safe. They were lying to their friend, but they were protecting her too.

Simone knew she could make the choice easier for Félix. She understood the wild, ambitious part of him. She had seen it so clearly, so strongly, that first night after the bar. It was what had made her kiss him. There was part of him that was an enigma, that seemed willing to do anything. Perhaps it was simply that he had the same volatile energy she possessed — the fire in the belly, the passion. The part of him that desired to be known, to make his mark on the world, to be more than the son of a *saunier*. It occurred to her that perhaps the dynamic of the three of them worked because it was balanced by Saskia's softness, her groundedness. One day they would be able to tell Saskia the truth. When things had calmed down and Juliette was safe. They would tell her then.

'We will tell her, eventually we will,' Simone said, gently placing her hand on his shoulder. 'And, Félix, you want more than anything to escape this place. Come with me to Paris. I am going to help Camille and Juliette, with papers, everything they need for a new life in the Lot Valley. I know people who can help and be very discreet. You don't grow up in a family like mine without knowing such people.'

Camille's eyes flashed. She could sense too that they were close to convincing Félix. 'I have an aunt who lives on a small, remote farm in the Lot, who I know will keep Juliette safe. I'll go to Paris to be with my mother while things cool off and then I'll join them. We'll start new lives. Henri may find me in Paris, but he can no longer threaten me. He has lost his ace card, and I don't care what he does to me, as long as Juliette is safe.'

'Come with us to Paris,' Simone said. 'I can help you too. I have a friend, a film director, very well known, who is casting for his latest movie. I really think you need to meet this man.'

Félix looked up at her and his face was pained, but there was something else there now. Maybe it was relief that the decision had been made for him. Perhaps it was hope. And Simone knew that, while it was not in the way she truly desired, perhaps he had at last chosen her.

CHAPTER 24

I reach the villa and the tears have dried on my face. I feel encrusted with the salt from the marshes – it's in my crevices, a thin film on my skin. Its briny prickle is all I can smell and feel, as though Félix has seeped into every pore. A fresh wave of pain washes through me and I know I'll never escape the scent and feel of him while I'm on this island.

The car is gone. Maybe Dylan is out looking for us. Maybe he has finally heeded my wishes and left. I hope, but very much doubt, it's the latter. The lights in Madame Gardner's house are out. Thank God my girls are safe there.

I hide my bike behind a tree and let myself into the villa quietly, my senses attuned to any movement, any sign of life. My breath is shallow, and I feel goosebumps erupt along my arms as I move through the dark house. It had just started to feel like this villa could be my safe haven, but now it's dawning on me that I never knew the woman who left it to me.

I go to the kitchen where I've seen a flashlight in a drawer. I don't want to betray my whereabouts in case Dylan is out there in the dark, watching. The moon casts a thin light through long windows in the loungeroom and I find what I'm looking for. The manuscript is stashed under the lounge. I'm over halfway through but I've run out of time. I flick to the end. I flatten myself against the floor, scanning the words by torchlight.

I find the part I'm looking for and make myself read the words over and over. I might have doubted my translation if Félix hadn't told me the same thing an hour ago. Discovering Juliette under the table, hiding her at Camille's insistence. How bad things were with Henri.

Simone wrote about her mother, Hélène, and her last wish for Camille to be free of her violent husband. A secret love affair between Hélène and Camille. Simone's struggle to reconcile her mother in her mind, her feelings of confusion and betrayal. But all I can register is my own confusion and the blunt shock of their joint betrayal – Simone and Félix and Camille all knew the truth and they didn't tell me. An animal noise comes out of my throat, and I throw the manuscript and it fans across the floor. There is a blackness edging in on me, pressing me down, making it hard to get air into my lungs. Black spots swim in front of my eyes and I feel like I might faint. I put my head between my legs and feel it pound with too much blood.

And then I'm rising, with a burning in my chest that makes me want to claw my own heart out. I scream, or maybe it's a roar, because the roar in my head is all I can hear.

'What have you done?' I shout, louder each time I repeat it. I don't know who I'm talking to. Or maybe I do. It's her. Simone. I want to find her in this big old house where she's been hiding, dead but not dead, haunting me, tormenting me, and shake her. I move towards the bookshelf and rip a book out. It thuds to the floor, and I rip out another, and then another.

'You left me on that beach ... surrounded by police ... grilling me like it was my fault ... that I'd done this to her. That I'd been distracted by my boyfriend. I'd been careless. Hopeless. Untrustworthy. And I thought you blamed me for her disappearance too. You never spoke to me again. You were the best friend I'd ever had, and you abandoned me. You left me to think I'd killed a child. A fucking *child*. I thought if anyone ever knew the real me ... what I was capable of ...'

I press my hand over my mouth. I bend over, crumple with the pain of what I've just said out loud.

'And it hurt more than Félix ... because we had something that didn't have to end – like love ... like stupid boyfriends.'

I've cleared an entire row of old books and I keep going, my nails catching on the fabric spines, tearing them like thin paper.

'But you ended it because you loved him, and you took him the only way you knew how. You offered him everything and he took it, he chose you, like you knew he would. You didn't want to be that girl who was just her power, her money, her influence, but that's what you ended up being.'

The last part comes out as a screech, and I fling a book across the room. I squat into a tight ball and put my face in my hands. The room spins and the only sound is my own ragged breath.

I realise I'm being insane. Books are scattered everywhere, I'm talking to no one, to ghosts. My voice is a whisper.

'Why did you bring me back here? Why did you leave this manuscript for me to find? What do you want from me? Redemption? Now you want me to absolve you of your crime?'

I don't even know if it is a crime, what they've done. It wasn't premeditated, but opportunistic, but surely ... They deceived not only me but the authorities, the police. Juliette's file would still be open, as missing people's files always are. Of course it's a crime.

An image comes to me of Juliette's grandmother in that sad café that Félix visits at night. Doesn't she deserve to know her granddaughter is alive? She may have given birth to an awful man who threatened to kill his three-year-old daughter just to keep control of his wife, but does that old woman deserve to die with the burden of not knowing? The same torment I've carried for all my adult years?

I could free her from that. I scramble onto my hands and knees and try to find the pages I've just read. The evidence. But there are books and paper everywhere.

I throw my hands up. 'What do you expect me to do with all this, Simone? Is this some kind of sick test? To see if I'll turn in Félix, the man I—' I can't even say it out loud. I feel the weight of this realisation land on me, and I stop scrabbling for the pages and close my eyes.

I return to the bookshelf and there is a single book left at eye level. It's a thin book of poetry. L'Oranger, *par Hélène Durant. The Orange Tree,* by Hélène Durant. I hold it between my palms. It's so slim, I could rip it in half. I want to. But I let it slip from my fingers and I sink to the ground.

There's a noise outside and I start, my body on alert suddenly. I crawl to the window and peek out. When I see who it is, anger crawls up into my throat and burns, as though fingers are pressing on the thin skin of my neck. Félix is standing in the garden, leaning on his bike.

My muscles tense involuntarily. I feel myself standing. I open the front door and walk out. The flats of my palms find his chest and I push him, hard, and he stumbles backwards in the dark.

'Forgive me, Saskia.' His voice is so soft it's almost a whisper. 'Please, can we talk? Please we can go somewhere?'

'Where do you want to go, Félix? To Juliette's grandmother's café? Shall we tell her the truth? That her beloved granddaughter is alive? Why do you go there every night? To make you feel less guilty?'

He shakes his head, despondent. 'You are right, yes, the guilt. But I don't know what else to do.'

The words are an ugly hiss from my mouth. 'I could destroy you, Félix Allard.'

I realise we're no longer speaking in French. I can't believe a few hours ago I was giving myself to this man, had somehow hoped to have some kind of future with him.

I gesture behind me. 'What is this place? A bribe? A pathetic attempt at a peace offering? Were you in on this too? The villa, the manuscript left in a drawer?'

I see on his face that he doesn't know about the manuscript.

'I know everything. Simone wrote it all down. Meeting us, that whole summer. She obviously had a crisis of morality before she died and left the evidence in the drawer of her writing desk for me to find.'

'Saskia, please, understand that I was trapped. Trapped between doing the right thing, and the thing that would save a little girl. My father hit my mother. I understood what it was like to grow up with that fear.'

'You never told me that.' My voice is softer. I feel an involuntary pulse of sympathy, but I push it away.

'I had no way of saying it out loud. It's too shameful, the things that go on behind closed doors in families.'

The weight of his words hits me like a physical blow, and I realise what I'm threatening. The truth would destroy

Juliette and Camille as well as Félix. I drop to the ground beside him, the heat of my anger suddenly cooled. I realise I'm shaking.

'Saskia, they convinced me that it would be better for you not to know, not to have the burden of the lie. They told me we would tell you, but then you left France, went home, and I suppose I thought that it would be better for you not to have that burden to carry if the police contacted you again. To leave what happened on the island behind and get on with your life.'

I laugh cynically. 'Instead you gave me the burden of thinking I caused a little girl to go missing and die. How could I forget? This island has haunted me, you and Juliette and Simone have haunted me my whole life.'

He reaches for me, but I deflect his arm.

'I'm so sorry. I thought I was doing the right thing, Saskia. I can see now that it was a mistake. That I should have come for you. That I should have fought harder for what we had. I didn't know that it was a fluke, a beautiful chance that we found so early in our lives. I was too young for it. I didn't realise that all the success in the world means nothing if there's no one to share it with.'

'Did you even leave messages for me? In Barcelona? Or was that a lie too?'

'I did. I left messages. You never called. I thought maybe you just wanted to move on with your life, after everything that had happened, and I could understand that.'

'But you're leaving something out,' I say, my voice small, cold. 'Simone loved you. It's on full display in her manuscript. And I knew, back then I could tell. So, you chose her in the end.'

He shakes his head. 'I was desperate to escape the island, the life my family expected of me. It is true, I chose what she could offer me. But I didn't choose *her*.'

I pull myself to my feet. I can't bring myself to look at him. 'It's the same thing,' I say, and I walk away from him without looking back.

He calls my name, but I shut the door behind me and lean against it. My eyes are burning with hot tears, my skin cold with sweat. I go to the fridge and take out a bottle of wine, pour myself a glass and drink it down, wait for the numbness to come. I look out the window. He is gone. My stomach twists and I can't tell if it's relief or regret.

I sit at the table under the window that doesn't close. I run my fingers over the swollen wood. It's where Juliette climbed in, the moment my life splintered in two. I resolve to have a tradesman fix it as soon as possible.

I hear a noise outside and see Dylan standing at the front door. He knocks, which surprises me. The door is unlocked. It's not an aggressive knock either, but a polite one as though he's a stranger calling. I feel a pang of emotion at this thought – of him being a stranger. I think of all the things we've been through together. An image comes to me of his face when Dee was born. The pride, the love. How can I leave this man who loves our daughters so much? I drain my glass and stand. I can feel the warmth of the wine lulling me. I am no longer shaking.

Dawn is breaking through a shell of cloud behind him, and I see that Dylan's face is pale. He's been crying. He moves towards me and pulls me to him. He smells like the washing detergent we use at home and a feeling, sweet and comforting, moves through me. He buries his face in my neck.

'Oh, thank God you're okay, Saskia. I thought you'd taken the girls. I thought you'd left me. I've been driving all over the island. I'm so sorry. I'll do better, I promise you. I'll be the man you used to love. I know I can be a dickhead sometimes, but I love my girls so much. I love you. I can't lose you. Please, please give me another chance, don't leave me. We can be good together again, like we used to be.'

I let him bury his head in my hair, kiss my fingertips. I feel guilt and shame collide inside me thinking where those fingers were only hours ago, and I wonder if I smell of another man, of salt.

He smooths my hair, wipes the tears from my face. I feel myself yielding. It is all too hard, this place, the truths it has given up, the secrets that have been floating to the surface, crystallising. And what can I do with the truth, with what really happened to Juliette? What is the right thing to do anyway? Would telling authorities that she's alive after all these years implicate Félix and Camille? Would they be charged with obstructing a police operation?

Would telling the truth bring me any relief? Would incriminating Félix give me any satisfaction? He is already a broken man.

But what of all the people who still don't know? Juliette's grandmother in her café? Her father? Does Henri have a right to know the truth, despite everything he did to his family?

I don't know where to put all of this inside me. I feel so tired suddenly, so overwhelmed by a burden that is not mine to carry anymore. The truth would only destroy more lives, and it would not make mine any better.

And what to do with this crumbling old villa that now feels like it's some kind of tragic compensation?

I think of Félix then, living in his own world of guilt, riding to that little café every night, unable to tell that despairing old woman the truth. I squeeze my eyes shut to stop the emotion that has flooded me.

No, it is over. C'est fini. There's nothing left for me here. This island has no claim on me anymore. When Dylan says the words, they are already on the tip of my tongue.

'Let's go home.'

CHAPTER 25

My husband is doing an impression of a famous French man with a walking stick. We are on his parents' deck drinking the French champagne we bought duty-free on the way home when I realised people would expect gifts upon our return.

The early afternoon air has a sharp chill to it and I'm so relieved to have left the simmering island heat behind, the oppression of all those unanswerable questions. The sounds and smells are so familiar – the clink of cutlery as my family eats, barbecued meat, woodfire, frangipani, eucalyptus. Home. Even my mother-in-law's strong perfume is a kind of balm against the surrealness of the past couple of weeks. His family laughs at his caricature of a French accent. Now he's telling them about the party and the boat. His parents are always impressed by excessive wealth, especially the exotic European kind.

Petra tops up my wineglass. 'You've been very quiet about the trip, Saskia.' She places her hand on my arm. 'Still jet-lagged?'

I flick her a weak smile, wishing she wasn't able to read me so well. The truth is, a thick exhaustion has taken hold of me that I don't know can still be blamed on my circadian rhythms.

I feel bad that I've been brushing off some of her text messages since our return. She's asking too many questions.

'So, did you find out why Simone Durant left you the villa? We've all been dying to know.'

I can't escape them anymore. My chest contracts, the tight fist balled inside is back. I shake my head and try to wash the lump in my throat away with wine.

I keep my voice light. 'Not really. I think she was a very rich and very eccentric, lonely lady. And there was the language barrier with her lawyer, of course.' *The language barrier.* I'm so thankful for that barrier. I am a different person in French. It's so easy to compartmentalise when you are two people. I've done it before.

I remember that I used to feel bad about lying to Petra. She's been my emotional compass for so long, but it doesn't feel like that anymore. I've weaned myself down to a small dose of my pills and my own compass is coming back. I know I'll probably never be entirely without medication, and that's okay, but I also know that I cannot live the rest of my life emotionally numb and disorientated. But tapering down has not been without pain. I wake with a pressure in my chest that I can't explain, as though I've been bruised at the centre. I get brain zaps that feel like electric shocks running through my synapses. Sometimes I feel everything so acutely that there's no room left for anything but the feelings. But now at least, I know my own emotions.

'Félix Allard was rather eccentric as well, by the sounds of it … and Dylan's colourful impression of him,' says Sal. 'But was he dressed beautifully? I bet he was. French men always are.'

Petra elbows Dylan. 'You'd better watch out, little brother. Félix Allard sounds like a catch – eccentric, with a cane or not. Is he single? Is he gorgeous?'

My eyes meet Dylan's. I shrug, feigning indifference, but I can't stop the colour creeping up my neck.

'Oh my God, Saskia you're blushing. I'm googling him.'

'No, don't, don't.' But it's too late. She's holding up an image on her phone for everyone to see.

'*Ooh là là,*' Petra says.

Sal raises an eyebrow and nods slowly in approval.

'Now I'm going to have to watch all his films. And when are we getting an invite to Saskia's French villa?' Petra turns to me, her hands pressed together in prayer. 'I presume you'll let us have one holiday there before selling? And introduce me to your French film star. Pretty please?'

I laugh, but there's a high, nervous note to it. 'You're all welcome to visit my villa, of course.'

My eyes flick to Dylan. *My film star. My villa.* His mouth twitches but his face betrays no emotion. He says nothing.

'I can see France hasn't improved Dylan's dress sense any,' his mother adds, indicating for him to top up her champagne glass. 'He still looks like he's just rolled out of bed.'

Dylan does as he's told and tops up her glass, but his mouth is drawn into a thin line and he's gone very quiet. His confidence of only moments ago has been deflated. He's been uncharacteristically subdued this past week. The power balance has shifted. There have been no criticisms, no offhand slights. No mention of, nor pressure to address, the enormous villa-shaped question between us. He's giving me time and space, I can see that. He's trying to be a better man. I've booked us in to couples' counselling, which we start next week, and Dee is going to see a psychologist. She's been eating at the table with us more often, and exercising a little less, which I hope is a step in the right direction. Neither of us has mentioned the night on the island when she and her sister stayed with Madame Gardner, the night she told me I could leave her father. Because surely she would prefer me to stay and work things out.

The island of wide salt flats and low hot skies has retreated into the territory of my dreams once more. I wake often at night, now that I am no longer heavily medicated. Without the tranquillising effect of the drugs, I have no defence against my subconscious. Sometimes I wake with a whisper of his language on my lips.

The days are short and cold, and in their weak, anaemic light it's as though those long, sun-soaked island days never happened. The girls have returned to school and I leave for my studio but find myself going elsewhere – walking along the beach mostly, unable to find the energy to create. Dylan has taken to complimenting my hair, which is slowly growing out, the dark dye fading to auburn.

'That was actually quite a nice lunch. I may have even missed your mother,' I say when we get into the car. I watch as Dee and Lara hug their grandparents goodbye at the front door. That lonely café on Île de Ré comes to me. 'Maybe we should have taken up their offer to have the girls overnight. Have a night to ourselves, a date night. It's been a while, and your parents really missed them, I think.'

I feel Dylan's hand on my leg and I put my own over it, feeling a contentment I haven't felt in a long time spreading through me. The car is warm, our clothes smell of woodfire and I'm pleasantly anaesthetised after several glasses of wine.

He leans over and kisses me on the cheek. He's been more demonstrative since we returned. He's told me he loves me often. I expect that's what he's about to say as he pushes a strand of hair behind my ear.

'Don't you dare humiliate me in front of my family ever again.'

His voice is even, calm, emotionless, and it takes a moment for my body to respond to the fact that it's a threat. But the pressure of his fingers gripping my leg is unmistakable. Adrenalin needles through me, but when I look into his eyes they're not cold, they are perfectly neutral, as though he's just told me we need to get petrol on the way home.

He releases my leg, turns from me, his head following the path of our children from his parents' front door to the car.

'It's freezing. Oh, it's so warm in here,' says Dee. 'Dad, can you put the seat warmers on in the back?'

'Sure, honey,' he says, and pushes the button.

'Granny said she's going to take us to high tea next weekend in the city,' says Lara. 'Can we go?'

I can hear the words, but no words are coming to my mind. I have lost all faculty for language. It feels like I am collapsing in on myself, going to that familiar place where I am made small. But as I start to feel myself shrink, something happens. A question floats to the surface of my mind. *Am I made of such flimsy scaffolding?*

'Sure La-La, I think that would be nice,' says Dylan. 'Mum was just saying you were about due for a sleepover at Granny and Pa's.'

I look at him. I can't hide the pain that must be plain on my face.

'Mum, are you okay?' asks Dee.

Our eyes meet in the rear-view mirror, and I see that she's sensed and understood the frisson in the car. There is fear, uncertainty in her voice, and something shifts inside me when I hear it. I feel something start to grow instead of contract.

'I think we're all tired,' says Dylan, his hand finding mine on my leg again. I don't draw it away, I sit there and let this new feeling expand in my chest.

As we drive, the cold winter landscape flashes past. My children and my husband are talking but I can't hear their words. All I can hear is a ringing in my ears, like a bell, like an alarm.

It's late afternoon when we get home. The girls settle on the lounge to play video games. I watch Dylan out of the corner of my eye as he laces his shoes for a run. I don't meet his eyes. I have mistaken his politeness, his lack of reprimand this past week, for respect. He was just biding his time, and now I am biding mine.

The house is quiet. I'm alone in the kitchen with the ringing in my head.

I find my suitcase, still in the laundry, half-full of clothes that need to be washed. The manuscript is stuffed in the front pocket. On the last page there's a phone number scribbled in black pen. I stare at it for a long time, but the ringing in my head will not stop. I know what I have to do. My hands are trembling as I press the buttons on my phone and wait.

'Hello?' A young woman's voice.

'Hi,' I hear myself say, trying to disguise my panic. What should I say? Perhaps they no longer go by the same names. It's been so long. 'Is your mum there?'

'Oh, hang on.' There's a rustling sound. '*Maman?*'

The young woman has a French-Australian accent. A perfect *mélange* of the two. And I know for sure then. It's Juliette. *She is alive. It's not my fault.* Something inside me releases, a relief that feels as acute as childbirth – the excruciating pleasure-pain of my daughters leaving my body and entering the world.

'Sorry, she's just stepped out. Can I get her to call you back?'

'Yes, no. No, it's okay,' I say. For a moment there is silence and I consider telling her who I am, the girl who used to look after her. The girl who used to love her. *Nounou Sass Sass*, but I realise that Juliette probably has no memory of that time, of that trauma. Her voice is free, clear, bright and unafraid. I remember the sound of my own daughter's voice in the car this afternoon. Lara and Dee will never be free because I am not free.

'*Salut,*' I say.

'*Salut,*' she replies.

A greeting that means both hello and goodbye.

*

I put the phone down. I'm sitting at the kitchen bench, the same place I sat when I opened Monsieur Rombard's letter. Now I hold Simone's manuscript in my hands. Its very existence is a question that needs to be answered. It is my past, it is a burden, a guilt that is not mine to carry anymore. It's heavy in my hands and in my heart, but I think I know a way to make it light. I kiss the tops of my girls' heads, tell them I need to get something from the studio, that I'll be back soon to make dinner.

The late afternoon light falls in strips along the polished concrete floor. It smells musty, like it's been shut up for weeks, which it has. The flowers on the centre table are dead and I throw them away.

I sit down at my desk and fan the pages of the manuscript out before me. Here is the truth, so damaging if I choose to release it into the world, so painful if I choose to cling to it, to conceal it inside. I think about the cost of that. Of how I've lived inside a cage of guilt my whole adult life. And now that I'm finally released, I don't want to be newly bound by anger, by hate.

I take a deep breath, pick up my scalpel and begin to cut.

It takes me several days and many hours. I find myself entering a dreamlike state, as I so often do when I create. I let that language flow through me, all those words written in French. I let the confusion, the anger, the pain come. I shape and cut and carve it. It flutters around me, tiny pieces of her, of him, of myself, falling to the floor. I think about the lightness of Juliette's voice on the phone. I think about Félix going to that little café every night to see Juliette's grandmother. I think about how Simone is no longer alive, but how hard it must have been for her to write these words.

I didn't know what I'd end up with, only that when I was done, Simone's manuscript, my past, and the evidence of what they did, would be gone.

I get to the last page. Under the phone number is an address. A PO Box in South Australia that has been handwritten in pen. I put down my scissors, turn the page over and begin to write.

Chère Camille,

I don't know if this is your address. Sometimes I imagine that it is and that you and Juliette are living a peaceful life in the Adelaide Hills. I can only imagine Simone left me your contact details for a reason. It has taken me a while to absorb the fact that Juliette is alive, to come to terms with the hurt and betrayal that comes with that knowledge. But I am happy she is safe. Sometimes I imagine what she must look like as a 29-year-old woman.

I've realised that there is no one else I can talk to except you. You knew Juliette would never be safe. And that is all a mother needs to know. I'm not a bad mother. For years I thought I was. I thought that I had let a little girl walk into the water and drown, or be abducted by some horrible man. It turns out that horrible men are not always strangers.

I didn't trust myself to care for my own daughters, but I know now that I was never a bad carer, that I am not a bad mother. I am broken, yes, but I will always, always be strong for my children.

I know now that I did nothing wrong. I was nineteen. I was brave. I see these qualities in my own teenager. She told me that I should leave her father. I didn't listen to her. I listened to him when he promised me he'd change, that he'd be better, but men like him don't change. This is what you realised. This is what you had to escape. We will never be entirely free in the way you and Juliette are now, but he belittled and threatened me for the very last time a few days ago.

I'm taking my girls back to the island. He will probably try to manipulate me, but I can no longer let him crush my spirit, crush my daughters' spirits. You and Simone have given me courage. I see now that Simone's villa was a gift. And an apology. And I understand why you did what you had to do twenty-six years ago. I forgive you. And I forgive myself.

Bisous,

Saskia

I find an envelope and stamp in my desk drawer and slip the letter inside.

I turn back to my scissors, but my work here is done. I pick up the fine scaffolding of my papercut sculpture. Simone's words are still there but they are inconsequential, scrambled, remade into something else. The paper fans out, settling lightly into the shape of an orange tree.

*

Le passé

From the age of fifty she knew that she was cursed, that death was waiting for her, just as it had been waiting for her parents. But it was not the same curse. She would not die dramatically, behind the wheel of a car as her mother, father and her great-uncle had. She would die of something altogether more pedestrian. She was not young. Not old either, but she had lived a life. She had Claude, the man who loved her as she needed to be loved. She had her cats. But after the doctors told her there was nothing more they could do, even with all the money she could offer them, all the places in the world she could go for treatment, she knew what needed to be done.

Simone stepped out of the taxi and the smell of salt and oranges wrapped her in their embrace, sweet and sour, like memory. She had only a small bag. In the end, you didn't need very much. She tipped the taxi driver so much that he raised his eyebrows and then smiled. Those smiles were things she had come to collect these past few months. She'd had Monsieur Rombard give so much of her money away. She had, when she was young, interpreted her mother's generosity as buying others' love. But she had come to understand that it was more complicated than that.

The villa, shrouded in the salt haze lifting off the sea, looked like a dream she'd once had that she did not want to wake from. But life was, of course, not a dream. Eventually you woke up and you had to face the stark daylight. You had to take responsibility for your life. For your choices. You had to live, and then you had to die, with your regrets.

Once she had thought she could buy the love of a young man, but love did not work like that. It was the one thing that in its truest form was given and received freely. And for this, she knew it as the most valuable thing on earth. She also knew that she was not a bad person. She had made a decision that had cost a lot. It was a decision that was both selfish and selfless. Because she was both these things. But regret had built and built, as secrets left too long to fester do. Until they must be told, let out of their painful cocoon. It was a price she was willing to pay. And she would pay it again. For her own mother. For a little girl and her mother. But in saving one girl she had damaged another.

She put down her bag in the lounge. She did not have a lot of time. She was tired in a way she never had been before. But she had brought all that she needed. Medicinal marijuana, a laptop, a printer. She had bread and oranges here, the things that had helped her survive during the worst of the chemotherapy. Claude could not believe that was all she wanted, when she was sick in bed. But he had not known what had sustained her soul when she was young.

She went into the kitchen and made herself coffee, strong and black, because she needed her mind to be alert. There was much to be done. She sat under the window that didn't close properly, running her fingers over the swollen wood, thinking of her mother.

She went upstairs and pulled on Hélène's kimono that still hung over the mirror and sat at her father's writing desk overlooking the trees and the sea. She opened her laptop and began to write. She had never written the novel she'd dreamed of writing, the book her father believed her capable of. She didn't have the patience for all that sitting, it turned out. But now, sitting was all she could do. They said you needed to live before you could write. She had lived a full life and, she realised, she had always had a story to tell. But it wasn't just her story. It belonged to all of them. And this was not a book that should ever be published. Or, maybe it should be. Because who after all, was the arbiter of the truth, something that money could buy, but only for so long. No, there was a girl with long red hair who had been preserved in her memory, seared into her. She had wondered about her so often over the years, but she'd convinced herself that this girl never thought about this tiny prism of time in the span of their lives. But now, as time concertinaed, and pressed around her like a bruise, she knew this could not be true. This book was for her. What she did with it was up to her. They had all once made a decision without her. But this was to give it back to her.

Days passed. Weeks passed. Claude understood her need to be there, surrounded by memories of her parents. He was a good man. They spoke at nights. He never once told her she must return home. Because he knew now, so close to the end, that control is life's ultimate illusion.

On the day that she wrote 'The end', her nurse, Monique, called to say that she should absolutely come home, to Paris. She was distraught, and Simone felt sad that she had upset this beautiful woman who had cared for her so well. Monique told her she was coming to take her off the island by the end of the week, whether she was ready or not, and Simone said okay.

The pain became difficult to bear once she had finished writing, even with the drugs. Fear gripped her deep in her gut, and consumed her at night. She used her last bit of strength to light a small fire in the barbecue in the garden. She took the freshly printed pages and stared into the flames. She was very close to burning all of her words. She did not know if she could leave this place, leave them behind. She knew she was trying to exert control. But she sat out there all night, wrapped in blankets under the stars until the flames died to embers. It felt like a baptism of sorts. A test she had passed. And then she went inside, took a pen, and wrote, on the very last page, a phone number and an address – her apology, a giving back of something that was not hers to keep anymore. She placed the manuscript in her father's desk drawer and felt something release inside her.

The sun was rising, and the light was soft. She was so tired. She went into the loungeroom and took the books from the shelf until she found the slim volume of poetry her mother had written and the heavy tome her father had edited. She lay down on the lounge and placed her parents' words over her heart. And, as she closed her eyes, she smiled, because she knew that a boy with dark eyes and a girl with red hair were on their way.

EPILOGUE

The house is by the sea. Orange trees flank its crumbling walls. The wind whispers through the pines and the sea answers. I have come back.

I have told no one where we've gone, except the recipient of the letter, posted the evening I wrote it. Not even Petra knows we're here.

Dylan will have guessed, of course, and I hope he knows that he's lost me forever. I left a note on the kitchen bench. A single sentence that he cannot have failed to understand.

You will never humiliate me in front of my family ever again.

The summer heat has ebbed and there is a new coolness to the air. The tourists have gone, and the beaches and cycle paths are deserted. I have never known the island outside of summertime. It feels more remote, more windswept, wilder. But it feels like it's all ours. The taxi drops us in front of the gate, and we brace ourselves against the breeze. We may not have brought enough warm clothes, but at least this time I have a key.

I notice the garden first. The grass has been mown and the overgrowing vines and shrubs cut back from around the house. There is no longer an algae bloom in the pool. For a horrible moment the thought occurs to me that perhaps Monsieur Rombard has rented the villa out. I slide the key into the lock, and it turns, and my shoulders drop in relief. There are no signs of life in the hall or loungeroom. But fresh flowers newly cut from the garden sit in a vase on the hall table. The floors have been polished, and everything smells like citrus and soap.

'Did you tell someone we were coming?' asks Dee, dumping her backpack on the kitchen bench. She opens the fridge. 'There's heaps of food in here.'

A tingle runs up my spine.

'Can we go down to the beach? We might see dolphins,' says Lara.

I've told her that we're having another French adventure, that her dad had to stay in Sydney for work, but Dee knows why we're really back here.

The sand stings our ankles as we slide down the dunes and arrive at the water's edge. We peel off our shoes and socks and begin to walk along the beach. The girls idle behind me, picking up shells, wading into the cold water. In my mind it was such a long way from the villa to Le Bois-Plage, but we're there before I know it. The wind whips our hair and gulls soar, bright against retreating storm clouds. The beach is wild, and we run along the tide line. I let the memories from this place wash over me like a long summer afternoon – Juliette's soft curls, tiny sandy hands, sipping Simone's tea from a thermos, bare backs on the warm sand. The feeling of Félix's skin on mine.

Lara is arranging shells into the shape of a turtle. I sit with Dee, our arms linked.

'I'm proud of you, Mum,' she says, resting her head on my shoulder. Her voice, for the first time in a long time is as clear and free as the soaring gulls above us. As clear and free as Juliette's.

I hug her to me and kiss her hair, fighting back the emotion building behind my eyes.

'You're so strong, Dee, stronger than you realise,' I say. She nestles into me. Her arms are no longer so thin, the shadows under her cheekbones are slowly fading. She's getting the help she needs. And Lara's anxiety might always be there a little, but so will I, with my scissors ready to shape a dreamscape to make her smile.

We stay at the beach until the very last of the light leaks away. The sun dips into the sea and the first stars prick the sky. Night is coming and the cold scatters goosebumps over our flesh.

We walk up the beach and scramble up the dunes to the villa. We dust the sand from our feet and add our shells to the collection I started in the jar by the door when we were here before.

The girls go upstairs to shower, and I move through the ground floor, securing the house. My heart feels like it stills when I reach the kitchen. The window above the table. The swollen frame that never closes properly. I notice the frame is a different timber. It's lighter and there is no peeling paint, no warped wood. I inspect it closer, run my fingers over the new carpentry. The window is completely closed.

There is no trace of those humid summers, the smell of rain and oranges seeping in from the garden. Or a little girl slipping through one hot afternoon to hide under the table like a cat. Or a woman who left a window broken because it reminded her of her mother.

Relief mixes with a kind of yearning, for everything I have lost, but also found. I reach over. I push the window open.

Something catches my eye. I notice there is one thin strip of wood that is still old, running vertically to the ceiling. The paint is flaking off like soft skin and I climb onto the table to feel the swollen wood under my fingers. Something glints in the delicate timber and I use my fingernail to pry it out. A tiny gold earring in the shape of a cat sits in my palm.

I swing around, expecting to see Simone standing here in the kitchen behind me. I notice a fresh baguette on the countertop and next to it a slab of yellow butter. There are oranges. And coffee. The smell of burned coffee and citrus surrounds me like an embrace.

A jar of *fleur de sel* sits unopened on the bench and I crack it open and breathe in its briny scent. It feels like something rare and delicate is forming around me like a salve, a protective shell, like being drawn to the surface, like floating in salt.

I sprinkle the fine, translucent crystals onto the benchtop and press my fingertip into them.

Je porte le sel à mes lèvres.

I touch the salt to my lips.

AUTHOR'S NOTE

I've explored some sensitive and personal issues in this story – anxiety and its medication, emotional abuse and coercive control, and eating disorders. I want to acknowledge that each of these conditions is complex and difficult and that the way they're portrayed here is through only one small window of experience. I also wish to send strength and hope to those who have lived or are living with these challenges.

For support and information, consider contacting the following organisations:

Mood disorders
Black Dog Institute, blackdoginstitute.org.au

Gendered violence
White Ribbon Australia, whiteribbon.org.au

Eating disorders
Butterfly, butterfly.org.au

ACKNOWLEDGEMENTS

These words were written on Guringai land and I would like to show my respect for the Traditional Custodians, Elders past and present.

There are so many people whose encouragement and belief meant that this book actually came to fruition. Firstly, thank you to my amazing publisher, Anna Valdinger, who was full of enthusiasm before I'd even finished the first draft.

Thank you, Tara Wynne, for taking on this book and believing in it.

Thanks to the wonderful editorial team at HarperCollins — Scott Forbes for unfailing attention to detail, and for that final, final read; Barbara McClenahan for generous input in the last days on the job; and Pam Dunne for finding all those little timeline issues. Thanks to Di Blacklock for her editorial guidance and keen insight into the story. Thank you to Louisa Maggio for creating the cover of my dreams (pun intended), and to marketing campaign manager Lucy Inglis.

Mille mercis to Stephane Bouclier and Kirsten Craze for checking the French and answering all my (many) questions. Any mistakes are purely my own.

Thank you to my trusted beta readers, Karina Ware, Kirstin Bokor, Ali Lowe, Danielle Townsend, and George Penney. I don't know what I'd do without your early, invaluable feedback.

Thank you, Bec McSherry, for the emotional support over cups of tea.

I think I would have given up somewhere along the way if not for the writer gang I've amassed over the years. You know who you are. Thank you for the honest and inspiring chats at book launches and events. You are all so talented and authentic and lovely.

Shelley Gardner, I hope you enjoy the character named after you – Madame Gardner – for the Northern Beaches Readers' Festival fundraiser. She came to me very naturally early on in the piece, as characters sometimes have the great fortune of doing, and I feel she's an integral and loving force in the book, a bit like your support of the Australian writing community.

A huge thank you to Varuna, the Writers' House, where I wrote a good chunk of this novel and finally found my groove and my confidence in it. What a gift to Australian writers this place is. Jacqui Ross, Gemma Noon and Helen Bodycomb, you ladies were a delight to share work, stories and wine with. Thanks to Helen too for the residency at the gorgeous Eastern Beach Art House at Geelong, where I started my structural edits. It wasn't quite the Varunion we were hoping for, but thank you for being so lovely and for bringing me soup when I was sick.

Thank you to my readers. Thank you to those who have taken the time to write to me this past year. You have made me believe that the connection between writer and reader is something so special and your messages of support help me through periods of self-doubt.

To the librarians and booksellers who hand-sell books and are so passionate about stories and words, you are the best.

Thank you to my classmates and teachers at the Alliance Française de Sydney for putting up with my very shaky French as I was re-orienting myself with the language.

To Jeanette, Richard, Anth and Beck, thank you lovely family for your unconditional love and support. A special thanks to Mum for all the countless times you help out, so I can go on retreats and research trips to get the writing done.

Ben, thank you for all your support and love and for believing in me. It means so much. And Soph, one day I'll take you to Paris, I promise.

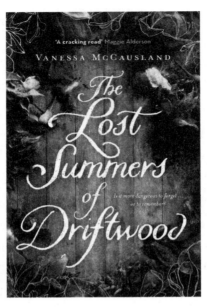

Is it more dangerous to forget ... or to remember?

Alone and adrift after a failed marriage proposal, Phoebe flees Sydney to her family's abandoned holiday cottage. On the slow-moving river, she is confronted with the legacy of her older sister's suicide, a year before. Why did Karin leave a note written in flowers and walk into the water?

Phoebe's childhood love, Jez, has moved back to the beautiful old house, Driftwood, one jetty down. He's married now and his home has become a refuge for an unlikely little community.

As the river begins to give up its secrets, Phoebe finds herself caught up in old feelings and new mysteries.

The Lost Summers of Driftwood is a story of lost loves, rekindled passions, tragedy and betrayal set against the backdrop of an idyllic south coast town.

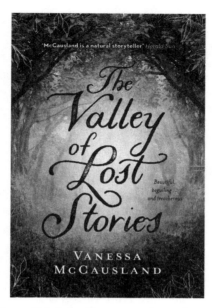

'McCausland is a natural storyteller' *Herald Sun*

The Valley of Lost Stories

Beautiful, beguiling and treacherous

VANESSA McCAUSLAND

Beautiful, beguiling … and treacherous

Four women and their children are invited to the beautiful but remote Capertee Valley, west of the Blue Mountains. Once home to a thriving town, only an enigmatic Art Deco hotel remains – and an unsolved mystery. In 1948, Clara Black walked into the night, never to be seen again.

As the valley beguiles these four friends, and haunts them in equal measure, each has to confront secrets of her own: Nathalie, with a damaged marriage; Emmie, yearning for another child; Pen, struggling as a single parent; and Alexandra, hiding in the shadow of her famous husband.

But as the story of what happened seventy years earlier unravels, one of the women also vanishes into this bewitching place, forcing devastating truths to the surface.

Two best friends, one summer night, and twenty years of silence …

Sylvie is a lover of words and a collector of stories, but she has no words for that night at the lighthouse. What happened to cleave her apart from her best friend and soulmate, Kase?

Sylvie yearns to rekindle their deep connection, so when Kase invites her to the wild Tasmanian coast to celebrate her 40th birthday, she accepts – despite the ghosts she must face.

As Sylvie struggles to find her feet among old friends, she bonds with local taxi boat driver Holden. But he is hiding from the world, too.

Through an inscription in an old book, Sylvie and Kase discover their mothers have a history, hidden from their daughters. As they unpick what took place decades earlier, they're forced to face the rift in their own friendship, and the question of whether it's ever okay to keep a secret to protect the person you love.